I AM AFRA
AFRA

Love ran through her mind. She wanted to be loved for herself, not wedded and bedded so a man could be an earl or beget sons. But how could she explain that? He would laugh at her foolishness. Oh, why had Shane died and left her to face this?

Hugh recognized the riot of emotions—fear, confusion, yearning, shame, sorrow—warring upon her face. His back stiffened and his lips hardened grimly into a tight line. Was she sorry to bed him? Was she mourning Shane? Would he always walk in the shadow cast by his infamous uncle?

Kathryn drew herself up self-righteously. "I shan't give Shane's daughter suckle and then lie with another man."

"Another man?" Hugh roared, grabbing her shoulders in an iron grip. "I'm your husband! Shane's dead and you live," he growled. "My wife will not tell me nay in my own home."

Kathryn watched his long-starved eyes devour her nakedness, his fury becoming scorching desire. Beneath his virile body and demanding kiss, she lay unresisting until his kiss stoked the embers of her passion.

"Katie," he murmured, seeing desire in her eyes.

"Oh," Kathryn moaned her long-denied need, her arms reaching out to hold him close.

Patricia H. Grasso

Emerald Enchantment

A DELL BOOK

Published by
Dell Publishing
a division of
Bantam Doubleday Dell Publishing Group, Inc.
666 Fifth Avenue
New York, New York 10103

ISBN: 0-440-20794-0

Printed in the United States of America

Published simultaneously in Canada

March 1992

10 9 8 7 6 5 4 3 2 1

RAD

This book is dedicated to three great ladies of romance (in order of their appearance in my life):

BERTRICE SMALL—

premier historical novelist. Your wondrous talent inspired me to write.

KATHRYN FALK—

the ultimate can-do woman. Your how-to book pointed me in the right direction to start.

TINA MOSKOW—

my editor, the soothing voice on the other end of the phone. Thanks for giving this unknown kid a chance.

PROLOGUE

London, England
November, 1563

"O'Neill!"

Turning around at the sound of his name, Hugh O'Neill scanned the crowded ballroom of Queen Elizabeth's Whitehall Palace. A distinguished looking, silver-haired man of middle years was slowly making his way toward him through the mob of gaily dressed courtiers.

"Lord Fitzgerald?" Hugh asked, extending his hand.

"Yes," Fitzgerald verified his identity but said no more, surprised by the other's appearance.

Crowned with a lustrous dark brown mane, the young Irishman stood six feet tall. Broad shouldered and narrow waisted, he possessed the well-muscled body of a soldier. His ruddy complexion and gleaming brown eyes announced his good health and easygoing humor. Hugh O'Neill at twenty-seven radiated charismatic power, an irresistible force that time would magnify.

"Are you newly arrived from Ireland?" Hugh asked with a smile, amused by the older man's scrutiny.

Lord Fitzgerald nodded and glanced around to be certain no one was listening. "Burke sends word that your newest O'Neill cousin will look fetching in pink. You might consider sending a christening gift."

Hugh grinned broadly at the news. His uncle Shane hadn't produced an heir, and another claimant to Tyrone was still in the future. Unbidden, the image of his uncle's wife—copper haired, green eyed, vulnerably young—formed in his mind. Acquainted with his uncle's notorious temper, Hugh almost felt sorry for the petite English beauty who'd fascinated him at court the previous year. *Almost.*

"I beg your pardon?" Hugh became aware the other man was speaking.

"I said," Lord Fitzgerald repeated, "my daughter Fiona is standing over there. I'd like you to meet her."

"I'd be honored."

The two Irishmen started to make their way through the crowded chamber but found their path blocked by Sir Henry Sidney. "Lord Burghley wishes to speak with you," he said to Hugh.

Promising to return soon, Hugh excused himself and left the chamber with Sir Henry. Without speaking, the two walked through the maze of dimly lit corridors to the prime minister's office.

"Good evening," Burghley greeted them, then motioned them to sit down. Sir Henry and Hugh sat in the chairs facing his desk. "The latest news from Ireland is Shane O'Neill sired a female, not the hoped-for heir," Burghley said, watching the younger man's reaction.

Hugh's mouth dropped open, his expression registering surprised relief. "Keeping me informed is most kind of her majesty," Hugh said. "Do I have permission to return to Ireland and take my rightful place in Parliament?"

"The time is unripe for that." Trusting his usually unfailing instincts, Lord Burghley decided the young man had been genuinely surprised. No spies were in this O'Neill's employ. "We must give your uncle time to comply with our negotiated terms or risk placing young Kathryn Devereux in an untenable position."

"I am eager for the day I can claim my seat in the Dublin Parliament and demonstrate my loyalty to my queen," Hugh said smoothly, "but I defer, of course, to her majesty's greater wisdom."

Lord Burghley smiled, pleased. At least *this* O'Neill would serve the crown faithfully.

1

Dublin, April 1567

Irish mist, he thought, *shrouds the deeds of saint and sinner alike . . .* It felt good to be home at long last.

Wending his way through Dublin's roads to the home long denied him, Hugh O'Neill enjoyed the feel of the purifying mist on his face and thought about his long-awaited homecoming.

Avenging the murder of his father, Matthew, and his brother, Brian, would be Hugh's first business in Ireland. Matthew, Shane O'Neill's older but illegitimate half brother, had quarreled with Shane over the leadership of Ulster when their father died. The Dublin Parliament favored Matthew's claim while Shane enjoyed popular support in Ulster. The stalemate between the feuding brothers ended when Shane's men ambushed and killed Matthew.

Next Hugh's sword would strike his cousin Turlough to revenge his older brother Brian's death. While Shane was in London negotiating peace with the queen, Turlough had murdered Brian. Executed by Shane's order, Hugh knew without a doubt.

The best part of this intended revenge was that the English would not oppose him; without reservation, the Dublin Parliament would uphold his claim to Tyrone. Believing him loyal because he'd been fostered in England and become part of her court, Queen Elizabeth had given Hugh her blessing.

"Do whatever you must to rid Ulster of our enemies," the queen had bade him.

And that is her majesty's first mistake, Hugh thought. Living in England a thousand years could never alter the heart of an Irishman.

"Good Christ, but I detest Ireland's climate," Sir Henry Sidney complained, interrupting his companion's reverie. "Do the sun and the stars never appear in the sky?"

"It rains in England too," Hugh reminded him.

"So it does, my friend, but England's rain is . . . is—"

"Drier?"

"Friendlier," Sir Henry finished.

Leaving the road, the two men turned onto the private lane leading to the O'Neill mansion's courtyard. "Did I ever tell you," Hugh asked abruptly, "how my family won its crest, the Red Hand of Ulster?"

"No, I don't believe I've heard that one."

"In a contest to claim Ulster's fertile lands," Hugh began, "the O'Neill and the O'Donnell chieftains raced boats across Lough Neagh. Whoever touched the shore first would win. Seeing he was about to be beaten, my illustrious ancestor cut off his hand, threw it ashore ahead of the O'Donnell, and proclaimed himself the prince of Ulster."

Sir Henry glanced sidelong at his companion. "Charming tale."

"I wonder which of us present-day O'Neills would make that sacrifice?"

"Well, if you're foolish enough to be tempted," the Englishman snorted, "don't cut off your sword hand. You might need it."

Hugh chuckled softly. "Thanks for the advice."

Walking into the mansion's main foyer, Hugh was satisfied that all was as it should be. Refurbishing and maintaining the house after Brian's death had been well worth the money he'd spent.

Hugh led Sir Henry into the study, poured two drams of whiskey, and handed one to the Englishman. There was a knock on the door, and it opened to admit a plump, middle-aged woman.

"Peg?" Hugh asked.

The housekeeper nodded and pulled a sealed paper from her pocket. "The viceroy's man delivered this today for Sir Henry Sidney." She handed the missive to Hugh who passed it to Sir Henry. "Can I bring you something to eat?" Peg asked before turning to leave.

"No, that'll be all for tonight," Hugh said, dismissing her.

After breaking its seal, Sir Henry read the missive, then looked up and smiled. "The viceroy says there's no danger to you yet. Shane O'Neill is occupied elsewhere."

"Where?"

"Executing a *surprise* attack on the O'Donnells."

"How does Russell know?" Hugh asked, his expression devoid of emotion.

Sir Henry shrugged. "Most likely, he has a well-placed spy in Ulster."

A well-placed spy in Shane's household, thought Hugh. *Perhaps a lovely English bride? A discontented clansman?*

"You're welcome to pass the night here," Hugh said in invitation.

"No," Sir Henry refused, picking up his cloak. "Russell wants to meet with us tonight at Dublin Castle."

"Tonight?" Hugh grimaced, then smiled at the other man. "I've waited fifteen years to come home. I suppose another few hours won't matter."

On the site of the ancient stronghold of Haskulf the Dane stood the symbol of English power in Ireland. A large quadrangular building, Dublin Castle was a fortress, a government building, a prison—the heart of English oppression.

Hugh and Sir Henry followed a young English soldier through a maze of dark corridors to the council chamber, their only light the torch the soldier carried. Anxious, Hugh wondered why they'd been sent for at such a late hour. Was it really an urgent meeting or did assassination await him there?

Their escort knocked on the council's door, then opened it and ushered them inside. Hugh smiled quizzically at the three familiar faces that looked up at their entrance.

"Sit down," said Sir William Russell, Queen Elizabeth's viceroy.

Nodding a greeting to Lords Fitzgerald and Burke of the Dublin Parliament, Hugh sat down at the table and turned to the viceroy. "What urgent matter requires meeting at this late hour?" he asked as an aide handed him a glass of whiskey.

"Your victory over Shane O'Neill is at hand," Russell answered, then nodded to his aide who opened the door and gestured to someone outside.

A MacDonnell warrior strode briskly into the chamber. In his hands he carried a foul-smelling sackcloth.

"Put it on the table," the viceroy ordered. Then, "Open it."

"Good God!" Lord Fitzgerald exclaimed.

"Bloody shit," muttered Lord Burke.

Hugh blanched as the severed and tarred head of a man was revealed. "What is this?" he demanded.

The viceroy counted out one thousand marks from a Treasury strongbox and handed it to the warrior. An aide escorted the MacDonnell courier to the door.

"You don't recognize your uncle Shane?" the viceroy asked. Without waiting for a reply, he turned to the aide and ordered, "Skewer it on a pike and mount it on the northwest gate. Let all Dublin see the punishment for treason against the crown."

Momentarily stunned, Hugh stared at the tarred head, but then his arrogant O'Neill pride surfaced and set the blood in his veins to boiling. His hand dropped to his dagger, but Burke touched his arm in a friendly warning.

I would have challenged Shane honorably, Hugh thought, *and buried him in a manner befitting a fallen prince of Ulster, not mutilated his body. Ulstermen have long memories; this needless atrocity will cost the English more than they thought to pay.*

"Well?" the viceroy said.

"We've finally bested Shane O'Neill," Sir Henry said to Hugh, "but you don't look pleased."

Hugh inwardly gritted his teeth and pasted a smile on his face. "All is well with the world, Henry, but I've been cheated out of exacting my own revenge."

The viceroy chuckled. "To the best of my knowledge, disappointment won't kill you."

Dungannon, Ulster, Ireland

Shane O'Neill, the hope of the rebellious Ulstermen, was dead. As if the heavens mourned his passing, bleak clouds of gray drooped sadly in a low overcast sky.

Dressed completely in black, Kathryn Devereux O'Neill knelt in front of her husband's grave and tried to pray, but her thoughts kept drifting to the uncertainty of her future. Shane was gone, leaving her to fend for herself, their four-year-old daughter, and the child growing inside her body. How could she ever tell her children that what lay beneath the sod was their father's headless corpse? Or that Shane's own cousin had betrayed him, setting into motion the events that ended in his brutal murder? On the other hand, how could she not tell them the truth? And where should they go? Should she return to her family in England or remain in this heathen land for the sake of the heir she carried?

"What should I do?" Kathryn cried, desperately confused.

"Are you speaking to me, Mama?" asked Maeve. Kathryn's daughter was a miniature replica of herself, complete with red hair and emerald-green eyes.

"I'm speaking to Da," Kathryn answered.

The little girl looked around and then back at her mother. "I don't see Da."

"That doesn't mean he isn't here," Kathryn replied. "You don't see the sun today, but it's up there in the sky; and you can't see your new brother, but he's here inside my belly."

"I've been waiting so long. When will I see him?"

"I've already told you several times," Kathryn answered. "He'll be with us in the autumn."

"And Da too?"

"No, Da's gone to heaven." *Small chance of that happening,* Kathryn thought and held out her hand to her daughter. With Maeve in tow, she left the graveyard.

Patrick and Conal O'Donnelly, kinsmen and warriors in the service of Shane O'Neill, waited in the courtyard for Kathryn. "There's no doubt in my mind," Conal said. "Turlough will proclaim himself the O'Neill and march into Dungannon."

"Hugh is in Dublin," Patrick remarked, watching Kathryn and Maeve walk down the path from the graveyard. "He has more right to Tyrone than Turlough."

"If we pledge ourselves to Hugh," Conal said, "we could get the chance to avenge Shane's death."

"What about Katie and Maeve?" Patrick asked, glancing sidelong at his brother. "We've sworn to protect them."

"Katie will decide to go home," Conal said. "Dungannon has nothin' to offer her, especially when Turlough arrives."

"Do you think Hugh would help us get her to England?"

"I don't know," Conal replied, "but it's worth a try. You stay here with Katie, and I'll ride to Dublin."

Spying the two men, Maeve dashed toward her favorite of all the O'Neill clansmen. *"Uncle Patrick!"* she called. Laughing, Patrick scooped her into his arms.

"Da's gone to heaven," Maeve told him. "And I'll see my little brother—I forget when."

"Is that so?"

Maeve nodded. "Mama said it."

"Then it must be so," Patrick agreed. "How about a kiss?" Maeve planted a smacking, wet kiss on his lips.

"What about me, colleen?" Conal asked. Leaning over, Maeve pecked his cheek, and Patrick grinned at her apparent lack of enthusiasm for his brother.

"There's an urgent matter we must discuss," Patrick said to Kathryn.

Taking Maeve from his arms, Kathryn set her on the ground, saying, "Run inside. Maude or Polly will give you a drink." When the little girl had vanished, Kathryn looked expectantly at the brothers.

"Turlough will return to Dungannon," Patrick told her.

"Dispatch him! I want him dead."

"It's not that easy," Conal said. "Turlough will be the new O'Neill."

"What about *my* child?"

"Shane named Turlough his tanist, his successor, and had no chance to recant before he died," Patrick explained. "The family supports him."

"Turlough deserted Shane," Kathryn cried, incredulous. "The O'Neills would follow a traitor?"

"His duplicity is unprovable," Patrick argued. "Besides, the O'Neills can't wait for Shane's son to be born and grow. The family needs a leader to keep the English at bay."

"Are my children in danger?" she asked.

"Harmin' Shane's widow and children is an action even Turlough wouldn't dare," Conal assured her.

"What should I do?"

"Stay put for the present," Patrick advised her, "at least until we judge which way the wind blows."

"I'm leavin' for Dublin to arrange your escape," Conal told her, "in case you feel the need."

"Do nothin' to antagonize Turlough," Patrick warned, watching his brother walk away.

"What do you mean?" Kathryn asked guardedly. She would die before bedding the lecherous swine who'd tried to rape her.

"I mean," Patrick answered, "break your cute little habit of baitin' the man."

A smile touched her lips, the first in many days. "I'll try," Kathryn promised, "but it won't be easy. With Turlough, I fear, it's either yield or antagonize."

"And I'll help," Patrick said.

Riding at breakneck speed, Conal arrived in Dublin a

few days later and learned that Hugh was living in the house built by his grandfather, Conn O'Neill, first earl of Tyrone, for those times when his presence in Dublin was required. He rode to the O'Neill mansion and presented himself to the housekeeper who ushered him inside.

Hugh, exuding his irresistible aura of power, rose from his chair and walked around the desk to confront the O'Neill warrior. "Well?" Hugh prodded when Conal stared in silence at him.

"I am your kinsman Conal O'Donnelly from Ulster," Conal introduced himself. "Shane O'Neill is dead."

"I know," Hugh replied, assessing this previously unknown clansman. "Ignoring his head on a pike proved impossible for me."

Conal went down on one bended knee. "I pledge you my fealty and that of my brother Patrick," he declared formally.

"Rise," Hugh said, then extended his hand to the other man. "Your brother was always Shane's favorite, and if I remember correctly, possessed the keenest sense of humor."

"That's Patrick. His humor is keen while you're sharin' a jest but painfully sharp when aimed at you."

"Why isn't he here to pledge fealty himself?"

"Patrick remained in Dungannon to see to the welfare of Shane's widow and daughter," Conal answered. "We promised Shane we'd keep her safe."

The image of the English beauty from whom he'd once stolen a kiss formed in Hugh's mind. *Petite and curvaceously slim—creamy complexion unmarred by freckles—brilliant copper hair resembling a fiery sunset—a small, upturned nose topping an infectious grin—startling emerald eyes that rivaled the green of Ireland.* "How fares the lady?" Hugh asked.

Conal shrugged. "Shane's murder was a terrible shock. Their daughter, Maeve, is four and Lady Kathryn is with child."

"Any news of Turlough?"

"We think he'll soon be ridin' into Dungannon and proclaimin' himself the new O'Neill. Lady Kathryn detests the man and could even be in danger. Turlough's attempted rape of her before the battle at Farsetmore caused the rift between Shane and him. Shane never made it home and had no chance to name another successor. Can you help us get her to England?"

"My housekeeper will give you a place to perch while I digest this information," Hugh hedged, his expression unreadable. "We'll speak again in the morning."

After Peg escorted Conal from the chamber, Hugh poured himself a whiskey and raised it to his lips. There came a rap on the door. At his call, it opened to admit Sir Henry Sidney. "Are you ready?" the Englishman asked.

"For what?"

"We're expected at Lord Fitzgerald's."

"Make my excuses, will you?" Hugh said. "I've just received a message concerning an urgent family matter." He noted the Englishman's interested expression, then added, "I'll tell you about it after I've considered the matter."

"Lady Fiona will be disappointed," Sir Henry remarked. "She hoped to renew the acquaintance you'd begun in London."

"Disappointment won't kill her," Hugh replied, "or so the viceroy once said. Tell Fiona I'll visit soon, if possible."

With a grunt, Sir Henry acknowledged Hugh's quip. "As you wish."

Alone again, Hugh gulped his whiskey down and poured another, then relaxed in the chair in front of the hearth. *What should I do about Shane's pregnant widow?* he wondered. *Leave her to Turlough or help her get to England? Neither choice is appealing if she manages to drop a boy and stalemates my claim to Tyrone.*

Hugh sipped his whiskey and pondered Kathryn's future. A provocative idea leaped into his mind, its utter simplicity making him laugh.

"I know exactly what to do with you, Lady Kathryn," he said to the empty chamber, "and you will cooperate." With anticipation gleaming in his dark eyes, Hugh stood and walked to his desk, then poured another whiskey and raised his glass in salute. "To Kathryn Devereux O'Neill— would that all of life's problems were as easily solved!"

2

Unaware that she and her children had become valuable pawns in the soaring ambitions of two men, Kathryn gazed out her chamber window at the sparkling spring morning. Who could have guessed that on a day as alive as this, Shane would be dead? And, more importantly, she would be forced to face Turlough alone. Not quite alone, Kathryn corrected herself and looked down at the courtyard below.

Patrick, as jumpy as a lone Englishman in Ulster, paced back and forth. A messenger had ridden into Dungannon the previous night, and Turlough was expected that morning. Patrick had cautioned Kathryn to stay hidden during the day so that he could gauge Turlough's intent. Acting as a buffer, Patrick would plead her ill with the child she carried, but Kathryn must show herself at supper or risk arousing Turlough's anger.

In the distance Kathryn saw a troop of men approaching. Turlough's *gall-oglach* were fierce-looking warriors. Mercenaries chosen to protect the O'Neill chieftain because of their mighty bodies, the men wore shirts of mail, iron caps, bright-colored trews that ended at their knees, and leather leggings. Cut short above the eyes, their hair hung long on their necks. They wore swords at their sides and carried battle-axes in their hands.

Patrick caught Kathryn's attention and motioned her away from the window. She scurried across the chamber and leapt into her bed.

Polly, her tiring woman, raced into the chamber. "My lady," she whispered. "Turlough is almost here."

"Yes," Kathryn replied, "but whispering's unnecessary."

Dungannon's housekeeper, Maude, marched into the chamber and looked at her daughter, ordering, "Polly, fetch the pot and then get a compress for Katie's head." She turned to Kathryn, explaining, "There's nothin' less seductive than a pukin' woman." At that, lady and tiring woman dissolved into giggles.

Riding into Dungannon's courtyard at a dignified pace, the new O'Neill chieftain surveyed everything in sight. Turlough was a giant of a man, standing well over six feet. Large but not fat, his muscular huskiness gave proof to many years of vigorous training. His very size instilled respect, if not fear, in the most toughened of soldiers. Fair skinned, sporting sandy blond hair and blue eyes, Turlough was as handsome as he was big. When he smiled, his face became deceptively boyish.

All that was Shane's is mine, Turlough thought with satisfaction, *except for one copper-haired wench, but I'll soon remedy that.*

Patrick approached Turlough and went down on one bended knee. "I pledge you my fealty," he said formally, his gaze never wavering from the other man's. Patrick hoped God would forgive the terrible lie he spoke, the breaking of faith being such a heinous offense.

Surprise registered on Turlough's face. "Those words

are far different from the last you spoke," he said, enjoying the other man's discomfort.

"As the eldest O'Donnelly and hereditary marshal of the O'Neill forces, my unquestionin' loyalty belongs to the O'Neill chieftain, whoever he may be," Patrick returned. "Acceptin' my pledge will gain you my unwaverin' steadfastness and sword arm until I draw my final breath."

"I can understand a man not wishin' to break faith," Turlough replied. "The O'Donnellys have always been loyal warriors in the O'Neill's service. Rise up—I harbor no grudge."

When they entered the main building's foyer, Turlough could no longer contain his desire. "Fetch Katie," he ordered, heading for the study.

"That's impossible at the moment," Patrick told him.

That stopped Turlough in his tracks. He whirled around, his eyes wide in angry disbelief. His right hand automatically reached for the sword at his side.

"I mean no disrespect," Patrick added hastily, his eyes fixed on the hand resting upon the sword hilt. "Feelin' ill in the mornin' is the way of breedin' women. Lady Kathryn sends her regrets until a later hour."

"I've waited five years but no longer," Turlough exploded, marching toward the stairs. "Excuses won't help her now."

Resisting the urge to slit the man's throat, Patrick dashed after him and placed a restraining hand on his arm. "I must speak with you before you see Katie," Patrick said, and when Turlough hesitated, added, "besides, a pukin' woman is the most incredibly unattractive sight, especially first thin' in the mornin'. Unless you've a notion to hold her head?"

Once inside the study, Turlough sat in his late cousin's favorite chair. "Well, what is it?" he demanded.

Patrick's gaze locked on Turlough's. "I would know your plans for Katie," he said, certain his death was at hand.

"You dare question the O'Neill?" Turlough barked, incredulous.

"I want assurance of her safety."

"She won't be harmed," Turlough replied, then added with an uncharacteristic smile, "in fact, I've decided to marry her."

Only mildly surprised by his intent, Patrick asked, "May I advise you?"

"*You* would instruct *me* on the ways of women?" Turlough was certain Patrick's wits had somehow been scattered.

"No, I'd never do that." Patrick forced a chuckle. "Since Shane's death, I've passed many hours consolin' Katie and would advise you on the most peaceful path to follow, assumin' you prefer she be willin'."

"I prefer her willin'," Turlough conceded, "but willin' or no, I'll have her."

"Carryin' Shane's child while he lies in yonder graveyard is makin' her outlook bleak," Patrick lied. "Proceed slowly and woo her gently."

"I've no time for courtin'," Turlough snapped, exasperated. As the O'Neill, he deserved immediate satisfaction.

"If you prefer her willin', then make the time," Patrick counseled. "Katie responds well to kindness."

Turlough stared at Patrick and considered his words. "I'll try it for a couple of days," he relented finally.

"Katie trusts me," Patrick went on. "The more time you allow, the more time I'll have to whisper your many virtues in her ear."

"So be it," Turlough agreed, "but I won't wait forever."

Kathryn emerged from her chamber just before supper. A vision of bereavement, she wore a black gown with a modestly high neck, a ruff of white lace the only brightness breaking its gloom. The paleness of her skin contrasted sharply with her gown, making her appear ill. Her hair had been pulled back severely, braided and then twisted into a knot at the nape of her neck. Dark circles beneath her eyes betrayed her sleepless nights. Except for her wedding band, Kathryn wore no jewelry, yet her beauty was undiminished, merely her frailty accentuated.

Kathryn started down the stairs. Her legs trembled almost uncontrollably, but her expression betrayed no emotion. Apprehensive, she hesitated at the bottom, then squared her shoulders in proud determination and headed for the study.

"Enter," Turlough called when she knocked on the door.

Kathryn shuddered at the sound of his voice but opened the door. Drinking whiskey, Turlough relaxed in a chair with his booted feet propped up on the desk. Kathryn's legs buckled at the sight, and she grabbed the door for support.

Turlough leapt up and kept her from falling, then helped her to a chair. He went down on one bended knee in front of her, and his enormous hands reached out to cover hers. "I'm sorry about Shane and sincerely regret my unseemly behavior when I . . ."

Attempted to rape me, Kathryn thought.

". . . unleashed my natural, manly desires," he finished.

Kathryn nodded, her expression sad, but her thoughts murderous. *Bastard!* she fumed inwardly. *If you had fought at Shane's side, the battle at Farsetmore would have ended differently, and Shane would have had no need to seek refuge with the MacDonnells at Dunluce Castle. His death is as much your fault as theirs.*

Certain her eyes betrayed her thoughts, Kathryn looked down and saw the dagger attached to his belt. Resisting the powerful urge to draw and plunge it deep into his chest, she tore her gaze away from it.

"As head of the family," Turlough continued, patting her hand, "I swear, by all that is holy, to protect you and Shane's children."

"Protect?" she echoed. "But who would harm us?"

"Hugh O'Neill would dare anythin' to become earl of Tyrone," Turlough told her. "The death of Shane's children would certainly serve his purpose, and your queen would forgive her favorite O'Neill almost any trespass. But there's no cause for worry. I'll guard your safety myself."

And who will protect us from you? Kathryn thought, but said, "I felt, in spite of everything, we could always depend upon you."

Encouraged by her words, Turlough gazed deeply into her incredible eyes and was neatly caught, mesmerized by those emerald jewels. He longed to pull her into his arms, mold her body to his, and mark her as his own, but because of Patrick's advice, checked the urge and suffered the sweetest torment he'd ever known.

"Shall we sup?" Kathryn asked, breaking the spell.

Seated beside Turlough in the crowded great hall, Kathryn stared at the table laden with bread, butter, and honey. Unable to swallow a bite, she glanced at Turlough who smiled and filled her wine goblet. Kathryn forced herself to return his smile, then lifted the goblet and sipped the wine.

Maude arrived with supper's first course of barley soup garnished with bits of boiled pork. "You're lookin' as fit and fine as ever, my boy," she complimented Turlough, boldly appraising him.

"And I feel better than I look," he boasted.

"To the touch?"

"Ah, Maudie! If I was a mite older, you'd be in deep trouble."

"You'd be the one in trouble," Maude shot back. "In my youth, several priests turned gray listenin' to my confessions." Turlough's laughter boomed like thunder throughout the hall.

Leaning against the wall near the entrance, Patrick watched the high table throughout the meal and prayed that Kathryn would not react like a typical woman, losing control. Unhappily, Patrick noted Kathryn's lack of appetite. When Turlough pointed at her plate and said something close to her ear, Patrick's heart pounded and his hand fingered the hilt of his dagger. Certain they were about to be slaughtered, Patrick watched in amazement as Kathryn stood to leave the hall. Sympathetic concern was etched across Turlough's face.

"The babe makes me queasy," Kathryn whispered, passing him on her way out.

Relieved, Patrick relaxed against the wall and closed his eyes. The danger would begin again the next day and every day until he could get Kathryn away from Dungannon.

"You've given me sound advice."

Patrick's eyes flew open at the sound of that voice.

"This courtin' is a frustratin' business," Turlough complained. Then he asked in a low voice, "Do you know of a suitable woman?"

Patrick smiled. "You could visit Maura."

"Maura?"

"You remember, Shane's mistress in the village."

"You've served me well this day," Turlough said, delighted by the prospect of sampling Shane's wife and mistress. "I won't be forgettin'."

Patrick grinned at him. "I'm certain of that."

After Turlough had gone, Patrick left the hall unnoticed and made his way upstairs. Without bothering to knock, he slipped into a bedchamber and stopped short, charmed by the sight that greeted him.

Kathryn sat in the tub in front of the hearth while Polly scrubbed her back. Hearing a noise, both women whirled around. Coloring a dark shade of pink, Kathryn gasped and sank lower in the water. Polly cast him a reproving look.

Patrick straddled a nearby chair. "I'm sorry for disturbin' your bath," he apologized, wearing the most unrepentant smile, "but we must speak while Turlough is otherwise occupied."

"Occupied how?" Kathryn asked.

"Visitin' Maura."

"I knew she was good for somethin'," muttered Polly.

"Turlough is plannin' on marryin' you," Patrick reported.

"*Marry?*" Kathryn cried. "I won't do it and he can't make me."

"Correct," Patrick replied, "but he can make you wish that you had." Kathryn paled at the implication.

"I've advised him to travel the slow road to you," he continued. "Understand this, Katie. Every road ends somewhere. Do you go or stay?"

"I go," she answered without hesitation. "Have you heard from Conal?"

"Not yet." Patrick's gaze drifted to Polly. "Are you with us, colleen?"

"I'm with you."

"No letters to England informin' them of your arrival," Patrick warned Kathryn. "And do not antagonize the man. We play a dangerous game, and may God's mercy protect us from discovery."

Patrick stood and crossed the chamber to the door, then

paused and looked back. "And may I add, Katie," he teased, "you've a very fetchin' backside." He was gone before the washing cloth hit the door.

Kathryn managed to almost totally avoid Turlough for several days. Each evening she supped with him in the great hall and then retired to an early bed. The O'Neill warriors claimed Turlough's days while Maura claimed his nights.

Kathryn's daily routine included walking to the graveyard each morning. Kathryn believed that tending Shane's grave and offering prayers for his salvation was her duty. That she had good reason to despise the man was unimportant. Kathryn would kneel at the grave, arrange a bouquet of fresh flowers from the garden, and pray for his departed soul.

"Little did we know those many years ago how prophetic your words would be," Kathryn said aloud one morning, unaware of being overheard.

"Ahem!" a deep voice sounded beside her. Startled, Kathryn whirled around, her hands flying up to ward off an attack.

"I did not mean to frighten you," Turlough apologized, towering over her.

Unable to speak, Kathryn nodded in acknowledgment. One hand clutched her heaving bosom as if it could calm the frantic pounding of her heart.

"Of what prophetic words do you speak?" he asked.

"On our wedding day," Kathryn said breathlessly, "Shane asked me to bring flowers to his grave each day. It was a jest."

"Or premonition." Turlough held out his hand. "Come away from here. I want to speak with you." He helped her to stand, and together they returned to the study.

"A messenger arrived late last night," Turlough told her.

"Hugh O'Neill and his men are causin' mine no end of trouble. I'll be leavin' in the mornin' for a fortnight or so."

Kathryn's spirits soared at the news of his departure, but her expression remained impassive. "What kind of trouble?" she asked.

"Nothin' for you to worry about," he replied. "Patrick will stay behind to guard your safety. When I return to Dungannon . . ." Turlough hesitated a moment, then forged ahead. "Because of my tender regard for Maeve and you, I've decided we will marry. I'm certain Shane would have wanted it so."

Although she'd known his plans, Kathryn was flabbergasted. Speaking the words made it all too real. He'd betrayed her husband, bedded his mistress, and then expected—*no, decided*—to marry her! Longing to slit his arrogant throat, Kathryn stared down at her lap and tried to hide her anger.

"I cannot accept your proposal," she said, then peeked up at him.

Turlough's eyes glinted dangerously.

"On the other hand," Kathryn amended quickly, "I'm not rejecting your proposal either. Everything has happened too fast. I'm so confused." With a woebegone expression she hid her face in her hands and wept.

Seeking to comfort her, Turlough knelt in front of her and stroked her arm.

"Shane's so recently gone," Kathryn whispered. "Birthing a healthy child is all I can think about. Can you understand such womanly troubles?"

"Of course." Turlough was so thoroughly frustrated that he'd the urge to slap, not bed her. "Weakness bein' the way of women," he said, "it's natural you're upset. Consider my offer. The best medicine for your heartache could be a quick remarriage."

Or your untimely death, Kathryn thought mutinously, but said with a tremulous smile, "I promise to think long and hard." Encouraging his trust, she planted a chaste kiss on his cheek and murmured, "I'll miss you."

Turlough caught her against his chest, but reluctant to risk frightening her, dared no more.

Patrick and Kathryn stood together in the courtyard on that warm and sunny first day of June and waited to bid Turlough farewell. When he stood in front of her, Kathryn extended her hand and forced a smile as sunny as the day.

"We'll miss you, especially Maeve, who's begun thinking of her uncle Turlough as the most important man in her life." Kathryn rambled on, worried he'd kiss her, or worse, change his mind about leaving. "I've planned a special treat to sweeten her loss."

"Loss?"

"First Shane, and now you must leave."

"But I'll be returnin'," Turlough reminded her.

Kathryn smiled warmly. "Understanding the difference is difficult for a child."

"What's the treat?" he asked.

"A picnic."

"Wanderin' about is dangerous," Turlough warned.

"We won't go far," Kathryn explained, fearing he'd delay his departure. "Patrick and Polly will accompany us."

Nodding permission, Turlough drew her close. His lips brushed hers and he kissed her cheek. "I'm hopin' Maeve's mother will also miss me," he whispered against her ear.

Feigning shyness, Kathryn looked away. Turlough smiled at the rosy blush staining her cheeks, then mounted his horse and led the O'Neill warriors away.

"Well done," Patrick said, then chuckled in sublime relief. " 'Twas *very* well done, Katie."

"I've already washed my face today," Kathryn complained, wiping her mouth on her sleeve. "Now I must scrub it again and pray his filthy touch rinses off." Laughing, Patrick offered her his arm and escorted her inside.

Later, they set off on their outing. Leaving the main estate behind, they walked at a leisurely pace, and when Maeve tired, Patrick offered his shoulders for her pleasure. Kathryn remarked on the distance they'd walked but was told the perfect spot for picnicking was just a little farther. Rounding a bend, they saw a coach and two men by the side of the road up ahead.

"*Conal!*" Kathryn cried and ran toward him.

Relieved she was safe, Conal hugged her, then introduced the other man as Sean and opened the door of the coach. Polly climbed inside, then took Maeve from Patrick.

"Let's go," Patrick said, turning to Kathryn.

"I don't understand," she said, bewildered by what was happening.

"We're bound for England," Conal told her.

"I can't leave now," Kathryn protested. "I've brought nothing with me! What about clothing?"

"We couldn't escape in secret if we stopped to pack our bags," Patrick snapped. Her needless delay endangered their lives. "Climb in and be quick about it."

Kathryn did as she was told.

3

Misty and silent, the starless night greeted Hugh O'Neill when he stepped into the courtyard. In the fog-shrouded distance, a coach turned onto the lane leading to the mansion. When it came to a halt, Hugh stepped forward and opened the door. "Patrick O'Donnelly?" he asked.

"In the flesh."

Hugh looked at the other occupants of the coach, his attention fixed on one in particular. "Is she ill?"

"We slipped her a mild sleepin' draught," Patrick answered. "She thinks we've anchored off Barnstable Bay, and I'm not lookin' forward to tellin' her differently."

Hugh's gaze fell on Maeve, sleeping in Polly's arms. "And the child?"

"Too much adventure wearied her."

"I'll take Lady Kathryn," Hugh said. "You carry the child."

Hugh reached up and lifted Kathryn into his arms, then turned toward the mansion. Instinctively seeking his warmth, Kathryn nestled against his chest. The intimate gesture surprised Hugh. He paused for a brief moment and stared down at the hauntingly lovely face that had smiled at him in a thousand dreams.

Upstairs, Hugh walked into one of the bedchambers facing the rear gardens and gently placed Kathryn down on the bed. Right behind him, Peg gestured to Patrick and Polly to bring Maeve into the adjoining chamber.

I hope she's as biddable as she is lovely, Hugh thought, leaning over to get a closer look. Without thinking, he reached out and brushed a stray lock of copper hair from her face.

Green eyes opened, and Kathryn stared at the masculine face, merely inches from hers. Her eyelids closed again, and she drifted into drugged sleep.

How could this beautiful vision have loved his uncle? Hugh wondered, an unfamiliar and wholly unpleasant pang of jealousy stabbing him. For that matter, how had she even survived his notoriously impulsive temper?

As if caught in a nightmare, Kathryn whimpered in her sleep. A solitary tear rolled down her cheek.

"Rest easy," Hugh whispered, his fingertips brushing the teardrop away. His deep, masculine voice seemed to quiet her. Hugh turned to leave and discovered, to his great embarrassment, the others were staring curiously at him.

Kathryn finally awakened at mid-morning the following day. Groggy, she looked around the chamber with detached interest and noted its rich furnishings. Remarkably rich accommodations for an English inn, she thought, but the memory of her arrival eluded her.

In spite of her queasiness, Kathryn sat up. Glancing at her night shift, she wondered why she wore a gown that wasn't hers. To whom did it belong? And why couldn't she remember arriving at the inn last night? What was happening to her? Was she losing her wits?

Polly opened the chamber door and beckoned to someone waiting outside. Patrick walked in and crossed the chamber to stand at the foot of the bed. When she looked at him, Kathryn's eyes mirrored her confusion.

"Katie . . ." Patrick hesitated, reluctant to complete the task at hand. Cocking her head to one side, Kathryn looked at him through blurred vision.

Unnoticed, Hugh stood in the doorway and watched the scene unfolding. His sharp eyes swept his unknowing hostage and noted her confusion. Kathryn shook her head as if to clear the cobwebs from her mind, and her luxurious mane of hair swirled around her like a fiery veil. Enchanted by the sight, Hugh relaxed against the doorjamb.

"Katie," Patrick began again, then glanced at the doorway. Following his gaze, Kathryn gasped in surprise.

"Good morning," Hugh said cheerfully.

"Y-y-you!" Kathryn jerked the coverlet up to her chin.

"Hugh O'Neill, at your service." He bowed with exaggerated gallantry. "I'm flattered you remember me."

"Where am I?" Kathryn demanded, turning back to Patrick.

"Dublin," he answered, inwardly cursing the other man's impatience.

"You've betrayed me! You vile, contemptible . . . !" Kathryn's body nearly shook with rage. Unmindful of her scanty attire, Kathryn leapt out of bed and faced them like a hostile warrior. How best to make her escape?

"This is the safest place for Maeve and you," Patrick tried to explain. "Hugh—"

"Seek refuge in the lion's den?" Kathryn cut him off. "You blockhead! This O'Neill wants my children dead."

Kathryn glanced at Polly, ordering, "Get Maeve. We're leaving."

Enjoying his guest's wild dramatics, Hugh chuckled softly and motioned Polly to stay where she was. When

Kathryn glared at him, his chuckle gave birth to a mocking laugh.

Kathryn grabbed the brass candlestick from the bedside table. Clutching it, she advanced on her captor.

"Try to stop me," she threatened, "and I'll kill you."

The mocking laughter died. Motionless, Hugh waited for her attack, his gaze fixed on hers.

"*Stand aside,*" Kathryn screamed, panicking at his silent refusal to retreat. She raised the candlestick to strike, but Hugh grabbed her wrist. Inches apart, their gazes met and clashed.

"If I had wanted you dead," Hugh told her, "believe me, madam, you would be."

Realizing Kathryn's complexion suddenly matched the green of her eyes, Hugh flung the candlestick aside, grabbed her around the waist, and rushed her across the chamber. Kathryn's stomach heaved and emptied its meager contents into the chamber pot. Weakened, she leaned heavily against his legs.

"You'll be fine," Hugh assured her. "The sleeping draught turned your stomach." He helped her back to bed and left, taking Patrick with him.

"I want my daughter," Kathryn insisted, trying to rise.

"Maeve's safe." Polly forced her mistress to lie back on the bed.

"You knew." Kathryn accused her.

"Would you have preferred remainin' with Turlough?" the other girl countered. "At least, Hugh played no part in Shane's murder."

"Oh, go away." Kathryn turned her back in dismissal and promptly fell asleep. Polly sighed with relief. The worst was over. The tempest had passed. If only she could be certain that bringing Kathryn to Dublin had been the right thing to do.

The draperies were drawn aside the next morning, and sunshine invaded the chamber. Moaning, Kathryn burrowed deeper beneath the coverlet.

"It's time to join the ranks of the livin'," Polly announced loudly.

"Have you no mercy?" Kathryn struggled to sit up. A knock on the door drew her attention, but before she could answer, it flew open.

Maeve dashed in, jumped on the bed, and gave her mother a gigantic hug. Kathryn's mood lightened immeasurably as she gazed at her daughter's beaming face.

"I like it here," Maeve told her. "Uncle Hugh's nice, not like Uncle Turlough."

"*Uncle Hugh?*" Kathryn echoed, brushing a stray lock of copper hair from her daughter's face. She forced herself to smile, saying, "I'm very glad you like it here, sweet."

"Uncle Hugh said I'm named for a great Irish queen," the little girl continued, her green eyes sparkling with excitement. "I'm to be queen of Ireland someday. Uncle Hugh promised."

"How wonderful!" Kathryn hugged her daughter. "I'm certain you'll be the grandest queen ever, and far better than Elizabeth Tudor."

"Elizabeth who?"

A chuckle sounded from the doorway, drawing their attention. With his arms folded across his chest, Hugh leaned against the doorjamb.

"Good morning," he greeted Kathryn. "Feeling better?"

Uncertain of what to do, Kathryn stared at him. Should she fear him? If he meant them no harm, why had he abducted them?

Well built, Kathryn unconsciously inventoried Hugh's person. *Eyes that sparkle when he smiles—a charming smile . . .*

"Mama, say good morning or you'll be rude," Maeve chided in a loud whisper.

"Good morning." Kathryn blushed at where her thoughts had drifted. "I'm much better."

Uninvited, Hugh stepped into the chamber and sauntered over to the foot of the bed.

"*Do* come in, *Uncle* Hugh," Kathryn drawled, irritated.

"Come along, Maeve," Polly said. "Let's go order breakfast and a bath for your mother."

As he stared at Kathryn, Hugh's smile froze on his face. Peg's overlarge night shift had slipped, and one of Kathryn's shoulders was bared, giving her a seductive appearance.

What the devil is wrong with me? he asked himself, feeling his groin tighten. *Many comely wenches have graced my bed, and they weren't there because I'd abducted them.*

Hugh scowled and looked away, but almost immediately, his gaze was drawn back to her irresistible shoulder. *Sweet Jesu!* he swore silently. She was as tempting as original sin!

Kathryn's gaze followed his. Scarlet with embarrassment, she yanked the offending night shift up.

"We've much to discuss, but I'll be gone most of the day," Hugh said, wondering if her rosy blush went all the way down to her . . . He cleared his throat, banishing the thought from his mind, and asked, "Will you sup with me?"

"As you wish." When the supper hour arrived, Kathryn had no plans to be in Dublin, never mind supping with him.

"Until this evening, then." Thinking she would cooperate after all, Hugh started to leave but paused at the door, saying, "You've the freedom of the house but don't entertain any foolish notions. You'll be closely watched." Then he was gone.

Kathryn leaned back against the headboard and stared at the door. *What business does he have with me? Could he be persuaded to help me get to England? Closely watched? The arrogant bastard!*

Despairing at her shabby appearance, Kathryn paused at the top of the stairs and smoothed an imaginary wrinkle from her skirt, the one she'd worn on her escape from Dungannon. Though freshly laundered and once quite becoming, the skirt was faded and the linen blouse as simple as a peasant's. *The very thing one wears to a picnic,* she thought with a resigned sigh. But there was nothing to be done for it now.

Kathryn squared her shoulders and, unaware she was sealing her fate for all time, started down the stairs. As she descended to the foyer, her thoughts in turmoil tripped over each other. *What business does this O'Neill have with me?* she wondered for the hundredth time. *Does he seek my permission to steal my children's birthright?* She would yield nothing. On the other hand, she admitted to herself, he had been kind. Perhaps, feminine sweetness would persuade him to help her get to England.

Kathryn hesitated at the bottom of the stairs and looked around the deserted foyer. Peg appeared from nowhere and gave her a tentative smile, then escorted her to the family dining chamber.

Hugh turned, smiling, when the door opened. Clad in chestnut-brown breeches and jerkin with a creamy, silk shirt beneath, Hugh was informally yet elegantly attired. His brown eyes sparkled and his ruddy complexion glowed with good health.

Avoiding his stare, Kathryn glanced around the chamber. The room reeked of masculinity. Exquisite tapestries depicting the hunt hung on the walls, and heavy draperies covered the windows. A cheery fire had been lit in the hearth to ward off the evening chill. Hugh was at ease in the rich surroundings, a fact that did not escape Kathryn.

Hugh crossed the chamber and offered her his arm, then escorted her to the table. "You're looking well, my lady."

"I beg forgiveness for my attire," Kathryn said, high color rising upon her cheeks. Compared to him, she felt positively ragged. "I—we left Dungannon in haste and—"

"It's a problem easily solved," Hugh interrupted, dismissing her apology with a wave of his hand. "I'll take care of it in the morning."

"*No!*" Kathryn cried. "You must not."

"I insist." Hugh was infuriatingly pleasant, trying to keep her off balance until she agreed to what he wanted.

Kathryn opened her mouth to protest but was thwarted by Peg's arrival with their supper. The housekeeper presented them with stuffed and roasted hen, greens in oil and vinegar, braised leeks, and wine.

Kathryn decided it would be easier to set him straight when his stomach was full and his mind sluggish. Giving her full attention to the meal, she ate slowly and occasionally stole a glance at Hugh, who seemed never to take his eyes from her.

"What business did you wish to discuss?" Kathryn asked, breaking the silence.

"Mixing business with pleasure is not a good practice," Hugh chided her with a mocking smile. "You must cultivate more patience, my lady."

How dare he scold one! Kathryn thought, her anger rising like a sudden gust of wind. Not daring to rebuke him, she seethed in silence.

"There'll be time enough for business after we've

supped," Hugh added. Lifting the wine goblet to his lips, he noted the mutinous set to her jaw and hoped she wouldn't explode.

"I stand corrected, my lord," Kathryn replied with a smile, remembering her vow of sweetness.

Hugh choked on his wine. The vinegar in her eyes belied the sugar on her tongue. Hugh realized he'd underestimated this slip of a girl, as evidenced by her tight self-control. Thinking his plans would best be served if she relaxed, Hugh refilled her wine goblet.

"I'm told you visited my stables today," Hugh remarked pleasantly. "Entertain no foolish thoughts, my lady. Horse thieving in Ireland is punishable by death."

Kathryn choked on *her* wine. "I don't believe *borrowing* is punishable by death," she countered. "Besides, as you said, mixing business with pleasure is a bad idea."

Hugh's lips quirked in amusement. "I stand corrected, my lady. Please call me Hugh—all my friends do. And you?"

"Me, my lord?"

"And what do your friends call you?"

"Lady Kathryn."

Hugh arched a brow at her. "Tell me about yourself, *Katie.*"

"Lady Kathryn. Remember?"

Hugh's lips quirked. "Tell me about your life in England and your family, *Lady Kathryn.*"

"There's not much to tell," she answered. "Basildon Castle has been the home of the Devereuxes since the days of the Tudor, the queen's grandfather. As a reward for his loyalty and service to the Tudor, my great-grandfather married my great-grandmother, the heiress of Basildon Castle. My father met and married my mother when he was in France on old King Henry's business."

Forgetting herself, Kathryn smiled and added, "They married without the king's permission."

Hugh smiled. "Your father must have been a brave man."

Kathryn nodded. "Being in love with love, King Henry forgave his favorite fourth cousin. When father died, we became wards of the queen."

"We?"

"My brother, sisters, and myself."

"How many sisters do you have?"

"Two—both younger. What about you?"

"I'm alone," Hugh answered. "Part of old King Henry's policy required the Irish chieftains to send their sons, willing or not, to England to be educated in one of the noble households. Molded into Englishmen, in a manner of speaking."

"If you're more at home in England, why return to Ireland?" Kathryn asked, though she already knew the answer.

"My father, Matthew, was Shane's half brother," Hugh told her. "His *older* half brother. A rumor spread that Matthew was illegitimate and unable to inherit, but bastard or not, my grandfather Conn O'Neill named my father his successor. The Dublin Parliament supported his claim to Tyrone while Shane enjoyed popular support in Ulster."

Kathryn looked away. "I've heard the tale."

"Then you know Shane's men killed my father, and when my older brother sued for his rightful title, he also suffered an untimely accident."

"D-did my husband m-murder your brother?" Kathryn stammered.

"Shane was visiting the Tudor court when Brian died," Hugh told her, refilling her wine goblet.

"Who murdered Brian?"

"Turlough."

Knowing her late husband had probably ordered the execution, Kathryn lost her appetite but forced herself to sip the wine. *Hugh certainly had valid grievances against Shane. Were Maeve and she about to be slaughtered because of her husband's crimes against this man?*

"Did you love him?" Hugh asked, unable to stop himself.

"W-what?"

"Did you love my uncle? Were you happy?"

"How dare you!" Kathryn's flaring anger banished her fears. "My life with Shane is none of your business."

Hugh grinned. "Again, my lady, I stand corrected."

The remainder of the meal passed without argument. Speaking of inconsequential matters, Hugh managed to draw a smile or two from his beautiful guest. Kathryn's wine goblet never emptied, and by supper's end, her head was spinning. Hugh stood and offered Kathryn his arm, then escorted her across the foyer to his study.

Emboldened by the wine, Kathryn openly appraised the chamber. A desk sat near a window, and opposite the door, an inviting fire had been lit in the hearth. Two comfortable-looking chairs had been set there.

Hugh ushered Kathryn into one chair, then sat in the other. He looked at her and wondered how best to begin.

"Why was I brought here?" Kathryn asked, solving his problem.

"Insuring your safety was of utmost importance," Hugh answered smoothly. "The second reason is . . . as soon as possible, we will marry."

Not another one, Kathryn thought. Her vow of womanly sweetness fled her mind. "I beg your pardon," she said, "but have you taken leave of your senses?"

"You will marry me," Hugh repeated, his voice low, emphasizing each word.

"Ignorance must be a family trait," Kathryn snapped.

"Your family or mine?" Hugh shot back.

"I shan't quibble nor will I wed you." Kathryn glared at him, but the grim set to his mouth frightened her. Baiting her captor was extreme folly.

"Please understand," she pleaded. "I am recently widowed and have no desire to remarry."

"Recently widowed and remarried is preferable to a great many other things," Hugh said coldly. "Wouldn't you agree?"

"Are you threatening me?"

"Heaven forbid!" *First the chit is meek*, Hugh thought in growing disgust, *then she's the boldest of vixens—whatever suits her purpose at the moment.* He took several deep, calming breaths and then continued, "I mean, being the countess of Tyrone is preferable to being homeless or at Turlough's mercy."

"Countess of Tyrone?" Kathryn echoed. "You speak in riddles."

"Listen carefully," Hugh said, leaning forward in his chair. "You have no place in England. Your mother has remarried, and when your brother's grown and wed, Basildon Castle will be his wife's domain. You'd live as a poor relation. The queen might wed you to an Englishman, but would he cherish your children, sired by an Irish rebel?" Hugh let that hang in the air for a brief moment, then admitted, "A union between us would benefit both of us."

"How so?" asked Kathryn.

"The queen refused to name me earl because of Shane," Hugh replied, "and the reverse was true for him." Reluctant to promise her what he must, Hugh stood and walked to his desk, then poured himself a glass of whiskey and turned around to look at her. "If we unite, the queen will acknowledge me the earl of Tyrone, and if you deliver a son, I will name him my heir."

"The queen is no fool," Kathryn said. "She would refuse us permission to marry."

"What makes you think I don't already have her permission?" Hugh countered.

"If, as you say, England has no place for my children and me," Kathryn returned, "I could return to Dungannon. Eventually, my son will inherit anyway."

"Return to Turlough? I think not."

"Turlough only desires what Shane possessed," she told him.

"Very perceptive," Hugh said, admiring her logic. "It's a rare woman who's blessed with uncommon beauty and a keen mind."

Kathryn bristled at his condescending attitude and gave a fair imitation of the Irish lilt. " 'Tis lucky I am to have met the rare man who appreciates both."

"It was a compliment," Hugh said, refusing to be provoked, then went on, "Turlough is the O'Neill and, I am told, wants to marry you. If you return to Dungannon, he'll marry you or kill you trying."

That was true. Patrick had implied as much. Kathryn knew she was losing this battle of wits. "Why would you want to help Shane's widow and children?" she asked. "He murdered your father, possibly ordered your brother's death."

"There's no other way. Together we win; separately, we cancel each other out."

Kathryn stood up and crossed the chamber to stand in front of him. "You would actually name Shane's son your heir?"

"Yes."

Turning away, Kathryn considered his words for several long moments. "I'll think about it," she finally said.

Hugh's hand shot out and whirled her around. Their bodies were only a few disturbing inches apart. "You will do it," he insisted.

"I will think about it." Kathryn tried to pull away.

Hugh dropped his hand, allowing her freedom, and when he spoke, his voice was softly persuading. "There's no time for thinking. I would take you to wife before Turlough steals you back to Dungannon."

Kathryn hesitated. She hadn't thought of that possibility. What alternatives were left to her? "You would sign a legal agreement naming Shane's son your heir?" she asked.

"I've already said as much," Hugh replied, knowing he'd won.

"In the presence of suitable witnesses?"

"Yes." Hugh's gaze dropped to her breasts, and for a moment he thought of the long, long nights they'd share as man and wife.

"If I did agree," Kathryn asked, recognizing *that* look, "what of the marriage itself?"

"I don't understand."

Embarrassed, Kathryn turned away and considered her words, then ventured, "I—I assume it will be a marriage in name only."

"That assumption is incorrect, my lady. The marriage will be in fact." When she refused to look at him, Hugh gently forced her to meet his gaze. His voice held a note of finality but was not unkind. "You will live with me, sleep with me, and bear my children. Our union will be consummated. You know it must be so."

Unsettled by his words, his nearness, his masculine

scent, Kathryn stammered, "C-c-consummated after my s-son is b-born."

"Immediately following the vows."

"I refuse to have my unborn child disturbed."

Admiring her spunk, Hugh considered her words and wondered briefly how her eyes appeared when she was aroused. "A compromise is in order," he conceded. "Our marriage will be consummated immediately, and then I will defer until you've recovered from birth. It's more than fair."

"You will sign a legal agreement to that effect?"

"No, madam, I will not," Hugh roared, glaring into her green witch's eyes. "My personal life, or lack thereof, will not be common knowledge." *Sweet Jesu! She was a viper masquerading as an Englishwoman!* How she survived his uncle's notorious temper would be a mystery until his final day. "And what the bloody hell are you staring at?"

"Froth."

"Froth?"

"Yes," Kathryn answered, feigning innocence. "You see, the few maddened creatures I've seen froth about the mouth area, and I was looking for the—Oh, I'm sorry if I've insulted you."

Unaccustomed to losing control of his temper, Hugh regained his composure slowly. He silently counted to ten, then added another twenty for good measure.

"If you throw yourself at my feet and beg for my attentions," he promised, "you won't receive them until the babe is delivered. You have my word as a gentleman." He looked her up and down, then added, "It won't be difficult."

Kathryn smirked and walked away. She knew marrying meant subjecting herself to his whims and desires. If only she could go home . . . But Tyrone was her son's birthright, and she wanted her son to inherit. What to do? Better this O'Neill than Turlough or an unknown Englishman, she supposed.

Kathryn turned around, her sudden movement surprising Hugh who'd been admiring her backside. Her eyes narrowed at his perusal, but she said nothing. She walked back to stand in front of him.

"Very well," Kathryn agreed.

Hugh relaxed, then smiled. "Shall we seal the bargain with a kiss?"

Kathryn stiffened and stepped back a pace. "When the contract is signed," came her icy reply.

Gazing into her upturned face, Hugh became lost. Her eyes were the green of Ireland, lush and inviting, warming his blood, enticing. He stepped forward a pace, his face coming closer and closer until his mouth covered hers—touching, tasting, probing her sweetness.

Unable to move, Kathryn felt herself falling under his spell, a warm feeling pervading her senses. Behind her head, Hugh's hand refused to let her go.

"Release me," she breathed.

He would not.

It was then Hugh felt the cold caress of steel on his throat and broke the kiss abruptly. "How—?"

"I pinched it at the noon meal." Clutching the knife, Kathryn stepped back a few paces, but her gaze was drawn back to his lips. What had possessed her?

Gathering the shreds of her dignity, Kathryn handed him the knife, then turned on her heels, and stalked out. She walked across the foyer and then raced up the stairs two at a time, chased by Hugh's shout of laughter.

Beautiful, brave, and intelligent, Hugh marveled, admiring Kathryn's spunk. An Englishwoman possessing all three admirable qualities was beyond his ken, yet here she was in his own home. And soon to become his wife!

Hugh knew one thing for certain. Life with this slip of a woman would never be boring.

4

Hugh lingered over breakfast the next morning with Patrick, Conal, and Sean. When Peg walked into the hall to clear away their plates, Hugh told her to sit down. He had important news to share. The four retainers looked at him expectantly.

"Lady Kathryn and I will be married as soon as possible," Hugh told them. Stunned silence met his announcement.

Patrick was the first to recover. "Does *she* know?" he asked wryly.

"She accepted my proposal last night." Cocking a brow at them, Hugh added, "Apparently, Lady Kathryn's been blessed with beauty *and* intelligence, not to mention good taste." Great hoots of laughter erupted from the men, and Hugh good-naturedly joined them.

"I've sent a message to Fiona Fitzgerald's dressmaker," Hugh said to Peg. "When Madame Bujold arrives, send her upstairs to Lady Kathryn."

"You awakened the poor woman in the middle of the night?" Patrick asked.

"No." Hugh grinned broadly. "I sent her a message yesterday."

The four men laughed with glee, but Peg was unamused by their masculine arrogance.

"Save the lecture," Hugh said, catching her reproachful frown. "Can we be ready for a small reception in two weeks' time?"

"Yes."

"Good. Prepare the chamber adjoining mine for Lady Kathryn but don't tell her of the move yet."

The housekeeper stared at him in shock. What he was suggesting was indecent.

"My intentions are honorable," Hugh assured her, throwing his hands up in a gesture of innocence. "It will save us the trouble of moving her later. Off with you now." Peg left, all the while snorting indignantly at his blarney as if he really expected her to believe him.

"Make arrangements with Father Dunn at St. Mary's, but specify the banns must be waived," Hugh instructed Sean, turning to him. "If he can manage that, St. Mary's will receive a generous donation. If not, tell him we'll go elsewhere."

Bribing a priest, Patrick marveled. Even Shane would not have dared to compromise a man of the cloth, albeit for the purpose of expediency. Seeing Hugh O'Neill in action was an amazing sight.

"If the banns are read," Hugh explained, turning to Patrick and Conal, "Turlough will try to recover Kathryn before the marriage. It's best to be cautious where he's concerned." When they nodded in agreement, he went on, "I'm putting the two of you in charge of security here. One of you must always be about and prepared for Turlough's worst."

"If anythin' does go wrong," Patrick said, standing to leave, "Conal will be at fault." Itching for a fight, Conal followed his brother out.

Sir Henry Sidney arrived at that moment and sat in the chair vacated by Patrick. "I got your message," he said, stifling a yawn. "What's so urgent?"

"I'm getting married and need your help," Hugh answered.

Surprise registered first upon the Englishman's face, then amusement. "Getting married and need my help?" Sir Henry echoed. "Should I prop you on top of your bride?"

Hugh chuckled and shook his head. "I need a betrothal agreement drawn and ready for signing this evening."

"Who's the bride?" Sir Henry asked.

"Kathryn Devereux O'Neill." Hugh watched the other man's reaction. "Uncle Shane's widow."

Sir Henry was surprised. "The late earl of Basildon's daughter?"

"Do you know her?"

"No. Why the rush?"

"The lady's reluctant," Hugh admitted, "but won't change her mind once the contract is signed." Then Hugh dangled an irresistible tidbit in front of the other man's ambition. "Once Kathryn and I are married, we'll petition the queen for Tyrone. To prove my good faith, I'll help quell disturbances directed against the crown. At my own expense, of course. That should please her majesty. Don't you agree?"

Sir Henry nodded, thinking his own expediency would please the queen. "Give me the pertinent articles, and my clerk will draw the contract. I'll return with it this evening."

"Thanks, Henry. Peg will serve you breakfast in my study. I'll join after I've checked Kathryn's progress with the dressmaker."

Upstairs, Hugh raised his hand to knock on the door,

but hoping to find Kathryn in a state of undress, lowered it to the doorknob, and walked in.

It was his lucky day, Hugh decided, delighted by the enchanting sight that greeted him. Polly was looking at the dressmaker's sketches while Maeve stared in obvious boredom out the window; Mme. Bujold was measuring Kathryn, who was scantily clad in a chemise.

Unnoticed, Hugh stood near the door and devoured his intended with his eyes.

Kathryn's small feet supported supple, shapely legs that brought Hugh's mesmerized attention to her slim but curvaceous hips and beckoning thighs. Hugh nearly drooled at the sight but frowned when his gaze drifted up to her gently rounded belly, a reminder of his uncle. Kathryn leaned over to speak to Mme. Bujold, who knelt in front of her, and two ripening breasts threatened to spill from the top of her chemise.

Hugh sighed at the sight, wishing time sported wings and weeks could pass in the blink of an eye. *There is a God in Heaven,* Hugh concluded, *and for unknown reasons, He's more than pleased with me.*

Kathryn looked up and saw desire—hot, glowing, intense—in his smoldering gaze. She felt vulnerable, naked beneath that scorching scrutiny. Kathryn thought of the previous evening's kiss, and a hot flush spread over her suddenly trembling body.

"Uncle Hugh," Maeve called, turning away from the window.

Laughing, Hugh went down on bended knee to receive her bone-crushing hug.

"Mama says we're staying here forever," the little girl gushed. "I love you, Uncle Hugh. May I have my own horse?"

"Maeve," Kathryn cried in a stern voice.

Hugh smiled, thinking a woman's wiles were instinctive, not learned. After casting the mother an admiring look, Hugh hugged the child, saying, "Perhaps, but only very good girls are gifted with ponies."

Always bargaining, Kathryn thought snidely.

"Polly, have Patrick escort Maeve and you to the stables to visit the horses," Hugh said, ignoring the look of displeasure on his intended's beautiful face. Happy with her orders, the tiring woman smiled and left with Maeve to find Patrick. Hugh winked knowingly at Kathryn. That he should use Polly's fondness for Patrick to his own advantage made Kathryn seethe.

Past her prime, Mme. Bujold was a small, well-made woman. Her hair was brown and scattered with wisps of gray. Her soft hazel eyes radiated kindness and a good sense of humor. The dressmaker was remarkably tolerant of other people's scandals, malice being foreign to her heart's nature.

"Lady Kathryn is lovely," the dressmaker commented, turning to Hugh.

"Yes, I'm a lucky man." Hugh smiled lazily as he perused his intended's scantily clad body.

"The lady is also lucky," Mme. Bujold complimented him, looking at "the lady" for agreement.

"Yes." Kathryn looked away, her face crimson with embarrassment.

"Come and see the sketches I've brought," the dressmaker urged, gesturing to the bed where she'd placed them.

As Mme. Bujold droned on endlessly about styles and fabrics and colors, Hugh put his arm around Kathryn's bared shoulder. Conscious only of that hand on her shoulder, Kathryn stood between them but heard not a word they spoke. When his fingertips began a slow caress, shivers of wild sensation raced throughout her body.

"Lady Kathryn needs everything," Hugh was saying to the dressmaker, unaware of the havoc he was wreaking. "She'll need three or four gowns immediately, and the wedding gown with accessories must be finished in two weeks' time. The remainder may be completed at your leisure. Any problem with that?"

"All will be as you wish," the dressmaker assured him.

Without warning, Hugh pulled Kathryn into a sideways hug and placed a chaste kiss on her temple. "Sir Henry's waiting for me in the study, sweetheart. The agreement will be ready for signing this evening." With that, he walked away but paused at the door as if just remembering something. "Madame Bujold, be certain to make very wide seams."

Kathryn gasped in horrified embarrassment. The dressmaker looked at him quizzically, puzzled by his instructions.

"Lady Kathryn is pregnant," Hugh said baldly.

"Ah," Mme. Bujold sighed, assuming he was the proud father. A smile of understanding spread across her face. *"L'amor!"*

"Oui, l'amor!" Then Hugh was gone, but as he strolled down the corridor, the sound of his laughter drifted back to them.

"Madame Bujold, do you have a gown I could wear this evening?" Kathryn asked when she regained her composure.

The dressmaker paused in her work and frowned, then brightened. "There is a gown that was promised to—"

"I'll pay triple for it," Kathryn interrupted, her generosity surprising the other woman. "You see, I've nothing to wear this evening."

Sympathetic to the beautiful woman's plight, Mme. Bujold decided her need was greater and nodded. "I'll return with the gown this afternoon and make the necessary alterations." The dressmaker smiled. Lady Fiona Fitzgerald would be furious about losing a man and a gown to the same woman. How delicious!

When she descended the stairs that evening, Kathryn looked coolly magnificent and as regal as a queen in a mauve-colored gown with long, flowing sleeves. Its bodice was form fitting and the squared neck cut daringly low, much too low to suit her taste. If only she had her jewels! *Or a blanket!*

Kathryn frowned at her exposed cleavage, then smiled as a wicked idea formed in her mind. This arrogant O'Neill had had the audacity to order a bridal gown before he had a bride. The rascal needed to be taught a lesson. She would honor the pact they'd made, but drool as he would, Hugh O'Neill would receive no more than his due.

Kathryn's confidence faded into nervous indecision as she walked toward the study. *Escape would be impossible once the papers were signed. Wouldn't it? Should she stay here or take Maeve and run? But where could they go? She'd fled Dungannon with nothing.*

Kathryn squared her shoulders and knocked on the door. Hugh opened it and instantly recognized the doubtful expression on her face. His hand shot out and claimed hers. He drew her inside and nudged the door shut as Sir Henry Sidney and Patrick rose from their chairs.

"You're looking quite beautiful this evening," Hugh complimented her, trying to put her at ease. "The gown is especially lovely, my dear."

"I'm glad you approve," Kathryn replied with a winsome smile. "For immediate delivery, Madame Bujold has charged you triple its worth."

Sir Henry and Patrick chuckled, but Hugh remained silent. His lips quirked, and amusement shone from his eyes. The lady was proving more defiant than he'd ever imagined, and there was nothing Hugh loved more than a challenge.

"My lady, I would make Sir Henry Sidney known to you," Hugh introduced them. "Sir Henry and Patrick will witness our agreement."

Kathryn extended her hand to the Englishman, saying, "I'm pleased to make your acquaintance, my lord."

"I can't begin to tell you how glad I am that Hugh has the good sense to marry an Englishwoman," Sir Henry said.

Hugh led her to his desk, and after signing the marriage contract, held the quill out to her, saying, "Make your mark here, Katie."

"I won't affix my name to a document I haven't read."

"You read?" Hugh was genuinely surprised.

Insulted, Kathryn cast him a reproving look. "I took lessons with my brother's tutor. Besides, I've many talents of which you are unaware."

"I hope so," he murmured, his gaze dropping to her cleavage.

Kathryn blushed scarlet to her roots. Hard pressed to swallow their mirth, Sir Henry and Patrick turned away.

"All is in order," Hugh assured her. "There's no need to read it."

"I insist," Kathryn challenged.

"You don't trust me?"

"Hardly."

That did it. Hugh handed her the document and walked away, but his gaze never left her. Kathryn read it carefully and more slowly than was necessary. Everything appeared in order, not that she'd actually expected him to renege. Vexing Hugh had been her intent.

Allowing precious little time for thinking, Hugh was beside her again, urging her to sign. As soon as she affixed her name to the document, Sir Henry and Patrick stepped forward to sign. Afterward, Hugh poured each a dram of whiskey.

"To Lady Kathryn, the loveliest colleen my eyes have ever seen," Hugh toasted her, raising his glass in salute, his gleaming brown eyes holding her captive. Sir Henry and Patrick drained their glasses, and feeling strangely pleased by his words, Kathryn gifted her betrothed with a dazzling smile.

"Let's sup," Hugh said.

"Would you mind if I spoke privately with Patrick?" Kathryn asked. Hugh nodded and left with Sir Henry.

Kathryn walked over to Patrick and looked up at him. Her eyes were soft and repentant. "I beg your pardon for my cruel words yesterday," she apologized.

"There's nothin' to forgive," he said with a smile.

"Am I doing the right thing?"

"Only God knows, but I do believe your best chance is with Hugh."

"I keep thinking that, no matter the price, Shane's son should inherit Tyrone," Kathryn said, desperately needing his concurrence.

Patrick touched her hand, saying, "I agree that he should."

"Life with Shane was a nightmare," Kathryn confided. "His blatant womanizing ruined my naive hopes for a loving marriage, but his violent temper and ready fist devastated me. And this marriage will put me at the mercy of another O'Neill husband who could possess the same miserable traits as his uncle."

"I swear to protect you," Patrick replied. "However, I do believe that Hugh and Shane are as different as night and day. If I'm wrong, I'll help you escape to England."

"Where would I be without you?" Kathryn whispered, clasping his hands. "Will you give me away at the wedding?"

"I'd be honored." Patrick's voice was hoarse with emotion and unshed tears glistened in his eyes.

In the private family dining chamber, Patrick relinquished Kathryn to Hugh who escorted her to the seat beside his. Sir Henry and Patrick sat opposite them.

Peg arrived with their supper. There were shrimp with snail butter, pheasant in game sauce, boiled potatoes, lettuce and cucumber in a vinagrette, and a rich burgundy wine.

"The wedding will be a simple affair," Hugh was saying to Sir Henry.

"I asked Patrick to give me away," Kathryn interjected.

"An excellent choice." Hugh's voice was warm with approval.

Perhaps she *should* place her trust in him, Kathryn thought, meet his kindness with kindness. "What preparations shall we make, my lord?" she asked.

"The arrangements are already made," Hugh answered, patting her hand. "All you need to do is attend."

Kathryn frowned and grumbled, "When?"

"What?"

"If all I need to do is attend," Kathryn said, her voice laced with sarcasm, "tell me when, and I shall do so. *Perfectly.*"

Hugh's eyes narrowed on her, and the other two at the table pretended deafness. "I meant no insult," Hugh said. "Undertaking strenuous activity in your condition is dangerous, and Turlough remains a very real threat until the ceremony is performed."

His logic made her feel exceedingly foolish. "The babe makes me overly sensitive," she murmured by way of an apology.

"I understand." Hugh smiled and stroked her hand as if she were a child, inadvertantly stoking her anger.

Peg returned with a dessert of fresh strawberries with clotted cream, but Kathryn, her thoughts in turmoil, only toyed with her food. She was being made to feel the outsider at her own nuptials. She lost all interest as the men's conversation drifted to politics and war.

"The Maguire's been harassing our troops again," Sir Henry was saying.

"Is that so?" Hugh said, feigning disinterest.

"Yes," Sir Henry went on. "The queen may be forced to send someone over to put an end to it. Russell can't be everywhere at once, you know. And—"

"It's been a long day," Kathryn interrupted, rising from her chair. She'd had enough of fighting and dying to last several lifetimes and would listen to no more. "I bid you good night."

Hugh was on his feet in an instant and grabbed her hand. "Make yourselves comfortable in my study," he said to Sir Henry and Patrick. "I won't be long." Turning to Kathryn, he said with a smile, "I've something to show you."

Kathryn was at odds with herself as she walked upstairs with Hugh. Her anger at his arrogant, condescending attitude would not die easily. As if his handsome face could answer the unanswerable, Kathryn glanced sidelong at him. For the rest of her life, she would climb these stairs with this stranger who was to be her husband. What did the future hold for her? For them?

Instead of depositing her at her chamber, Hugh led Kathryn into another, much larger room on the opposite side of the rectangular corridor. Polly was waiting for her there. Puzzled, Kathryn raised questioning eyes to his.

"This chamber is more suitable for the mistress of the house," Hugh explained.

Kathryn's lingering hostility evaporated beneath the warmth of his unexpected thoughtfulness. Her expression softened. "How kind of you," she murmured, her gaze sweeping the spacious chamber.

The four-poster, curtained bed was enormous and decorated with a velvet coverlet and matching curtains. Colorful tapestries adorned the walls of the room, and in front of the hearth sat two comfortable-looking chairs. Luxuriant, imported carpets covered the floor.

Kathryn noticed a certain oddity about the room. In England, her chamber had one entrance, and Dungannon's had two. Without counting the corridor door, this chamber sported three.

As if sensing her thoughts, Hugh opened the first door. "This will nicely closet all those gowns for which I'm paying," he said, cocking a brow at her. Kathryn's delighted laughter filled the chamber.

"A sitting room overlooking the gardens," Hugh said, opening the second door.

Perhaps life would be good after all, Kathryn thought, realizing he was trying to please her. "And that one?" she asked, pointing to the third door.

"My bedchamber." Hugh grinned guiltily like a boy caught in a prank.

Kathryn frowned.

Watching them, Polly was unable to stifle a chuckle and received the blackest of scowls from both.

"My thanks for your kindness," Kathryn said. She extended her hand in dismissal, but Hugh drew her close and planted a chaste kiss on her cheek, then left.

With Polly's assistance, Kathryn disrobed and donned the silken night shift that Mme. Bujold had brought her that afternoon. She walked across the chamber and watched the dancing flames in the hearth. Turning her back on the cheery fire, Kathryn stared in thoughtful consideration at the door connecting her chamber with her betrothed's.

"Will there be anythin' else?" Polly asked before leaving.

"As a matter of fact, there is something," Kathryn said, a puckish grin lighting her face. She marched across the chamber to the bedside table and began pulling it toward the connecting door, calling over her shoulder, "Grab those chairs."

"W-what?" Polly's expression mirrored her bewilderment.

"I said, drag those chairs over here."

Kathryn shoved the table against the offending portal, then strengthened her makeshift barricade with the two chairs. "The O'Neills are an arrogant lot," she explained to her horrified tiring woman. "This one is no exception."

Much later, after bidding Sir Henry and Patrick a good night, Hugh climbed the stairs to his own chamber and thought with immense satisfaction that his plans were finally falling into place. Passing Kathryn's chamber, Hugh heard a noise and stopped. Muffled sobs.

Uncertain of what to do, Hugh stared at the door. Had he done something or *not* done something he should have? Should he offer her comfort?

Hugh reached out and turned the doorknob. *Locked.*

In his own chamber, Hugh headed straight for the connecting door. He reached out and turned the knob, but the door would not open beyond a crack.

"Go away," Kathryn cried from the other side. "How dare you try to enter my chamber!"

She certainly didn't *sound* in need of comforting.

Hugh frowned and stepped back a pace, then corrected her, "*My* chamber. This house belongs to *me*. Why were you weeping?"

"That's none of your business! Unlike this house, my thoughts are my own," Kathryn informed him. "I'm not your property."

Not yet but soon, Hugh thought and smiled to himself. Forcing a sternness into his voice, he ordered, "Be warned, madam. That barricade comes down in two weeks' time."

Boom! Something heavy crashed against the other side of the door.

Walking away, Hugh began undressing for bed, but his eyes were drawn to the connecting door and his thoughts to the furious woman—*exquisitely beautiful, furious woman*—on the other side.

How could he hope to unite the clan chieftains and force the English dogs from Ireland's sod if he was unable to manage his own betrothed wife?

"Be damned," Hugh muttered, dismissing his own question. An Irishman always knows what the English are thinking. He sat down on his bed and stared in growing consternation at the offensive door. Would that a man could understand a woman's mind so well!

5

"I don't want to learn how to ride," Polly whined. "Horses frighten me."

"Riding is a necessity," Kathryn insisted. "Your first lesson will be immediately."

Polly paled but said nothing.

As the two women walked toward the stable yard, Kathryn enjoyed the sun's warm caress on her face. This was only the second day of sunshine she'd been able to enjoy since her arrival in Dublin. The others had been gray and bleak, almost as bleak as her mood.

During her unhappy marriage to Shane, Kathryn had found peace in riding and missed Dungannon's countryside. Unused to inactivity, Kathryn yearned to take a horse from the stables and ride until she dropped from exhaustion. And then she devised this foolproof plan to make her desire a reality. She'd be gone and back before Hugh even realized she was missing.

"Saddle your most docile horse for Polly," Kathryn ordered the O'Neill head groom. "I'll take that lovely mare over there."

Seamus, the groom, stood motionless for several seconds and debated what he should do. His instincts told him the lord would disapprove of his betrothed riding out.

"Is something wrong?" Kathryn asked.

"No, my lady," he replied. Then he went for the horses.

Several O'Neill warriors watched with interest as the two women led their horses out of the stable. Kathryn explained the proper method of mounting and then made Polly recite the process back to her.

"Correct," Kathryn said. "Now mount up."

Quaking in fear, Polly turned to the horse but was unable to lift herself up. The watching warriors laughed and Kathryn became more determined. She refused to let these men embarrass her.

"I'll help you," Kathryn said.

"Help me?" Polly cried. "Liftin' me will hurt the baby."

"Nonsense! I said I'll help you." Kathryn's voice was stern and Polly knew she must obey.

Summoning all her strength, Kathryn boosted Polly into the saddle. With a triumphant smile, Kathryn looked at Hugh's men who pretended not to notice, then expertly mounted her own horse.

Prancing around the stable yard, Kathryn demonstrated the proper use of the reins and how to give instructions to a horse. Then she insisted Polly try it alone. The Irish girl proved a quick learner.

"Stay here and practice what you've learned," Kathryn ordered. "I'm going for a short ride."

"No," Polly protested. "You—"

Kathryn trotted off, giving her tiring woman no time for further objections.

Torn between concern for her mistress and the terror of riding after her, Polly decided this was no time for cowardice. She nudged her horse forward, but a masculine hand seized her reins.

The hand belonged to Patrick. He frowned and hauled her off the horse, then looked in the direction Kathryn had ridden. Hugh was riding hard after his betrothed.

Kathryn struggled wildly when she was grabbed and lifted from her saddle.

"You little fool," a familiar voice growled in her ear.

Kathryn looked at her abductor and saw Hugh's furious face. Apparently, her intended tour of Dublin was canceled.

"Trying to escape, my dear?" Hugh asked.

"And leave Maeve behind?" Kathryn countered.

Nothing more was said. Hugh did not trust his anger enough to speak, and Kathryn fumed in silence.

In the stable yard, Patrick reached up and lifted Kathryn from Hugh's great stallion. Instantly, Kathryn rounded on Hugh.

"And just what did you think you were doing?" she snapped.

Hugh's simmering temper boiled over. "Leaving these grounds before our marriage is forbidden to you," he ordered, towering over her. Hugh flicked a glance at his men who were openly watching, hanging upon every word. "Do you understand?"

"I was merely teaching Polly to ride," Kathryn said, mortified at being scolded in front of an audience. "I won't have a tiring woman who needs to be pulled around in a cart." She stamped her foot for emphasis.

"Leaving my protection is dangerous. Turlough might get you."

"With any luck, the *bogeyman* will get you!" Kathryn tried to brush past him, but his hand shot out and grabbed her upper arm.

"Don't hit me!" she cried, flinching.

"Hit you?" Hugh echoed in surprise. "Do you think I'm a monster? Why would you think I'd strike you?"

Because Shane hit me, Kathryn thought. The horrifying memory of that fateful day at Dungannon's dungeon came rushing back to her. Her husband had beaten her so badly that she'd miscarried their second child. And here was another O'Neill, reaching for her in anger.

Shane, Hugh realized. His uncle had obviously been free with his fist. Though this beautiful little shrew was in dire need of a sound spanking, beating women went against Hugh's nature.

Sympathy for what she'd suffered at his uncle's hands shone from Hugh's brown eyes. "At least, have a care for the babe you carry," he said in a quiet voice.

Stubbornly proud, Kathryn abhorred the pity she saw on his face. "Your concern is quite unnecessary. Who knows better than I what limits should be placed on my activity?"

"Having borne a single child," Hugh countered, "does not an expert on childbearing make."

"And how many children have *you* borne, my lord?" she shot back. "I've carried three."

"Three? What happened to the second?"

"I fell," Kathryn snapped, steeling herself against that painful memory. She refused to break down in front of an audience.

"Off a horse?" Hugh asked in an effort to make his point, then instantly regretted his words.

Kathryn flinched as if she'd been struck. "My previous life is none of your business!"

"Understand this, madam," Hugh said tightly. "Stitching baby clothes is the most strenuous thing you will do until the babe is delivered."

"Go to hell." Kathryn turned to leave.

"Where are you going?"

"Pardon me, my lord. Are the gardens also forbidden to Maeve and me?"

"No."

"Good." Without another word, Kathryn turned on her heel and stalked off.

For a brief moment, Hugh watched the angry sway of her hips, then delighted his men by rounding on Patrick. "Teach Polly to ride," he ordered the other man. "Lady Kathryn desires a tiring woman who can sit ahorse."

Cursing silently, Patrick scowled at a shyly smiling Polly. When his gaze dipped to her generous breasts, Patrick grinned broadly. Teaching Polly to ride could prove a pleasant task after all.

Kathryn, dressed in her picnicking outfit, sat on the grass in the garden and leaned against a tree. She closed her eyes and inhaled deeply of the fragrant scent pervading the air.

I am Hugh's prisoner, Kathryn thought darkly, her nerves as frayed at the seams as the clothing she wore. Though the prison was luxurious, she was, nevertheless, his prisoner.

Kathryn opened her eyes. Maeve stood in front of her and held out her hand with an offering. Kathryn laughed until salty tears rolled down her face and her breath came in quick, painful gasps. Clutched in the little girl's hand were Hugh's carefully tended flowers, pruned at the roots Kathryn accepted the gift, wove the long stems into wreath, and then placed it with great ceremony upon her daughter's head.

"Now you must have a crown," Maeve said, delighted with her mother's trick.

Kathryn wove another wreath. Summoning all the pomp and circumstance of a coronation, Maeve set the flowery crown upon her mother's head.

"Uncle Hugh needs one," the little girl insisted.

"I doubt Uncle Hugh desires a crown of flowers, my pet. Gold would be more to his liking." Seeing her daughter's crestfallen expression, Kathryn added, "On the other hand, perhaps he'd like one of these in the meantime." Maeve's expression brightened, and Kathryn began to weave.

Alone in his study, Hugh was working at his desk when Peg knocked and entered. "Lord Fitzgerald and Lady Fiona are here," the housekeeper announced.

"Send them in, Peg." Hugh hoped Fiona Fitzgerald would cause no problems with Kathryn. Wearing a cordial smile of welcome, he greeted his guests at the door and ushered them inside.

Past his prime, Lord Fitzgerald was a striking man with a full head of silver hair and not an extra ounce of fat on his aging body. He'd been blessed with keen intelligence, a boon to the Dublin Parliament. Softhearted leniency for his only child was his one outstanding flaw.

Poised like a princess at her father's side, Fiona Fitzgerald was the essence of feminine beauty. Her dark brown hair, sapphire-blue eyes, pouting rosy lips, and ivory complexion were the lyrics of many a troubador's song, every man's dream maiden. Rivaling her startling beauty was her arrogance, the natural by-product of an overindulgent father.

"Sorry for the intrusion," Lord Fitzgerald apologized. "After receiving your wedding invitation, Fiona insisted we meet your betrothed. You'll soon discover, my boy, how bothersome the ladies can be when their minds are set upon a thing."

"I'm beginning to see the truth of that," Hugh replied, thinking of Kathryn's desire to ride. "Please be seated."

Lord Fitzgerald and his daughter sat down in front of

the hearth while Hugh brought another chair from the far side of the chamber.

"I'll call Kathryn," he said, turning to leave.

As Hugh reached the door, Kathryn with Maeve in her arms did too. Before he could utter a word, Maeve crowned him and Kathryn roared with laughter.

"Are your servants always this brazen?" Fiona asked snidely.

"Oh!" Kathryn peered into the study. "We didn't know you had guests."

Hugh took Maeve from her arms, saying, "I'd like to present Lord Fitzgerald and his daughter, Lady Fiona."

Kathryn curtseyed to Lord Fitzgerald, then glanced at Hugh. His flowery crown sat lopsided on his head. In a gesture suggesting intimacy, she divested him of the wreath and smoothed an errant lock of his hair, then sat on a stool beside his chair. Smiling, Kathryn looked at Fiona but was stunned by the unmasked hatred in the other woman's startling blue eyes.

"I wish you happiness in your forthcoming marriage," Lord Fitzgerald said, enchanted by the noble beauty that young O'Neill had somehow managed to ensnare. *I wish I were thirty years younger*, he decided as Hugh passed him a dram of whiskey.

"Your late father was the earl of Basildon," Fiona remarked, her sharp eyes appraising the other woman's charms and seeking flaws.

"Yes, my brother is the earl after him," Kathryn replied stiffly, uncomfortable with the intense scrutiny.

"I first became acquainted with Hugh in London," Fiona said, then gifted him with the warmest of smiles. Her expression turned wintry cold when she looked back at Kathryn and added, "We spent many hours together there."

Hugh shifted uneasily in his chair, and Lord Fitzgerald coughed his discomfit.

Feeling the interloper, Kathryn wondered about the connection between Hugh and Fiona. And that, for some unknown reason, made her stomach churn.

Pleased by the other woman's troubled expression, Fiona went for the kill. "As a matter of fact," she went on, "my father expected that Hugh and I would marry."

Lords Fitzgerald and O'Neill coughed simultaneously, drawing the ladies' attention. "Fine whiskey," Fitzgerald commented. "A bit strong, I think."

"Yes," Hugh agreed.

Kathryn seethed at the Irishwoman's implication and stared at Hugh, willing him to look at her. He would not. Turning back to her beautiful adversary, Kathryn said coldly, "As an Englishwoman, I'm certainly fond of my homeland. During my stay in London, however, I found the town to be filthy—filled with trash." An impish grin touched her lips as she placed heavy emphasis on the word *trash*.

Fiona's face mottled with anger at the obvious insult. Lord Fitzgerald sputtered and spat a mouthful of whiskey into his glass.

Hiding his smile, Hugh relaxed in his chair. The English rose had prickly thorns and could protect herself.

"I was sorry to learn of your late husband's passing," Lord Fitzgerald offered in a poor attempt to change the subject.

"Who was your late husband?" Fiona asked.

"Shane O'Neill." Kathryn's voice was no louder than an aching whisper.

"Shane O'Neill!" Fiona cried. "He's only been dead three months!"

Kathryn's face drained of color and her eyes clouded with pain. Hugh watched her worriedly.

Noting his tender concern, Fiona continued heartlessly, "I must warn you, my dear. The news of such a hasty remarriage will drive Dublin's gossips wild. And to your late husband's nephew? They'll say an earl's daughter should have more sense of propriety." Feigning innocence, she added for good measure, "My, how scandalous! Imagine, such a short bereavement."

"I'm sorry your sense of propriety has been offended, *my lady*," Kathryn snapped, leaping from her stool so fast that Fiona flinched back in her chair. "You see, earls' daughters are taught manners, which apparently were lacking in your education. If you will excuse me . . ." Yanking her daughter's hand, Kathryn stalked out of the study.

"How dare you!" Lord Fitzgerald barked at Fiona.

"Have I said something wrong?" Fiona turned innocent eyes on her father.

Furious, Hugh stood up, saying, "I must go to Kathryn. Peg will see you out."

"I'm sorry," Lord Fitzgerald apologized.

"It's not your fault, sir," Hugh said, then rounded on Fiona. "Your malicious spite far surpasses your incredible beauty. Good day."

Dreading the scene he knew was to come, Hugh climbed the stairs on leaden feet and damned Fiona Fitzgerald with all his heart. Kathryn had just begun to accept her fate and make the best of it. Now he'd probably be forced to start over with her.

Damn Fiona, Hugh cursed silently. *And damn Shane O'Neill too!* For an unknown reason, Kathryn's marriage to his uncle bothered him.

Hugh knocked on Kathryn's bedchamber door, but silence was his answer.

He knocked again.

No answer came.

Uninvited, Hugh opened the door and walked inside. Kathryn stood with her back to him and stared out the window. Hugh crossed the chamber and stood beside her.

Kathryn refused to acknowledge his presence.

Hugh reached out and gently turned her face to look at him. Tears streaked her cheeks. With his fingertips, Hugh brushed them away.

"I knocked," he said.

"I know," she replied.

"Why didn't you answer?"

"I mistakenly believed you'd go away."

Hugh smiled at that. "I'm sorry for what happened downstairs."

"Lady Fiona is correct. We should postpone the wedding or—"

"Fiona Fitzgerald is no lady," Hugh cut her off. "And she knows nothing of the circumstances surrounding our marriage."

"She's a beautiful woman."

"That she is."

"What is your connection to her?" Kathryn asked, unable to bite back the question.

"I've no connection with Fiona. While in London, I was one of several men acquainted with her. For God's sake, that she cat is prowling for a title, not a husband." Hugh grinned infuriatingly. "Could you be jealous?"

"Never," Kathryn said.

Still smiling, Hugh pulled her against his hard masculine length and lowered his head to claim her lips.

"Let me go," she demanded as his lips descended to hers.

"Never." Hugh's mouth covered hers in a tender, possessive kiss.

Kathryn pressed her hands against his chest and tried to push him away, but Hugh granted her no quarter. One of his hands at the small of her back held her firmly, molded her body to his. The hand at the back of her neck kept her lips captive beneath his.

The kiss was gently persuasive. Hugh nibbled lightly at the corners of her mouth, seeking and getting her shivery response.

Kathryn's struggles ceased. When her arms crept up his chest to entwine his neck and pull him closer, the tempo of the kiss changed, became ardent and demanding. Gaining entrance to her mouth, Hugh's tongue explored and tasted and teased. Trembling with long-denied desire, Kathryn met his thrusting tongue with her own.

"Yield to me," Hugh whispered hoarsely, breaking the almost magical spell.

Disgusted with herself, Kathryn jumped back and stared dazedly at his lips. *What had possessed her?* Heedless of consequence, Kathryn drew back and slapped him with all her might.

Surprised, Hugh stared at her for a moment. He touched his smarting cheek, then grinned and sauntered across the chamber to the door.

"Was that slap because of Fiona, my kiss—or your lusty response?" Hugh teased, then ducked out of the room. As the door closed behind him, the now quite battered brass candlestick crashed against it and fell harmlessly to the floor.

"Keep that up, madam," Hugh called from the corridor,

"and Dublin's candlestick makers will be rich beyond avarice."

"Knave," Kathryn muttered to herself, turning in a huff to stare out the window, her thoughts troubled.

Though her marriage to Shane had been far less than happy, Kathryn mused, he deserved the respect of a decent period of mourning. Three months was most unsuitable, even . . .

Scandalous! That tormenting word pounded painfully in her mind.

She would not go through with this. But how could she not? The agreement had been signed and witnessed.

Escape. Leaving undetected without Maeve would be easy, but she wasn't about to leave her daughter behind. That was unthinkable.

Feeling trapped, Kathryn closed her eyes and sighed deeply in a poor attempt to calm herself. In the next instant, her sparkling green eyes flew open as an outrageously risky escape plan formed in her mind.

It just might work, Kathryn decided, the corners of her lips turning up in the hint of a smile. If caught, she'd have a credible explanation. After all, Maeve and she would merely be playing a child's game, a natural thing for a mother and daughter to do together.

The next afternoon, Kathryn sat in front of the dark hearth in her chamber. With her were Polly and Maeve. Setting aside her embroidery, Kathryn yawned and stretched.

"It's past time for Maeve's nap," Kathryn said to her tiring woman.

"No nap," Maeve piped up from where she played on the floor.

"I'll put her down," Polly offered.

"Don't bother," Kathryn said. "Maeve and I will rest together. Take time for yourself."

"No nap, Mama," Maeve insisted as Polly left the chamber.

When the door clicked shut behind the tiring woman, Kathryn flashed her daughter a dazzling smile. "No nap, my pet? So be it."

"What?" Maeve was surprised. The game of "no nap" had been won too easily.

"How about playing a game instead?" Kathryn suggested.

"Game?" Maeve echoed.

"Hide and sneak," Kathryn said.

"Hide and seek?"

"No, precious, hide and sneak."

"How do we play?"

"We sneak from hiding place to hiding place," Kathryn explained. "If we reach Dublin Castle before Uncle Hugh finds us, we win the game."

Maeve clapped her hands together in excitement. Though her mother was usually entertaining, she'd really outdone herself this time.

"*Shhh!*" Kathryn hushed the little girl. "No one at all must hear or see us leave."

"Why?" Maeve whispered loudly.

"Because the servants will tell Uncle Hugh where to find us."

"But that's cheating!"

"Unfortunately, Uncle Hugh is not above cheating. Are you ready?"

Looking very much like her mother, Maeve smiled impishly and nodded, and they crossed the chamber to the door. Opening it a crack, Kathryn listened.

Silence.

Kathryn opened the door wider, then poked her head out to peer up and down the corridor. No one was about.

Turning back to her daughter, Kathryn placed her index finger across her lips in a gesture for silence. Solemn faced, Maeve immediately imitated her, and Kathryn nearly choked as she tried to swallow the laughter bubbling up in her throat. Hand in hand, they tiptoed down the length of the deserted corridor until they reached the stairs. No sound came from the foyer below.

With Kathryn in the lead, mother and daughter started down the stairs. They paused at the bottom to listen. In the great hall, the servants prepared for supper, and the sound of men's voices drifted into the foyer from the courtyard. The back entrance into the garden was their only avenue of escape.

Turning to the left, Kathryn led Maeve to the foyer's rear door and pulled her into the garden. Leaning against the cool, stone side of the mansion, Kathryn breathed a sigh of relief. At least, they'd made it outside.

Lifting her head in the air as if trying to catch the scent of danger, Kathryn scanned the deserted garden and wished she knew where Hugh was. Which way to go? The path on their left led to the stables, and to the right were the kitchen, ovens, and servants' quarters.

"See that rosebush over there near the wall?" Kathryn whispered, crouching down beside her daughter. "We'll hide behind it. Remember, not a sound."

Kathryn and Maeve scampered noiselessly across the manicured grass and crawled behind the rosebush. "Isn't this fun?" Kathryn asked.

"Oh, yes," Maeve answered. "What do we do now?"

"Wait."

"Why?"

"So Uncle Hugh won't find us before we get to Dublin Castle."

"I get it!" Maeve cried.

"Shush!" Kathryn silenced her daughter. "No talking."

"But why?" Maeve whispered.

"Someone will hear us and tell Uncle Hugh where we are."

"Oh."

For half an hour, mother and daughter sat uncomfortably behind the rosebush. Maeve finally broke the silence.

"I'm so thirsty, Mama."

"We'll drink a victory toast when we get to Dublin Castle," Kathryn whispered. "Won't that be grand?"

Maeve nodded without enthusiasm. Another half hour passed excruciatingly slowly.

"Mama?"

"What?"

"My bum hurts," Maeve complained.

Kathryn smiled. "Climb upon my lap."

Maeve scrambled onto her mother's lap. Kathryn held her daughter lovingly in her arms.

"Mama?" With disarming green eyes, Maeve gazed up at her.

"Yes, my pet?"

"I want my nap."

"Close your eyes, my child," Kathryn said with a smile. "Mama will keep you safe while you sleep."

Maeve closed her eyes. Two seconds later, she opened them again. "Mama?"

"Yes?"

"I love you."

"And I love you even more," Kathryn said.

Maeve closed her eyelids. In a very few minutes, the child's breathing evened, and Kathryn knew she slept.

Two hours later, Mme. Bujold and two of her assistants alighted from a coach in the courtyard and went inside. Peg escorted them upstairs, but Kathryn's chamber was deserted. After looking in Maeve's chamber, the great hall, the library, and the study, Peg headed for the courtyard where Hugh was speaking with several of his men.

"My lord," Peg called, obviously alarmed, "I can't locate Lady Kathryn and Madame Bujold is waitin'. Little Maeve's disappeared too."

"They're supposed to be restin'," Polly piped up, standing with Patrick a few feet away.

"Search the house again, Polly," ordered Hugh. "Peg, check the vicinity of the kitchen and ovens. Go to the stables, Conal, and be certain no horse is missing." Grim faced, he turned to Patrick, saying, "We'll search the garden. Be sure to look under every bush and shrub for that viper masquerading as an English lady."

Behind the rosebush, Kathryn regretted her foolish plan to escape to Dublin Castle. Her legs felt cramped, her buttocks had numbed, and her arms ached from holding her daughter.

Kathryn sent up a silent prayer of thanks when Maeve's eyelids fluttered open. At least, her aching arms could relax.

"Sit beside me," Kathryn whispered to Maeve who moved off her mother's lap.

"*Ouch!*" Maeve yelped as a thorn pricked her backside. "A snake bit me, Mama!"

"*Shhh!*" Kathryn looked down at her daughter.

"The only serpent under that bush is your mother," sounded Hugh's voice. "Come out now."

Kathryn closed her eyes against the pair of gleaming black boots in front of the rosebush. When she opened them a moment later, another pair of black boots stood there.

"Come out, I said."

Maeve laughed and crawled from behind the bush, then grinned at Hugh and Patrick. "You win, Uncle Hugh," she cried. "Now you must sneak to Dublin Castle before Mama and I find you. We'll close our eyes and count to ten."

Behind the rosebush, Kathryn groaned. Her daughter had just ruined her credible explanation.

"We'll play tomorrow," Hugh told Maeve. "It's almost suppertime. Patrick, have Polly tend Maeve's backside."

Patrick held out his hand to the little girl, and they headed for the house.

"The game is up," Hugh told the rosebush. "Show yourself."

"I'm coming," the rosebush grumbled.

Humiliated and smudged with dirt from head to toe, Kathryn crawled from behind the rosebush. Without a word, Hugh grabbed her upper arm in a painfully tight grip and pulled her toward the mansion. Once inside, he dragged her like a common criminal past the watching eyes of his servants into his study. The door shut behind them with an ominous click.

"You, madam, have the brains of a sheep," Hugh said, pointing an accusing finger at her.

Rubbing her bruised upper arm, Kathryn whirled away, then turned back to him, spouting venom. "And you, my lord knave, have the tongue of a serpent, the morals of a rabbit, and the manners of a swine. You are rude, crude—"

"*Enough!* Hugh shouted, silencing her, then smiled. "I believe I have the general idea." He gestured to a chair. "Please, be seated and we'll discuss this mutiny gently."

"I prefer to stand."

"I said, sit down."

With all the aplomb of a queen, Kathryn sat down and carefully arranged her dirty, grass-stained skirt around her. After folding her trembling hands in her lap, she looked up with a haughty, contemptuous expression on her face.

The lady is good, Hugh thought, admiring her spunk. Grown men had been known to cringe at his anger, but this slip of a woman had the courage to try to outface him.

"Why did you attempt escape?" he asked, scowling at her.

"Why did I . . . ? My lord, with all due respect, you must *think* before asking stupid questions."

"Enlighten me," Hugh said, ignoring her sarcasm.

"Lady Fiona—" Kathryn began.

"Fiona Fitzgerald is a spiteful bitch," Hugh cut her off. "We've been through this several times, Katie. I admire your wish to honor my uncle's memory, but because of Turlough, our marriage cannot be delayed. Besides, the contract has been signed."

"Contracts may be broken," Kathryn replied. "Vows cannot."

"The queen has blessed our union," Hugh lied. "She expects us to wed posthaste."

Turning away, Kathryn sulked in silence. Hugh pulled a chair close to hers, then sat and took her hands in his.

"Look at me," he said, and when she did, asked quietly, "Is marriage to me so abhorrent, then?"

Kathryn's expression softened. "No."

With her hands clasped in his, Hugh knelt on bended knee in front of her and smiled. "Will you do me the great honor of becoming my wife?" he asked, his piercing gaze holding hers captive.

Touched by his tenderness and unable to speak, Kathryn

nodded. Never in her young life had she been courted, only ordered to wed.

"Good," Hugh said briskly, then stood. Kneeling to anyone made him distinctly uncomfortable. "You may enjoy the freedom of the house and grounds, but riding is forbidden until the babe is delivered. I will have your word that you will not try to leave again."

"You would accept my word of honor?" Kathryn asked, surprised by his trust.

"Of course. Will you give it?"

"Yes, I swear."

Hugh looked her up and down, then smiled at her tattered appearance. "Run along and wash those smudges from your cheeks before supper."

Kathryn grinned puckishly, then stood and walked with him to the door. There she paused, saying, "Just one thing more."

Hugh waited.

"I want you to stop lunging at me for kisses every time we're alone," Kathryn told him.

Hugh nodded agreement.

"I will have your word on it."

"I swear I will refrain from lunging at you for kisses . . ."

Accepting his word, Kathryn inclined her head, and the door clicked shut behind her.

". . . until the vows are spoken," Hugh finished his thought, then decided to tell Patrick to watch her. Discreetly, of course.

6

The morning of midsummer night's eve, Hugh and Kathryn's wedding day, dawned sunny and warm. After bathing, Kathryn dressed with the assistance of Polly and Peg, who paused to admire their finished creation. Excited, Maeve gamboled around and around until her mother felt like a maypole.

Magical midsummer night's eve, Kathryn thought wryly, when mischievous spirits descend upon humankind to do their worst. Seeking his due, the most puckish of all will arrive in this chamber tonight.

Kathryn looked like summer's most glorious, vibrant blossom. Her pale yellow silk gown had long, flowing sleeves and squared neckline, cut low to reveal the crevice between her breasts. Slashings on its skirt and sleeves displayed a sheer silk underskirt and blouse. Intricate embroidery of golden threads and seed pearls accentuated the neckline and slashings. Her luxuriant copper hair had been pulled back and woven into a French love knot. Around her neck Kathryn wore a double strand of perfectly matched pearls with a magnificent jeweled clasp, her wedding gift from Hugh.

A noise sounded from the other side of the connecting

door, and the three women turned in that direction. Peg rushed across the chamber, opened the door a crack, and peered at Hugh.

"What do you want?" she asked.

"Lady Kathryn—if you don't mind."

"But I *do* mind," Peg replied. "She's indisposed." She tried to shut the door but was thwarted by his booted foot.

"Will you be wantin' to bring bad luck down upon this household, my lord?"

"No."

"Then go away. Seein' the bride before the weddin' is bad luck."

"No cheating, Uncle Hugh," Maeve called, making the women laugh.

Hugh withdrew his foot, and the door slammed shut in his face. With an oath, he turned away and stalked out of his chamber, his destination St. Mary's Church.

Awaiting their cue to enter the chapel, Patrick and Kathryn stood in the small antechamber at the back of St. Mary's. Trembling and pale, Kathryn jumped when the door creaked open.

"It's time," Conal said, then vanished.

"Pinch your cheeks, Katie," Patrick ordered when she raised uncertain eyes to his. "You resemble a ghost."

"You'll better understand my feelings on the day of your own marriage," she replied, pinching her cheeks. "In fact, I look forward to that day."

Patrick held Kathryn's hand and drew her into the chapel. She hesitated at the end of the aisle, but the hand holding hers made flight impossible. Forward was the only way to go.

Oblivious of the wedding guests, Kathryn glided down the aisle toward Hugh, who stood with Father Dunn in front of the flower-adorned altar. Reaching them, Patrick raised her shaking hand to his lips and then relinquished her.

"Relax," Hugh whispered, squeezing her hand. He led her into the inner sanctuary, and together they knelt in front of Father Dunn.

Responding mechanically from a lifetime of attending mass, Kathryn heard not a word as the priest's prayers became a faraway drone and anxious thoughts usurped her senses. *Was it too late to stop the ceremony? What would Hugh do if she turned around suddenly and ran back down the aisle?*

Realizing such thoughts were absurd, Kathryn gazed sidelong at Hugh and forced herself to concentrate on his admirable traits. He was handsome and intelligent—kind —generous—patient—an excellent kisser . . . As she thought of the physical intimacy they would share, her gaze slid down his masculine form.

"Lady Kathryn?" Father Dunn prompted.

Hugh snapped his head around to look at her. The dreamy glaze in her eyes gave proof to the amorous bent of her thoughts. Hugh swallowed his laughter with difficulty. *The little hypocrite!*

"Answer Father Dunn," he whispered out of the side of his mouth.

Startled from her reverie, Kathryn blushed and looked at the priest. "I beg your pardon?" she whispered.

Comely but dull witted, Father Dunn thought. He smiled benevolently and cleared his throat. "Do you, Kathryn Marie O'Neill, take this man, Hugh Owen O'Neill, to be your lawful wedded husband?"

"I do."

Father Dunn nodded at Hugh, saying, "Place the ring on the bride's finger."

Hugh started to slip the band on her finger but stopped unexpectedly. Silent fury appeared on his face.

Kathryn's gaze traveled from his forbidding expression to her finger. She gasped, her eyes widening with horror. She was still wearing Shane's wedding band!

"I'm sorry," Kathryn managed to choke out. She quickly removed the offending ring, but having no pockets, placed it on the third finger of her right hand.

Hugh placed his wedding band on her finger, then looked at the priest who was clearly appalled by what had transpired. "She's a widow," Hugh explained, his face mottled with angry embarrassment.

"You may face the assembled faithful," Father Dunn said after declaring them man and wife. When they turned to face their guests, the priest announced, "My lords and ladies, I present Lord Hugh O'Neill and his wife, Lady Kathryn."

What folly have I committed? Kathryn wondered, her stomach lurching sickeningly. There would be no escape for her now.

"I'm sorry," Kathryn apologized again, looking up at her husband.

"It's forgotten," Hugh replied. "We won't mention it again." Placing her arm on his, he escorted her down the aisle, out of the church, and into the coach that awaited them.

The O'Neill mansion's great hall was artfully decorated with flowers from the gardens. Inside the entrance, the bride and groom stood together to greet their guests.

Relieved that her husband's good humor had been restored, Kathryn was enjoying herself. Refusing to relinquish her hand, Hugh raised it to his lips every so often and smiled into her beguiling green eyes. To the casual observer, the O'Neills appeared a love match, though both would have been surprised to hear themselves so described.

"Lord and Lady Burke," Hugh introduced the couple standing in front of them. "Close friends of mine."

Of an age with Hugh, Lord Burke was a handsome man, tall and well built, his swarthy complexion proclaiming his Norman ancestry to all the world. Petite and fair but far advanced in pregnancy, Lady Burke was the opposite of her husband.

When the couple moved on, Hugh told Kathryn the Burkes already had two sons at home in Connaught. Having lingered in Dublin to attend their wedding, Lord and Lady Burke would almost immediately be returning home to await the birth of their third child.

Hugh gave Kathryn's hand a reassuring squeeze when Lord Fitzgerald and his daughter stood before them.

Fiona's dress was sapphire blue, matching her eyes, and cut daringly low to expose her enticing cleavage. Around her neck she wore an exquisite sapphire-and-diamond necklace, its jeweled clasp beckoning masculine eyes to follow the crevice beneath it and discover her silken woman's flesh.

Kathryn compared her own bosom to the other woman's and came out sadly lacking.

"I wish you happiness," Lord Fitzgerald said, shaking Hugh's hand, then gestured to the couple right behind him. "This is my niece Aisling, and you know, of course, her husband, Lord O'Brien."

Lady Aisling O'Brien was an incredibly beautiful young woman. Sapphire-eyed like her cousin Fiona, she had hair the color of spun gold and a silken, peach-hued complexion. Shockingly, Lord O'Brien was old enough to be her grandfather. Theirs had been an arranged marriage, and with any luck, Lady Aisling would soon become a wealthy young widow.

Ignoring Kathryn, Fiona smiled at Hugh, but his gaze was fixed on his bride. Then she moved on with her father.

Queen Elizabeth's viceroy was one of the last guests to offer congratulations. Approaching mid-life, Sir William Russell was short and stocky. He detested the Irish but was impressed with English titles, even coveted a more important one for himself.

"You've made an excellent match, O'Neill," Sir William said, then smiled at Kathryn. "When the queen's granted your petition, you and your lady will be feted at Dublin Castle."

"We'll look forward to it," Hugh replied. "You'll do us the honor of sitting at the high table?"

Sir William nodded and moved on.

"One who seeks a title must petition the queen," Hugh told Kathryn when she raised questioning eyes to his. "A formality in our case."

Kathryn sat at the high table between her husband and the viceroy. Having given the bride away, Patrick sat on Hugh's right and Sir Henry Sidney sat to the left of Sir William. Freshly baked bread, thick honey, creamy butter, and a generous supply of both red and white wines lay on the table.

The servants set the feast's first course of shrimp in snail butter and boiled oysters in front of them. Hugh served Kathryn a bit of shrimp before helping himself. One of the O'Neill men-at-arms called for the bridal couple to feed each other oysters, insuring potency in the marriage bed, and Kathryn blushed. Hugh laughed, as much at her embarrassment as at the man's jest.

"Allow me," Hugh said, raising an oyster to her lips.

Kathryn remembered another wedding feast like this

and froze. She struggled valiantly to hold back the tide of tears welling up in her eyes.

Hugh put his arm around her shoulder and drew her close, asking, "What is it?"

"Nothing," she lied, then lowered her eyes, unable to meet his gaze.

"Tell me what distresses you," Hugh demanded softly. "I want no secrets between us."

"I fed Shane oysters when—" Seeing her husband's eyes harden coldly against her, Kathryn hesitated for a brief moment and then tried again to explain. "The memory of his brutal ending . . . I—I'm afraid that you—"

"Suggesting the bridal couple eat oysters is customary," Hugh told her. "There's nothing to fear."

"Oh."

Hugh leaned closer and planted a kiss on her lips. The wedding guests cheered wildly, making Kathryn blush.

The sumptuous meal continued without event. The second course consisted of roasted sides of beef, braised lamb shanks, and whole roasted suckling pigs. Flaky pies filled with duck, lark, pigeon, and sparrow came next. Bowls of lettuce, scallion, and radish were consumed. Tempting the guests, the desserts—sweet cheese, molded jellies, fresh strawberries with clotted cream, iced wedding cake—arrived last.

After the servants cleared the remains of the meal, the O'Neill men-at-arms pushed the tables aside to clear a large section of the hall. Hugh and Kathryn danced first but were soon joined by their guests.

Kathryn danced with Patrick and Sir William. Hugh reclaimed her and suggested they make the rounds of their guests, but nearing the hall's entrance, drew her into the foyer.

"Peg's fetching Maeve," he explained, gesturing to the

stairs. "I've something to show you." The little girl bounded down the stairs, and Hugh ushered them outside into the gardens.

"Patrick!" he called.

Maeve's green eyes, so much like her mother's, widened with joyful surprise when the O'Neill warrior appeared, leading a black Shetland pony. In the next instant, Maeve dashed toward Patrick, who laughed and swung her onto the pony, then led them around the garden.

"You certainly know how to please the ladies," Kathryn remarked, her eyes gleaming at the sight of her daughter's happiness.

"For your sake, madam, I hope so," Hugh said. But noting her paleness, he added, "There'll be no bedding ceremony. Go and prepare yourself. I'll deliver Maeve into Peg's care."

"Thank you," Kathryn said.

Pleased with himself, Hugh smiled at her retreating back.

Kathryn found Polly waiting in her chamber. At the sight of Kathryn's expression, strained with apprehension, Polly decided silence would be the best policy. She unpinned her mistress's brilliant coppery mane and brushed it out, then helped her disrobe and don the alluring night shift created by Mme. Bujold for this special night.

"Leave me," Kathryn said. "I would be alone for a few minutes."

"You made a beautiful bride." Polly walked toward the door.

"Polly?" When the other girl turned, Kathryn pointed to the bed, garlanded with flowering branches in keeping with an old pagan fertility rite. "There was no need. I'm already with child."

"I'm just makin' sure another goes into the oven when this one's done."

Alone, Kathryn stood in front of the pier glass and studied her reflection. Her night shift had been created from almost transparent ivory silk and shot throughout with shimmering golden threads. Form fitting around the bosom, the gown hung loose across the belly and hips to disguise her pregnancy as much as possible. Sleeveless, its bodice was cut low and held together in the front by three ribbons of gold satin. With her shimmering night shift and shining copper hair cascading around her, Kathryn looked like a pagan goddess of old in the flickering firelight.

I'm no innocent maid to be frightened, Kathryn told herself, trying to calm her frazzled nerves. *I've made a bargain and must keep it for my children's sake.*

Dressed in a silken bed robe, Hugh entered silently through the connecting door and approached Kathryn from behind. He placed his hands upon her shoulders. Their eyes met in the pier glass. The dark, scorching intensity of his gaze made Kathryn whirl around to face him. All thoughts of children and bargain fled her mind.

Noting her fear, Hugh did not give Kathryn a chance to think.

Gently but firmly grasping her upper arms, he pulled her against his lean, masculine frame and lowered his lips to hers in a passionate kiss that melted into another.

"My sweet, beautiful wife," Hugh whispered against her lips, then lifted his head to gaze into her mesmerizing green eyes.

It was then he saw two silent tears streaming slowly down her cheeks.

Determined to receive his due, Hugh untied the first golden ribbon, freeing her lush breasts, and devoured them with his eyes. He untied the second ribbon, but when his hand moved to the third, he felt the gentle swell of her belly. *Shane's child!*

Disgusted by his own lust, Hugh swore softly and stepped back. "Go to bed," he ordered and turned away.

"But—"

"Nobody must suspect our marriage is unconsummated," Hugh cut her off. "We'll share the bed tonight. Go to sleep before I change my mind."

Bewildered but relieved, Kathryn leapt into the bed and pulled the coverlet up to her chin.

Frustrated, Hugh sat on the chair in front of the hearth and thought about his wife.

He wanted her. Badly. Of that, he had no doubts. And he'd wanted her for a good, long time.

Five years earlier, Hugh had come face-to-face with the newly married Shane and Kathryn at the Tudor court. Hugh had been instantly attracted to his uncle's beautiful, fifteen-year-old bride. Later that long-ago evening, he'd managed to catch her alone and steal a kiss from her.

Unfortunately, Shane had found them together and put an abrupt end to that first, wonderful kiss. Shane had threatened Hugh's life for the hundredth time and then slapped Kathryn.

Since then, Kathryn had smiled at Hugh in a thousand dreams. And now, she was his wife.

Shane stopped me then, Hugh thought, *and his unborn son stopped me tonight.*

No, Hugh corrected himself. *It was those tears.* After living with Shane, Kathryn was afraid and needed time. Waiting until she delivered her child was such a small favor to grant her. After all, they would be married a long, long time.

Hugh awakened early the next morning. Kathryn still slept, snuggled intimately against him. Studying her tranquil expression, he decided she was more an angel than a temptress. His gaze roamed the length of her scantily clad body, and to his chagrin, Hugh felt his manhood stirring.

The sliest of smiles appeared on his face. Why not take his pleasure on her now? After all, she had agreed to consummate their marriage.

Hugh reached for one plump, tempting breast. A horrifying thought popped into his mind, and his hand halted in midair just before touching a large, dusky nipple. Was this fleeting pleasure worth a lifetime of listening to her denounce him as dishonorable?

No! Hugh quickly withdrew his hand.

Sexual frustration is not fatal, Hugh told himself, *merely unspeakable torture.* For safety's sake, he eased from the bed and sought refuge in his own chamber.

Verging on consciousness, Kathryn moved restlessly around the enormous bed and instinctively sought the body that had warmed her through the night. She opened one eye first and then the other, but found herself alone.

The door flew open suddenly, startling her. Polly walked in and cast her a knowing look. "Your bath is set up in Lord O'Neill's chamber," she announced.

"Where is m-my—Lord O'Neill?" Kathryn feigned nonchalance.

"Playin' squire to Maeve in the garden." Polly's lips quirked at her mistress's formality toward her new husband. "They've waited to breakfast with you."

Dressed in a peach silk gown with a modestly high neck and lacy ruff, Kathryn hurried downstairs but hesitated before entering the gardens. Embarrassed by her tears of the previous evening, Kathryn wondered, not for the first time since waking, if her husband planned to consummate their marriage that night. After all, she had agreed to it.

"Damn." Kathryn cursed her foolish nervousness and forced herself to step outside.

Leading Maeve on the black pony, Hugh turned and saw Kathryn standing there, shy and uncertain, a high blush staining her cheeks. Between facial hue and dress, she looked like a rare and beautiful blossom growing in his garden. Hugh had the strongest urge to pluck her.

"Good morn, my lady," he called, and bowed gallantly in her direction, then he signaled the waiting stable boy, and lifted Maeve from the pony.

"Mama, did you see me riding Soot?" Maeve asked, excited.

"Soot?"

"My pony!"

"Yes, sweet. You're an excellent horsewoman. But, wouldn't Midnight be a prettier name for so fine a pony?"

The child's green eyes flashed. Her small, turned-up nose was lifted high in swift consternation, looking very much like her mother when angered. "I like Soot," Maeve insisted, "and he's *my* pony."

"It's Soot then, my pet."

"Madam, your uncommon beauty shames these proud blossoms." Hugh flattered her outrageously, gesturing to the gardens.

"My lord, you should have been a poet," Kathryn returned, the hint of a smile flirting with her lips.

"A poet's riches are his words," Hugh said. "I prefer something far more tangible, not to mention valuable. Shall we breakfast?"

As the three entered the mansion, Hugh slipped his arm familiarly around Kathryn's waist. Surprised, she looked up and met his disarming smile.

"I trust you slept well?" he asked, leaning close.

"Y-y-yes," she stammered, her face as red as the most brilliant rose in his garden.

After putting Maeve to bed that night, Kathryn went directly to her own chamber. Rejoining her husband downstairs would have put her in a decidedly uncomfortable situation, and so she avoided it.

Polly was waiting in her chamber. After helping her mistress undress, she left, but not without a suggestive rolling of her eyes and wishes for pleasant "dreams."

Kathryn wondered how Polly had become so knowledgeable in the ways of the married. Patrick's doing, no doubt!

Once in bed, Kathryn glanced at the connecting door and thought of her husband. She could almost feel his powerful hands upon her, imagine his hardened, muscular body pressing her into the bed. Then the child within her fluttered, and she groaned at where her thoughts had wandered.

"What is wrong with me?" Kathryn asked the empty chamber. She heard a noise from the other side of the door and knew that Hugh was preparing to retire. Will he seek my bed or not? she wondered, uncertain which she really desired. Kathryn did appreciate his sensitivity to her feelings, but did he desire her so little that he'd not even try?

It was a long time before Kathryn found release from troubled thoughts in sleep.

Hugh climbed into bed and stared contemplatively at the connecting door. Was Kathryn sleeping or thinking of him? His heart wrenched at the possibility she might be thinking of Shane.

His wife had been warm and affectionate all day. Could she have changed her mind about sealing their bargain?

Fickle by nature, women frequently changed their minds. All he need do was open the door.

Then what?

Stubbornly proud, Kathryn would never admit the blasted bargain was a mistake. *Or would she?*

No! Hugh would not chance it. He'd no wish to force her or face her rejection.

Hugh rolled to his other side, but it was a long, long time before he, too, found sweet release in sleep.

7

"Mama, I want to ride Soot," Maeve said, playing in front of the hearth.

"No, Soot would catch his death of cold in this rain," Kathryn refused.

Standing at the window of her sitting room, Kathryn gazed in restless boredom at the rainy September afternoon and sighed. It would be two long and dreary months until she was relieved of her burden. Glancing down at her distended belly, she wondered how much larger she would grow and worried that she would remain a wondrously great object. Returning to her task, Kathryn once more sat in the chair by the fire and picked up the baby clothes she'd been sewing.

Polly walked into the sitting room, announcing, "Sir William Russell is downstairs."

"The viceroy?"

"Lord O'Neill and he are waitin' for you in the study."

"Stay with Maeve," Kathryn instructed Polly, rising slowly from the chair. Smoothing the skirt of her gown, Kathryn felt too misshapen to greet such an important guest and wished she was not so advanced in her pregnancy.

Downstairs, Kathryn knocked on the study's door and opened it. Hugh was at her side in an instant and led her to a seat in front of the hearth, then perched against the arm of the chair.

"Forgive my rudeness," Kathryn said to Sir William. "Curtseying is rather difficult for me these days."

"Nothing to forgive, my lady," the viceroy replied. "I've excellent news for you, but I've also heard something quite distressing today."

Hugh flicked a glance at his wife, then cast a silent warning at Sir William who missed it.

"Share the bad news first," Kathryn said with a smile. "The good news will make us feel better."

"Are you certain you're up to it?" Hugh asked solicitously, his eyes searching hers.

"Being with child does not mean I am a child or incapacitated," Kathryn snapped.

Hugh rolled his eyes in exasperated patience. There were times when his wife behaved like the petulant child she professed not to be.

"Lord Burke's wife passed away," Sir William told them, "giving birth . . ." His voice trailed off as his gaze fixed on Kathryn's belly, and he realized his blunder.

Both Hugh and Kathryn were several shades whiter.

"Damn," Hugh muttered, leaning over to look at his wife. "Are you all right?"

Visibly shaken, Kathryn nodded. Dying in childbirth had never entered her mind. Hugh reached for her trembling hand.

"And the good news?" Kathryn asked in a quavering voice.

"I'm terribly sorry, Lady Kathryn," Sir William apologized, then added with a smile, "or should I address you as countess?"

"What?" Hugh and Kathryn exclaimed simultaneously.

"Her majesty has granted your petition," Sir William announced. "On the first day of the new year, you will present yourselves at Dublin Castle to be invested the earl and countess of Tyrone."

Hugh beamed, then leaned down and planted a kiss on his wife's cheek. "Thanks," he whispered.

Kathryn smiled at him, mesmerized by the tenderness in his eyes. For a brief moment, both forgot about their guest.

Sir William cleared his throat. "However, there is a small condition."

"Go on." Hugh was suddenly all business.

"Come spring, Sir Henry Bagenal will arrive in Dublin to—"

"My stepfather?" Kathryn interrupted, surprised.

"Oh, yes. I'd forgotten that your mother and he wed last year. Or was it the year before? Anyway, Bagenal leads a force to rout the Maguire who, as you know, has been harassing our troops. You are expected to help, Hugh, at your own expense as you promised."

Kathryn opened her mouth to protest but felt Hugh squeeze her hand. Reluctantly, she remained silent.

"I am honored to aid her majesty and my father-in-law," Hugh told the viceroy. Bearing arms against his own kind was distasteful in the extreme, but he had no alternative.

"I'll see the message gets sent. Come January first, we shall be celebrating in your honor at Dublin Castle." Sir William smiled at them.

Kathryn politely returned his smile, but Hugh's expression remained emotionless.

"There is another matter I must discuss with you," Sir William added, looking at Hugh. "Privately."

"I'll go," Kathryn said. With her husband's assistance

she stood and walked to the door, saying, "I fear I'm falling behind in my sewing."

"Madam, persist in making baby clothes," Hugh teased her, "and there will be a shortage of blue cloth in Dublin."

Turning around, Hugh looked at Sir William who was staring dreamily at the door through which Kathryn had vanished. "Even heavy with child, she's exquisite," the viceroy remarked.

Hugh's lips quirked in amusement at the other man's besotted expression. "Thank you, I think."

"I mean, most women aren't that lovely under normal conditions," Sir William explained. "Lady Kathryn is even more beautiful with child."

"I must keep her that way," Hugh said. Then, "There's more to a woman than meets the eye, you know."

"I know no such thing," Sir William returned.

Hugh chuckled, then asked, "What's so important we must send Katie away?"

"I've had bad news from England." Sir William handed him a letter, addressed to Kathryn. "In view of your lady's condition, I decided to tell you privately."

"What is it?"

"Heather Devereux, your wife's youngest sister, was to be wed in France. The ship's been lost at sea, and she's presumed dead. I suppose that letter from her mother will tell you more. Knowing Lady Kathryn was with child, Bagenal included the tragic news in his missive to me and asked that I break it gently. Unhealthy for an expectant mother to become upset, you know. It marks the child."

"What happened?" Hugh asked, slipping the letter inside his doublet.

"Only God knows," Sir William said with a shrug. "The ship simply vanished somewhere between England and France. Probably went down in a storm."

"Damn it! How can news like this be gently told?" Hugh was silent for a moment, then said, "Telling Katie after the child is delivered seems to be the wisest course. After all, risking the babe won't bring her sister back from the dead. As a favor, don't mention this to anyone."

Sir William nodded. "You can depend upon my silence."

"And the queen can depend upon me," Hugh said, shaking his hand.

Sir William walked toward the door, saying, "I'll see that her majesty gets the message."

Alone, Hugh stared at the letter Sir Henry had given him. How could an innocuous-looking thing bear such tragic tidings? Should he tell Kathryn or not? If she somehow discovered the truth about her sister, Kathryn would hold him accountable for withholding this information.

His silence could be a mistake.

And, Hugh decided, losing the child would be Shane's loss, not his.

Hugh left his study and climbed the stairs to Kathryn's chamber. This time he knocked and waited for her answer before entering.

Sitting in a chair in front of the hearth, Kathryn smiled at him as he walked across the chamber toward her. Polly sat in the other chair while Maeve played on the rug at their feet.

Hugh dreaded shattering the peacefulness of this domestic scene.

"Polly, take Maeve downstairs," he instructed. "I want to speak privately with Lady Kathryn."

After they'd gone, Hugh paced back and forth in front of the hearth. Kathryn watched and wondered what she'd done now.

"What is it?" she asked, breaking the silence.

The anxious pacing stopped. Hugh opened his mouth to speak, then hesitated and looked away.

She trusts me, Hugh realized with a start when his gaze returned to her up turned face. He could not tell her. Losing the child might cause *her* death, and that would be unbearable.

"Well?" Kathryn prodded.

"I'll be interviewing two candidates for the position of nursemaid tomorrow," Hugh told her. "Since whoever I hire will be caring for Maeve and the baby, you will, of course, have final approval."

Kathryn nodded, pleased with his consideration. "What time shall I come to your study?"

"Ten o'clock."

"I'll be there."

Without another word, Hugh left the room and retraced his steps downstairs to the study. He crossed the chamber to the hearth and removed the offensive letter from inside his doublet, then tossed it into the fire. He would give Kathryn the bad news as soon as the baby arrived. There was little chance of her discovering the truth before then.

Kathryn arrived late for the first interview the next morning but just in time to save herself much heartache. She raced into the study without knocking and sat in the chair beside her husband's, then looked at the first applicant, who leapt to her feet, curtseyed, and sat down again.

"This is Maggie O'Malley," Hugh introduced the buxom blonde seated across from them.

Kathryn stared at this unlikely nursemaid. Eighteen-year-old Maggie O'Malley was blond and blue eyed, much too blond and blue eyed to suit Kathryn. Sharp green eyes dropped to the girl's ample bosom, much too ample for Kathryn's liking. When Kathryn's critical gaze returned to her face, Maggie smiled. Why, the slut even had all her teeth!

Her marriage was certainly no love match, Kathryn thought as she stared at the girl, and women were subject to the whims and fancies of their husbands. In her enlarged condition, she needed no serious rival for Hugh's favor. An ounce of prevention was worth ten pounds of cure.

"Maggie comes to us highly recommended," Hugh was saying.

"We've another woman to interview," Kathryn said to the girl. "We'll let you know."

After making desperate cow eyes at Hugh, Maggie O'Malley stood and curtseyed to them, then left the chamber.

"Well?" Hugh asked in a hopeful voice.

"She won't do."

"Why not?"

"The wench looks more suited to a brothel than a nursery," Kathryn replied. "Call in the next one."

Shaking his head, Hugh went to the door and beckoned to the second applicant. Fifty and fat, Nellie Dowd walked in.

"She'll do," Kathryn said.

"*She'll do?*" Hugh echoed, astounded.

"Yes."

"But, you haven't even spoken with her," he argued.

Kathryn smiled at her husband. "Nellie is Peg's third cousin. Besides, Maeve requires a grandmotherly type nurse." She turned to Nellie, saying, "Come along. I want you to meet my daughter, Maeve." The door clicked shut behind them.

Hugh stared at it and wondered in confusion what had

just happened. Compared to his wife, dealing with the English was like a day of lighthearted picnicking.

The fertile seeds, planted in early spring, had grown by leaps and bounds. As the peasants in the countryside had harvested their crops, so too would Kathryn now that bleak November was upon them and her burden dropped.

Hugh had already left for Parliament on that dreary November morn when Kathryn, rotund yet radiant, walked downstairs to speak with Peg concerning the day's fare. As she crossed the foyer, Kathryn pressed a hand to the small of her back and tried to soothe its dull ache.

She would be glad when the babe was delivered and the sooner the better. Shrinking into her former shape by the time of her husband's investiture, less than two months away, was of utmost importance. That Hugh would then seek entrance to her bed never entered her mind.

Kathryn passed through the deserted great hall and went into the kitchen where Polly and Peg were treating themselves to warmed cider. Feeling a strange but not unfamiliar gushing sensation, Kathryn looked down in surprise. The housekeeper's gaze followed hers.

"The babe!" Peg cried, leaping from her chair. "We must get you upstairs."

"Polly, send Patrick to find Hugh at Parliament," Kathryn said calmly, relieved that her time was at hand. Unperturbed by what was to come, Kathryn slowly retraced her steps through the deserted great hall to the foyer and was followed by an anxious Peg.

Upstairs, Peg helped Kathryn undress and don the blue night shift made especially for her son's birth. Leaving her mistress, the housekeeper stoked the fire in the hearth. When she turned around, Kathryn was pacing back and forth across the chamber.

"Hie you to bed!" Peg screeched, alarmed.

"I won't seek that torture sooner than I must," Kathryn refused. "Make your preparations."

"The wife is as stubborn as the husband is wily," Peg grumbled, but did as she was told.

A short time later Hugh and Patrick returned from Parliament. Doffing his cloak without breaking stride, Hugh ran up the stairs two at a time and burst into his wife's bedchamber.

"You're not in bed!" Hugh exclaimed, surprised to find her standing in front of the hearth.

"I need a diversion," Kathryn said, turning toward him, her hands soothing the cramp in her belly. "Will you keep me company?"

Hugh clasped her hands in his, saying, "Of course, dear heart, but you should sit down."

"I don't want to sit," Kathryn snapped as the pain grew sharper. Tiny beads of sweat glistened above her upper lip.

"But I do."

Hugh sat in the chair in front of the hearth and gently drew her onto his lap, then wrapped his arms around her. Kathryn rested her head against his shoulder. They sat in silence and watched the flames dancing in the hearth. Kathryn gasped suddenly and groaned in the midst of a contraction worse than the others.

"I'm sending for a leech," Hugh said.

"*No!*" Kathryn forced herself to smile serenely. "Peg and Polly know what to do, but it's time I went to bed."

"I'll stay with you," Hugh offered, his face as pale as hers.

"No," Kathryn refused. "Find Patrick. He's been through this before and will help you pass the time."

On trembling legs, Hugh walked down the stairs to the foyer. He'd never seen a laboring woman and was shaken by its seeming agony, especially since the pain-racked woman was his wife. His thoughts drifted to the child— Shane's child—struggling to enter the world. Hugh knew he wanted his own son to inherit Tyrone, but he was bound to keep faith with the bargain. To do otherwise would mean the loss of the woman.

In his study, Hugh nodded at Patrick and sat in one of the chairs in front of the hearth. Offered a dram of whiskey, Hugh shook his head, saying, "Help yourself."

Easing into the other chair, Patrick gulped down the two drams of whiskey and grinned. "Whiskey's the only way to get yourself through childbirth," he said sagely.

"Women die in childbirth."

"Some do," Patrick agreed, and sprawling comfortably in the chair, advised, "Relax, my lord. You've a long wait stretchin' before you."

Hugh moaned as if in pain, then rose from his chair and got the flagon of whiskey. For hours, the two Irishmen sat in companionable silence and passed the whiskey between them, their thoughts on Kathryn caught in the throes of birthing her child.

Suppertime came and went. When the door opened suddenly, Hugh and Patrick looked up.

Grinning with joy, Peg stood there. "It's a right bonnie lass," she announced.

"What?" both men exclaimed simultaneously.

The housekeeper laughed at their astonished expressions, then repeated, "We've another lass to cosset."

Hugh leapt from his chair, a satisfied smile stealing across his handsome face. Chuckling with glee, he rubbed his hands together vigorously.

Patrick and Peg turned questioning gazes upon him.

"No son of Shane O'Neill will become earl after me," Hugh said, answering their puzzled expressions. "And I won't be breaking faith to see my own son take his rightful place." Hugh fairly danced out the door, and Peg was hard-pressed to keep up with him.

When he entered his wife's bedchamber, the scene Hugh found was not what he'd anticipated. Appearing frail and lost in the enormous bed, his wife held the squalling infant in her arms. Instead of greeting him with a joyous smile, Kathryn turned her face away, but not before Hugh noted the silent tears streaking her cheeks.

"Let's give them their privacy," Peg said, ushering Polly outside.

Hugh frowned and crossed the chamber to sit on the edge of the bed. Still, Kathryn refused to acknowledge his presence.

"Give her to me," he said, lifting the infant into his arms.

Hugh unwrapped the swaddling and inspected the baby. Her black hair and rosy complexion promised a rare beauty and proclaimed her the daughter of Shane O'Neill.

"Our daughter is bonnie," Hugh said, rewrapping the swaddling. "I will enjoy cosseting her."

Kathryn stared hard at him. Fresh tears welled up in her eyes and rolled down her cheeks.

Cuddling the baby against his chest, Hugh flicked a glance at Kathryn. "Tell me what pains you so."

"I did not birth a boy. You needn't have married me," she said, her voice laced with bitterness. "Our marriage is still unconsummated and can be easily annulled."

"I've no regrets and want no annulment," Hugh replied. "Fate has decreed that our own son become earl after me, and we've time enough to produce one."

"Pass her to me," Kathryn said with a tremulous smile, her spirits soaring as if an unbearable weight had been lifted from her soul.

Hugh's breath caught in his throat when Kathryn pushed aside the front of her night shift and offered a plump breast to her daughter. The baby quieted instantly. Her small mouth made suckling movements, and the tiniest of hands began kneading the warm, motherly flesh.

"What will we name her?" Hugh asked hoarsely.

"She resembles Shane," Kathryn said, her eyes on her daughter. "I'll call her Shana."

A pained expression crossed Hugh's face but was quickly banished before she looked up. "It's Shana, then," he agreed.

"Whether 'tis fitting or no," Kathryn said, "Patrick and Polly will be her godparents."

"An excellent choice." Hugh planted a chaste kiss on her cheek, and his eyes regained their sparkle. "I do hope Shana looks well in blue."

8

Radiant sun shone auspiciously on Hugh O'Neill's investiture day; indeed, his fortunate star was beginning its fabulous ascent. A mid-morning ceremony had been scheduled at Dublin Castle and was to be followed in the evening with a gala in honor of the O'Neills. The investiture ceremony was simple and brief. Afterward, its few participants, anticipating Dublin's grandest social event in many a year, went their separate ways.

When the O'Neill entourage returned home, Hugh invited Patrick and Conal to join him in his study for a toast. As he passed his most trusted men-at-arms their whiskey, Hugh flicked a glance at his wife. Kathryn cocked her head to one side and raised a perfect brow. With a slight incline of his head, Hugh acknowledged her silent challenge and poured a splash of whiskey for her.

"May we never fall from sweet Success's grace." Kathryn spoke first.

"To Christendom's most beautiful countess," Hugh complimented her outrageously.

"Good health and long life to the earl and countess of Tyrone," Conal offered.

Sparing a wink for Kathryn, Patrick ventured, "May the

earl of Tyrone and his countess prosper and be blessed with a house full of fine, strong sons."

Kathryn blushed but raised her cup with the men and drank. Having never tasted Ireland's water of life, she was unprepared for its violent jolt. Her eyes widened in surprise as the unexpected burning sensation raced from her lips to the pit of her stomach. She choked and gasped for breath.

Hugh slapped her back and cast her an "I-could-have-told-you-so" look. Removing the cup from her hands, he chided, "Shana must eat, and getting her drunk won't do."

"If Shana develops a taste for whiskey," Kathryn returned with an impish grin, "I'd say she's a true O'Neill." The three men chuckled, knowing it was truth.

"Rest before tonight's celebration, countess," Hugh teased. "Yawning in the viceroy's face is considered impolite. You're dismissed."

Sweeping him a curtsey befitting a king, Kathryn bowed her head in feigned meekness and murmured, "As you wish, my lord earl."

"Arise, fair damsel." Hugh offered Kathryn his arm, and in a courtly manner, escorted her to the door. As she passed him, he slapped her backside and made her squeal.

"See to your brood, wench," Hugh ordered gruffly. Enchanted, he watched her cross the foyer to the stairs.

The time is ripe for my next conquest, he decided. From this night onward, the earl of Tyrone and his countess will share a bed.

"Wipe your noble chin, my lord earl," Patrick remarked when Hugh turned around. "You're droolin'." Conal and Patrick dissolved into laughter at the newest earl's besotted expression, and Hugh smiled.

Late in the afternoon, Kathryn bathed and then nursed Shana. She worried that it would be hours before she could feed her hungry daughter again, but could hardly contain her excitement about the gala at Dublin Castle.

Kathryn sat in a silk chemise and a tightly laced busk while Polly arranged her hair in a simple but elegant chignon at the nape of her neck. "Fetch those pads," she ordered the tiring woman. "I've no wish to be embarrassed by leaking nipples." After covering her nipples so the padding would not become exposed, Kathryn stepped into her gown, and Polly fastened the tiny, emerald-green buttons that secured the back.

"You're a sight, my lady," Polly gushed.

Kathryn looked at herself in the pier glass.

Matching the emerald-green of her eyes, the gown had been created in luxuriant velvet. As she studied her appearance, Kathryn grew anxious about her husband's reaction to the daringly low-cut neckline that exposed the tops of her breasts, almost to her nipples. Knowing Fiona and her cousin Aisling and many other lovely ladies would be present, Kathryn had ordered Mme. Bujold to create a neckline that would keep her husband's eyes from wandering elsewhere.

"Fetch my pearls," Kathryn ordered Polly.

Elegantly attired, Hugh walked through the connecting door at that moment. His velvet pantaloons and doublet were hunter green, and attached to the side of his belt was Conn O'Neill's ancient Celtic skean with jeweled hilt and sheath.

Approaching her from behind, Hugh smiled at her in the pier glass, and Kathryn turned around to face him. "You're stunning," he said. His gaze drifted to the tiring woman. "Put away the pearls, Polly, and leave."

Hugh bade Kathryn turn in a circle for his perusal, but when she faced him again, his approving smile had become an aggrieved scowl. "The gown is exquisite, but I refuse to expose my treasures to the greedy eyes of others." His voice rose in vexation. "The gown is unsuitable. Remove it at once."

"All the ladies will be garbed thusly," Kathryn argued, unhappy with his overbearing attitude.

"All the ladies are not my wife."

"I hope not." Undaunted, Kathryn smiled sweetly. *Too sweetly.* "Of course, I will remove it." Turning her back to him, she murmured, "The buttons, Hugh. Would you mind?"

Pleased with her rare obedience, Hugh raised his hands to the buttons, but her honeyed voice stopped him.

"I've nothing else to wear so I won't be able to attend. You must remember all the details and tell me about it when you return."

Hugh's hands froze in midair, then dropped to his sides. Watching his reaction in the pier glass, Kathryn knew victory was hers.

"Bah! You've a chamber full of gowns, but we've no time to spare." Hugh grumbled, "I'll probably spend the entire evening guarding you."

Kathryn whirled around and kissed his cheek.

"I've a gift for you," he said, pulling a jeweled box from his doublet.

Accepting it, Kathryn studied its precious jewels and fine craftsmanship. "Thank you. I'll cherish it."

"The gift is inside, silly."

Blushing at her own stupidity, Kathryn opened the box. A magnificent emerald-and-diamond necklace sparkled at her from its velvet-lined bed.

"Oh!" she exclaimed. "I—I—I don't know what to say!"

Hugh decided the necklace would nicely facilitate the transition in their sleeping arrangements. "Allow me," he offered, taking the necklace from her hands and placing it around her neck.

When he saw the emerald clasp winking at him from the deep, inviting cleavage between her breasts, Hugh struggled valiantly against an aggravated grimace. His hands lingered against the beckoning swell of his wife's enticing flesh, then traveled ever so slowly to her shoulders.

"Thank you," Kathryn murmured, his touch unsettling her. "But I have nothing for you."

"You've given me what's truly valuable, my title and a family."

Touched by his words but wishing she had a gift for him, Kathryn said, "Still, I would give you something more."

"In that case, I'll think about what I most desire," Hugh said. "I'll let you know."

Ignorant of his lusty intent, Kathryn failed to see the double meaning of his words, and with a smile, accepted his offered arm.

A rainbow's variety of colors filled Dublin Castle's great hall. All of Dublin's noble lords and their ladies wore their finest to welcome the newest among them. When Hugh and Kathryn arrived, the hall grew silent, and a sea of faces turned in their direction. Viceroy Russell's majordomo turned to the aristocratic assembly. "My lords and ladies," he announced, "the earl of Tyrone and his countess."

The noble crowd applauded. Viceroy Russell stepped forward and led them to the far end of the hall where they could greet their many well-wishers.

"Refreshments are in the adjoining chamber," the viceroy told them, eyeing Kathryn's cleavage. "The great hall is for dancing and, of course, you'll honor us by dancing first."

Hugh led Kathryn onto the area set aside for dancing. When the music ended, Sir William claimed Kathryn.

Smiling inwardly, she wondered how her husband could guard her while she danced with another man. As she danced with Sir William, Kathryn spied Hugh dancing with Lady Fiona and felt annoyed by the sight, especially when he caught her staring and grinned infuriatingly in her direction.

Hugh saw Lord Fitzgerald claim Kathryn for the next dance. Since Fiona seemed reluctant to let him go, Hugh danced with her again. His gaze frequently traveled the distance to his wife.

"Congratulations," Fiona said, trying to capture his wandering attention.

"Thank you." Hugh's gaze dipped to her alluringly displayed flesh. "You look dazzling tonight."

"I'm so disappointed that we haven't renewed our acquaintance," Fiona purred, her invitation unmistakable.

Hugh's gaze dropped from her face to her bosom, and his manhood stirred as if awakening from a long, stuporous sleep. Hugh inwardly cursed his lack of self-control, and then Kathryn.

My virginal wife is a sore vexation, he thought, but her maiden's act will end tonight. That coppery-haired virgin huntress will no longer prey upon my heart. *Nor other vital parts.*

Extricating himself from temptation's path, Hugh maneuvered Fiona across the chamber. The music ended, and they stood beside Kathryn and Lord Fitzgerald. One glance at his wife told Hugh she was unhappy with his choice of a dancing partner. Hoping his well-laid plans for her would not go awry, Hugh claimed Kathryn for the next dance. As she placed her hand on his, Sir William Russell approached.

"I need a private word with you," the viceroy said to Hugh who nearly groaned at his bad luck. "Lord Fitzgerald, of course, is welcome to accompany us." Hugh murmured an apology to Kathryn and left her with Fiona.

"Congratulations," Fiona sneered when the men had gone.

"Thank you, Lady Fiona," Kathryn returned, placing special emphasis on "lady."

Fiona, with unmasked hatred shining from the depths of her blue eyes, glared at her. "I understand congratulations are in order for the birth of your daughter," she parried, placing her own special emphasis on "daughter."

"Shana is two months now," Kathryn replied, choosing not to be baited.

Determined to hit her mark, Fiona added, "Hugh must be concerned about producing an heir for his earldom, especially since you've managed to drop only daughters thus far."

Kathryn's eyes became green shards of ice. She stepped threateningly closer to the dark-haired beauty just as the men reappeared.

"If you don't mind, I'd like to steal my wife for a few moments," Hugh said, sensing danger. Gently but firmly, he led her away, saying, "Turlough sends us his congratulations."

"Congratulations from Turlough?"

"And a reminder that he's still the O'Neill." Hugh squeezed her hand reassuringly. "I sent a reply saying I hoped he'd be as gracious when the family is mine."

"No good can come from antagonizing Turlough," Kathryn said.

"Trust me," Hugh said, drawing her close. "I promise no harm will befall the children or you."

"You cannot very well protect us," she observed, "if you are otherwise occupied with Fiona Fitzgerald."

"You sound amazingly like a jealous wife," he teased.

"I am not jealous."

"I tried to get away, but you were occupied with Lord Fitzgerald."

Kathryn flicked a glance toward Fiona, who was surrounded by several young men. "The slut probably planned it with her father."

Hugh chuckled. "You've nothing to fear, my hissing kitten. Fiona's a harmless nuisance in dire need of a noble husband who's young enough to keep her belly swollen."

Kathryn smirked and looked away. When she turned back to him, Hugh was nearly blinded by her radiant smile. "What say you, my lord earl?" she asked puckishly. "Shall we tempt Lady Fiona's sense of propriety?"

"You speak in riddles, my English sphinx."

"Over there." Kathryn's eyes gestured the direction. "Lord Burke is a very recently eligible, irresistibly handsome man and young enough to keep the fair lady occupied."

"A point well taken." Hugh grinned at her intended prank. "Shall we?"

Tall and well built, Lord Michael Burke was a handsome man with dark eyes that gleamed devilishly. Dressed in midnight blue, he appeared every inch the wealthy aristocrat he was.

As they walked toward him, Kathryn could understand why women were attracted to him. In her secret heart, she hoped nothing would come of their prank. If Fiona Fitzgerald won the affections of this fabulous specimen of manhood, there was no justice.

"Grand seeing you, Michael," Hugh greeted his friend.

"We were disheartened to learn of the loss of your wife," Kathryn said.

"Thank you." Burke smiled at them. "I broke mourning to offer my congratulations."

"Our thanks," Hugh said.

"Are your sons in Dublin?" Kathryn asked. "I'm certain my daughter Maeve would enjoy meeting them."

"No, they stayed at home."

"Perhaps we could join our families through marriage," Hugh suggested. "After all, we've two bonnie colleens and you've two sons."

"Shana is only two months," Kathryn cried. The two men smiled.

"If the daughters resemble their mother, I would be glad to join our families," Burke said. Kathryn blushed.

"I owe an obligatory dance to Fitzgerald's daughter," Hugh said as if just remembering. "Michael, would you keep Kathryn company?"

"With pleasure." Burke smiled at Kathryn who smiled back.

Hugh wondered for the briefest moment if he dare leave her with his handsome friend. Deciding his interests were safe, he left them to find Fiona.

"Losing a loved one is difficult," Kathryn said. "You must miss Lady Burke terribly."

"It's been hard on my sons."

"But not for you?" Kathryn asked baldly. The words slipped off her tongue before she could bite them back.

The question was too personal. For his friend's sake, Lord Burke hoped the lady's interest in her husband was not waning.

"I'm sorry," Kathryn apologized, embarrassed by her breech in manners. "I'd no intent to be rude. I've lost many loved ones, and grief is no stranger to me."

Kathryn looked away. Turning back to Lord Burke, she said without thinking, "In spite of our differences, Hugh has been kind. We'll be together a long time. Happily ever after, I hope."

Recognizing in her unguarded expression the budding love she harbored for his friend, Lord Burke was touched by the personal confidence. The lady may have been married twice, but she's still an innocent babe, he concluded mistakenly. Not a deceitful bone in her lovely body!

"My late wife and I shared no great love," Burke confided. "Ours was an arranged marriage."

Kathryn nodded, then changed the subject. "Do you know Lord Fitzgerald's daughter Fiona?"

"No."

Kathryn stretched her imagination. "Fiona's a true beauty, inside and out, and possesses the sweetest of dispositions. Since my arrival in Dublin, she's taken a keen interest in me."

"And she's made you feel welcome," Burke said with a polite smile, beginning to feel bored with their conversation. "It's good to know we Irish are a hospitable people."

"Why, there they are now," Kathryn cried, watching the dancers. "See Hugh with the dark-haired woman?" Then added, "The lady whose bosom is exposed for all to see."

Lord Burke turned so quickly he nearly knocked Kathryn over, but managed to steady her before she fell. He murmured an apology, but his dark eyes were fixed on the incredible vision dancing with his friend.

A Celtic siren, he thought. *If she's as lovely up close as she is from afar, I'll have her!*

The dance ended. Hugh maneuvered Fiona skillfully through the crowded hall. "Katie is with Lord Burke," Hugh chatted away. "Do you know him?"

"No," Fiona answered. Happy in her seeming triumph over the little English upstart, Fiona paid no attention to where he was leading her.

"You must meet him," Hugh said. Then he added in a hushed tone, "He's recently widowed."

"Really?" That stimulated Fiona's interest.

When the two couples met, Fiona smiled radiantly. Her sapphire eyes scanned Burke's handsome features, broad shoulders, and well-formed body, then returned to his face. His dark eyes gleamed as he boldly appraised *her* charms. When his heated gaze met hers, Fiona felt as if he'd stripped her naked and shivered at the delicious thought.

"Lady Fiona," Hugh began, then cleared his throat to hide his amusement. "I present Lord Michael Burke."

Fiona swept Burke a deep curtsey and artfully extended her hand. When he bent low over the offered hand, she felt an unexpected surge of heat enter her body where his lips touched. Fiona tingled with excitement. Never had a man so affected her!

Hugh turned to Kathryn, saying, "Shall we have refreshments, sweet?"

"Yes," Kathryn agreed, placing her hand on his arm. Without another word, they walked away, leaving Burke and Fiona smiling mutely—*and hungrily*—at each other.

Hugh and Kathryn spent the remainder of the evening dancing and toasting their success. The bud of love they shared, so easily seen by others, remained unnoticed to themselves. Occasionally, they scanned the noble mob for Burke and Fiona who, they noted, had eyes only for each other.

Giddy with excitement and wine, Kathryn drew Hugh into an isolated alcove. "It's late," she whispered loudly. "Shana must be in a fine temper without her food."

"The lass has certainly inherited her father's temperament," Hugh said dryly. "Nellie will comfort her until we return."

"But I have an urgent need to relieve my aching breasts," Kathryn complained.

Hugh chuckled. The ache in her breasts matched the ache in his groin. He tilted her chin up and gazed into her mesmerizing green eyes. "You're uncommonly beautiful, my countess."

"And you, my lord earl, are blessed with magnificent taste," Kathryn returned, batting her eyelashes at him.

"Are you feeling well? You've recently given birth and—"

"I'm full recovered from birthing Shana, but my breasts ache to be emptied."

"Excellent!" Anticipating the night's activities, Hugh almost laughed with glee. "Shall we leave?"

Kathryn nodded, oblivious to his lusty intent, and they made their way slowly through the crowd.

Intercepting them at the great hall's entrance, Lord Fitzgerald asked anxiously, "Have you seen Fiona? I can't locate her."

"I saw her earlier with Lord Burke," Hugh told him, then cast his wife a meaningful glance.

Taking his cue, Kathryn suggested, "Lord Burke may have escorted her home."

"There's no cause for alarm," Hugh added. "Burke will take good care of her."

"You're probably correct," Lord Fitzgerald said. "There's an interesting game of chance in the viceroy's study. If you see Fiona, tell her my whereabouts." As the older man hurried away, the O'Neills looked at each other and burst out laughing.

Dreamy with romance and wine, Fiona luxuriated in the exciting nearness of the very handsome, very masculine, and very wealthy man beside her. Snuggling against him, Fiona knew that her behavior was improper but banished the disturbing thought. What, after all, was the harm in letting him escort her home?

"Here we are, my beauty," Burke said as the unsprung coach came to a halt. He opened the door and climbed out, then turned to assist her. As she stepped out, Burke unexpectedly lifted her into his arms.

"This isn't my home," Fiona gasped, suddenly alert.

"It's *mine*," Burke said with a wolfish grin.

Shrieking in outrage, Fiona struggled against him, but her meager strength was no match for his. Chuckling at her efforts, Burke carried her inside the mansion, past the astonished stares of his men-at-arms and servants, and up the stairs to his chamber. He slammed the door shut with his foot, then dumped her ungently onto his enormous bed and laughed when she scrambled off the other side.

"Release me at once!" Fiona demanded. "I'll be ruined!"

"You're already ruined, dear heart," Burke returned, looking pleased with himself.

Fiona, her sapphire eyes glinting dangerously, crossed the chamber to accost him. "You vile, misbegotten—" she sputtered, then struck him full force across his face.

Burke returned her slap, more surprising than hurting her.

Fear replaced anger, and Fiona backed away.

"You're mad," she said in a horrified whisper, raising a trembling hand to her smarting cheek.

Burke grabbed her wrist and jerked her against his virile body, then shoved her onto the bed and ordered, "Don't move."

Running a hand through his hair in utter frustration, Burke decided he'd made an incredibly bad beginning. He sat down beside her on the bed and felt her body stiffen in fear. Smiling into her wide-eyed gaze, he said, "Anger complements your beauty."

Fiona's mouth dropped open in amazement at his bizarre change of mood.

"I'm as sane as you, my Celtic goddess," Burke assured her, hoping to still her fears. "I know what I want when I see it, and you, my irresistible one, I want."

"No," Fiona cried.

Burke put his arm around her shoulders and pulled her close, saying, "Indeed, my love, I will have you."

His closeness, his scent, and the feel of his hardened body conspired against her, and her resistance waned in the face of his ardent expression. "My father will demand satisfaction," Fiona warned.

"Call out his son-by-marriage?" Burke smiled. "I think not."

"Son-by-marriage?"

"Yes, my pretty puss," Burke said, his face inches from hers, sensing her weakening resolve and his victory near at hand. "You will marry me and play mother to my sons."

"I hardly know you," she protested. "Besides, you're in mourning."

"We'll marry in August," he countered, his arms encircling her body as if to hold her prisoner until then. "It's a decent interval for mourning and time enough to know me better. I'll accompany you home in the morning and announce our intentions."

Her eyes widened in understanding just as his lips claimed hers in a devastating kiss. Fiona was lost. She'd been kissed many times by many men, but none moved her as this one now did. Her arms traveled up his chest to entwine around his neck, and eagerly, she returned his smoldering kiss.

"After tonight," he whispered, his lips nibbling upon her

delightful earlobe, "you will look at me the way Lady Kathryn looks upon her husband."

"That bitch?" Fiona cried, jerking her head back.

Burke cast her a puzzled look. "It's exceedingly strange, my sweet, that Lady Kathryn sang of your virtues quite melodiously."

"She did *what*?" Fiona was stunned.

Burke shrugged his shoulders, saying, "Perhaps match-making suited the night's festive mood."

"Or maybe Lady Kathryn sought to turn my eyes from her husband."

"Cast those beautiful eyes upon another, and I will beat you without mercy," Burke growled, his eyes hardening coldly against her. "Understand?"

"Y-y-yes."

Burke gave her a rough shake. "Yes, what?"

"Y-y-yes, m-my l-lord." Fiona gulped nervously. Apparently, this man she desired was not one to be led. Oh, Lord! Into what folly had she stumbled?

"Good girl," he soothed, stroking her back, all menace gone from his voice. Though cruelty was contrary to his nature, Burke knew the sleek feline in his arms needed declawing. He pushed her back on the bed and hovered above her, promising, "Before this night is old, my puss, I will have you purring in my arms." His lips claimed hers, and his tongue ravished her mouth.

"Michael . . ." she breathed, and sighing her surrender, yielded to his talented ministrations.

Hugh and Kathryn, still chuckling over Fiona's disappearance with Lord Burke, returned home and walked up the stairs together. At the top, Shana's furious screams of hunger assailed them.

"I'll change and keep you company while you feed Shana," Hugh said, then disappeared into his chamber.

"Polly," Kathryn said, surprised when she walked into her own chamber. Dozing in the chair in front of the hearth, Polly jumped up at the sound of her mistress's voice. "You needn't have waited up for me."

"A tirin' woman's job is to await her lady," Polly said, stifling a yawn.

"Help me out of this dress," Kathryn instructed her, "and then fetch Shana." Polly left as Kathryn slipped into her night shift. Taking the pins from her hair, she brushed it out.

Clad in a silken bed robe, Hugh walked through the connecting door just as Polly brought in Shana whose cries of hunger had not abated. "It's late," he said to the tiring woman, watching his wife bare her heavy breasts and offer a juicy nipple to her daughter who attacked it with ferocity. "Seek your bed."

An air of intimate domesticity enveloped husband and wife. In the eerily shadowed chamber, Kathryn sat in front of the hearth like a pagan goddess, her copper hair cascading around her and glinting in the fire's light. Hugh was mesmerized by the picture she presented.

Glutted, Shana closed her sky-blue eyes, sated drowsiness overpowering her.

"I think she's drunk." Kathryn giggled, breaking the spell she's unwittingly cast upon her husband.

"I'll return her to the nursery," Hugh offered.

"And frighten poor Nellie by appearing in your robe?" Kathryn clucked, covering her breasts. "I'll return her." Lifting Shana without awakening her, Kathryn stood and carried her daughter out.

When she returned, Hugh stood in front of the hearth. Approaching him, Kathryn admired his handsome features and well-made form. Hugh smiled, put an arm around her shoulders, and drew her close. When she put her arm around his waist and leaned against him, Hugh thrilled to her gesture, so natural between husband and wife.

"It was a wonderful evening," Kathryn said, a feeling of security shrouding her senses as Hugh turned her to face him and lowered his lips to hers.

She responded.

He pulled her closer.

Their bodies touched.

Kathryn's lips parted willingly, allowing his tongue entrance to the moist warmth within. Her arms crept up his chest to entwine around his neck, and she pressed her body against his, seeking his strength.

A throbbing flame ignited between her thighs. As if from a great distance, Kathryn heard a woman's soft moan of desire. The humiliating realization that she was the woman seeped into her mind.

"No!" Kathryn cried and backed away.

Hugh frowned and stepped toward her. "What's wrong?"

"I—I can't." Kathryn continued her backward retreat.

An angry look crossed Hugh's face but was almost instantly replaced by a patient expression. He'd known that getting into her bed the first time might be difficult.

"From your own lips this very night came word of your full recovery, sweetheart," Hugh argued reasonably, advancing on her.

"I can't!" Kathryn found further retreat impossible. She had backed herself to the foot of the bed. Frustrated tears welled up in her eyes when she realized she had no escape, should it come to that.

Hugh stood in front of her, the dark intensity of his gaze

holding her motionless as she stared back at him. "Tell me what troubles you, Katie."

I am afraid, Kathryn thought, *afraid and confused.* Love ran through her mind. She wanted to be loved for herself, not wedded and bedded so a man could be earl or beget sons. But, how could she explain that? He would laugh at her foolishness.

Hugh recognized the riot of emotions—*fear, confusion, yearning, shame, sorrow*—warring upon her face. His back stiffened and his lips hardened grimly into a tight line. Was she sorry to bed him? Or was she mourning Shane? Would he always walk in the shadow cast by his infamous uncle?

Kathryn's pride was the ultimate victor over her rioting emotions. Unwilling to divulge her thoughts or the tender feelings she harbored for him, Kathryn drew herself up self-righteously. "I shan't give Shane's daughter suckle and then lie with another man."

"Another man?" Hugh roared, grabbing her shoulders in an iron grip. "I'm your husband!" He shook her violently. His hands slid down her arms and pulled them behind her back, easily trapping them there with one hand.

"Shane's dead and you live," he growled. As if to emphasize it, his free hand grabbed the bodice of her night shift and tore it savagely from her quaking body.

As if paralyzed, Kathryn watched his long-starved eyes devour her nakedness, his anger becoming scorching desire. When his hungry gaze returned to hers, she panicked and began to struggle.

"My wife will not tell me nay in my own home," he snarled, shoving her onto the bed, then fell upon her like a predator upon his quarry.

Frenzied with panic, Kathryn squirmed and thrashed about. Her hands attacked his face, but Hugh captured and imprisoned them above her head. Kathryn bucked madly. Hugh laughed without humor and waited for her to tire as he knew she must.

Kathryn's struggling subsided and the maddened bucking stopped, her only movement her heaving chest as she panted for breath. Defeated, green eyes watched him warily.

"Now I'll lay Shane O'Neill to rest," Hugh muttered. His lips swooped down and captured hers in a savage, bruising kiss, his tongue boldly pillaging the sweetness of her mouth.

Beneath his virile body and demanding kiss, Kathryn lay unresisting until his kiss stoked the embers of her passion. A delicious chill ran the length of her body and made her tremble. Unable to stop herself, Kathryn returned his kiss in kind, her honeyed tongue seeking his.

Hugh drew back and stared at her, but Kathryn looked away in shame. Releasing her arms, he touched her burning cheeks and forced her to meet his gaze.

"Katie," he murmured, seeing desire in her eyes.

"Oh," Kathryn moaned her long-denied need, her arms reaching out to hold him close.

Hugh planted feathery-light kisses upon her temples, eyelids, nose, and throat, then claimed her lips again in a gentle kiss. Leisurely, his lips glided down the delicate column of her throat, and his questing hands discovered the silkiness of her flesh. Hugh's lips traveled lower to her ripe breasts where they lingered, tasting of her incredible sweetness.

Hugh wanted to delay and savor his wife's surrender, but knew he could not. Already his masculine weapon was stiff and unyielding, primed for life's most intimate battle. His exploring hands drifted between her thighs and found the source of her pleasure, wet and throbbing, ready for his invasion.

Hugh shrugged off his bed robe and positioned himself between her thighs, then thrust forward and sheathed his sword to the hilt.

Kathryn cried out at his entry. Kittenish mewling sounds welled up in her throat, urging him to thrust again and again. With a cry, Kathryn arched and offered herself in primitive submission, her trembling body finding its primal pleasure.

Shuddering his pleasure, Hugh lost himself within her. In a fleeting flash of awareness, he knew the victor had become the vanquished. Regaining his breath, Hugh fell to one side and pulled Kathryn close.

"Stay," she whimpered.

"Yes," he answered, but her eyes had already closed in sleep.

Hugh studied his wife and realized he loved her beyond words. Sighing in dejection at the way she had fought him, Hugh decided she still loved Shane and vowed she would never learn of his own love. Sharing his tender feelings with her would be like placing a dangerous weapon in a child's hands.

Hugh awakened before dawn. Snuggled against him, Kathryn slept. Like a young boy with a new toy, he was unable to resist drawing the coverlet aside and feasting his eyes on the exquisitely beautiful woman who belonged to him. Her nakedness was an irresistible temptation. He reached out, his hand following the enticing curve of her hip. Glancing at her face, Hugh found disarming green eyes watching him.

"Kiss me," Kathryn whispered, and drew him against the softness of her body.

9

Winter ebbed and Kathryn's life fell into a pattern. Her daughters and housewifely duties filled her days, but the nights belonged to Hugh. Though they shared a bed each night, Kathryn became troubled.

She was hopelessly in love with her husband, but Hugh had never spoken words of love. Being considered a brood mare upon whom he could get an heir bothered her. That she had never spoken of love to her husband never occurred to her. In misery, each awaited a sign from the other and neither was willing to be the first to profess love.

The winter had seen other changes. After a certain O'Neill footman had shown great interest in Polly, Patrick had succumbed to her charms. A June marriage was planned.

News of another impending marriage scandalized the Dubliners. Rumor was that Lady Fiona Fitzgerald had disappeared with Lord Burke on the night of the O'Neill celebration. Frantic, Lord Fitzgerald had burst like a madman into Burke's bedchamber and found his daughter coupling with the handsome widower. Calling his daughter a slut, Fitzgerald had dragged her naked and screaming from the bed. It was then Lord Burke had gone for his sword, threatening to dispatch the older man if he did not unhand his intended wife. Lord Fitzgerald calmed somewhat at that and explained that the wedding night should be celebrated after the ceremony, not before. After telling his future father-in-law to prepare for an August wedding, Lord Burke had ordered Lady Fiona back to bed. Unwilling to chance a change of heart, Fitzgerald left at once to have the betrothal contract written and ready for signing that very night.

"Katie," Hugh called, interrupting her reverie as she walked alone in the garden and enjoyed the early spring day.

Kathryn turned around and stared in surprise at the man who stood beside her husband. *"Sir Henry!"* Kathryn lifted her skirts and ran toward her stepfather.

Sir Henry Bagenal opened his arms and Kathryn, weeping, nearly crushed him with her hug. "What's this?" he teased. "Do you weep with joy or sorrow?"

"J-joy," Kathryn sobbed. "I thought I'd never see my family again."

"You do have a husband and children," Sir Henry said. "Stand back and let me get a good look at you."

Sir Henry smiled with delight at what met his eyes, then remarked, "The essence remains, but a woman stands where the girl once was."

With tears glistening in her eyes, Kathryn clung to her stepfather, the first tangible piece of England she'd held in six long years. "Come inside. You've two beautiful granddaughters to meet." She pulled him toward the mansion, and Hugh followed behind.

At supper that evening, Kathryn sat between her stepfather and her husband at the high table. She talked more than she ate, starved more for information about England than food.

"Tell me about the family," she begged, tugging like a child at her stepfather's sleeve.

"Let the man eat in peace," Hugh said. "There'll be time enough after supper."

"Tell me all, Henry," Kathryn urged, ignoring her husband. "I want to know everything."

Sir Henry smiled with indulgence, understanding her urgent need. "Your brother is a page at court," he began. "A favorite of the queen's, I might add. Your sister Brigette is with child and happy with her Scottish laird. You knew she'd run from him?"

"No!" Kathryn giggled, then turned to her husband, saying, "You see, I'm not unique. Disobedience is a family trait."

Hugh laughed at her impish expression of glee.

"Mother is well and sends her love," Sir Henry went on, "but still grieves for Heather."

"Grieves for Heather?" Kathryn echoed, bewildered.

"We sent you the sad news months ago," Sir Henry said. Helplessly, he looked over her head at a grim-faced Hugh and instantly realized his blunder.

"What news?" Kathryn demanded, her face draining of color.

Taking her hand in his, Sir Henry told her, "Heather's ship went down on its way to France. There were no survivors."

"No survivors . . ." Kathryn's voice ached with emotion. She rounded on Hugh, whose unguarded expression confirmed her sudden suspicion.

Hugh would have spoken, but Kathryn drew back as if his betrayal were the deadly plague. Accusation leapt from her eyes, silencing whatever he would have said.

"Excuse me," Kathryn said to her stepfather, then stood and left the hall.

Upstairs, Kathryn changed into a night shift and dismissed Polly. Unable to sleep, she stood in front of the hearth and stared into the flames. *Hugh knew about Heather's death* pounded through her mind. Silent tears trickled down her cheeks. Did she grieve for her lost sister or the misplaced trust she'd given her husband?

A short time later, Hugh opened the door of his wife's bedchamber. Wishing he could undo what was past, he paused for a moment and studied her back.

Be damned! he decided, stepping forward. The sorry choice had been his and correct at the time.

"I'm sorry," Hugh apologized, placing his hand on her shoulder.

Whirling around, Kathryn shrugged off his touch. No longer would she play the fool.

"You knew about Heather," she accused him, her eyes glinting with contempt.

"Yes, but—" Hugh tried to defend himself.

"You played me for a fool. You vile, conniving, lying—" At a loss for more suitably insulting words to hurl at him, Kathryn turned her back in dismissal, but Hugh gently forced her to turn around and face him.

"Viceroy Russell told me about your sister," he admitted, "but I never played you false."

" 'Twas by omission a lie!"

"You were seven months pregnant and I feared for the babe," Hugh told her. She stared coldly through him, and he lost his patience. *"Christ Almighty!* Sickening with shock could have harmed the babe! Madam, would you have risked Shana's life for the truth of the matter?"

"No," Kathryn answered in an aching whisper, "but— but later . . ."

"Later my courage failed me," Hugh admitted. "Cowardice can overtake the bravest of men. I feared shattering our newfound happiness. So, I waited and waited for the right moment to tell you, but it never came." He drew her into his arms and tilted her face up. "Believe me, dear heart, I am sorry for your loss and even sorrier for adding to your grief. Forgive me. Please?"

"I forgive you," Kathryn said.

Hugh planted a chaste kiss on her lips. "Henry awaits me in the study. We've little time to formulate our strategy against the Maguire."

Kathryn nodded, but a troubled expression creased her forehead.

"Frowning causes premature wrinkles," Hugh teased, his index finger playfully tapping the tip of her upturned nose. He strode across the chamber but paused at the door to leer suggestively at her and warn with mock severity, "I expect to find you awaiting me in bed. Dare to disappoint me, wench, and you will suffer unspeakable torment, however tender it may be."

The corners of Kathryn's lips twitched, and when he saw her smile, Hugh left.

As soon as the door closed behind him, Kathryn's smile vanished. She sat in the chair in front of the hearth and stared, unseeing, at the dancing flames.

"Poor Heather." Kathryn sighed. "Lost to me forever."

Kathryn let her thoughts travel across the years to her earlier life at Basildon Castle in England.

Heather, the youngest of the three Devereux girls, had always complained that she was the only one in the family afflicted with freckles. And Brigette, their sister, had teased her without mercy. To Kathryn had gone the task of breaking up their fights.

It was Heather who had witnessed their father's gruesome murder at the hands of poachers, and she'd suffered for it. Scarcely a night passed without Heather screaming in torment, caught in the unspeakable nightmares that preyed upon her young mind.

Perhaps, Kathryn thought finally, *her baby sister had found a peaceful sleep in death.*

And Hugh! Kathryn's chest rose and fell in a deep, dejected sigh. She loved her husband, but he'd never mentioned harboring tender feelings for her. Now he was below planning strategy for war. *Like Shane!* Nauseating fear coiled around her heart. Hugh must not accompany Sir Henry. She didn't possess the inner strength to survive another loss. But how could she prevent it? Would Hugh heed her warning or discount it? Indeed, would he even listen?

A few days later, Hugh sat in his study and tried to work, but his mind drifted constantly to his wife. Her behavior of late had become odd. On more than one occasion, he'd awakened in the night to find her awake and obviously brooding over something. When asked what troubled her, Kathryn denied that anything was wrong.

A knock on the door intruded upon his thoughts. When his wife walked in and sat in the chair near his, Hugh wondered if his wayward thoughts had conjured the vision to his side.

"I'm sorry for interrupting you," Kathryn said. "I must speak with you about an urgent matter."

Hugh nodded, but Kathryn looked away and chewed nervously on her bottom lip.

Mustering her courage, she met his expectant gaze and said, "I—I think it unwise to accompany Sir Henry."

Hugh's first impulse, which he suppressed, was to inform his wife that war was a man's business, not hers. Instead, he asked, "Why don't you deem it wise, my sweet?"

Encouraged but flustered, Kathryn stood and paced the chamber. Recalling the many logical arguments she'd planned, Kathryn mentally formulated and then discarded each.

Watching her changing expressions, Hugh was hard-pressed to conceal a smile.

Kathryn turned to him suddenly, admonishing him, "Fighting your own kind isn't right." She hoped this was the correct approach. "The Maguire is the queen's problem. Let her solve it."

"She is."

"What?"

"The queen is solving her problem by sending Sir Henry and me to fight the Maguire."

"Don't play games with me." Kathryn's voice rose in frustration. "You understand precisely what I mean. It's not your problem."

"In order to be invested the earl of Tyrone," Hugh replied, "I agreed to fight."

"The price is too high," Kathryn cried, losing control of her taut emotions.

Hugh stood up and walked toward her, warning, "Never say the price of a man's birthright is too high."

"You're twisting my words."

"The subject is closed." His voice was low, but his eyes warned her to silence.

"Shane fought the queen's battles and I buried him." Kathryn sobbed as tears of defeat streamed down her face. "You won't come home alive either."

Hugh's expression gentled. "You fear for my safety?" he asked, drawing her close.

When she hid her face against his chest, Hugh stroked her back, explaining, "It's always frightening for women when their men go to war, but there's nothing to be done for it. I must go."

Horrified, Kathryn jerked away from him. His words were the same as Shane's before Patrick carried his body home slung across his horse. That she would hurt and mourn alone was Hugh's fault. Her fear became boiling anger. Needing to hurt as she had been, Kathryn lashed out with her only weapon, her words.

"Go and die for your queen," she shouted. "First Shane and now you—perhaps there's another O'Neill who'll seek to better himself by marrying me."

At that, Hugh slapped her. Kathryn stumbled against the door but managed to remain standing.

Hugh offered her a steadying hand. Kathryn flung the door open and ran, her hand holding her reddened, smarting cheek.

"Katie," he shouted.

"Shane beat me too," she cried, then disappeared up the stairs.

Patrick, Polly, and several other retainers had been loitering in the vicinity of the study and privy to the angry shouts and flight of their near-hysterical countess. Hugh, thinking to go after her, stepped into the foyer, then realized he had an attentive, grim-faced audience. Apparently, public opinion went against him.

"I did not beat her," Hugh growled when his gaze met Patrick's. "I slapped her."

Patrick said nothing, but his eyes judged him guilty.

"Go on about your business!" Hugh roared, sending all but one scurrying away like mice. He watched in satisfaction as his servants hastily obeyed. His gaze fell on Patrick, who stood there eyeing him.

"She's *my* wife," Hugh said. "I'll deal with her as I deem

fit." Turning on his heel, he marched into his study and slammed the door.

Mulling something over in his mind, Patrick stared at the closed study door for a few moments. With his decision made, he walked over to it and knocked.

"Go away," Hugh growled at the unwelcome intrusion.

Heedless of consequence, Patrick opened the door anyway and walked in.

"I said, go away."

Ignoring the invitation to leave, Patrick sat down across from Hugh. "Do you recall the day long ago when Katie tried to teach Polly to ride? You asked her if she'd lost her second child by fallin' off a horse?"

Setting his quill down, Hugh gave the other man his full attention. "Yes, I remember."

"Katie miscarried a boy-child because Shane beat her within an inch of her life for showin' kindness to his prisoner, Sorley Boy MacDonnell," Patrick told him. "I won't sicken you with the details."

"I didn't know," Hugh said. He felt like a monster for slapping her.

"If you hurt her again," Patrick threatened, "I'll kill you."

Hugh stiffened at his man's words, and with his hand resting on the hilt of his dagger, stood to confront him. "You've given me your oath."

Rising from his chair, Patrick stood almost nose to nose with Hugh. "I'm forsworn to protect Katie."

Hugh relaxed, and with an apologetic smile, said, "Actually, I abhor wife beating."

With a curt nod, Patrick started to leave but turned back at the sound of Hugh's voice.

"Patrick?"

Whack! Hugh's fist connected with Patrick's jaw, sending the warrior sprawling on the floor.

"That was for threatening me," Hugh said, holding out his hand to help the other man rise. "I'm no Shane O'Neill. Do not dare attribute his loathsome habits to me."

Patrick nodded and again turned to leave.

It was then Hugh extracted his real revenge for Patrick's threat. "By the way," he said casually, "I saw Jake the footman walking with Polly in the gardens just before supper last night. Is your wedding on or off?"

Without bothering to answer, Patrick flew out of the study, muttering, "That two-timin' witch. I'll put an end to her flirtin' ways."

When Hugh walked into the great hall that evening, Sir Henry was already seated at the high table. Kathryn's chair was empty.

Polly approached the two men. "Lady Kathryn is unwell and bids you sup without her." She looked pointedly at Sir Henry, adding, "My lady especially begs your forgiveness, my lord."

"What about my forgiveness?" Hugh asked.

"She never mentioned you, my lord," Polly answered, then left.

"All is not well between Kathryn and you," Sir Henry remarked.

"She believes it unwise to fight the Maguire," Hugh told him.

"She fears for your safety," Sir Henry concluded. "Her mother was of the same opinion concerning me."

"Katie believes my uncle's fate is mine."

"Ah." Sir Henry nodded. "I suppose, there are a few similarities. You must remember, my friend, Kathryn led a sheltered life."

"She's no longer a child," Hugh complained, "and should understand that a man must do what he must."

"Yes," Sir Henry agreed. "But women are weak by nature. I've known Kathryn since she was a child. Perhaps it's easier for me to be patient."

"What was she like?"

A faraway look glazed the older man's eyes, and he smiled at the memory. "Enormous green eyes too big for her face, copper hair blazing like a fiery sunset, a scrawny chicken's arms and legs . . ."

Hugh chuckled at the description. "She's filled out nicely."

Sir Henry smiled. "I've noticed."

"Was she always so stubborn?"

"As they grew, the three Devereux girls were obstinate, charming hoydens," Sir Henry answered. "As a matter of fact, the first time your uncle saw Kathryn, she was dressed in stable boy's clothing."

At that, Hugh burst out laughing. He wondered what his uncle, a notorious connoisseur of women's flesh, thought when he saw he was to wed a stable boy. Seeing Shane's expression would have been worth the risk to his own life.

Much later, hoping to find her awake, Hugh went to Kathryn's bedchamber. He stood beside the bed and stared at his sleeping wife. Weeping had swollen her eyelids. Knowing he'd caused her pain, Hugh filled with aching remorse.

Without a doubt, Hugh loved her, but he stood in indecision beside the bed. Should he undress and, as usual, sleep beside her, or wait until she apologized? With his shoulders sagging beneath weighty loneliness and aching remorse, Hugh turned away and walked into his own chamber.

When she awakened the next morning, Kathryn found herself alone. Certain that her husband's anger had kept him out of her bed, Kathryn decided to divorce her love from him. Accepting his death when Patrick carried his corpse home from battle would be easier.

At supper that evening, Kathryn sat between her husband and her stepfather at the high table. She participated little in the conversation, but listened intently when the men spoke of the forthcoming battle. Knowing they would be closeted in the study for hours to make their infernal plans, Kathryn excused herself at the end of the meal and sought the privacy of her own chamber.

After bathing and changing into a silken wrapper, Kathryn dismissed Polly and sat in the chair in front of the hearth. She tried to keep her mind a blank, but after a time, sensed a presence beside her and looked up.

With a tender expression etched upon his handsome features, Hugh stood there. Kathryn's heart quickened at the sight.

"Yes?" Her voice was cool.

"I must speak with you," Hugh said, then surprised her by kneeling and taking her hands in his. Anguished brown eyes met anguished green. "Forgive me for striking you. I swear I will never raise a hand to you again."

Kathryn accepted his apology with a nod, then stared at her lap where her hands rested in his. Long moments passed while he waited for her to speak. She yearned to hold him against her breast forever, but vowed to distance her heart from his. His apology did not change the fact that Patrick would soon carry his lifeless body home from battle. She had to survive that, if only for the sake of her children.

Summoning her strength, Kathryn looked up at her husband's hopeful expression. "Was there something else?" she asked coldly, her heart breaking.

"No." Downcast, Hugh stood and went to his own chamber. He never saw the hot, silent tears streaming down his wife's face.

During the next week, their relations were strained. Each night Kathryn kept a lonely vigil, hoping her husband would come but uncertain of what she would do.

Hugh did not again seek entrance to her chamber.

Several days later, Kathryn gazed forlornly out Hugh's bedchamber window. Below in the courtyard, men-at-arms were scurrying hither and thither, making final preparations to leave. Scanning the mass of busy warriors, Kathryn was unable to locate her husband. An almost unendurable yearning to go below and bid him farewell filled her breast, but she squelched the urge.

Strong hands touched her shoulders. Kathryn whirled around.

"I'm leaving now," Hugh said.

"Yes." Kathryn restrained the powerful urge to reach up and caress his face a final time.

Hugh planted a chaste kiss on her forehead, then drew back to gaze at the lovely face with which he'd become so familiar. He opened his mouth as if to speak, then shut it. Instead, he turned without another word and left the chamber.

As the door closed behind him, Kathryn glanced down at her trembling hands. *Dear Lord! How could she watch him ride away to his death, unaware of her love?*

"*Hugh!*" Kathryn flew out of the chamber, down the stairs, and out to the courtyard. Her cries pierced the air and silenced the men mounting their steeds.

Hugh dismounted when he spied her. Kathryn, her face

streaked with tears, leapt into his embrace. Hugh held her close as all eyes in the courtyard watched.

"Please come home alive," Kathryn sobbed. She buried her face against his chest.

"I promise," Hugh vowed, tilting her face up.

Bending his head, Hugh kissed her soundly, pouring all his love into that single, stirring kiss. As if the world contained nothing but themselves, Hugh and Kathryn clung to each other, the shadows they cast seeming to be one. Their smoldering kiss lengthened and became another. And another.

"I'm thinkin' we'll never get back if we don't leave," sounded Patrick's mocking lilt. The O'Neill warriors chortled loudly at their lord's expense.

Reluctantly, Hugh tore his lips from Kathryn's. Raising her hands to his lips, he kissed them lingeringly. For long moments husband and wife drank in the sight of each other but remained unquenched, thirsty for more.

"If we tarry much longer," Patrick quipped, "I'll be too old to fight." Again the crowded courtyard resounded with laughter.

Hugh gave Kathryn one more quick kiss, then mounted his horse, grumbling, "Damn you to hell, Patrick."

With a trembling hand raised to her passion-bruised lips, Kathryn stood in the courtyard and watched until they'd vanished from sight.

Though those around Kathryn kept her occupied, the depressing days following Hugh's departure passed slowly. Kathryn gave most of her attention to her daughters, but insisted on helping with the preparations for the marriage of Patrick and Polly.

Mme. Bujold, enlisted by Kathryn to create a wedding gown for the bride, became a frequent visitor to the

O'Neill mansion. Polly protested but Kathryn insisted, claiming the gown was a wedding gift.

Indeed, the best days of all were the days Mme. Bujold appeared at the mansion. Kathryn's chamber rang with feminine laughter as Mme. Bujold chronicled Dublin's latest scandals, privy as she was to that sort of information. A fondness sprang up between countess and dressmaker. More than a few times Mme. Bujold scolded Polly or Peg for failing to care for their mistress, for the countess had lost weight and dark circles of worry had appeared beneath her eyes.

One evening when Hugh had been gone nearly a month, Kathryn was attempting to soak away her worries with a leisurely bath. The door crashed open suddenly. Peg stood there, gasping for breath.

"T-the e-earl is h-home," the housekeeper panted. "In the courtyard."

Naked and dripping, Kathryn jumped up. "Polly, hand me the towel."

Polly held out the towel, but Kathryn jerked it from her hands. The two horrified women stared as Kathryn wrapped the towel around her more interesting endowments and tucked the two ends between her breasts.

"What are you doin'?" Polly finally found her voice.

Ignoring her, Kathryn ran across the chamber but found her path blocked by the housekeeper. "Stand aside," she ordered.

"You can't go down like that," Peg insisted.

"Stand aside or seek other employment in the morning." Shaking her head, Peg stood aside and watched her noble mistress fly half naked down the corridor. Shrieking Hugh's name, Kathryn raced down the stairs to the reception foyer below.

Accompanied by the viceroy, Sir Henry Bagenal, and

Patrick, Hugh walked into the foyer just as Kathryn reached the bottom of the stairs. Stunned, the men were rooted where they stood.

Gripping the slipping towel without breaking stride, Kathryn leapt into her husband's open arms. Hugh lowered his lips to hers.

Breaking the kiss, he surveyed his wife's scandalous attire, then threw back his head and shouted with laughter. "The fashions appear to have changed."

Kathryn's eyes glowed with happiness. "Did you win?"

"We won." Hugh carried her across the foyer to the stairs, then remembered the others and turned back. "Make yourselves comfortable in the study. I'll join you shortly."

Sir Henry smiled at the viceroy's shocked expression. "She is her mother's daughter," he said. "French blood heats her veins."

Passing Peg on the stairs, Hugh instructed her, "Bring food and drink for my guests." His eyes fell on Polly, and he teased her, "Shame on you, Polly. No towel for Patrick?"

Giddy with joy, Kathryn placed little, nipping kisses on her husband's neck and cheek. Hugh carried her into his chamber and slammed the door shut with his foot, then dumped her onto the bed and whipped the towel from her body. A low moan of hungry desire escaped him as he stared at her lush, silken flesh.

"Kiss me," Kathryn said, her arms beckoning in an irresistible invitation.

Goaded to tender action, Hugh pressed his mouth to hers, tasting of her honeyed lips that parted in the sweetest of surrenders to his probing tongue. "Forgive me," he rasped, loosening his suddenly restrictive codpiece. "I cannot wait."

Hugh fell upon her with a groan. She was already wet for him. Kathryn, crying her pleasure, climaxed almost immediately and Hugh followed quickly.

Gazing into her love-filled eyes, Hugh said, "We'll continue this later." He kissed her again and stared a moment longer into her gleaming green eyes.

"I love you, my countess."

"And I love you, my great earl."

Hugh tried to rise, but sleek thighs tightened around his waist. Refusing to release him, Kathryn flashed him an impish grin.

"You're *my* prisoner," she said, "and won't be returning downstairs."

"Prisoner of war, my irresistible wife?"

"No, husband. Prisoner of love."

10

On a warm afternoon in June, St. Mary's Church filled with O'Neill men-at-arms and retainers to witness the marriage of Patrick and Polly. Kathryn sat alone in the front pew and waited for Hugh. Acting as the bride's guardian, he would escort her to the altar where her nervous bridegroom waited with the priest.

The wedding was a simple affair, O'Neill men-at-arms and household staff being the only invited guests. Temporary help had been hired so that the servants could be served on this special day. Hugh had spared no expense for the two people most responsible for bringing Kathryn into his life.

Escorting the bride past the front pew, Hugh winked at Kathryn. Wearing a solemn expression, Hugh placed Polly's hand in Patrick's, but before stepping away, leaned close to his man and whispered, "Pinch your cheeks, Patrick. You resemble a ghost."

Patrick's gaze darted to Kathryn's smirking face. Knowing the joke was on him, Patrick smiled and relaxed.

An evening of feasting and dancing followed the ceremony. Sitting at the high table, Kathryn decided the day had been enjoyable, and all would remember it fondly. Of course, being all of the same household, no political differences marred the gaiety. Lord Burke's wedding would not be as pleasant.

"It's time the bride retired," Hugh said, joining her. Taking her hand in his, he raised it to his lips, adding, "Patrick grows impatient to bed his wife, and so do I."

Kathryn knew her husband was well into his cups. She smiled tolerantly and nodded, then stood and signaled to Peg that it was time to put the bride to bed. The ladies started to leave, but the sound of her husband's voice stopped Kathryn in her tracks.

"To the bride," Hugh toasted, swaying as he rose from his chair. The men in the hall raised their cups in salute. Draining his goblet, Hugh grinned at Patrick and boasted, "However, it's certain *my* mighty seed will reach its mark first."

"I beg to differ," Patrick challenged, rising unsteadily from his chair. "Will you place a wager upon the outcome of our efforts?"

"Your ladies will weary with the toilin'," a voice called out.

"Mine will not!" Hugh shouted.

"Nor will mine!" Patrick insisted.

"I'll hold the monies in escrow," Conal announced, advancing on the high table. "When I see which belly grows large with child, that man will receive the monies. Along with our heartfelt congratulations." The hall's rafters shook with masculine laughter.

"Agreed!" Hugh and Patrick shouted simultaneously.

Hugh's gaze wandered to the hall's entrance and came to rest upon his wife whose face was scarlet with angry embarrassment. He leered at her and bowed awkwardly in her direction. Silently cursing him, Kathryn lifted her upturned nose in the air, then whirled away and left the hall.

As the ladies finished tucking a frightened Polly into the bed, the men burst into the chamber. Patrick had already been stripped to his loincloth.

Kathryn giggled at the sight of his undress and teased, "You've a very fetching backside, Patrick."

Everyone laughed. For once Patrick was speechless and his face red with embarrassment.

"Come," Kathryn said to Hugh. "We mustn't let these newlyweds win the wager. Our winnings will purchase a new horse for me. Will it not?" Her honeyed tone belied the angry challenge in her eyes.

"Of course, dear heart," Hugh agreed. "If that's your desire."

After that, the chamber emptied quickly. Without taking his eyes from Polly, Patrick removed his loincloth, slid into the bed, and drew her into his embrace. Feeling her stiffen, he gently caressed her face.

"Open your eyes," he ordered, and when she obeyed, smiled reassuringly into her dark eyes. "Now, colleen. Before we escaped Dungannon, did your mother speak of the marriage bed?"

"No," Polly answered. "She said good girls had no need of such knowledge before their weddin' day."

Patrick sighed. His bride's ignorance would make his task more difficult. If he ever saw Maude again, he'd be sure to give her a large piece of his mind.

"Do you know what happens between a man and a woman?" he asked.

"Of course. Lady Kathryn told me."

Silently, Patrick blessed Kathryn and vowed to pray for her each time he attended mass, which wasn't very often. "And what did she tell you about the marriage bed, sweetie?"

"There's naught but pleasure awaitin' me with a virile

man like you," Polly told him. "She said I must trust you in all things."

"And do you trust me, sweetheart?"

"Yes, but if you don't stop talkin' and start doin', the earl and his lady will be takin' our hard-earned coin."

Patrick threw back his head and shouted with laughter. "May the Lord grant me the patience to survive such a naughty chit." He lowered his lips to hers and claimed his bride.

The revelry continued in the great hall until dawn. To everyone's amusement, not only were the bride and groom safely tucked in bed but also the earl and his countess. Myriad wagers were placed with Conal upon the outcome of the household's lusty contest.

Wishing the endless rain would cease, Kathryn sat in front of the fireless hearth in her chamber late one morning in early July. Maeve and Shana played on the floor at her feet.

As Kathryn's thoughts drifted to her husband, a smile stole across her face. Hating to lose at anything, Hugh was vexed because she'd not conceived immediately upon his command. Though he exerted herculean effort, Hugh was unable to control this situation.

Kathryn glanced down at her offensively flat belly, and her mauve-colored gown tickled a vague memory. Then she chuckled. Lady Fiona would have a fit if she knew she'd lost not only a potential husband but a new gown as well.

When Hugh walked in unexpectedly and sat down, Shana looked up and pointed a tiny finger at him. "Da— Da," she chirped, then giggled, proud of her increased vocabulary.

Kathryn froze. That her daughters would think Hugh

was their father had never occurred to her. Faced with it now, Kathryn decided their conclusion was logical, and she was not at all displeased.

Maeve, refusing to be outshone by her younger sister, climbed on Hugh's lap and hugged him. Raising her disarming green eyes to his, she asked, "Uncle Hugh, would you be my da?"

"I'd be proud to be your da," Hugh answered easily, "but you must never forget your real da. Shane O'Neill was a brave man, a patriot of incomparable worth. When Shana's older, you must tell her about him. Do you promise?"

"I do," Maeve vowed, her eyes large with wonder. No one had ever mentioned her real da before, and her memories of him were vague shadows, there but beyond her reach.

Hugh kissed the tip of Maeve's upturned nose and sent her back to play, her confidence in her superiority over her sister restored. He looked at Kathryn, whose eyes glistened with unshed tears. "Christ's blood, Katie! There's no need for tears. Unless you're with child?"

"I'm not weeping."

Hugh smiled. Resting his head on a hand, he studied her through half-closed eyes. "Are you happy?" he asked casually.

Taken aback, Kathryn countered, "Why do you ask such a question?"

"Being a country girl at heart, you'd be more comfortable living at Dungannon."

"Dungannon?"

"Lords Fitzgerald and Burke are meeting with me today," Hugh told her. "With their help, I am making arrangements for us to live at Dungannon."

Kathryn was bewildered. "But—but Turlough's at Dungannon."

"Yes, he is."

Kathryn's eyes narrowed with suspicion. "What are you planning?"

Hugh grinned like a naughty boy, a mischievous gleam lighting his eyes. "Why, I'm planning to become the O'Neill," came his matter-of-fact reply.

Kathryn gasped, horrified that he would confront Turlough. "Why must you go to war? I'm content to live as I am and—"

"Diplomacy is always preferable to war," Hugh interrupted.

"What have Lords Fitzgerald and Burke to do with this?"

"They will give me the opportunity to speak with Turlough."

"You are the earl of Tyrone," Kathryn argued. "Why is becoming the O'Neill so important?"

"Once I lead the clan," Hugh revealed, his voice rising with passion, "I will unite the other chieftains. Together, we will force the English from Ireland's shores."

Shocked, Kathryn stared at him. After more than a year of marriage, her husband was still a stranger to her. He'd seemed so friendly with the viceroy and others. She'd never known he'd harbored such intense feelings.

"I—I—I'm English," she stammered.

"If you behave yourself," Hugh said with a smile, "I'll make an exception in your case."

Kathryn did not return his smile. "You're not so different from Shane."

"My uncle always bypassed diplomacy."

"Perhaps he knew diplomacy would fail. Do you actually believe Turlough will relinquish control of the family?"

"No." Hugh stood, and looking down at the girls, changed the subject. "Maeve is certainly her mother's daughter. She climbs enticingly upon my lap and then asks for favors."

"Oh." The corners of Kathryn's lips turned up in a winsome smile.

Hugh pointed a finger at her. "You, madam, had best hurry and get with child or I'll lose a great deal of coin."

Humph! Kathryn thought after he'd gone. My husband, in his masculine arrogance, thinks he has only to order it so and I will get with child. I'm surprised he hasn't informed me of what gender he desires. Better he should call to the birds from yonder window and order them to stop singing!

Soon Kathryn's mood grew somber, her anxiety about Turlough coming to the fore. Through sheer strength of will, she banished the terrifying thoughts. Nothing she could do would prevent the future from arriving.

Shaking the rain from their cloaks, Lords Fitzgerald and Burke arrived that afternoon in the foyer of the O'Neill mansion. Hugh stepped out of his study to meet them, but a cordial greeting died on his lips when he saw the other person with them. He arched a questioning brow at his friend.

"Fiona begged to accompany us," Burke explained with a smile. "She wants to visit with Lady Kathryn."

Hugh looked at Fiona, whose face was pale and drawn in high anxiety. Whatever the vixen was about, Hugh hoped his wife would forgive him.

"Peg," Hugh instructed the housekeeper. "Escort Lady Fiona to Lady Kathryn's sitting room. She's there with the girls."

Kathryn rose from her chair in surprise when the Irish beauty, carrying two boxes, walked in. Fiona smiled stiffly, but her gaze wandered to Polly and Nellie and the children.

"I—I w-wish to speak with you, Countess," Fiona said hesitantly, her expression pinched with stress.

Seeing no hint of insult or sarcasm in her words, Kathryn motioned Polly and the others to leave.

"Let the children stay," Fiona requested. "I've brought them gifts."

"Please be seated," Kathryn said, her voice devoid of cordiality. She wondered what trouble the other woman was brewing. Fiona accepted a chair and Kathryn returned to hers, but her gaze traveled to the door where Polly was loitering, reluctant to leave her mistress with the well-known witch. Kathryn's determined stare finally sent Polly from the chamber, and with an unsmiling face, she turned to Fiona who fidgeted uncomfortably.

"I've brought dolls for your daughters," Fiona said, opening the boxes. Squealing with delight, Maeve accepted hers and presented Shana with her own.

"To what do we owe this unexpected pleasure?" Kathryn asked dryly.

"I—I have never apologized to anyone," Fiona began, "b-but I wish to b-beg your forgiveness for my . . . my previous behavior."

"Why?" Kathryn asked, certain there was a hidden motive.

Fiona's words had the ring of recitation as if she'd been thoroughly coached. "I love Michael and have known true happiness with him. Hugh and you brought us together. My behavior has been unpardonable and you could never possibly regard me as a friend, but I *am* truly sorry."

Surmising what such a speech had cost in pride, Kathryn regarded the other woman for a long moment. "I accept your apology."

"Why, apologizing isn't nearly as difficult as I had imagined," Fiona gushed, pleased she had seen the humiliating thing through to its finish.

"Like many of life's experiences, the first is the worst," Kathryn remarked. "Practice makes it easier."

"How wise you are!"

Kathryn laughed at her abrupt change in attitude, and Fiona joined her. Soon the two noblewomen were chatting away about a subject dear to Fiona's heart, her forthcoming marriage to Lord Burke.

Fiona stopped speaking suddenly and stared at Kathryn. "Your gown is lovely," she complimented her, "but it seems oddly familiar."

"It should seem familiar," Kathryn said, the corners of her mouth twitching with merriment. "You ordered it from Madame Bujold last year, but knowing my need was greater, she sold it to me."

Fiona's sapphire eyes widened, and her expression ran the gamut—surprise, anger, amusement. Knowing the joke was on her, Fiona smiled uncomfortably and then chuckled, but Kathryn enjoyed the heartiest laugh she'd had in months.

Entering the chamber to inform them that Lords Fitzgerald and Burke were leaving, Polly stopped short at the startling sight of bitter rivals enjoying a jest. Polly stayed with the girls while Kathryn escorted Fiona below. Watching them, the tiring woman shook her head in confused disbelief.

Astonishing the three men in the foyer, Kathryn and Fiona chatted like old friends as they descended the stairs. Lord Burke cast his betrothed a surprised yet pleased look. He'd been extremely doubtful she could carry it off, even with his superior coaching.

"What was that about?" Hugh asked when the others had gone.

Kathryn smiled and stepped into his embrace. "Fiona apologized for her obnoxious behavior."

Hugh smiled at that.

She kissed his chin, then said, "Tell me about your meeting."

"Ply me not with your insincere kisses, wench," he growled with mock ferocity, then planted a kiss on her lips. "Turlough and I will meet at the Burke wedding."

"Oh, no!" Kathryn cried. "I've no wish to see Turlough!"

"There's nothing to fear," Hugh tried to reassure her. "I will be at your side."

Standing in front of the pier glass, Kathryn noticed Hugh in the doorway that connected their chambers. She smoothed an imaginary crease from her gown and returned his scrutiny. His doublet and pantaloons were tawny colored and his shirt was made from cream-colored silk. Hugh wore Conn O'Neill's jeweled skean on his belt.

"Does my beauty leave you speechless?" Kathryn asked. "Or do you detect some flaw of which I'm unaware?"

"Summer's most vibrant blossom does indeed leave me speechless," Hugh complimented her, walking toward her.

Resplendent in peach and gold, Kathryn appeared more like a Celtic princess of yore than any Irish colleen he'd ever seen. Peach silk with a low-cut bodice, the gown glittered with threads of gold embroidered on flowing sleeves and skirt. Enhancing the pagan aura, her fiery hair cascaded to her waist in the Irish fashion. Around her neck gleamed her husband's most recent gift, the magnificent Celtic torc worn by the O'Neill's chosen woman. Kathryn was ignorant of how Hugh had come by it, but he'd insisted she wear it.

"Ah, wife!" Hugh sighed. "I feel sorry for the other la-dies who'll be present today."

Kathryn grinned. "We are a handsome couple, are we not?"

"Remember, dear heart," he teased as they left the chamber. "Pride goeth before a fall."

Following the ceremony at St. Mary's Church, the wed-ding guests went to Lord Burke's mansion where the re-ception was to be held. In the great hall, the O'Neills joined the line of the bridal couple's many well-wishers. When they stood in front of the smiling groom and radiant bride, Kathryn was surprised by Fiona's affectionate hug, and Hugh wondered if his friend had tamed the dark-haired vixen.

"Congratulations." Hugh extended his hand, then glanced sidelong at his wife, hoping she wouldn't mark his next words. "Would you care to make a small wager, Mi-chael?"

"Hugh, how dare you!" Kathryn exclaimed, a blush ris-ing on her cheeks, then turned to Fiona. "Do not let your husband wager against mine. One of us will end with a swollen belly."

"There's pleasure in the making," Fiona said, her sap-phire eyes sparkling like jewels.

"Perhaps when you're settled, you'd care to call upon me?" Kathryn invited her.

"I'd like that." Fiona was genuinely pleased. She'd never truly had a friend.

"We'll speak later about that wager?" Burke whispered to Hugh.

Unaware the bride was already with child, Hugh nodded agreeably. He was confident he could make a great deal of easy money.

The O'Neills found their places at one of the tables

laden with freshly baked bread, creamy butter, thick honey, and a generous supply of wine. Kathryn glanced around as the sumptuous feast began and was relieved that Turlough had not been seated in their immediate vicinity.

Dinner's first course of baked trout, shrimp swimming in snail butter, and of course, boiled oysters arrived. The guests seated at their table laughed when Kathryn ordered her husband to go lightly on the oysters and Hugh encouraged her to eat more of them.

Mutton stuffed with garlic, roasted beef dripping in its own juices, braised lamb shanks, and whole roasted suckling pigs were served next. Accompanied by a variety of seasonable vegetables, flaky pies made with lark, pigeon, dove, and sparrow followed. Molded jellies, fruit pies, and iced wedding cake were served last.

Hugh noticed Turlough sitting across the hall with a pretty, dark-haired woman and nudged Kathryn. "Who is she?" he asked. "Do you know her?"

"It's Maura," Kathryn answered flatly.

"Maura?"

"Shane's mistress."

Hugh covered Kathryn's hand with his. He was sorry he'd asked and even sorrier for what he was putting her through. Another way to meet with Turlough could have been planned, he thought, feeling a twinge of guilt.

The feasting ended and the dancing began. Kathryn's mood lightened. She was once more enjoying herself, almost forgetting Turlough's presence. As she danced with Hugh, the most distressing feeling of being watched pervaded her senses.

Scanning the crowd, Kathryn saw Turlough staring at her. His predatory smile confounded her. She missed a step and bumped into Hugh whose arms were there to steady her.

"What's wrong?" he asked.

"Nothing," she lied. "Let's walk around."

Aware that something was wrong, Hugh offered his arm. An aide to the viceroy intercepted them as they were leaving the dancing area and told Hugh that the viceroy wished to speak with him. Hugh looked at Kathryn who was clinging to his arm. "Will you be all right?"

"Of course." Kathryn smiled bravely, though she wasn't feeling especially courageous.

After wandering to the opposite side of the hall from where she'd seen Turlough, Kathryn decided to go outside to the gardens. With the meeting close at hand, Turlough would not leave the hall.

"Good evenin', countess." A strong hand touched her shoulder.

Kathryn whirled around. Her eyes widened in alarm, and she suddenly felt faint.

"When I learned of your marriage to him, I wanted to slit your lovely throat," Turlough growled. "At the moment, however, you've nothin' to fear. I only wish to speak. Privately."

Turlough grasped her upper arm and forced her into an isolated alcove. Blocking her view of the hall, he loomed over her. "You led me quite a merry chase, my dear."

"So?" Kathryn returned boldly. "You've found another to take my intended place."

"Jealous?"

"Hardly."

"You do remember Shane's mistress Maura?" Turlough's smile was cruel. "Maura is warm and willin', everythin' you're not."

Kathryn refused to rise to the bait, but her composure was rapidly slipping away. What could be keeping Hugh? She tried to see past the big Irishman's frame. Turlough grabbed her hand, his touch surprisingly gentle. Raising questioning eyes to his, Kathryn recognized his burning desire and tried to pull away, but his grip was steel. She was trapped.

"You're hurting me."

"I want you, my elusive dove," Turlough said huskily. "I'll have you yet." One massive hand reached out to caress her cheek. His smoldering gaze mesmerized her, kept her from fleeing. Slowly, his eyes raked her body, and then returned to her face.

"Even now you wear the symbol of your submission," he told her, then smiled at her obvious confusion. "The torc around your neck proclaims you the O'Neill's chosen. I am the O'Neill and will possess you, even if I must chain you naked to my bed."

"Never," Kathryn insisted.

Turlough laughed harshly. He turned abruptly and walked away, contemplating the many pleasurable hours he would have, bending her will to his.

Shaken, Kathryn scanned the hall but was unable to locate her husband. Leaving the chamber, she sought refuge in the gardens. The solitude would calm her badly frayed nerves. After a time, Kathryn realized Hugh would return to the hall and worry about her disappearance. She retraced her steps, but as she neared the mansion, a figure stepped from the shadows and blocked the path. Startled, Kathryn stopped short but then recognized the figure.

"Stand aside," Kathryn demanded.

"Your title means nothin'," Maura said. "Turlough is the O'Neill now. And mine. We'll see you punished for destroyin' Shane."

"Turlough's your *what*?" Kathryn asked. "Has he married you? Or are you merely sharing his bed, as you did with my husband and so many others?"

Maura raised her hand to strike. With surprising swiftness and strength, Kathryn intercepted her hand. It was then she noticed the necklace that Maura wore.

"That necklace is mine," Kathryn cried. "Remove it at once."

" 'Twas yours but now 'tis mine." Maura fondled the necklace of gold tauntingly. "Turlough's gifted me with everythin' you left behind."

Kathryn lunged forward to tear the necklace from the other woman's throat. Caught off guard, Maura could do nothing to protect herself.

A hand appeared from nowhere and grabbed Kathryn's. Its grip was steel, yet she clung fiercely to the other woman.

"Release her," Turlough ordered.

Kathryn's grip on the necklace remained firm. She did not even bother to glance at the man beside her. Before Kathryn could protest the Irish girl's thievery, Hugh's voice called out, "Unhand my wife!"

"Tell her to release Maura," Turlough said, his hand dropping away.

"Let go of her, Katie."

"No," Kathryn refused. "That necklace is mine."

Turlough chuckled insultingly at his kinsman's inability to control his own wife.

"Let go!" Hugh shouted, his face livid.

Her hand fell away. Instead of seeing to her husband, Kathryn looked at Turlough. "My grandmother gifted my mother with that necklace, and she gave it to me when I married. The necklace has been in my family for many generations and belongs to Maeve, your godchild."

Staring into the fathomless pools of green that were Kathryn's eyes, Turlough felt himself drowning in their depths. "Remove the necklace," he ordered.

"But—" Maura began to protest. Her gaze shifted from Kathryn to Turlough. His expression was deadly. Reluctantly, she removed the necklace.

Angry at his show of weakness, Turlough lashed out and struck Maura with the back of his hand.

Hugh snarled and stepped closer, appalled by his kinsman's cruelty.

"This wench is mine," Turlough growled. "See to your own."

A long, tense moment of silence passed.

Turning away, Hugh led Kathryn to a secluded area where she could compose herself. Leaning against a tree, he drew her into his embrace. Silently, they stood there until he felt her relax in his arms.

"It will be war," Hugh said, then felt a shudder pass through her body. "Was the necklace so important?"

"I could not allow that woman to keep what belongs to my daughter," Kathryn answered. "Besides, the slut was lucky Turlough happened by or I would have done worse than strike her."

Hugh shook his head and playfully tapped the tip of her upturned nose, chiding, "You're a bad lass, Katie O'Neill. A woman obeys her husband in the presence of others. Your disobedience will be punished. Severely."

Hugh's mouth swooped down and covered hers in a "punishing" kiss.

11

March 1569

Green eyes fluttered open.

By the chamber's dimness, Kathryn knew it was too early to begin the day. She shivered and thought of stoking the fire, but lingered in bed. A frown troubled her expression as she stared at her sleeping husband's back. What new problem would arise that day in the endless, bloody conflict with Turlough?

As last September had begun, so too had the ever-escalating power struggle between the O'Neill kinsmen. A large troop of Hugh's warriors had been sent into the Ulster countryside to harass Turlough's men, and spies had been positioned in Ulster's villages. Even the O'Neill's stronghold at Dungannon was not impregnable.

Finally, through the efforts of his increasingly efficient network, Hugh had begun to win support from his relatives in the north. Furious, Turlough retaliated in kind, and the bitter struggle between kinsmen became a *danse macabre* that would end ultimately with the death of one.

Kathryn banished the terrifying thought from her mind. A smile flirted with the corners of her lips. Hugh had grudgingly paid Lord Burke the money due him for winning the ridiculous wager of whose wife would get with child first. However, his mood had lightened considerably at the prospect of collecting from Patrick.

Four months pregnant, Kathryn prayed fervently for a boy. Hugh had foolishly made another wager with Lord Burke. The man whose wife delivered a boy would receive a great deal of money from the other, and Kathryn dreaded living with her husband if he lost the wager. On the other hand, if they delivered babes of the same sex, both Fiona and she would be relieved.

Sliding out of the bed, Kathryn shivered in the morning chill and raced across the chamber to stoke the hearth's dying embers back to life. Scurrying back into bed, she snuggled against the broad expanse of Hugh's back. A mischievous gleam lit her eyes.

Kathryn slipped her arm across her husband, her hand seeking and finding his sleeping manroot. It stiffened beneath her gentle, probing touch. Kathryn sighed, content to lie there, snuggling and fondling her husband.

"Ohhh!" Kathryn was flipped onto her back.

Hugh loomed over her, a devilish glint lighting his eyes. "Your tickling awakened the dragon."

"Are you truly a dragon?" she asked, stifling a giggle, her eyes large with feigned fear.

"No, my tempting morsel. There's your hungry dragon."

Her gaze followed his. Hugh's manhood was erect, poised for attack.

A knowing gleam replaced the feigned fear in Kathryn's eyes, and she reached out to guide him into her warmth. Catching her hands, Hugh drew them above her head and held them captive with one strong hand.

"Katie," he murmured, his face close to hers. "You've eaten from the tree of knowledge and would taste its fruit once more."

"Love me," she whispered.

Hugh smiled lazily and placed feathery-light kisses on her lips, temples, eyelids, and the tip of her upturned nose. When his mouth returned to hers, Hugh unleashed his irresistible power. His kiss demanded and received her shivery response as his due.

When Kathryn's lips parted in invitation, Hugh's tongue invaded and ravished the sweetness within. Exploring and tasting, their tongues swirled around and around in a seductive dance.

Hugh caressed her flushed cheek. His hand traveled to her breasts and teased their dusky peaks to tautness. Leaving her nipples aching for more, his hand caressed her belly, then dropped lower.

"Summer's heat lies forever between your thighs," he whispered huskily.

Kathryn sighed.

Hugh claimed her mouth. His scorching lips singed her cheek and devoured her neck, offered in trusting submission, then moved downward. Desperate with desire, Kathryn clutched him to her breast. Hugh suckled greedily upon a large, dark nipple, making her moan and thrust her hips enticingly.

Hugh chuckled deep in his throat, then lavished his attention on her other breast. Tauntingly, his tongue tickled its way across her fluttering belly. Smiling with love, Hugh rose up and knelt between her parted thighs.

"Take me," Kathryn breathed, craving his possession.

Hugh lifted her hips but did not enter. He raised her legs and drew them over his shoulders, then buried his face between her thighs.

"Ohhhh—" she cried.

Hugh's tongue teased the silkiness of her inner thighs, then dipped into the essence of her womanhood and tasted its incredibly sweet nectar. Consumed by this sensual torture, Kathryn moaned and surrendered to the maddening sensations. His tongue slashed upward to the jewel of her womanhood. Kathryn thrashed wildly, kittenish mewling sounds welling up from her throat.

Hugh built her tension to a dangerous peak, and when she exploded, her most intimate depths throbbing with ecstasy, his manhood replaced his tongue. With a groan, Hugh buried himself into her exquisite sheath. Kathryn's throbs of pleasure overwhelmed him. Hugh groaned and shuddered, spilling his seed.

Except for their labored panting, stillness pervaded the chamber. Hugh fell to one side and drew Kathryn into his embrace, then kissed her forehead and gazed deeply into her eyes.

"Ravisher of women," she accused.

"Dragon-slayer," he shot back.

Kathryn's gaze darted to his groin. Flaccid and harmless lay her husband's proud symbol of manhood. Kathryn giggled, and locked in embrace, they laughed so hard salty tears streamed down their faces.

"Mark my words," Kathryn warned, wiping the tears from her face. "You'll be complaining when my abused body is too large to slake your lust upon."

"Humph!" Hugh snorted. "Do you think, my mouthy wench, that yours is the only tempting body in Dublin?"

"Oh!" Kathryn raised her hand to strike.

Hugh intercepted the blow and enveloped her in his embrace. "If you can carry this burden," he promised, one hand stroking her belly, "I can wait out the drought."

"I love you," she said.

Hugh smiled into her shining eyes, then planted a kiss on her lips. "And I love you," he replied. "Parliament convenes today. What do you have planned?"

"Parliament, my lord?" Kathryn asked archly, feigning suspicion. "I'm visiting Fiona. You know the Burkes are leaving for Connaught soon to await the birth of their child."

"Correction, dear heart. To await the birth of their *daughter*. Take the coach, sweet."

"I'll ride."

"Katie, take the coach or stay home," Hugh ordered. "I want no unnecessary risks taken with my son."

Thinking it was such a little thing, Kathryn capitulated easily. "If it makes you feel better, I'll take the coach."

He rewarded her with a kiss.

Far to the north at Dungannon, Turlough sat in his study in the middle of a war council, its purpose to more effectively harass the English. With him were Calvagh O'Donnell and Sorley Boy MacDonnell, archenemies of the previous O'Neill, Shane.

"Restricted as we are to five hundred men-at-arms," O'Donnell asked skeptically, "how can you make war against the English and protect yourself from Hugh O'Neill?"

" 'Tis an impossible task," MacDonnell interjected.

Turlough smiled confidently at them. "My war with Cousin Hugh is rapidly approaching an end."

Surprised, Sorley Boy and Calvagh glanced at each other. Neither had received this information from his own spies, but rather the opposite. Hugh O'Neill and his men were making great advances.

"I've set a trap into which my cousin is certain to fall," Turlough explained. "Its bait is irresistible."

"And what might that be?" Sorley Boy asked with renewed interest.

Turlough chuckled, pleased with himself. "Come into

the hall and eat. You will see this valuable bait before the week is gone. Then you'll understand."

"Is it extremely painful?" Fiona asked, searching her friend's eyes for the truth of the matter.

Arriving at the Burke mansion, Kathryn had been ushered into Fiona's sitting room and there presented her with an embroidered coverlet, made especially for the baby. Kathryn had noted her friend's pallor and known something was wrong but had refrained from questioning her. Fiona would confide her worries if she wished. Now Kathryn understood what troubled her.

"Is what extremely painful?" Kathryn asked, a naughty imp entering her soul. After all, Fiona had previously delighted in making *her* anxious.

"Curse you," Fiona said, her hand nervously stroking her enormous belly. "Answer to the point."

"Yes, it's painful," Kathryn admitted, then decided to be merciful. "But not unbearably so. When your child is at your breast, you'll fill with joy and forget the pain."

"Are you certain? Or are you trying to lift my spirits?"

Kathryn smiled at her suspicion. "If the pain was unbearable, would the world be so peopled?"

Fiona brightened. "I never thought of it that way. But, I fear my figure will never return to what it once was."

"There's nothing to worry about," Kathryn assured her. "Mine returned posthaste."

"And my accursed husband," Fiona continued her list of complaints. "Before I conceived, Michael always called me his 'Celtic siren,' but now I'm his 'mother duck' because of the way I walk. I never imagined I would feel this outrageously large and ungainly."

"You do resemble a mother duck when you walk," Kathryn said, her eyes sparkling with laughter.

At that, Fiona burst into tears.

"Do not weep," Kathryn said, stifling her merriment. "All women heavy with child acquire the duck's gait. Why, it's a universal truth."

"R-really?" Fiona sobbed, wanting desperately to believe her.

"I swear," Kathryn vowed, crossing two fingers at the lie. "Think positively. Your burden's at an end, but I've still five months to endure. If you return to Dublin before my time, you'll see that I will be waddling like a duck."

"You always make me feel better," Fiona said, drying her tears.

"It's late," Kathryn said, standing. "I must leave. You'll send word when the babe's delivered?"

"Yes." Fiona started to rise from her chair.

Gesturing her to sit, Kathryn leaned down and pecked her cheek. "Do not forget to send word. Hugh is impatient to learn the child's gender."

Fiona smiled, saying, "Godspeed."

Lost in thoughts of her husband, her daughters, and the new baby, Kathryn walked outside to the courtyard where her coach was waiting. As he opened the door, the O'Neill footman turned his head away in a sudden cough, but his hand was there to help her up.

The door slammed shut. Kathryn settled herself in the unsprung coach, then leaned back, and closed her eyes wearily. She tried to keep her mind a blank and seize for herself a few moments of quiet relaxation before her husband and daughters began their demands for attention.

"Christ's blood!" Thrown off the seat, Kathryn sprawled on the floor of the coach as it suddenly picked up speed. If drinking was the cause of this reckless driving, she'd see the driver's head adorning a pike at Dublin Castle!

With difficulty, Kathryn managed to crawl back on the

seat and hold on as best she could while the racing coach relentlessly pitched her about. Kathryn slid across the seat to the window and looked out, then became alarmed. They were traveling in the opposite direction from the O'Neill mansion, and Dublin would soon be left behind.

Trying to attract her driver's attention, Kathryn banged frantically on the inside hood. No response.

After a seemingly endless time, the coach jerked to an abrupt halt. Kathryn fell on the floor again, and tears of pain and fear sprang to her eyes.

Purposeful footsteps approached. The door swung open. Wearing the O'Neill livery, a stranger with an ugly scar running the length of one side of his face stood there.

"Step out," he growled.

Kathryn shrank back.

He reached in to pull her from the coach but, hearing several horses approaching, turned away. Kathryn's hopes for rescue were dashed when the sounds of fighting were not forthcoming.

Accomplices, she thought. *Someone's snatching me for ransom. Or worse!*

"Countess?" A familiar-looking man stood in the coach's open door.

"Liam!" Kathryn cried, but relief was short-lived. Her mouth dropped open as she recalled this former warrior of Shane's was now Turlough's man.

"Come, countess," Liam said, holding out his hand. Stunned, Kathryn was unable to move.

"Come along now," he repeated. "We're bound for Dungannon."

"No!" Kathryn kicked out wildly when he reached for her, but Liam caught her flailing limbs and dragged her toward the door.

"Please," she pleaded.

Seeing the many men surrounding them, Kathryn knew she had no hope for escape. Grasping her upper arm, Liam forced her toward a horse.

"Please don't do this," she begged.

"Mount!"

"For the love of God!" Kathryn cried. "The ride to Dungannon will kill the child I carry!"

Liam studied her distraught face for the briefest moment. Regrettably, he had his orders. Removing his cloak, he wrapped it around her, saying, "Do as you're told, countess, and your baby will be unharmed." Liam lifted her onto his horse and mounted behind her. The long journey to Dungannon had begun.

The late-winter sun was setting in the western sky by the time Hugh arrived home from Parliament. Walking into the great hall, he spied Patrick sitting in front of the hearth and joined him there. While they waited for the evening meal to be served, the two men drank mugs of ale and chatted.

"Supper's ready," Peg interrupted, a worried look on her face, "but Lady Kathryn has not returned. Should I hold it back?"

"Something's happened," Hugh said, rising from his chair.

"Could she have been taken ill, do you think?" Patrick asked.

"Fiona would have sent word." A frown clouded Hugh's features. "Gather some men. We're going to the Burkes."

A short time later Hugh and a group of his men-at-arms rode into the courtyard at Lord Burke's mansion. Leaping from his mount, Hugh ordered his men to wait there and hurried inside. He headed straight for the great hall where supper was being served.

"Where's Katie?" Hugh demanded, reaching the high table. Lord Burke turned to his wife.

"She left hours ago," Fiona cried, becoming alarmed.

"How?"

"Coach," she answered as Patrick and Burke's master-at-arms hurried into the hall. "She told me her coach was waiting in the courtyard."

The Burke master-at-arms cleared his throat, drawing their attention, then spoke in a hushed tone. "One of the stable lads found three bodies with their throats slashed."

Lord Burke leaped from his chair. Hugh's gaze darted to Patrick.

"They're ours," Patrick confirmed.

"Christ!" Hugh swore.

"Who would dare murder your men and snatch your wife?" Burke asked.

"Turlough," Hugh spat, turning to leave. "Patrick, send Sean home to summon the rest of the men. All routes leaving Dublin must be searched, but we'll concentrate most on those going north."

"I'm coming," Burke said, then shouted to his men-at-arms to follow.

The night was cold, but nary a single man complained, knowing full well each passing moment brought with it less chance of finding the countess. Hugh concentrated his forces in the northern sector surrounding Dublin, and less than an hour later, they discovered his abandoned coach.

"That bastard!" Hugh kicked the coach, blaming himself for his wife's predicament. If only he'd let her ride that day instead of insisting she take the coach.

"We can't be certain it's Turlough," Patrick said.

"Damn you!" Hugh shouted. "We're riding for Dungannon now."

" 'Twould be suicide," Patrick said. "*If* Turlough snatched Katie, you can be sure it's *not* for ransom."

"Yes," Burke agreed. "What better way to entrap you?"

"Alert our spies in Ulster," Patrick advised, "and based on their intelligence, formulate a rescue plan."

"He's snatched my pregnant wife," Hugh snapped. "We're bound for Dungannon now."

Lord Burke exchanged a meaningful look with Patrick who nodded in understanding. "You aren't riding anywhere tonight," Burke said, drawing a surprised look from Hugh.

It was then Patrick captured Hugh's arms behind his back, making it easier for Lord Burke whose fist connected with Hugh's jaw, rendering him unconscious.

"You're braver men than I," Conal remarked. "When he awakens, the earl will be none too happy."

Dirty and weary and sick, Kathryn still sat proudly erect on her horse as they approached Dungannon's courtyard. Determined to retain her dignity, she'd refused to shed a single tear since the first night of her abduction.

Surprisingly, Liam had been solicitous of her throughout the long journey, always remaining close by her side. When Kathryn had grown so tired she could barely sit in the saddle, Liam had taken her upon his own mount. Resting her head against his chest, Kathryn had slept fitfully.

Glancing at the lead rein on her horse, Kathryn decided that, in spite of everything, she still had things for which to be grateful. If not for Liam, death would have been her fate.

Inside the courtyard, Liam dismounted and lifted her from the saddle. Kathryn glanced around in puzzlement. Their progress had surely been noted, yet the courtyard was nearly deserted.

"What are you doing?" Kathryn cried when Liam grabbed her hands and tied her wrists together with a cord.

"I'm sorry," he whispered, "but I must."

Kathryn nodded, accepting his apology. After all, he was only following Turlough's orders.

Noting her bedraggled appearance, Liam felt a surging rush of pity mingled with respect for the proud, young noblewoman so ready to forgive his trespass. With extraordinary dignity, Kathryn had borne numerous indignities on the long journey to Ulster.

"Come." Grasping her upper arm, Liam nudged her forward.

I am the countess of Tyrone and will betray no fear, Kathryn repeated to herself over and over again like a chant. They entered the main building and walked toward the great hall, which was alive with noisy activity. Kathryn hesitated in the hall's entrance, but Liam tightened his grip on her arm and forced her forward.

Silence descended eerily upon the chamber as captor and captive walked through the crowd toward the high table. The three Irish chieftains looked up from their conversation and stared in silence as the unlikely couple advanced on them.

When Kathryn stood before them, Turlough smiled with satisfaction and relaxed back in his chair. The evening had just become very interesting.

Ignoring him, Kathryn stared hard at Sorley Boy MacDonnell whose eyes widened with surprised recognition. The green eyes shining from her smudged face reminded the MacDonnell of the enormous debt he owed her for saving his life years before. Her attention drifted to Calvagh O'Donnell, whom she'd never met.

"Good evenin'," Turlough greeted her. "I'm glad you could visit."

Forced to acknowledge his presence, Kathryn finally looked at Turlough. Her eyes shot angry defiance at him and her lips curled in a silent snarl.

As filthy as she is, Turlough thought, *the bitch is yet overly proud. But, by this time on the morrow she will be properly meek and submissive.*

"Gentlemen, I present my irresistible bait," Turlough said, his arm sweeping a gesture toward her. "Lady Kathryn O'Neill, countess of Tyrone, my cousin Hugh's wife."

Turlough smiled and nodded his head deferentially at Kathryn before continuing. "Countess, I present Calvagh O'Donnell and Sorley Boy MacDonnell."

Kathryn stared boldly at each of the Irish chieftains responsible for Shane's destruction. "Pardon me for failing to curtsey," she said, wearing the sweetest of smiles, "but I'd as lief pay homage to pigs."

Turlough's smile vanished. Each man in the hall was aghast at her suicidal folly. The MacDonnell chuckled suddenly, breaking the tension and drawing a surprised look from Turlough.

"The lass is brave as well as beautiful and witty," Sorley Boy said.

Turlough nodded, and a collective sigh of relief sounded in the hall as if the many warriors had been holding their breath.

"Why have I been brought here against my will?" Kathryn demanded.

"You know the answer to that, my dove," Turlough replied, boldly appraising her body, his desire apparent to all.

"Release me at once," Kathryn shouted, anger covering her hot embarrassment.

Turlough threw back his head and laughed. Everyone but Sorley Boy MacDonnell joined in.

Aware that most of Shane's former men-at-arms were in the hall, Kathryn thought to elicit sympathy for her cause. "What manner of man makes war against a pregnant woman?" she asked loudly, shrugging the cloak off her shoulders.

Turlough's gaze darted to her belly. "I make war against the English," he said.

"Then why have you abducted Shane O'Neill's widow?" Kathryn shouted.

"Silence!" Turlough leapt from his chair and banged his massive hands on the table. "You're Hugh O'Neill's wife, *not* Shane's widow."

"Shane would still be alive," Kathryn shot back, "but for you diabolical three. You, Turlough, deserted your own kinsman and let him go alone to Cushendun to die. Now you break bread with his sworn enemies? How you sicken me!"

Turlough opened his mouth. Before he could speak, another angry voice was heard.

"You English witch!" Maura screeched, materializing from nowhere. "Now you'll pay!"

Before she could be stopped, Maura slapped Kathryn. Though the enmity between these two beauties was well known, that a village lass would strike a countess shocked the spectators in the hall.

Again, Maura moved to attack.

With clasped hands, Kathryn took a backhanded swing that caught the other woman on the side of her face and sent her reeling. At a nod from Turlough, one of his warriors captured Maura before she could recover and press another attack.

"Keep your whore at bay, else she dies," Kathryn threatened, glaring at Turlough.

Finding vast humor in the discrepancy between fragile woman and stout words, Turlough laughed.

Kathryn swayed, her strength depleted, fatigue riding over her like a wave. Sensing her collapse, Liam placed a steadying arm around her shoulders, and Kathryn leaned heavily against him.

She's dead on her feet, Turlough marveled, *yet boldly baits and outfaces me—retains her noble dignity. What a fitting mate for a man such as I!*

"Escort Maura to her cottage," Turlough ordered his man, then shouted when she opened her mouth to protest, "*I* am master here and all will obey." None too gently, Maura was led from the hall.

"That also includes you, countess." Turlough's attention returned to his beautiful captive. "You will have your old chamber back. Everythin' is as you left it."

Kathryn was surprised, then her ire rose to the fore. Enjoying luxuries would not win her the men's sympathy.

"A prisoner in a fine chamber?" Kathryn mocked. "I thought prisoners of war were sent in chains to the dungeons."

"You may yet get the chains, sweet," Turlough replied, eliciting ribald laughter from his men. His voice grew stern, tired as he was of useless verbal fencing with an overly bold captive. "You are mine to do with as I will. I want you ensconced in your old chamber. Understand?"

Kathryn was silent, but rebellion shone from her eyes.

"Do you cherish that brat you carry?" Turlough snapped, annoyed by her unwavering defiance.

"Yes," Kathryn croaked, her eyes wide with fear.

"Answer my question," Turlough demanded, his eyes gleaming with the knowledge of her one apparent weakness. "Do you understand your situation?" When she nodded, he smiled benignly, pleased by her submission.

Maude, Dungannon's housekeeper and Polly's mother, charged into the hall. She drew Kathryn into the security of her comforting arms, asking, "Are you unharmed?"

"I fear for the child I carry," Kathryn said, leaning against her old friend.

Rounding on Turlough, Maude glared at him as if he was nothing more than a terribly naughty boy. Knowing he was helpless against her, Turlough rolled his eyes in disgust. How could he possibly intimidate the old harridan? She'd known him since he'd come into the world. How could he threaten a woman who'd wiped his ass and changed his napkins? He was the O'Neill but powerless against such a force as Maude, and the sly old witch knew she could take certain liberties that he'd never allow others.

"Bathe and feed her, then put her to bed," Turlough ordered. "Afterward, lock her in and bring me the key. Liam, escort them upstairs."

"Free her hands," Maude demanded. How she wished Turlough was still young enough to paddle!

At a nod from Turlough, Liam cut the cord binding Kathryn's wrists.

"Come," Maude said kindly. "I'll be takin' good care of you now."

Kathryn smiled faintly at the older woman and stepped forward. Buzzing, as loud as a swarm of bees, sounded in her ears. The chamber spun dizzyingly, its occupants becoming blurred figures. Determined to show no weakness, Kathryn forced herself forward several more steps, then crumpled as a haven of black nothingness enveloped her.

Liam caught her before she hit the floor and lifted her into his arms. Maude cast Turlough a withering look, then preceded Liam out of the silent hall. Kathryn's bravado and fragility had touched the toughened soldiers' hearts of those watching.

Upstairs, Liam carried Kathryn into her old bedchamber and placed her on the bed. Then he left to do Maude's bidding, ordering food and a bath for Kathryn.

As soon as Kathryn regained consciousness, her tears began to flow and her body shook with the force of her sobs. Maude gathered her into her arms and held her until she quieted.

When the tub was ready, Maude bathed Kathryn and sensed her spirits reviving. In spite of the church's teachings, the housekeeper thought wryly, there was nothing in life more soothing to the soul than a steaming tub. Confession finished a poor second.

Clad in one of her old night shifts, Kathryn was helped into bed. Maude insisted on feeding her the hot stew a serving girl had brought.

For the first time in a week, Kathryn felt clean and well fed. She leaned back against the pillow and said, "Polly and Patrick have wed."

Maude smiled. "I know."

"B-but how?"

Maude mouthed the word *spies,* then pressed a finger to her lips in a gesture to drop the subject. Pulling the coverlet up to Kathryn's chin, Maude stroked her pale cheek in a motherly fashion, asking, "When is the child due?"

"August." Kathryn blinked back the tears welling up. "My girls will miss me." She closed her suddenly heavy eyelids. "Shana . . . is . . . Shane's . . . image . . ."

Kathryn succumbed to the deep and dreamless sleep of

the weary. After a long moment, Maude stood and left the chamber, locking the door behind her.

High-ranking guests and lowliest castle folk had long since gone to their beds and pallets when Turlough, clad in a bed robe, walked into Kathryn's chamber through the connecting door. No movement or sound came from the bed.

Crossing the chamber, Turlough stood beside the bed and studied his sleeping captive. *How lovely she is!* he thought. *Her copper hair is like a brilliant, dazzling sunset and her sweet angel's face disguises her blatant stubbornness. Beneath those delicate lids hide green eyes, startling eyes as fathomless as the sea. A lesser man than I would drown in their misty depths.*

Turlough's manroot stiffened, and he smiled to himself at the bent of his masculine instinct. *It doesn't matter that she ran from me*, he decided. *Katie is mine and only death will separate us now.*

Turlough slipped off his bed robe, and a more exquisite specimen of manhood did not exist. Larger than most in his proportions, Turlough possessed the hardened, muscular body of a soldier, a well-honed weapon. His broad shoulders tapered to a reasonably narrow waist and hips, giving him the strength of a giant as well as agile grace. His features were attractive, only the absence of compassion in his cold blue eyes preventing true handsomeness. To view Turlough was to gaze upon the mighty essence of masculine power.

Drawing the coverlet back, Turlough eased onto the bed. It creaked, protesting his weight, and Kathryn swam up gradually from the depths of unconsciousness. When he moved to pull her into his arms, she awakened; and when he touched her shoulder, her eyes flew open.

Danger! screamed her suddenly alert senses.

Kathryn leapt from the bed just when he would have claimed her.

"No!" Kathryn cried, backing away on trembling legs, her eyes large with fear.

Her tousled, defiant appearance only added to her irresistible appeal. Turlough enjoyed minor feminine challenges; he loved to feel the conqueror with both types of swords.

Turlough drew the coverlet back so she could better view her fate, then nonchalantly rested his arms behind his head as if she was of no consequence. "Get back into bed," he ordered.

"No," Kathryn snapped, her expression changing to horror at the sight of his enormous shaft. Seeking escape, she glanced around like a small, cornered animal. Where could she run to? The bed stood between her and the door!

"Disrobe and get into bed." Turlough forced a sternness into his voice, but made no move to force his will. He was thoroughly enjoying this game of cat and mouse.

Kathryn's instinct to fly overwhelmed her. She dashed frantically for the door. As she ran past him, Turlough jumped out of bed and grabbed at her, tearing the night shift from her back.

Kathryn's scream pierced the night's silence. She yanked wildly at the locked door, then whirled around to face her attacker.

For several long moments predator and prey stalked each other with their eyes. Turlough perused her nakedness. His mouth watered at the sight of her pregnancy-heavy breasts with their dark nipples, fearfully erect as if highly aroused. Curvaceous hips and swollen belly conspired to give Kathryn an appealing voluptuousness.

Turlough stepped closer.

In a daring maneuver, Kathryn flew at him. She hoped

to duck at the last possible moment and escape beneath his arm, but her ploy failed.

Turlough slammed her back against the door.

Like a blind man studying a beloved treasure, Turlough caressed her burning cheeks. Ever so slowly, his hands slipped down her neck to her shoulders, then dipped lower. When he cupped her breasts, Turlough's moan was pure lust. His hand slid to her rounded belly, curved hips, and the warmth between her thighs.

"Please," Kathryn whimpered. "My baby . . ."

Ignoring her plea, Turlough pulled her roughly into his embrace. His mouth swooped down, capturing hers, and his tongue plundered the sweetness within.

Revolted, Kathryn struggled fiercely. Turlough grabbed her hair and jerked her head back, his eyes warning her to submit. Kathryn spat in his face.

Turlough's reaction was instant and vicious. He slapped her with the back of his hand, then lifted and slammed her against the door. Intending to impale her on his engorged manhood, Turlough forced her legs around his waist.

"D-do this," Kathryn sobbed brokenly, "and I—I'll k-kill myself."

Turlough released her, and clutching her belly, Kathryn fell with a thud to the floor. Disgusted, Turlough stared down at her. She was finally his, but not satisfactorily. He wanted her willin', if not eager.

Weeping, Kathryn lay unresisting when Turlough lifted and carried her to the bed. Uncertain of what to do, Turlough stared helplessly down at her and decided to do nothing. He walked over to the hearth and sat down in a chair.

The sounds of sobbing grew fainter and fainter, then finally ceased. Turlough breathed a sigh of relief, then ground his teeth in frustration. *There has to be a way to make Kathryn willing—The babe! She'd begged my mercy for the sake of the bastard's brat!*

Wearing the slyest of smiles, Turlough stood and walked through the connecting door into his own chamber.

12

🍀

As usual, Maude rose early the next morning and prepared a light breakfast for the two visiting Irish chieftains to eat in their chambers. Carrying two trays, the housekeeper started up the stairs just as the first of the men-at-arms straggled into the great hall to break their own fast. Carefully, she set one tray down in front of the O'Donnell's door and the other beside the MacDonnell's, then started to retrace her steps down the corridor.

"Psssst!"

Hearing a sound behind her, Maude stopped and turned around. Bemused, she cocked her head to one side at what she saw. The MacDonnell was beckoning her into his chamber.

Maude hesitated a fraction of a moment, but realized she was no young wench to fear entering a man's bedchamber. She retraced her steps and slipped into the room. The door clicked shut behind her. Facing him, Maude opened her mouth to speak, but he pressed a finger to his lips.

"Last evenin', Lady Kathryn's safety seemed important to you," the MacDonnell began. He hesitated at her indifferent stare, then pressed on, "In fact, you seemed fond of her."

Maude eyed him suspiciously and nodded.

"The O'Neill raped her last night," the MacDonnell said baldly. "I heard her screams."

Maude's eyes widened in horrified dismay. She tried to move past him to the door, saying, "I must see to her welfare at once."

"Hold," he ordered, blocking her way. "Tell Lady Kathryn that I'll help her, but my aid must be discreetly given. When I leave tomorrow, I'll send a message to her husband. The O'Neill is expectin' a rescue attempt, so it will take a while to get her safely away. In the meantime, she must do nothin' that will cause him to kill her. The O'Neill is a dangerous, unpredictable man. Do you understand?"

"Yes." Maude nodded.

"Be certain Lady Kathryn also understands," the MacDonnell warned. "I can't be riskin' my position for a dead woman."

"Don't worry about that, my lord," Maude returned. "Lady Kathryn will heed my orders or I'll kill her myself."

The Irish chieftain grinned broadly, then opened the door, and Maude slipped out.

Balancing a breakfast tray on her left forearm, Maude unlocked the door to Kathryn's chamber a short time later and stepped inside. As she hurried across the chamber to the bed, Maude scowled blackly at the torn, discarded night shift lying on the floor. Turlough's unbridled lust could very well have killed Kathryn and her unborn child.

Setting the tray on the bedside table, Maude pulled the coverlet up to Kathryn's chin and studied the sleeping woman, her heart breaking at the sight. Kathryn's face was bruised, her lip swollen, and purple smudges of fatigue circled her eyes.

Maude eased herself onto the edge of the bed and touched her. Kathryn threw up her arm as if to ward off a blow.

"It's me," the housekeeper whispered.

"Maude?" As Kathryn awakened, terrible desolation appeared in her eyes.

"The swine's not harmed you, has he?" Maude asked, stroking her hair. Scarlet with shame, Kathryn shook her head.

"We've not much time, so listen carefully," the housekeeper whispered. "The MacDonnell is sympathetic to your cause and will help."

"Help me escape? Today?"

"Not today, lass. When he leaves tomorrow, he'll send a message to your husband. Then a plan will be devised. It wouldn't do for your husband to be caught in Turlough's trap."

"How long will that take?" Kathryn asked.

"That's not for me to be knowin'," Maude replied, "but you mustn't give Turlough a reason to kill you." Kathryn paled beneath her bruises, and one hand dropped to cover her belly protectively.

"I'm certain murderin' you is not his purpose," the housekeeper added.

" 'Tis fuckin'!" Kathryn spat.

Seeing the unholy hatred shining from startling green eyes, Maude made the sign of the cross, then scolded, "Shame on such language from a countess. Remember— resist Turlough and the greater is your chance for harm."

"Are you suggesting I submit?" Kathryn was shocked. "I'd sooner be dead."

"Don't be sayin' that," Maude cried, crossing herself

again. "There's nothin' more final than death. Think of your daughters and husband. Would you leave them mournin' while you lie with Shane in yonder grave?"

"I loathe Turlough! How could I possibly—?" Kathryn broke off, appalled by the thought of actually *allowing* the monster's touch.

"Life has a charmin' way of forcin' us to do thin's we don't like," Maude said. "Promise you won't be fightin' him."

Chewing anxiously on her swollen lip, Kathryn looked away. *Suicide is mortal sin,* flashed the religious teachings of a lifetime. And fighting Turlough could be construed as suicide. But what if Hugh did not want her afterward? What if he took her babies and cast her out? Touching her belly, Kathryn decided to hide behind her pregnancy as long as she could.

"I'll try," Kathryn said.

"Promise."

"I promise."

"Good," Maude said, then stood. "Now eat the food I've brought."

Kathryn sat up and wrapped the coverlet around herself, then turned to the tray and saw the mug filled with white liquid. "You know I hate milk," she complained.

Maude smiled with relief. If Kathryn could complain about the milk, she'd be fine. "You're breedin'," the housekeeper reminded her. "Down it all."

Grimacing, Kathryn picked up the mug, pinched her nostrils together and drank.

"You'll be wantin' to rid yourself of the swine's scent," Maude said. "I'll order a nice hot tub."

With her stomach full, Kathryn leaned back in the scented, steaming tub and looked at Maude, who sat in a chair facing her. Closing her eyes, she steeled herself for the inevitable confrontation with Turlough. Or perhaps she could sit in the tub until she shriveled up and disappeared. The silliness of the thought made Kathryn smile.

When she opened her eyes, Maude was frowning at something behind her. Looking around, Kathryn followed her gaze. Turlough stood in the doorway.

"Oh!" Kathryn sank lower into the tub.

"Good mornin'." Turlough sauntered across the chamber toward her.

Too embarrassed to look up, Kathryn kept her eyes lowered as Turlough studied the enchanting picture she presented. Her tousled, copper hair had been pinned on the top of her head, but recalcitrant wisps of fire escaped and streamed down in an adorable fashion. A becoming blush colored her cheeks, the rosy hue extending down her throat and stopping just short of her breasts, which played a teasing game of peekaboo beneath the bath water. Yet, Turlough knew those timidly lowered eyes glowed with defiance, never meekness.

"Leave us," Turlough ordered curtly, looking at Maude.

"I'm bathing," Kathryn protested.

"Yes, I see," he said, then sat in the now empty chair and stretched his long legs out.

"Am I to be granted no privacy?" Kathryn challenged.

"No, dove, not from me." Turlough leaned forward in the chair. "I had no wish to cause you pain, Katie. If you hadn't fought me last night, I would not have been so—so rough."

"I understand," Kathryn replied, her eyes lowered in simulated meekness, "but I refuse to have my child disturbed."

The bastard! she cursed inwardly. *As if it's my fault he tried to rape me!*

Kathryn refused to meet his gaze lest he accurately

gauge her true thoughts. Turlough was many despicable things, but a stupid man he was not.

Surprised by her more agreeable attitude, Turlough wondered if she might not be pliable after all. What the minx needed was a *real* man to put her in her proper place. If so, he could afford to be generous.

"Though it was much of your own doin'," Turlough said, feeling expansive, "I apologize for any pain my—my eagerness caused you. After the babe is delivered, we'll consummate our—our relationship. I am forgiven, dove. Am I not?"

"Yes." Steeling herself to appear suitably shy, Kathryn lifted her gaze to his.

"Excellent! Now I'll help you wash."

"*No!*" Her refusal was too quick, and the warmth in his eyes cooled with suspicion.

"Playing the tiring woman is unnecessary," Kathryn amended. "You need do no penance for what is already forgiven."

"But I insist."

At his first touch, Kathryn stiffened with revulsion.

"Relax," he whispered, feeling the tenseness in her muscles as he lathered her back. "I won't hurt you."

As one of his powerful hands skillfully massaged her back, Turlough embraced the front of her body, his free hand coming to rest on her shoulder. Kathryn's eyes closed as her stress-tightened muscles relaxed. Almost imperceptibly, she leaned against the arm supporting her body, her rigid muscles loosening beneath the insistent kneading.

Startled by a surprisingly gentle touch upon her breasts, Kathryn opened her eyes. Turlough was watching her reaction. *He's testing me,* she realized, then looked away, scarlet with embarrassment. Forcing herself to submissiveness, Kathryn made no protest against his caress. Peeking from beneath her lowered lashes at the massive hand stroking her flesh, Kathryn was shocked and humiliated to see her nipples hardening.

"Look at me," Turlough said huskily. When she obeyed, he asked, "You won't fight me again?"

"No." Kathryn swallowed the revulsion she felt.

Turlough lowered his lips to hers. His tongue demanded and received entry to the sweetness hidden behind her lips, and the kiss deepened. Kathryn felt revolted but consumed by a more powerful force.

"Stand," Turlough ordered softly, helping her rise. "Your beautiful nipples beg to be sucked."

"But you said—" Kathryn protested.

"I know what I said," he cut her off, then smiled slyly. "But I did not swear to leave you untouched."

"You conniving pig!" The words slipped off her tongue before she could bite them back.

"Do you cherish the bastard's brat?" Turlough snapped. "Or will you fight me again?"

Kathryn looked away and said nothing. For the sake of Hugh's heir, she would suffer the swine's touch.

Satisfied, Turlough lowered his head. His lips swooped down claiming one tempting nipple, tasting its incredible sweetness. At the same time, one large paw teased the other.

"You're wet for me," Turlough murmured as his finger found the precious pearl hidden in the folds of her nether lips.

Kathryn shuddered with revulsion. Turlough mistakenly believed she was aroused. However, the O'Neill was a busy man and had no time at the moment to dally with her.

"You'll rest today," Turlough said, composing himself,

his hands falling away from her body. "My guests leave in the morning, and tonight you will play my hostess."

Turlough yearned to take her immediately but reminded himself she was only a woman and available whenever he wished. Leaving her standing in the tub, he crossed the chamber but paused at the door, his hungry gaze feasting on her bounty. "Wear the emerald silk gown tonight."

"Emerald silk?"

"The one you wore on Beltane, the first time I met you." Turlough smiled at the memory. "Maude will get it out."

"But—"

"You'll dress to please me," he interrupted. "That beautiful body of yours understands it's mine, even if your mind has not accepted it." Then he was gone.

Humiliated, Kathryn stood motionless in the tub. Hot tears of shame trickled down her face. She felt sullied by his disgusting touch. Hugh would not want her now and she could not blame him. He would claim their child and cast her out.

Kathryn climbed out of the tub and dried herself. Retrieving her night shift from the floor, she saw its torn condition and dropped it. Naked, she climbed into bed and closed her eyes, but was unable to cast aside her troubled thoughts of what would happen when night descended, its darkness shrouding the sins of weak, mortal man.

Anxious about her charge's condition, Maude rushed in several moments later. "He caused you no harm?" she asked worriedly.

"Merely my pride."

"Good." Maude chuckled, her mirth surprising Kathryn. "To the best of my limited knowledge, I've never known injured pride to be fatal."

At suppertime that night, Kathryn stood poised at the top of the stairs. Her thick, copper hair fell loose to her waist, and she wore the emerald silk as Turlough had commanded. Recalling the gown had been one of her late husband's favorites, Kathryn sighed. Apparently, Turlough had also admired it.

The bodice was snug, the intervening years and pregnancies having ripened her figure. The emerald silk barely covered the dusky tips of her enlarged breasts. Looking down at her exposed bosom, Kathryn was perplexed about what to do. She felt positively naked.

A crafty imp entered her soul. Virtually defenseless, she need not make things easy. Kathryn pulled her fiery hair forward and draped it artfully over her bosom. *There!* she thought with satisfaction, at least I am somewhat protected from curious eyes.

A throaty chuckle that could only be Turlough brought her to alertness. Looking up, Kathryn saw her captor climbing the stairs.

"I was comin' to escort you below," he said.

"I—I—" Kathryn faltered. "The door was unlocked. I was uncertain."

"Your breasts were meant to be admired," Turlough said, brushing aside her hair and exposing her creamy mounds of flesh. Embarrassed, Kathryn flushed a vivid scarlet. Smiling, Turlough offered his arm, and they descended the stairs in silence.

The great hall was bustling with the men-at-arms of three clans. Uncomfortably, Kathryn felt every eye upon her as Turlough escorted her to the high table. She felt like pirates' booty, a prized possession proudly displayed.

Turlough seated Kathryn on his left, and Calvagh O'Donnell sat on his right. Almost immediately, Sorley Boy MacDonnell appeared and sat in the empty chair on

Kathryn's left. Relief washed over her, knowing a friend was close. The food and drink began arriving, and feeling less the center of attention, Kathryn relaxed.

"A toast to Lady Kathryn," Turlough said, raising his goblet. Following his lead, the other Irish chieftains raised their goblets in salute.

Kathryn stared straight ahead and refused to acknowledge their dubious honor.

"Drink," Turlough said, placing a hand on her shoulder. "It will relax you."

Kathryn met his gaze, his eyes warning her he'd tolerate no defiance. Nodding, she picked up her goblet and drank.

Pleased with her submission, Turlough smiled his approval and caressed her shoulder. Leaning close, he nuzzled her neck and whispered against her ear, "Smile and play the gracious hostess."

Swallowing her pride, Kathryn looked first at Calvagh O'Donnell. "Good evening, my lord. I hope you find everything to your liking."

"Good evenin', Countess," the O'Donnell replied, his gaze fixed upon her breasts threatening to escape from their confinement. "Dungannon's bounty is . . . exquisite."

Kathryn blushed crimson, and Turlough chuckled at her embarrassment. Controlling her rising ire, Kathryn turned to Sorley Boy MacDonnell and forced a smile. Masking his compassion, the MacDonnell met her smile with an icy stare.

"I see you've bent the wench to your will," the MacDonnell said to Turlough.

"Aye. All she needed was a real man to lay her in her place." The three Irish chieftains laughed at their own vulgar wit.

Burning with humiliation, Kathryn could no longer deny

her anger, would tolerate no more. She stood up abruptly. "If you—*gentlemen*—will excuse me?" Kathryn spoke with exaggerated politeness.

"Sit down," Turlough ordered. "Unless you wish to be the spectacle again this evenin'?"

"I refuse to sit here while you discuss me as if I were deaf or had no feelings." Kathryn's voice rose in anger.

"We're sorry," Turlough apologized, his tone condescending. "Sit and eat. You need to keep up your strength."

"Please, sit," the MacDonnell said. "I meant no insult."

Kathryn hesitated, then sat down again. The men began to eat. Soon they were ignoring her presence, speaking openly of their plans to harass the English as soon as Turlough's difficulties with Hugh ended. Kathryn perked up at the mention of her husband's name, but noticing her interest, Turlough signaled the others off that subject.

Distracted, Kathryn ate little, only when ordered to do so by Turlough who watched her every movement. As the meal ended, she noted the hall's occupants had become rowdy with drink. Not only had her supper companions drunk a great deal, but her own tension had lessened. Under Turlough's command and scrutiny, Kathryn had drunk two goblets of wine, making her heady.

Turlough reached out and drew her close. "I count the moments until we are alone, my dove," he murmured against her ear. Kathryn stiffened at his words.

"Kiss her!" shouted one of the men-at-arms from somewhere in the chamber. His lusty suggestion was followed by others.

"Aye, kiss her!"

"Tame the vixen!"

"Take her!"

"Take her on the table!"

Laughing at their enthusiasm, Turlough pulled Kathryn into his steely embrace. Instinct screamed at her to flee, but quelling it, Kathryn smiled seductively at him. She was determined to play the game well and eventually win the war that raged between them. To his surprise, Kathryn entwined her arms around his neck.

"Allow me," she murmured, drawing his head down to hers. Kathryn's lips were moist and already parted in invitation when they touched his. Wantonly, she thrust her tongue into his mouth, assailed his senses without mercy, held him enthralled in a languorous sensation.

Who is controlling whom? Turlough wondered. Without warning, the current of the kiss changed. Turlough's tongue chased Kathryn's back inside her mouth. When he broke the kiss, Kathryn fell back in her chair. The men cheered their chief's prowess wildly, but Kathryn struggled to keep from wiping her mouth on her sleeve.

"Are prisoners now seated as guests of honor?" Maura asked, standing in front of the high table.

"Begone." Turlough dismissed the Irish beauty with a wave of his hand. "Return to your cottage."

"You would set that English slut in my place?" Maura stepped closer to Kathryn. "The witch belongs in yonder graveyard."

"Liam!" Turlough shouted. Instantly, his man appeared and grabbed Maura who struggled in his arms. "Take the bitch home and see she stays put," he ordered, then winked. "Even if you must *personally* guard her all night."

Boisterous laughter filled the hall. Grinning broadly, Liam scooped Maura up and flung her over his shoulder. He gave her buttocks a few resounding whacks, ending her struggles, then sauntered toward the door.

"I must escort Lady Kathryn to her chamber," Turlough told the two visiting chieftains, then stood. "We'll speak again before you leave." Turning to Kathryn, he offered his hand. She placed her trembling hand in his and let herself be guided out of the hall.

Upstairs, Turlough locked the chamber door and lunged for Kathryn, pulling her into his powerful embrace. One of his massive hands prevented her escape as his lips swooped down and claimed hers.

Seeking a reprieve, Kathryn jerked her head back, caught her breath and asked, "Will you call Maude to assist me?"

Turlough smiled lazily. "I will play the lady's maid this night."

"Y-you promised." Silent tears of despair welled up in her eyes. "P-please, my baby."

"Tears?" Turlough mocked, his voice colder than the bitter winds of winter. "My touch moves you to tears?"

Frightened, Kathryn looked away and said nothing.

"Do you fear me?" he asked, tilting her face up to gaze into her disarming green eyes.

"No," she lied.

Turlough smiled at the obvious lie and sauntered toward the door. Kathryn's voice stopped him in his tracks.

"May I visit Shane's grave?" she asked. "As his widow, duty demands that I tend it."

Turlough stared at her for several long moments. "I'll think on it," he evaded, then left without another word.

Dejected, Kathryn stared at the locked door and wondered what Hugh was doing and thinking at that very moment. *If not for the baby growing inside me,* she thought, *I would end my worthless life and spare his honor.*

A cacophony of sounds coming from the courtyard below her chamber window awakened Kathryn the next morning. What was happening outside? Then she remem-

bered. The MacDonnell was leaving Dungannon. Soon
help would arrive. But how long would that take? How
long could she keep Turlough at bay?

Kathryn decided to be alert for other avenues of escape.
After all, freeing herself would be less dangerous for
Hugh.

Filled with hot water, the oak tub had already been set
in front of the hearth. Kathryn pulled the coverlet back,
stood, and wrapped it around herself. She sat down on the
edge of the bed and reached for the bell rope, but the
chamber door opened.

"Good mornin'," Maude greeted her. "I've good food
here and you must eat it all." The housekeeper set the tray
on the bedside table, then busied herself with straighten-
ing the room.

Leaning closer to the tray, Kathryn inventoried its contents. There were freshly baked bread, hard-cooked eggs,
ham, cheese, and two mugs. One mug was filled with nut-
brown ale and the other with milk.

"I've a choice today?" Kathryn asked, eyeing the two
mugs.

"The ale's for him," Maude answered.

Surprised, Kathryn looked up. Standing in the doorway
connecting their chambers, Turlough admired the fetching
picture she presented—tousled hair, sleepy expression,
flawless skin wrapped haphazardly in the coverlet.

"Called in the reinforcements?" Kathryn asked, casting
a sidelong glance at Maude, whose lips twitched with suppressed amusement. "I never expected such an unworthy
maneuver from you."

"A bit waspish this morn?" Turlough asked, collecting a
chair and strolling across the chamber. He placed the chair
close to the bed and sat down. "I was thinkin' it would be
pleasant to break the fast together."

Pleasant for whom? Kathryn thought. Her gaze met his, and she pointed at the milk. "I shan't drink that and torture won't work."

"She's breedin'," Maude called from the other side of the chamber.

Turlough looked from Maude's determined stare to Kathryn's stubborn expression, then shrugged his shoulders. "Drink the milk, Katie."

"Are you the O'Neill or no?" Kathryn snapped. "Who's in charge here?"

Turlough leveled an icy glare at her. His eyes narrowed and his lips tightened in anger.

"I'll drink it." As she reached for the mug, Kathryn spied the housekeeper's triumphant smile. Her anger flared.

"Ooops!" The mug slipped through Kathryn's fingers and crashed to the floor, the milk spilling out.

"You did that a purpose," Maude accused, charging toward them.

The cunning little witch! Turlough thought, squelching the urge to laugh. Vowing Kathryn would drink a mug of milk, even if it was her final earthly act, Turlough forced a sternness onto his face. Of course, *he* never drank milk and sympathized with her dislike, but he had commanded her to drink. Kathryn had disobeyed his order and he would not allow that, no matter how much he yearned for her exquisite body. The chosen of the O'Neill must be obedient.

"It was an accident," Kathryn capitulated. "Fetch another, and I'll drink it." She'd not risk her chance for freedom over something as trivial as milk.

"Spoken like a true Irishman," Turlough remarked as Maude left the chamber.

"How so?"

"Rebel and submit. Live to rebel again another day. 'Tis the Irish way of life."

After he'd gone, Kathryn bathed and dressed in a soft woolen skirt and linen blouse, then wandered to the window and peered down into the courtyard. The two visiting Irish chieftains and their warriors were ready to leave. Turlough, Liam, and several other O'Neill men-at-arms stood in the midst of the departing warriors. As the O'Donnells and the MacDonnells turned their horses to begin their long journeys home, a smile flitted across Kathryn's face.

Before I'm finished with him, Kathryn vowed as she hurried across the chamber, *Turlough will be begging my husband to take me back.* The door was unlocked. Kathryn raced down the stairs and outside into the courtyard.

"What are you doin' here?" Turlough asked.

"You promised I could tend Shane's grave," Kathryn answered.

"I promised nothin'. I said I would think about it."

"Well?"

Turlough smiled benignly. "Madam, you need an escort and I am busy at the moment."

Kathryn's smile drooped a little. "Liam?"

"My men are also busy."

"Maude?" she persisted.

"Maude has household duties." Turlough scowled at her. "We've work to do. People cannot stop their chores to loiter with you among the dead."

"There must be someone," Kathryn cried desperately. A solitary tear trickled down her cheek.

Turlough's firm resolve weakened. "Liam!" he shouted.

"Yes?" answered his man, standing beside him.

"Find that witless stable boy," Turlough ordered gruffly, trying to mask his embarrassment at being undone by this slip of a girl. Liam winked at Kathryn and headed toward the stables.

Happy with her victory, Kathryn bestowed a dazzling smile upon her captor. "Thank you, my lord," she said sweetly, her eyes mocking him.

Irritated, Turlough knew he'd been manipulated, but his consternation became a sly smile. "You may demonstrate your gratitude later this evenin'," he returned, then chuckled at her dismayed expression.

Kathryn judged the stable boy stood on the threshhold of adolescence, perhaps twelve or thirteen years old. Taller than she by several inches, he was thin and gangling. Though his light brown hair was common enough, the boy had an angelic face and startling blue eyes. Frightened by the O'Neill's summons, the boy hung his head, and Kathryn realized he was mentally slow.

"Look up, Tim," Turlough ordered, and instantly, the boy obeyed. "This is Lady Kathryn. You will escort her to the graveyard today and any other day she desires. Understand?"

"Y-y-yes," Tim answered, staring openmouthed at the copper-haired vision. When the *vision* smiled at him, Tim blushed furiously and hung his head.

"Shall we?" Kathryn extended her hand, and the countess and the stable boy walked away hand-in-hand.

"I'm thinkin' the lady will soon be enjoyin' *another* conquest," Liam remarked, watching them go, then laughed.

"Go on about your business," Turlough said in a gruff voice, then stalked off.

Leaving the courtyard proper, Kathryn and Tim passed the O'Neill family chapel adjacent to the graveyard. Noting his nervousness, Kathryn tried to put him at ease.

"When Shane O'Neill was my husband, Dungannon was my home," she said. "Do you remember me?"

Tim stopped short and stared curiously at her. Vague recognition lit his eyes. "Y-yes, my lady." Tim blushed, adding, "I c-could never forget you 'cause you're so pretty."

"How gallant!" Kathryn exclaimed. "As I recall, you once took a bad fall. Have you recovered completely?"

"I feel good," Tim answered, confusion clouding his eyes, "but people say I'm not the same. The O'Neill said my wits were scattered, but I can't remember anythin' like that happenin'."

At the graveyard, Kathryn walked to Shane's final resting place, but fearful of graveyards and ghosts, Tim hung back. If a person wasn't careful, Tim knew, the spirits of the dead would gladly carry him away, nevermore to be seen.

Kathryn knelt in front of Shane's grave and stared at his tombstone as if in a trance, seeing not with her eyes but with her mind. Shane's face, as he had been in life, loomed before her.

It's peaceful here, Kathryn told him, speaking not with her lips but her heart. *I haven't come for a long time because I was forced to run from Turlough. You have another daughter. Shana is your image . . .*

With tears streaming down her face, Kathryn sobbed, "Oh, Hugh . . ."

"Weep not, my lady!" Overcoming his fear of the dead, Tim rushed to Kathryn's side, knelt beside her, and grabbed her hand. "Please, do not weep." Without thinking, he brushed her tears away with one of his dirty hands, leaving her cheeks smudged.

"Tim is your very best friend," he said brightly.

"Thanks," Kathryn said, then smiled sadly at him. "I'll be your very best friend too."

Tim grinned, eager to please. "Tomorrow I'll be stealin'

flowers from the O'Neill's garden, and you can leave them here."

"I'd like that." Then, thinking of Turlough's gardens being slowly denuded, Kathryn burst out laughing and Tim joined her.

13

Everyone at the O'Neill mansion suffered long and anxious days, but no one suffered more than Hugh. Haggard with worry, Hugh seemed to have aged ten years in the days following his wife's abduction. Tormenting fingers of guilt gripped and wrenched his heart until he could neither eat nor sleep. Having sworn to protect Kathryn and failed, Hugh knew the never ending agony of hell would be easier to bear than this.

At first Hugh was furious that his plan to ride to Dungannon had been thwarted, but finally saw the sanity in his friends' logic.

Well trained and expert at their craft, his spies in Ulster sent word that Turlough had, indeed, abducted Kathryn. She was unharmed, and though closely watched, allowed a small measure of freedom.

Hugh, Lord Burke, Patrick, and Conal closeted themselves in the study for hours, formulating and discarding rescue plans. Hugh insisted a plan be devised that would not endanger Kathryn, but knew in his heart that none would be found.

"My lord," Peg interrupted, drawing their attention to

the doorway. "A Francis MacDonnell demands to speak with you about Lady Kathryn."

Four astonished faces fixed on Francis MacDonnell, the same warrior who'd delivered the severed head of Shane O'Neill to Dublin Castle, as he brushed past Peg.

"Be seated," Hugh said, then nodded at the house-keeper to leave.

Remembering Shane's untimely death at Cushendun, Patrick and Conal exchanged meaningful looks and eyed the MacDonnell's son suspiciously.

"I've a message from Sorley Boy MacDonnell," Francis said.

Hugh leaned forward in his chair, saying, "Speak."

"The O'Neill is holdin' your wife—"

"We know," Patrick snapped. "How did you get this information?"

"Let the man speak," Hugh said.

"I saw the countess with my own eyes," Francis contin-ued, surprising them. "We were at Dungannon when they brought her in. The O'Neill is expectin'—and hopin', I might add—you'll ride to her rescue. A direct assault would be suicidal. In one week's time, my father will meet you in Antrim."

"This is another MacDonnell trick," Patrick blurted out. "Like Shane's murder."

"I swear 'tis no trap."

"Is your word as good as your hospitality?" Conal sneered. After all, the MacDonnells had offered Shane their hospitality, then poisoned him and sent his severed head to Dublin Castle.

"Why should Sorley Boy help me?" Hugh asked, suspi-cious.

"My father's not helpin' you," the young man replied. "He's helpin' your lady to whom he is indebted."

For a long moment, all were silent. Hugh's eyes clouded with pain, and when he spoke, his voice was an agonized whisper, "How—how was she when you saw her?"

"The countess's bearin' was as majestic as a queen's," Francis told him. "She exhibited great courage, the likes of which I'd never thought possible in a woman." Pitying the other man's obvious anguish, he added, "Your lady was bein' well kept."

Hugh nodded, then looked at Conal. "Deliver this man to Peg. Tell the men we ride at dawn." Turning back to Francis, he said, "My housekeeper will give you a hot meal and a perch where you can rest."

"Ride where?" Patrick asked when the door closed behind the two men.

"Antrim."

"Then we'd better be prepared for the unexpected," Patrick advised. "The MacDonnell could be part of Turlough's trap."

Hugh nodded, but knew he'd no other alternative. "It's a risk we must take."

Silent until now, Lord Burke stood and announced, "I'm leaving but will return with my men at dawn."

"No." Hugh's voice stopped him. "You won't be riding to Antrim, my friend. Fiona's due to deliver any day. You—"

"I can do nothing but hold her hand," Burke protested.

"Remain in Dublin," Hugh said. "If it's a trap, you'll be free to notify the viceroy or the queen, whoever possesses the might to free Katie. I won't leave my wife and child to Turlough's mercy, even if I must reach from the grave." With a nod of understanding, Lord Burke left and Patrick went to make preparations for their departure.

Hugh poured himself a whiskey and sat down in front of the hearth. *This is my fault*, he concluded for the thousandth time. How could he face Katie again? What fear and agony had she suffered at Turlough's hands?

"If he's dared touch her, I'll—" Frustrated, Hugh hurled his glass into the fireplace.

Kathryn's days fell into a pattern. Each night Turlough subjected her to his repulsive touch, and though she allowed him no satisfaction, guilt festered within her. As Turlough reveled in the silken feel of her, Kathryn professed her hatred of him. Even she was shocked by the hideous insults and jeers that poured from her lips. That he'd never struck her surprised Kathryn even more. Perhaps, she concluded, rapture rendered him deaf.

Each morning Kathryn appeared in the courtyard, and Tim would be waiting, clutching the flowers he'd stolen from the gardens. Hand in hand, they walked to the graveyard, and when they returned, Tim said farewell until the following day.

Though Tim was her official escort, Kathryn knew the O'Neill warriors watched them. Any deviation from their normal procedure would bring Turlough's wrath down upon Tim and her.

From a distance, Maura watched the unlikely couple and recognized Tim's expression as besotted. Determined to rid herself of her detested rival, the Irish beauty considered how best to use the boy's infatuation to her own advantage.

Walking back from the graveyard one day, Tim touched Kathryn's hand and blushed when she looked at him. "D-Daisy has new pups. In the s-stables. D-do you want to see them?" he asked, then dropped his eyes in embarrassment.

"Why, Tim, I'd love to see Daisy's pups."

When they entered the stable yard, nobody stopped them. Kathryn knew that someone had probably already gone to inform Turlough, and he would be furious that she'd gone there without his permission. *Damn him!* She was weary of constant confinement and refused to be cowed.

Tim led the way into the stable's dimness, back to one of the last stalls. It smelled of horseflesh, leather, and puppies. As her eyes became accustomed to the darkness, Kathryn peered into the stall. There sat Daisy, an immense stormy-gray Irish wolfhound, surrounded by ten wriggling balls of gray fur.

Side by side, Kathryn and Tim knelt to watch the pups' playful antics. Ten fluffy balls of gray fur staggered and rolled and leapt excitedly against, over, and under each other to investigate these monstrous, alien objects. Attacked by this army of scampering beings, Kathryn and Tim laughed, enjoying the jumping and licking and nuzzling bestowed on them. One of the pups limped, and Kathryn pointed it out.

"He was born that way," Tim told her, "but I—I d-dare not tell the O'Neill."

"Why not?"

"Crippled hounds are useless for huntin'. The O'Neill would have him drowned."

"*No,*" Kathryn cried. "I won't allow that."

Never doubting she could save the pup from certain death, Tim grinned with relief. "When he's weaned, would you like him for your own?"

"Yes, and I'll take good care of him."

"Madam," Turlough shouted, walking into the stables with Liam. "What do you do here? Return to your chamber at once!"

Kathryn paled, but Tim spoke up boldly. "I—I brought her here," he said, earning himself a forbidding glare.

She's bewitched a witless stable boy, Turlough fumed. *I should keep her locked in her chamber lest she nurture other allies.*

"Y-y-your lady is s-sad," Tim stammered, frightened by the murderous expression directed at him. "The pups made her laugh. Is it wrong?"

Turlough looked at the pups for the first time. "You did no wrong," he said, patting the boy's shoulder. "Lady Kathryn may visit the pups again if she wishes."

Kathryn and Tim exchanged smiles.

"That one is lame," Liam pointed out.

"Get rid of it," Turlough ordered.

"*No!*" Kathryn cried. Surprised by the fierceness of her outburst, the two men stared at her. Kathryn caught Turlough's hand in hers and turned pleading eyes upon him.

"Please," she begged. "Tim promised I could have the crippled pup for my own."

"You'd make a useless dog your pet?" Turlough asked in disbelief.

Standing behind him, Liam swallowed a chuckle. He knew the pup was as good as the countess's pampered pet. The O'Neill would deny nothing—barring freedom—to the object of his desire.

"It's not a fittin' gift," Turlough argued, dismissing her words with a casual wave of his hand.

"I want that pup," Kathryn insisted, then rubbed her cheek against his callused hand. "Please?"

Turlough melted at her gesture. "Very well," he agreed, certain her sentimentality was due to her breeding condition. "Come along now."

"My thanks," Kathryn murmured, then smiled at Tim. "I'll see you tomorrow."

Tim gazed longingly at her retreating back.

"Now, my boy," Liam teased, seeing his besotted expression, "you'd not be tryin' to steal the O'Neill's lady away from him, would you?"

"No." Tim blushed with embarrassment and guilt.

"That's a good lad," Liam said, patting the boy's shoulder in camaraderie. " 'Twould be unhealthy to do so."

As Maura had known it would be, the stable yard was deserted that evening, the O'Neill's men having gone to the great hall for supper. Carrying a covered earthenware bowl, Maura searched for Tim. She walked into one of the stables and found him finishing his chores.

"I was lookin' for you," Maura said, advancing on him.

"Lookin' for me?" Tim looked up, surprised. He'd always admired this pretty lady from afar, but had never known she'd noticed him.

"I've made more stew than necessary and wondered what to do with it," she lied. "Then I thought of you, how you're such a fine lad and all."

"Me?" Tim grinned, flattered by her words.

"Yes, Tim, and I've brought this delicious stew for you." *The boy is stupid*, Maura concluded. Winning and using his trust to her own advantage would be easy.

"I'd like us to be friends," she said. "Would you like to be my friend?"

"Yes." Tim was happy but could not quite believe his good fortune. Now he'd have two friends. Pretty ones too! The O'Neill's men wouldn't tease him anymore. In fact, they'd probably be envious and more respectful.

Maura handed Tim the bowl, then sat beside him on the floor, and watched as he ate. Smiling at his obvious relish of the stew, Maura hid her disgust at his deplorable manners.

"It's good," Tim said, his mouth full.

Maura's stomach lurched at the sight.

"You're very pretty," Tim complimented her, his admiration clear in his voice. This time Maura's smile was genuine but vanished at his next words. "Of course, Lady Kathryn is prettier, but you're pretty too."

"Do you like Lady Kathryn, then?" Maura asked, resisting the powerful urge to thrash him.

"She's my very best friend," Tim boasted. "I'm givin' her one of Daisy's pups. The O'Neill said I could."

"That's kind of you. Indeed, you must be Lady Kathryn's very best friend."

"I am." Tim shoveled more stew into his mouth. Some of the broth dribbled down his chin. Using the back of his hand, Tim wiped it away and cleaned his dirty hand on his shirt.

Maura closed her eyes and gulped down her nausea. "Would you like to come to supper at my cottage tomorrow?" she invited him, regaining her composure.

Tim's blue eyes lit up at the prospect. "Could I?"

"Of course, silly, I'm invitin' you." Maura smiled, but then her expression grew serious. "You must swear not to tell anyone. People would misunderstand—if you know what I mean." Her look was blatantly seductive, but seeing his blank expression, she realized he was ignorant of what she meant.

"You must keep our friendship a secret, else we cannot be friends." When the time came, Maura wanted no accusing fingers pointing at her.

"I can hold a secret," Tim bragged. "Of course I can."

"Excellent! Come to supper tomorrow evenin'." Maura stood, took the empty bowl from his hands, and went on her way.

Heart-swelling joy consumed Tim. Never had he thought to be blessed with so many friends!

The next afternoon Turlough climbed the stairs and strode purposefully down the corridor to Kathryn's chamber. Without knocking, he opened the door and walked inside, but found the room empty. Irritated, Turlough retraced his steps downstairs in search of Maude who was just exiting the pantry.

"Where is she?" Turlough demanded.

"Gone to the graveyard," Maude answered without breaking stride.

One of his massive hands reached out and halted her progress. "But it's afternoon," Turlough protested.

"How clever to notice the time of day," the housekeeper snapped. Supper was fast approaching and she'd work to do. She was much too busy to be bothered by a grown man who behaved like a moonstruck boy. No doubt he'd turn petulant if supper was late. Men could be such children!

Smiling like a sleek cat who knows its prey is cornered, Turlough instructed her, "Prepare a light supper for two. Lady Kathryn and I will be closeted in her chamber this evenin'."

Turlough walked outside to the courtyard and started down the path to the graveyard. Kathryn had been his hostage for weeks, but there was still no sign of Hugh. Did not the greatest of earls cherish his wife? Why didn't Hugh come to Kathryn's rescue so he could neatly lay him next to Shane?

Tim stood near the graveyard's entrance. The boy's eyes shone with love and devotion as he watched Kathryn, her head bowed in prayer, kneeling in front of Shane's grave. In his mind, Kathryn ran a close second to the Virgin Mary.

Nodding at the boy, Turlough walked toward Kathryn who was unaware of his presence. With her copper hair flowing loose almost to her hips and her head bowed in prayer, Kathryn was a living picture of serene innocence. Anyone seeing her could never imagine the height to which her stubborn temper could soar. But Turlough knew better.

"Return to your chamber," Turlough ordered, his husky voice intruding upon her prayers.

Curse and rot him! Kathryn thought, surprised by his voice. He'd given her permission to attend Shane's grave. Was she not to be given the privacy to do so?

"I'm not finished here," she said without looking up.

Turlough, annoyed by her defiance in front of a stable boy, grabbed her arm and yanked her to her feet. "I said to return to your chamber."

"And *I* said I wasn't finished," Kathryn insisted, trying to pull away. "I'm praying for Shane and your pleasure will await mine."

"Your prayers are wasted," Turlough growled, giving her a violent shake. "I'm alive and want you now."

"You murdering son of a swine," Kathryn cried. "I wish you were dead too!"

At that, Turlough struck her with the flat of his hand, then grabbed her staggering body, and kept her from falling.

"Don't touch her!" Tim shouted, running toward them.

Like a lightning bolt came the sudden flash of steel as Turlough drew his dagger and pointed it at Tim, whose wild attack was abruptly halted by the gleaming death that awaited him. Kathryn gasped, horrified, the danger to Tim dousing her anger like a bucket of icy water.

"Please, he doesn't understand," Kathryn pleaded, her hand staying the death thrust. Seeing Tim harmed for her sake was a thing she could not bear.

Turlough cast a long, measuring look at Kathryn but kept the dagger pointed at Tim.

"I'm sorry," she apologized, tugging on his arm. "The baby makes me irritable. I meant no disrespect."

Soothed by her placating words but unwilling to let the stable boy's insubordination pass unpunished, Turlough stood in indecision and stared at Tim.

"I will be grateful for any mercy you show him," Kathryn said.

Turlough's head snapped from Tim to Kathryn. Their gazes locked. Green eyes promised submission.

"And the venom you spew in my ear?" Turlough asked.

"Shall cease," Kathryn promised. She knelt beside him, submitting to his will. "I beg of you, have mercy."

"Get up." Turlough yanked her to her feet. "Yield to me."

"Upon my honor, I yield."

"Women have no honor."

Kathryn swallowed her anger and vowed, "I swear upon the lives and souls of my daughters."

Turlough sheathed his dagger and turned on Tim. " 'Tis indeed your lucky day, boy. This lady and your scattered wits have saved you. *This time.* Remember my warning. Do not again interfere with your lord's will. Now return to the stables."

Tim hesitated, torn between his devotion to Kathryn and his fearful respect for the O'Neill. He looked at Kathryn for guidance.

Understanding his dilemma, Kathryn smiled reassuringly, saying, "I'll be fine, Tim, and will see you tomorrow."

Reluctant, Tim nodded at her and left the graveyard.

"Thank you," Kathryn said, watching him walk away. "I could not have borne his death on my account." She stood on tiptoes and planted a kiss on Turlough's cheek.

Turlough was stunned. It was the first time Kathryn had

voluntarily reached for him. He looked down at her face and winced, noting a bruise forming where he'd slapped her. Marring her beauty was not his intent. For once in his life, guilty remorse subdued his great arrogance. Confused by this unfamiliar and uncomfortable feeling, Turlough turned away and saw the flowers adorning Shane's grave.

"Where did you get those?" he asked, gesturing to the flowers.

"I appropriated them from your garden," Kathryn answered. "Are you angry?"

"No, appropriate all the flowers you want."

I hate you, Kathryn thought. She'd behaved foolishly and endangered Tim. Her ruthless captor would never punish her directly, but strike out at those she loved best. Surrender was more endurable than the heavy burden of Tim's death.

Turlough and Kathryn left the graveyard. As they passed through the courtyard, several men-at-arms noticed the angry bruise rising on Kathryn's cheek. Their initial amusement at Turlough's abduction and treatment of her had faded. Though the bravest among them merely mumbled his displeasure, more than a few were wholly disgusted. After all, Kathryn was Shane O'Neill's widow and the mother of his children. Shane's former warriors remembered her many kindnesses to them, and all would testify to the dignity with which she'd borne her present ordeal.

When the supper hour arrived, Tim left the stable yard and walked down the path that led to Maura's cottage in the village. Pale and nervous, he worried about the unsettling events at the graveyard. Had he done wrong? The O'Neill was his master, and as such Tim owed him his loyalty and obedience. On the other hand, his devotion to

Kathryn demanded that he defend her in spite of the danger. The conflicting emotions overwhelmed him.

Lost in troubled thoughts, Tim knocked on the door and entered at Maura's call. He handed her his usual offering of gallantry, a bouquet of flowers stolen from the O'Neill's gardens. Since the night Maura had brought him the stew at the stables, Tim had been her nightly supper guest, but heeding her warning, went to the cottage after the others had gone to the great hall.

Downcast, Tim sat at the table. Feigning disinterest, Maura noted the change in his demeanor and set a bowl of potato and leek soup, garnished with tiny bits of ham, in front of him.

Maura sat in the other chair and started to eat, but her eyes never left the boy's face with its downhearted expression. "What's botherin' you?" she asked. "Is the soup not to your likin'?"

"It's not that," Tim answered. "Somethin' puzzlin' happened at the graveyard today."

Maura squelched the look of eagerness threatening to appear on her face. "Good friends share their troubles," she said. "Perhaps I can help."

"The O'Neill came to the graveyard to fetch Lady Kathryn," he told her. "Sayin' he'd wait no longer, the O'Neill ordered her back to her chamber and struck her when she refused." Tim's expression mirrored his confusion. "Why should she return to her chamber? It wasn't supper time."

Maura's frown was genuine. The English witch was getting from Turlough what she was not and wanted. A more advantageous opportunity to activate her scheme would not be found.

"The O'Neill wanted to rut Lady Kathryn," Maura said bluntly, shocking the boy.

"Rut? Like the animals?"

"Of course. How do you think babies are made?"

"B-b-but," Tim stammered, "she didn't want to go with him."

"I can well understand that." Maura gave him a knowing look.

Tim fell easily into her trap. "Why?"

Emphasizing the horror that had awaited Kathryn in her chamber, Maura leaned across the table and spoke in a hushed tone. "The O'Neill has a stallion's cock that hurts the women he chooses to rut."

"No!" Tim cried, leaping up so quickly the table was nearly upset. "I must save her!"

Tim raced for the door, intent on saving his very best friend. Before he could escape the cottage, Maura halted his flight and drew him back to the table.

" 'Twouldn't do to get yourself killed," she scolded. Then added in a kinder voice, "If it's what you really want, I'll help you and the lady."

Relief flooded Tim's features. "But, how can we save her?"

"Do you trust me?"

"Yes," Tim answered without hesitation.

"I can arrange for Lady Kathryn's escape," Maura said. Then warned, "But you cannot tell her we're helpin' her cause."

"Why not?" he asked. "It would make her happy."

"Thwartin' the O'Neill be risky business, boy, and to keep us safe, Lady Kathryn would refuse our help. Do you see?"

Tim nodded. "I understand."

Two days passed. Sending word that she was ill, Kathryn had not appeared in the courtyard for her daily excursion to the graveyard.

With stolen flowers in hand, Tim paced back and forth anxiously. Would she visit the graveyard that day? Or was she still suffering from the O'Neill's rutting? His head ached from the unaccustomed thinking and planning. Intent upon his worries, Tim failed to see the object of his intense concern until she greeted him.

"Good morning," Kathryn called, walking across the courtyard.

Tim's blue eyes filled with a mixture of relief and joy. He handed her the stolen flowers, and seeking an outward sign of the O'Neill's cruelty, studied her appearance as they started down the path toward the graveyard.

Kathryn was pale, but except for the fading bruise on her cheek, her face was unmarred.

"Does it hurt, my lady?" Tim blurted out. Then, shamed by his boldness, he lowered his gaze and fixed it on her belly.

Kathryn stopped short, looked at him curiously and followed his gaze. "It hurts a great deal," she answered, assuming he spoke of childbirth.

Tim groaned inwardly. He'd the fiercest urge to skewer the O'Neill on a sharp sword. How could a great man like the O'Neill be cruel to such a kind, gentle lady?

"I—I—I'd like to help," Tim said.

"That's unnecessary. I can manage." Kathryn hid her amusement at his strange yet touching offer. For the birth of Hugh's heir, a midwife would be more suitable than a stable boy.

"You help me by being a true friend," she added. "I will always cherish your friendship, my gallant protector."

Kathryn smiled and touched his scarlet cheek. Embarrassed but pleased and proud, Tim returned her smile.

At the graveyard Kathryn knelt in front of Shane's grave, crossed herself, and began to pray. Suddenly, a shadow fell across the tombstone. Startled, she whirled around, her hands flying to her chest.

"Tim, you surprised me," she cried, seeing the boy kneeling beside her.

"I must speak to you, my lady, now we are away from the O'Neill ears." Tim glanced around furtively, assuring himself they were alone.

"Yes?"

Tim looked away, afraid if he met those piercing green eyes, she would know he was lying. "As I was walkin' home from the village last evenin', a stranger stopped me. He knew we were friends and gave me a message for you."

"A man?" Kathryn asked. "What did he look like?"

Tim shook his head, saying, " 'Twas too dark to see him clearly."

"And the message?" Kathryn's heart pounded furiously with excitement.

"Meet him here after dusk on Friday. Arrangements have been made." Looking into her dazzling green eyes, Tim almost confessed that he was the one who would help her escape, but remembering Maura's warning, held his tongue. All would be for nothing if he did not.

Hugh is somewhere near, Kathryn thought, her eyes sparkling with a vibrancy Tim had never seen, beguiling him. "Will you do something for me?" she asked.

"Anythin'! After all, you're my very best friend."

"Promise you won't mention this to anyone," Kathryn said.

"I swear upon my sainted mother's soul."

"That's a good boy." Kathryn touched his cheek. "Would you like to live in Dublin with my husband and me?"

Tim was surprised. "Y-y-you'd take me with you?"

"Gladly, if you've the inclination. Think about it."

14

On the day Kathryn received the message from the mysterious stranger, Hugh and his warriors rode into the MacDonnell's camp in Antrim. With a smile of greeting upon his lips, Sorley Boy MacDonnell stepped forward and shook Hugh's hand. In those brief seconds, each man tried to gauge the other. Behind Hugh, the O'Neill warriors stood on guard, their hands resting on the hilts of their swords.

" 'Tis no trap," Sorley Boy said, trying to relieve the tension that crackled around them. "I am a man of honor."

"I believe you," Hugh replied. "I have, of course, taken precautions to keep you that way." At the other man's questioning look, he added, "If your word proves false, the whole of Bess Tudor's forces will shortly be breathing down your neck."

A frown crossed the MacDonnell chieftain's rugged features, then vanished. Sorley Boy chuckled. "You must be a man of great wisdom such as myself. Were I wearin' your illustrious boots, I would've done the same." He gestured to his tent, saying, "Come inside and we'll refresh ourselves."

Followed by Patrick and Francis MacDonnell, Sorley

Boy and Hugh walked into the tent. After pouring generous cups of whiskey, Sorley Boy gestured Hugh to sit, and the two men eyed each other.

On short acquaintance, Sorley Boy thought, Hugh O'Neill seemed calmer than his troublesome relatives, Shane and Turlough, and appeared less impulsive, more like his grandfather Conn O'Neill in temperament. His eyes shrewd with intelligence, Hugh exhibited a cautious cunning. Whether Hugh O'Neill boded good or ill for Ireland remained to be seen.

On short acquaintance, Hugh thought as he stared at the older man, the MacDonnell seemed honorable. Unpolished but intelligent and practical, Sorley Boy MacDonnell appeared strong enough to hold the reins of his clan but incapable of firmly grasping the reins of a war-torn Ireland. In battle, a good man to fight beside.

"The countess once saved my life," Sorley Boy said, making himself comfortable on his cot. "I'm helpin' her because of that."

"What's your plan?" Hugh asked.

"The assault on Dungannon must be swift and silent," Sorley Boy replied. "With your men disguised as mine, surprise is our best advantage. You, however, must ride as my prisoner. If we're intercepted by Turlough's men, I'll say I'm deliverin' you to him."

" 'Tis entirely too risky," Patrick blurted out. "I don't like it."

"We've few choices," Hugh said, turning to his man.

"Slipping a dagger in your back would be just as easy as it was with Shane," Patrick reminded him. "The MacDonnells are untrustworthy."

Young Francis MacDonnell growled, outraged at the insult, and reached for his sword. With a casual wave of his hand, the MacDonnell chieftain stopped his son.

"Your man has good reason to distrust us," Sorley Boy admitted, "but Shane O'Neill's execution was not by my order."

Hugh nodded, accepting the man's word. Not that it really mattered. Hugh had been planning his uncle's demise anyway.

"It's your choice," Sorley Boy said, leaning toward him. "Remember—if Turlough's dispatched, you become undisputed head of the O'Neill clan."

"That thought already crossed my mind," Hugh said.

"As the O'Neill, what would be your goals for Ireland?" Sorley Boy asked.

The topic was treason. Unwilling to voice his thoughts in front of an audience, Hugh shifted uncomfortably and flicked a glance at Francis MacDonnell. Catching his son's eye, Sorley Boy indicated he wanted privacy.

At a nod from Hugh, Patrick left too. Though Patrick was privy to Hugh's ideas, his presence at the confidential meeting would needlessly insult the younger MacDonnell.

Hugh swallowed a gulp of whiskey, looked the older man straight in the eye and said, "Tell me how my wife saved your life."

The MacDonnell drained his whiskey and leaned back. "Let me see," Sorley Boy began. " 'Twas about four or five years ago—"

"Lord MacDonnell?"

Startled by the feminine voice, Sorley Boy MacDonnell moved. "Who's there?" he called, getting slowly to his feet.

"The O'Neill's wife."

The MacDonnell walked to the iron bars, and Kathryn held the candle up so he could see her. Speechless, the aging Irish chieftain stared at the incredibly beautiful face peering at him.

"My lord, are you seriously hurt?"

No answer.

"My lord?"

"It's a pleasure to make your acquaintance," he said finally. "But what the hell are you doin' here?"

"I've brought you warmed water, salve, and food," she told him. His mouth dropped open at that.

"Lady O'Neill," Sorley Boy explained, thinking her lovely but dim witted. "I'm a prisoner here, not your guest. Aidin' your husband's enemy can only win his wrath."

"You aren't my husband's enemy," Kathryn replied. "Queen Elizabeth is his enemy, and yours also."

"Perhaps, but I doubt your husband would approve of what you're doin'."

Without bothering to answer, Kathryn wet a cloth in the warmed water and handed it through the bars. With a smile, the MacDonnell accepted it. Next came the salve. When he finished, Kathryn passed him bread, ham, cheese, hard-cooked eggs, and a skin of wine.

"Why are you doin' this?" he asked, chewing on a bit of ham.

"For my husband, of course."

"For O'Neill?" The MacDonnell was surprised by her words.

"Ireland's a wild place," Kathryn explained. "If Shane is ever in need of kindness, I hope you'll think of me and return my kindness to him."

"O'Neill is a lucky man to hold the love of a woman like you."

"My lady, we must not linger," Polly whined.

Suddenly, the door above them crashed open. Kathryn and Polly whirled around. Standing at the top of the stairs was Shane, his face contorted in rage.

"You betraying bitch!" Shane roared, running down the

stairs. Patrick followed behind and pleaded with him to stay calm.

Kathryn was paralyzed, her gaze never leaving her husband's face. Reaching her, Shane struck out with his fist and sent her flying several feet away to fall on the floor. Polly screamed and Patrick grabbed his arms from behind.

"Not your fist, man!" Patrick yelled in his ear. "You'll kill her!"

"Stay out of this." Shane shrugged his man off.

Weeping, Kathryn huddled on the floor where she'd fallen. Shane yanked her up by her hair and struck again, then threw her against the wall. Trying to protect herself, Kathryn faced the wall.

"Please," she begged. "Please don't hurt me."

Reaching for her, Shane hesitated until the MacDonnell inadvertently stoked his rage.

"O'Neill!" Sorley Boy shouted from his cell. "You're a fool!"

As Kathryn slid down the wall, Shane yanked her up and whirled her around. He raised his fist to strike. Unexpectedly, Kathryn struck out first and kneed him in the groin. Shane doubled over with pain, and she raced toward the stairs, seeking escape.

Halfway up, Kathryn felt a hand grabbing her ankle, pulling her back. "Patrick!" she cried, finding nothing to hold. "Help me!"

Grabbing him from behind, Patrick pulled with all his might, and Shane fell back, still clutching his wife's ankle.

Kathryn toppled sideways off the stairs. With a nauseating thud, she landed on her belly and lay motionless on the stone floor below.

"Oh, God!" Shane moaned, kneeling beside her. He turned her over. Kathryn's nose and lips were bleeding like a river, and ugly bruises were already rising on her pale skin.

"She's losin' the baby," Patrick said flatly.

Shane's gaze darted to her bloodstained skirt, the tell-tale spot of red growing larger with each passing second. "Find Maude," Shane ordered as he lifted Kathryn into his arms.

"Early the next mornin'," Sorley Boy finished, "your man—Patrick, is it?—came to the dungeon and released me. Your uncle even provided a horse and enough supplies to get me back to Dunluce Castle."

Grim faced, Hugh remarked, "And so, you repaid my wife's kindness by murdering her husband."

"I've said, 'twas no order of mine that laid Shane O'Neill low," Sorley Boy said. "I was gone from Dunluce at the time. My blockheaded son thought to avenge my treatment at the hands of your uncle. Do you suppose there'll be war between us because of this?"

"No, your son merely robbed me of the pleasure of dispatching my uncle," Hugh admitted.

Sorley Boy nodded, then asked, "And now will you answer my question?"

"Question?"

"What be your goals for the O'Neills and Ireland?"

"My long-range plans for Ireland do not include Bess Tudor," Hugh revealed.

"Such as?"

"Rebellion. Irish must govern Irish."

"Fine words, to be sure," Sorley Boy remarked, unimpressed. "But how can that be accomplished?"

"The northern and southern clans must unite," Hugh said. "We'll train our men in secret, as many as can be enlisted—"

"The English allow us to keep only five hundred warriors," Sorley Boy interrupted. "Not enough for victory."

Hugh smiled. "We're allowed five hundred warriors *at one time*," he corrected. "After five hundred have been trained, we'll drop their names and make room for another five hundred. Again and again and again."

"A simple yet sage idea." Grinning, Sorley Boy decided he liked this young upstart. The man was destined for greatness. "Bein' forbidden to import lead, how do we arm these myriad warriors?"

"Unfortunately, the keeps and castles of Ireland are in sad need of repair," Hugh told him, drawing a puzzled look from the other man. "Separately, each chieftain will suffer severe roofing problems. The lead will be obtained by special permission, but upon its arrival, transformed into ammunition."

"The English queen favors you enough to grant this permission?"

"My wife's brother is a favorite of her majesty's."

"You could become the most famous of all the precedin' O'Neills," Sorley Boy commented. Ireland's future appeared brighter. "If you're with me, that is."

"Do you doubt I'd risk anything to recover my wife?" Hugh asked. "Above all, Katie is my first priority."

"Ah, Lady Kathryn." Sorley Boy sighed, then smiled at a memory. "When they brought her in, she refused to curtsey. Said she'd as lief pay homage to pigs."

Hugh smiled. A thoughtful pause halted their conversation as both conjured the vision of a copper-haired, green-eyed, and extremely willful lady in their minds. Hugh's gaze met and held Sorley Boy's.

"How fared she when you saw her?" Hugh asked.

Good God! the MacDonnell thought, seeing the anguish in the younger man's eyes. Though Hugh O'Neill probably began his marriage to gain his title, he'd ended by loving the woman.

"Well?" Hugh prodded.

"She was bein' cared for as befittin' a woman of nobility," Sorley Boy evaded.

"*Damn you!* That's not what I meant!"

"I know what you meant." Sorley Boy decided he'd better speak truthfully lest the man be startled when he next faced his wife. "Your suspicions are well founded; Turlough raped your wife. I heard her screams, but intervention at that point would've been suicidal. There was nothin' I could do, and there's nothin' to be done for it now. What's done is past."

Drained of color, Hugh's face contorted in frustrated rage. He opened his mouth to speak, but the MacDonnell cut him off.

"Lower your heat, man," Sorley Boy warned. "Strategy requires the coolest of heads." He stood and changed the subject, saying, "Your men are as weary as mine. We'll rest here for a couple of days and then be off."

"Agreed," Hugh said, standing up. "I'll need the time to alert the spies I've placed there." The two men shook hands and walked outside.

Friday arrived. Breaking her usual routine, Kathryn did not visit the graveyard in the morning. Failing to appear for supper that night would arouse no suspicion if she feigned illness during the day. Apprised of this in advance, Tim had been instructed to appear in the courtyard that morning as usual and pretend surprise when she failed to appear. Kathryn even contrived to make Turlough himself deliver the message that she was sick.

Thinking about the scene with Turlough that morning

and how easily he'd been manipulated made Kathryn smile . . .

"My stomach is weak," she'd complained, "and my head a bit dizzy. Please tell Tim I won't be visiting the graveyard today."

"You want *me* to carry a message to that witless boy?" Turlough asked, incredulous.

"You pass through the courtyard on your way," she replied. "Would it hurt your pride so to speak to a boy who idolizes you?"

Perhaps he did owe the boy a debt, Turlough had thought. Since the day at the graveyard when Tim had foolishly jumped to her defense, Kathryn had been on her best behavior, appropriately respectful, meek, and submissive.

"A point well taken," Turlough had agreed. "Consider it done."

Dusk's shadows were lengthening. Sprawled on her bed, Kathryn decided her plan had progressed nicely. She'd lain in bed the whole day and done a fine piece of playacting. As soon as she sent an unsuspecting Maude away for the evening, Kathryn would don her old stable boy clothing that she'd found at the bottom of her rosewood chest. By the time she was missed, she'd be safely away with Hugh.

Kathryn reached out and tugged on the bell rope. When Maude appeared a few minutes later, Kathryn smiled wanly and asked, "Will you tell Turlough I'm too sick to come down tonight?"

"Yes." Maude reached out and touched her forehead. "I'll bring you a tray after the men are served."

"*No!*" Kathryn cried. "I—I mean . . . Don't bother yourself. I'm not hungry."

"Sick or no, the babe needs nourishment," Maude insisted. "I'll be hearin' no arguments. Understand?"

"Yes." Kathryn hadn't shared her plans because the older woman would have tried to dissuade her from the dangerous escape. Now, Kathryn hoped Maude had the sense to not sound the alarm when she returned and found the chamber empty.

As soon as the door closed behind the housekeeper, Kathryn leapt off the bed and dashed across the chamber to the rosewood chest. Recklessly strewing its contents every which way, she dug to the bottom and pulled out her old stable boy breeches, shirt, stockings, cap, and riding boots.

Her heart pounded and her hands shook, stubbornly refusing to begin changing her clothing. What if someone, especially Turlough, entered while she was changing? How could she explain?

Indecision gripped Kathryn. Should she transform herself into a stable boy now or carry her disguise and change behind the chapel?

Now, Kathryn decided. Disguised as a stable boy, she had a better chance of escaping undetected. Where was the sense in carrying her disguise if she was unable to get out of the door?

Kathryn pulled off her night shift and donned her shirt and stockings, then groaned in dismay. The breeches were too tight across her swollen belly. There was nothing to be done for it. She fastened the breeches as far as she could, and hiding her belly, wore the shirttails outside. She pinned her hair on top of her head and covered the flaming tresses with her cap. Finally, Kathryn pulled on the black leather riding boots and headed for the door.

Pressing her ear against it, Kathryn listened for activity in the corridor. There was none. She opened it a crack and peered out. No one was about. Steeling herself with a deep breath, Kathryn took that fateful step into the corridor and closed the door.

Hugging the wall with her back, Kathryn stayed hidden in the shadows as she glided down the dimly lit corridor to the top of the stairs. The noise from the great hall reached her ears, and she halted. Should she leave by the front or the back? The rear of the castle would be alive with servants, but at the front she might fall prey to any of Turlough's men arriving late for supper.

Kathryn started down the stairs, her back to the stone wall until she reached the bottom. The path across the foyer to the front door was clear. Unless someone loitered outside in the courtyard, she would make it.

Constricting fear coiled around her chest, making breathing difficult, but her feet moved of their own volition. On tiptoes, Kathryn scurried silently across the foyer like a capering mouse, and in one swift motion, opened the door and flew outside. The courtyard was deserted.

Dashing around the building to the right, Kathryn entered the gardens and leaned against the stone wall. Her heart pounded frantically and her breath came in short, raspy gasps. Inside the warmth of her body, the baby kicked its displeasure. To hide her paleness, Kathryn smudged her face with a handful of dirt, then cut across the garden to the rear of the chapel and slipped into the graveyard.

As Kathryn was blackening her face with dirt, Maude left the pantry and started down the corridor toward the foyer. Turlough, annoyed at having to fetch Kathryn, walked out of the great hall but spied the housekeeper and waited at the bottom of the stairs.

"I'm bringin' Katie a tray," Maude offered by way of an explanation. "She's feelin' poorly."

Turlough grimaced at the news. "Did she visit the graveyard today?"

"Are you deaf, boy?" Maude snapped. "The girl is sick and hasn't left her bed the whole day long."

"I'll deliver this," Turlough said, taking the tray. "We'll see how sick she really is."

"Don't you be frettin' her," Maude scolded.

"Return to your kitchen," Turlough ordered, aggravated by her lecturing tone. "I'm a man full grown and know what I'm about."

"Humph!" Turning on her heel, Maude retraced her steps down the corridor.

Marching into the deserted bedchamber, Turlough saw the wildly scattered clothing littering the floor, then saw the empty bed. Shouting for Liam and Maude, he raced downstairs into the hall, and when they hurried forward to answer his call, thrust the tray into the housekeeper's hands.

"The bitch has flown," Turlough said, "but I don't think far. Maude, check inside." He turned to Liam, saying, "I'll check the graveyard and you go to the stables."

As Turlough was bellowing for Liam and Maude, Kathryn slipped through the graveyard. The night was moonlessly dark and she was unable to see more than a few feet in front of herself. Her fright-heightened senses alerted her to every nuance of sound.

Then it came, the neighing of a horse. Kathryn blindly walked toward the sound and nearly collided with one of the two waiting horses. Much to her surprise, Tim stood where she had expected to see Hugh.

"What do you do here?" she asked. "Are you coming with us?"

"I—I—I'm helpin' you escape," Tim answered. "There never was any stranger, nor message either."

Bitter tears of disappointment sprang from Kathryn's eyes and streaked her smudged cheeks. She was smart enough to realize that a pregnant woman and slow-witted boy would never make it to Dublin alone. This was extreme folly, and dangerously so.

"I'm not leaving," Kathryn said, wondering how to sneak back to her chamber without being detected. "I thought my husband had sent the message."

"We've no time for tarryin'," Tim insisted as if she hadn't spoken. "We must be off."

"Risking Turlough's wrath is too dangerous," she argued.

"But I want to help my very best friend," Tim said, grabbing her upper arm. "Let's go."

Kathryn tried to pull away. Suddenly, the boy's grip loosened and his eyes widened in pained shock. As Tim toppled over, Kathryn tried to break his fall, but his weight forced her to her knees. It was then Kathryn saw the dagger protruding from his back.

"*Holy Mother!*" she cried. "*Tim!*"

His eyes vacant in death, Tim was beyond answering.

"Oh, God," Kathryn wailed over the fallen boy.

Turlough reached to retrieve his dagger. Kathryn moaned as the hand of destruction pulled the dagger out of Tim's back and wiped its bloody blade on the dead boy's shirt.

Kathryn looked up. Turlough towered over her like a terrible god of vengeance. As Kathryn stared into the cold, dispassionate eyes of death, her instinct for survival surfaced. She leapt to her feet and ran.

With two long strides, Turlough grabbed and whirled her around, then struck out with his fist, catching her near the top of her cheekbone. Reeling from the blow, Kathryn staggered back, but Turlough grabbed her upper arm and kept her from falling. Again he struck and blood gushed from her nose and lips.

"You treacherous bitch," he growled, dragging her down the path toward the courtyard. More unconscious than not, Kathryn was beyond protesting.

"Liam!" Turlough shouted, passing through the crowd of gaping warriors in the courtyard. "Get the horses and that stable boy's body in the graveyard!"

Wringing her hands in worry, Maude waited inside the foyer and gasped, horrified, when she saw Kathryn's bleeding face and Turlough's deadly expression. Without a word, Turlough marched toward the stairs, and Maude raced after the gruesome couple.

So abruptly did Turlough turn around to face Maude that Kathryn fell to her knees. He yanked her up, nearly dislocating her shoulder, but ignored her cry of pain.

"Shroud Tim's body," Turlough ordered. "We'll bury him in the mornin'."

"Holy Mother of God!" Maude cried, making the sign of the cross. Her gaze shifted to Kathryn. "The lass is hurt."

"I'll take care of this she devil," Turlough said, then pulled Kathryn, whimpering but unresisting, up the stairs.

Once inside the bedchamber, Turlough threw Kathryn to the floor as if she was an unspeakably vile thing. Through blurred vision, Kathryn gazed up the long length of the wrathful giant glaring with unmasked hatred down at her.

"Please don't hurt me," she pleaded.

Turlough snorted in disgust, then walked away to retrieve one of her discarded chemises. He dampened it in the water basin and returned to where she lay, trembling in fear. She shrank away when he squatted down beside her.

"Move and I'll kill you," Turlough threatened, grabbing

her upper arm in a punishing grip. None too gently, he wiped the blood and dirt from her face, then examined her split lip and blackening eye. Kathryn was not a pretty sight at the moment, but she'd bear no scars.

"You were escapin'."

"No." Kathryn tried to back away.

Turlough's powerful grip held her in place. "Are you accusin' that boy of kidnappin'? Attempted rape, perhaps?"

"No!"

"It doesn't matter now. He's dead."

The harsh reality of Tim's brutal murder slammed—harder than Turlough's fist—into Kathryn. *"You bastard!"* she shouted into his face, insane fury replacing the fear in her eyes. "Loathsome swine!"

Turlough raised his hand to strike but halted its progress in midair, then lowered it. "You're the guilty one," he said. "You led that poor boy to the slaughter. Live with that, if you can." Turlough smiled coldly at her stricken expression, then stood and left the chamber, being careful to lock the door behind him.

"No," Kathryn protested to the empty chamber. She buried her face in her hands and sobbed brokenly, "Oh, T-Tim. I never meant . . . Forgive me."

Spring teased Dungannon's inhabitants the next morning. The sun shone and the western wind caressed the land gently. Peace pervaded the air, so at odds with the violence of the previous evening.

Turlough stood in the graveyard and watched Tim's shrouded body being lowered into its final resting place. Uncertain of what had been transpiring the previous night, Turlough knew the boy had been no match for his prowess, even had he been armed.

Cold logic pointed at Kathryn as the instigator, enticing

a dull-witted child into helping her escape. A gentlewoman like Katie would never use a child's affection to her own advantage, Turlough thought. Or would she? Perhaps he should thrust the bitch into the darkest dungeon lest she entice a more able man to do her bidding.

No matter, Turlough decided. There was nothing to be done for the poor boy now. Shrugging off his feelings of guilt as easily as a cloak, Turlough turned away from the grave and cast Tim's murder from his mind.

That stupid fool, Maura fumed, standing near the graveyard's entrance. She should have known the idiot would fail.

As Turlough walked toward her, Maura masked her seething fury beneath a placid expression. "It wasn't your fault," she said when he reached her.

Occupied with thoughts of Kathryn, Turlough absently patted her shoulder, saying, "You're a loyal lass."

Preening at his touch, Maura believed that all was not lost. "You're welcome to visit my cottage," she invited him. "Bein' away from the pryin' eyes of your men would be relaxin'."

For a brief moment, Turlough studied the beautiful face turned up to his but then refused. "Another time, perhaps. Duty demands that I see the countess now."

"She's the guilty one and should be punished," Maura hissed, startling him with her hatred. "Shane lies in yonder grave because of her. Now Tim. The Englishwoman's a witch and must be burned before we're all destroyed!"

"Shane lies in yonder grave because the MacDonnells murdered him," Turlough corrected. "Return to the village and forget such foolishness."

Maura stalked away in a huff. She would not let Kathryn steal this O'Neill from her. Obviously, the English witch had cast a spell on Turlough, Maura concluded, else she would have been Dungannon's lady by now.

As Turlough was watching Tim's body being lowered into its grave, Maude unlocked the door to Kathryn's bedchamber. Scanning the chamber, she saw the garments strewn wildly around.

Holy Mother of God! Maude exclaimed inwardly, then looked toward the bed where Kathryn slept. Why did she do it? The MacDonnell had warned her to do nothing until arrangements could be made with her husband. Now she lay bruised and battered, and the boy dead.

Maude walked across the chamber and set the breakfast tray on the bedside table, then sat on the edge of the bed and looked at the sleeping face in the day's harsh light. Kathryn's bottom lip was swollen, an ugly scab beginning to form where it had been cut, and her eye, black and swollen, was a worse sight than the lip.

Kathryn stretched and moaned, every muscle vehemently protesting the movement. Her face and body ached horribly, and she wondered if she was dying. Kathryn opened her eyes and stared into the housekeeper's face.

"You're a sight to behold," Maude said. "How do you feel?"

"Like the mortally wounded," Kathryn answered, her hands dropping to her belly. Something was terribly, horribly wrong, but she was unable to remember exactly what.

"The babe is with us," Maude assured her.

Relieved, Kathryn tried to smile, but the effort was too painful. "Fetch me a night shift, please."

With Maude's help, Kathryn pulled on the night shift and used the chamber pot. Reluctant to return to bed, Kathryn stood at the window overlooking the deserted courtyard.

"Where is everyone?" she asked.

"Buryin' Tim."

Tears welled up in Kathryn's eyes and streamed down her battered face. Her loyal friend! If only she hadn't hesitated, Tim would still live. His death was her fault. Covering her face with her hands, Kathryn shook with the force of her sobs, and weeping made her stomach churn and heave.

Maude rushed her across the chamber to the pot. When Kathryn's spasms ended, the housekeeper helped her back into bed, then dampened a washing cloth and gently wiped the sweat from her aching face.

The door crashed open. Marching purposefully across the chamber, Turlough motioned the housekeeper to leave.

Maude stood up and rounded on him, warning, "Go gently, boy. The lass is hurtin' and unable to survive more of your tender courtin'."

Frowning, Turlough stared at Kathryn and winced inwardly at the sight of her battered face. Perhaps he should not have handled her so roughly, but she'd been attempting to escape.

"You won't be visitin' the graveyard again," Turlough said. "Indeed, you'll consider yourself lucky to leave this chamber."

Kathryn turned her face into the pillow and wept. Without thinking, Turlough sat on the edge of the bed and touched her shoulder in an effort to console her. Gradually Kathryn quieted, her breathing evened, and she slept.

Why did she try to escape? Turlough wondered, genuinely perplexed. Indeed, why had she flown from Dungannon and married the bastard's son? Every woman he'd ever known had considered him the ultimate catch. Honorably, he'd offered her marriage and been rejected, but that didn't matter anymore. He would never relinquish her until death claimed one of them.

Three days passed. Downcast, Kathryn gazed out her chamber window at the morning, also downcast.

Turlough had questioned her several times about that fateful night, but convinced that Tim could not have plotted her escape on his own, Kathryn had repeated the same tale over and over of persuading the boy to steal her a horse so she could escape. Whoever had masterminded the plan had been trying to help, and another death for her cause would be unbearable. Kathryn gladly shouldered the blame, and in the process, frustrated Turlough, who sensed she was lying. The most intriguing question was who had it been? Who would dare cross wills with the head of the O'Neill clan?

Kathryn sighed in dejection. Another long day alone in her chamber loomed before her. The door had been unlocked since the previous day, but doubtful she would be allowed any freedom, Kathryn had not ventured out. Now she was truly a prisoner.

Maude knocked and entered to retrieve the untouched breakfast tray, but pitying the young woman's isolation, stayed to tidy the chamber. The housekeeper worried about Kathryn's withdrawal and apparent lack of interest in what was happening around her.

Kathryn turned away from the window and spoke so abruptly the housekeeper jumped. "Maude?" she asked. "Where is Turlough?"

"In the hall."

"Good." Kathryn headed for the door.

"And where do you think you're goin'?" Maude asked, surprised.

"To speak with him."

" 'Twould be unwise," Maude cautioned. "Don't be

givin' Turlough the opportunity to remember you're here and feelin' better."

"I doubt he's forgotten I'm here," Kathryn said, opening the door. "Besides, I'll go mad if I stay in this chamber another minute."

At the top of the stairs, Kathryn hesitated. Was she doing the right thing? Or was this folly? Slaying her was the worst Turlough could do, and considering the way she felt, that might be a blessing.

Kathryn squared her shoulders, lifted her chin a notch and started down the stairs. Her bravado faded as she neared the bottom, and on leaden feet she walked toward the great hall. Standing at the entrance, Kathryn took a deep, calming breath and stepped inside. No one noticed her. On trembling legs Kathryn advanced on the high table where Turlough sat, deep in conversation with Liam.

As she passed them, the warriors stopped talking and watched her. Sensing the sudden change in atmosphere, Turlough looked up and saw Kathryn standing in front of him.

When Liam stood to offer her his chair, Turlough snapped, "Sit down!" Scarlet with embarrassment, the man obeyed instantly.

Staring at Kathryn, Turlough recognized her apprehension. *I can almost smell her fear,* he thought with satisfaction.

Deathly pale, Kathryn stepped back in near panic. Going to the hall had been a terrible blunder. Oh, why hadn't she listened to Maude? Turning around, Kathryn tried to retreat, but the cold voice of authority rang out.

"Halt," Turlough ordered. When she faced him, he said, " 'Twould seem you've somethin' important on your mind, or Maude would not have disobeyed my order by allowin' you to leave your chamber."

"She could not stop me," Kathryn said, absolving the housekeeper of wrongdoing.

"Yes, you are a stubborn wench," Turlough agreed. "Now, what is it you want?"

Kathryn hesitated, wishing she'd remained in her chamber.

"I haven't all day. What do you want?"

Mustering her courage, Kathryn stepped forward a pace and in a loud but quavering voice, said, "I w-want to v-visit the graveyard."

Turlough threw back his head and shouted with laughter, then looked around at his men and back at her. "Surely, you jest."

"No, I am—"

"Damn it!" Turlough snapped as his powerful hands came crashing down on the table. Without taking his gaze from her, Turlough stood and advanced on her. Kathryn returned his stare unflinchingly.

The wench has great courage, Turlough thought, *or else she's a fool.*

"You attempt escape via the graveyard and now want my permission to go there again?" Turlough's voice rumbled with contempt. "Madam, you amaze me."

"I beg you," Kathryn pleaded, and without thinking, reached out and touched his hand. "It's important."

Where she touched him burned. For several long moments, Turlough stared into her mesmerizing eyes, fathomless pools of green. Aware that his men were watching this interesting byplay, he said, "Enlighten us. Why is visiting the graveyard so important? Planning another escape, my dear?"

"I must tend my husband's grave and—"

"Your husband is in Dublin. Remember?"

"—and Tim," Kathryn went on as if he hadn't spoken. "I must apologize. Please . . ."

Glancing around the hall, Turlough saw sympathy etched on the faces of his men. How could he refuse such a touching request in the presence of a sympathetic audience?

"Very well," he agreed reluctantly, grasping her upper arm and leading her out of the hall. "I'll walk you outside."

In the courtyard, Turlough turned her around to face him and threatened, "You'll be watched, and if you try to run away, I'll kill Maude."

"I understand," Kathryn said. "I'd like flowers. May I go to the gardens first?" When he nodded, Kathryn started to turn away but stopped, remembering Daisy the wolfhound and her young family. "Has someone been caring for Tim's dogs?"

"The hounds belong to me," Turlough said. "As does everythin' else in Dungannon." His eyes softened as he looked down at her, and he reached out, his touch on her cheek surprisingly gentle. "Everythin'."

After tending Shane's grave, Kathryn walked the short distance to Tim's grave, knelt in front of it and arranged the flowers she'd taken from the garden. Making the sign of the cross, she bowed her head and began to pray for the boy's departed soul, but soon her troubled thoughts surfaced.

"I'm sorry," Kathryn whispered. "You lie in an early grave because of me. If only I hadn't hesitated, argued—" Overcome by guilty remorse, she broke off with a sob.

Those struck down by death are freed from life's miseries, she thought, *while those of us left behind are sorrow's tortured prisoners.*

Lost in her misery, Kathryn failed to hear another's approach. Standing up, she turned to leave but found dark, hate-filled eyes glaring at her. Kathryn cried out, startled.

"Aye, you're a witch with them green cat's eyes," Maura hissed, then made a protective sign of the cross. "I won't let you destroy this O'Neill like you did the other."

"Stand aside," Kathryn ordered sharply.

Motionless, Maura silently refused to move. A satisfied smile touched her lips as she noted the other woman's bruises.

"Stand aside, or you'll regret it," Kathryn threatened.

The English witch is no longer pretty, Maura thought, then laughed and walked away.

Kathryn watched her go. Walking down the path toward the courtyard, Kathryn felt lonelier than she'd ever been before. Surrounded by enemies, she found it difficult to believe Dungannon had once been her home.

15

As she'd done each day for the past week, Kathryn stopped at the graveyard entrance and looked around. In spite of the sun's warmth, a chill of unease tickled her spine and made her shiver.

Nothing seemed unusual. Banishing that awful feeling of being watched, Kathryn stepped inside the graveyard and walked toward Tim's grave.

She knelt in front of the grave and arranged the fresh-cut flowers she'd brought, then made the sign of the cross and prayed for the boy's departed soul. Intending to leave without visiting her late husband's grave, she stood and turned around.

"Oh!" Kathryn cried, startled.

With her lips curled in a silent snarl, Maura stood a few feet away. Kathryn, stunned by the wild light in the other woman's eyes, stepped back a pace.

"Castin' spells won't help you now," Maura said. "You should've fled when you had the chance."

"You planned my escape with Tim."

Maura stepped threateningly closer, and in a flash of movement, raised her hand to strike. Before the dagger's glimmering blade hit its mark, Kathryn grabbed her wrist and pushed with all her might. Maura, caught off balance, fell with a thud to the ground.

Shouting for help, Kathryn ran toward the graveyard entrance, but pregnancy slowed her movements. She tripped over her skirt and fell, her hands protectively clutching her belly as she went down.

Maura was upon her in an instant, and the two bitter rivals grappled in the dirt. Kathryn tried to fend her attacker off but tired quickly, and faltering, was wrested onto her back.

The gleaming dagger slashed downward, slicing the air.

With a burst of energy born of desperation, Kathryn rolled to her right and threw her arms up to ward off the fatal blow. The blade caught the palm of her left hand, and a torrent of blood gushed out.

"*No!*" Kathryn screamed.

Again Maura raised the dagger to strike. A hand appeared from nowhere and grabbed her wrist, halting its deadly descent.

"Connivin' slut," Turlough growled, knocking the blade out of her hand. He twirled her around and backhanded her, sending her sprawling on the ground.

Turlough turned back to Kathryn but caught the glint of steel from the corner of his eye. He kicked the dagger out of Maura's hand and grabbed her around the neck, squeezing and squeezing the life's breath from her body.

Kathryn stared in horror as Maura's struggles lessened, then ceased. Shaking with fright, she leapt to her feet and ran toward Tim's grave, shrieking, "Help! Someone help me!"

"Come back," Turlough shouted, then swore in irritation and started after her.

Kathryn whirled around and around, desperately seeking a hiding place. It was then she felt her throbbing hand

and looked down at her bleeding palm. Blood covered her skirt and blouse.

"Oh, God," she moaned, falling to her knees.

"I'm not going to hurt you," Turlough said, standing beside her. He removed his jerkin and wrapped it around her hand, then lifted her into his arms and hurried down the path to the courtyard.

"Maude!" Turlough called as he climbed the stairs. He gingerly set Kathryn down on her bed and turned to the housekeeper, explaining, "Maura tried to do her in."

"I'll need hot water," Maude said, glancing at the blood-stained jerkin. "Send someone up with my needle and thread." Noting Kathryn's white complexion and half-closed eyes, she called over her shoulder, "And send up a goblet of warmed wine and my sleepin' herbs."

Downstairs Turlough did as Maude had ordered, then decided it was a good time to dispose of Maura's body. He walked outside to the courtyard.

"Hey!" one of his men shouted, running up the path from the stables. "We've a problem—"

Whoosh! Whoosh! Whoosh! A barrage of arrows sliced the air. One caught the warrior's shoulder, felling him. Another, bearing the earl of Tyrone's personal insignia, pierced the ground in front of Turlough's boots.

Dungannon's courtyard filled with MacDonnell and O'Neill warriors. Taken by surprise, Turlough's men laid down their arms.

"Good day to you, cousin," Hugh said, appearing from nowhere to confront his wife's captor.

"I've been expectin' you," Turlough replied. "It's a good day for dyin', is it not?"

"If you've the inclination to meet your Maker," Hugh said, drawing his dagger. Regardless of allegiance, the warriors in the courtyard stepped back to watch the two feuding kinsmen.

Turlough chuckled without humor and drew his own dagger. Compared to him, the earl of Tyrone seemed puny, certainly no match for his superior size and strength.

Hugh and Turlough circled each other in a danse macabre. Each tried to gauge the other's strength and weakness. Turlough's reach was longer, but Hugh's frame proclaimed his agility.

"Come on, you son of a bastard," Turlough challenged. "You've got to get past me to reach your wife."

Without warning, Hugh leapt closer. He flicked the point of his blade across the other man's cheek, drawing first blood, and danced away.

"Are you shavin' or killin' me?" Turlough asked, sounding more confident than he actually felt. "Come closer and fight like a man."

Hugh refused to be baited. Killing a man like Turlough required a cool head. *And luck*.

Only the occasional grunts of the combatants and the whooshing of their blades broke the silence in the courtyard. Again and again they clashed and separated, neither able to win an advantage.

Suddenly Turlough jumped into the arc of his cousin's reach. Hugh swung wildly with his dagger and missed his target, and Turlough leapt back.

Hugh went after him. Expecting such a maneuver, Turlough used his booted foot to swipe his cousin's legs out from under him. Hugh, caught off balance, went down and lost his dagger in the fall.

In an instant Turlough was upon him. Just before the gleaming dagger slashed his throat, Hugh stayed that hand of death and strained with all his strength to keep it away.

"You're as soft as a girl from all those years of licking English boots at court," Turlough jeered.

Answering the insult, Hugh savagely kneed his cousin's groin. Turlough cried out and toppled sideways off him. Hugh rolled away, retrieved his dagger, and leapt to his feet.

Sweating and panting, the two men began circling each other again, taking occasional swipes at each other and then dancing away. When the end came, it was swift and unexpected.

"Beddin' Katie is worth the risk of dyin'," Turlough taunted, trying to goad his opponent into a foolish move. "So hot and willin' for it—"

Hugh growled in a rage and leapt inside the range of Turlough's reach. Glinting steel slashed the air in an arc toward his chest. Hugh feinted to one side, switched the blade from his right hand to his left in a lightning flash of movement, and hurled it toward the other man's throat. In one swift motion, he dived to the ground, rolled away and leapt to his feet.

Stunned, Turlough dropped his weapon and his hands clutched at the dagger protruding from his throat. With a bloody gurgle, Turlough toppled over and lay still.

Then it came. An agonized wail pierced the air.

Kathryn! Hugh, chased by Patrick, ran inside and followed the sound of his wife's cry up the stairs. The pain-filled wail was abruptly cut off as they reached the bed-chamber door.

"Open up!" Hugh shouted, banging on the locked door.

"Maude, are you in there?" Patrick called. "It's me— Patrick. Open the door."

The bolt clicked and the door opened. Hugh and Patrick brushed past the housekeeper. Unconscious, Kathryn lay on the bed.

"What are you doing to her?" Hugh demanded, rushing across the chamber to his wife.

"Stitchin' her hand," Maude answered matter-of-factly. "She fainted."

Intending to gather his wife into his arms, Hugh started to sit on the edge of the bed, but Maude stopped him. "See to your men and let me finish my work here. When she comes around, I'll be givin' her a sleepin' draught to take the edge off the pain. It won't harm the babe either."

Then Maude rounded on Patrick, saying, "Well, boy, as soon as my back was turned, you sneaked off and married my daughter. The least you can do is get out of here."

Patrick grinned. "With all due respect, Maudie, I didn't marry Polly to make you my mother-in-law." With that parting shot, he headed for the door.

Hugh leaned over and kissed Kathryn's forehead. "Thank God," he said, then left the chamber.

"Amen to that," Maude murmured, picking up her needle.

Blaming himself for his wife's pain, Hugh retraced his steps down the stairs to the courtyard. He stepped outside. Someone had removed Turlough's corpse, and the warriors milled about, uncertain of what to do next.

Liam approached Hugh and knelt in front of him, saying, "I, Liam MacMartin, pledge my life and my fealty to the earl of Tyrone—the new O'Neill."

Wild cheering erupted from the O'Neill warriors, and Hugh stared at the man kneeling before him. Another of his goals had been realized, but his heart was strangely empty. Success without his wife by his side meant nothing.

"Arise," Hugh said to Liam.

In turn, each of Turlough's men pledged his life and loyalty to Hugh. When the last of them had finished, Hugh directed a group of men under Conal's supervision to prepare for Turlough's burial in the morning.

"How fares Lady Kathryn?" the MacDonnell asked, sidling up to Hugh.

"Not well."

"Poor lass," Sorley Boy sympathized. " 'Twill take time for recovery, but she's young, strong, and feisty of spirit."

"I hope so," Hugh replied.

Intending to request Hugh's hospitality for the night and leave at dawn for Dunluce Castle, Sorley Boy opened his mouth to speak but nothing came out. A lone rider, wearing the MacDonnell colors, careened at breakneck speed into Dungannon's crowded courtyard. Heedless of the O'Neill warriors who'd drawn their swords and encircled Hugh, the young man leapt off his horse.

"Angus!" the MacDonnell exclaimed, surprised by the unexpected sight of his kinsman. "What do you do here?"

The O'Neill warriors relaxed. At Hugh's nod, they allowed the young man safe passage to his clan chief.

"A terrible disaster has befallen Dunluce," Angus cried, his eyes wide, conveying the yet-unnamed horror. "Lady MacDonnell ordered me to fetch you and her husband home."

"What happened?" Sorley Boy asked. "Speak up."

"Dunluce's kitchens fell into the ragin' sea," Angus said, his voice filled with horror.

"*What?*" The MacDonnell was unable to believe what his ears heard. The O'Neill and MacDonnell warriors inched closer. They wanted to hear this unbelievable tale of destruction.

"In from the sea roared a fierce tempest with heavy rains and wild winds," Angus recounted in a highly dramatic tone. "Somehow, the kitchens got dislocated from the keep and—and fell into the sea!"

The listening warriors, believing the MacDonnell messenger half crazed, gaped at him with open mouths.

"Your son's lady knew not what to do," Angus said with a shrug of his shoulders. "Supper was late and we'd few left to serve it."

Sorley Boy MacDonnell threw back his head and shouted with laughter. "Since we've many hours of sunlight left," he said, turning to Hugh, "my men and I will be on our way."

"Come inside and refresh yourselves at least," Hugh invited him.

"That we will," Sorley Boy accepted. "I'm supposin' no supper will be awaitin' me at Dunluce."

"Sean, be certain the MacDonnell horses are fed," Hugh called to his man. The new O'Neill clan chief led his first guests into Dungannon's great hall.

Two hours later, Hugh escorted Sorley Boy MacDonnell back to the courtyard and wished him well on his long journey home, then retired to the O'Neill's private study. With him were Patrick and Liam. Deciphering Dungannon's badly kept accounts wasted the whole afternoon. That Turlough had been a better soldier than administrator became blatantly apparent to the three closeted within the study.

Hugh had a difficult time concentrating on the business at hand. His thoughts frequently traveled the short distance up the stairs to Kathryn. Was she awake or asleep? What was she thinking? Did she know he was here? Could she ever forgive him for his carelessness?

Supper time arrived. Hugh longed to fly up the stairs to Kathryn, but duty demanded on this of all nights he sup in the great hall with his men. Forcing himself to walk toward the great hall instead of the stairs taxed his inner strength.

Hugh excused himself when supper ended and leisurely

strolled out of the hall, stopping to chat and joke with groups of his men along the way. Sauntering into the foyer, Hugh saw it was deserted and quickened his pace, then took the stairs two at a time until he stood outside his wife's chamber.

Hugh opened the door and stepped inside. Maude sat in a chair beside the bed where Kathryn slept. Crossing the chamber, Hugh stared at his wife. Kathryn was pale and the evidence of abuse still marred her features. Maude had wrapped her injured hand in gauzy white linen.

"I gave her that sleepin' draught," the housekeeper told him. "She'll be feelin' better in the mornin'."

"Thank you," Hugh said. "Seek your own rest now."

"Well, I shouldn't be leavin' her alone," Maude protested.

"I'll be with her."

Maude eyed Hugh skeptically.

"I *am* her husband."

Maude nodded, albeit reluctantly, then stood and left the chamber.

Hugh removed his leather boots and jerkin, then rolled his shirtsleeves up. He sat in the chair beside the bed, stretched his legs out, and studied the object of so many days of worry. Leaning forward in the chair, Hugh rested his chin in his hands and wondered what deep secrets Kathryn dreamed in the heavy mist of her drug-induced sleep.

The corners of Kathryn's lips twitched and turned up in a smile, but then a frown chased the smile away. Murmuring unintelligible words, Kathryn rolled away from him and then back a moment later.

Hugh studied his wife's face. Her dreams appeared unpleasant.

When a solitary tear trickled down her cheek, Hugh sat

on the edge of the bed and gathered his sleeping wife into his arms. He stroked her back soothingly, and that seemed to quiet her. Gently, Hugh pressed her back on the bed, lay down beside her and gathered her into his arms.

How could he erase from her mind the hideous memory of what she'd suffered at Turlough's hands? Hugh wondered, his thoughts as troubled as his wife's dreams. How did he dare ask her to forgive and love him again?

It was a long, long time before Hugh closed his eyes in sleep.

16

Early the next morning Maude walked into Kathryn's chamber and lightly shook Hugh's shoulder. When his eyes flew open, she placed a finger across her lips in a gesture for silence and pointed toward the connecting door.

Hugh nodded and eased from his sleeping wife's side. After retrieving his discarded boots and jerkin, he padded across the chamber and followed the housekeeper through the door.

"Buryin' Turlough and Maura is a chore that's best done early," Maude said. "Warmed water for washin' is over there. I'll be stayin' with the countess 'til she wakes." With that, the housekeeper disappeared through the connecting door.

Hours later, Kathryn stood at her chamber window and gazed forlornly at the courtyard below. As if drawn to a magnet, her eyes locked on Hugh where he stood speaking with Patrick. Love for her husband ached in her heart and throbbed more painfully than her injured hand.

Turlough's lust had sullied her, Kathryn concluded, and Hugh would never want her again. At first opportunity, she would offer him an end to their marriage and go home.

Her heart wrenched at the thought, but she refused to live with a man who was unable to return her love.

Hugh glanced in the direction of the window and saw her standing there. Without another word, he walked abruptly away from Patrick in mid-sentence.

Bewildered, Patrick looked up and spied Kathryn just as she stepped back. *Ahh!* he thought, a wry smile touching his lips. For this, he would take immense pleasure in roasting the earl.

Without knocking, Hugh walked into the bedchamber, and Kathryn whirled around to face him. Husband and wife stood motionless for several moments, unaccountable awkwardness seizing both.

He appeared unchanged, Kathryn thought as she stared at him, but fatigue was finely etched beneath his eyes. Could he forget what Turlough had done and love her again?

Perusing his wife, Hugh noted the night shift and robe that clung to her body. Her recently brushed hair sparkled like fire in the sunlight from the window behind her. His gaze fell on her bandaged hand. Could she forgive him for what had been done to her and love him again?

Hugh crossed the chamber and sat in one of the chairs in front of the hearth, then motioned Kathryn to join him. "Are you feeling better?" he asked when she sat in the chair beside his.

"Yes," Kathryn answered without looking at him, afraid of the scorn she'd find in his eyes.

She despises me, Hugh decided when she refused to look at him. He cleared his throat nervously and said, "We must speak of the future."

Kathryn studied her lap with great interest. Her heart pounded, and she knew she had to speak before her meager courage and resolve fled. A clean break would be best for both of them. And yet—

"Look at me when I speak to you," Hugh interrupted her thoughts.

Kathryn looked at him through eyes clouded with pain. And Hugh almost wished she'd look away.

"I—I want to go home to England," Kathryn told him.

"You are my wife and your place is with me," Hugh said, the sternness in his voice disguising his agony. He would never let her leave. In time, he would win back her love and trust.

Kathryn was confused but hopeful. Didn't he want to be rid of her? "But—"

"Do you actually believe I would grant you leave to go while you carry Dungannon's heir?" As soon as the words had passed his lips, Hugh realized it was the wrong thing to say and longed to call them back.

Crestfallen, Kathryn paled. Her husband wanted her for the child she carried. And after the babe was delivered? What then? He would keep the child and cast the mother out.

"When do we return to Dublin?" Kathryn croaked, striving to hold back her tears.

"Next year."

"W-what?"

"I am the O'Neill, and my place is in Ulster with the family," Hugh said. "My son must be born here, among his own."

"What of my babies?" Kathryn cried. "I can't live without my girls."

"Don't fret yourself, sweet," Hugh said with an indulgent smile. "Of course, Maeve and Shana will be brought here."

"Don't fret myself?" Kathryn snapped, leaping to her

feet. She glared at her surprised husband, saying, "Do you think Dungannon is filled with happy memories, you unfeeling bastard? I won't stay in this evil place." In a flash of shining, copper tresses, Kathryn whirled away and stalked across the chamber to the window.

Hugh studied his boots with undue interest and said nothing. Several silent moments passed. Finally, he stood up and walked across the chamber to stand behind her. "I'm sorry, Katie. Can you forgive me for what you've suffered?"

Bewildered, Kathryn turned around and caught the unmasked anguish in his eyes. "It wasn't your fault."

Relief flooded his features, and his eyes cleared. Hugh reached for her uninjured hand, intending to escort it to his lips, but she shrank back.

"Please," Kathryn choked, pulling away. She yearned for his touch but was afraid to accept it.

"As you wish," Hugh said stiffly, then turned to leave. Tears, unseen by Kathryn, welled up in his eyes. Outside the chamber, Hugh paused for a moment and wiped a lone tear from his cheek. He took a deep breath to regain his composure and walked down the stairs to resume his duties as the new O'Neill clan chief.

Claiming her hand pained her, Kathryn remained hidden all day in her chamber and at supper time ate a lonely, solitary meal. When Hugh asked her to accompany him on a tour of the estate the next morning, Kathryn refused without even bothering to offer a plausible excuse.

Exiling herself to her chamber, Kathryn yearned to be with her husband but was ashamed to face the O'Neill warriors who'd witnessed her degradation at Turlough's hands. Guilt ridden, Hugh was reluctant to force her, but each passing day rubbed away another layer of his patience.

And so it went for several days.

Then came the evening when Hugh's patience ran out. He wanted his wife back by his side.

Determined to force the issue, Hugh fortified himself for the oncoming battle with two glasses of whiskey. Leaving his study, he climbed the stairs and walked into his wife's bedchamber without knocking.

The image of serene motherhood greeted him. Kathryn sat in front of the hearth, sewing baby clothes. Hugh crossed the chamber quietly and stood beside her.

"You startled me," Kathryn gasped, looking up. One of her hands flew to her breast. "I thought you would be at supper."

"And so I shall be, my dear. I've come to escort you."

Kathryn looked down at her sewing and frowned, saying, "I think not. My hand—"

"You're fine," Hugh said. "Besides, I wish to sup with you."

"I'm not hungry," she lied, meeting his gaze.

"Of what are you afraid?" he asked.

"Nothing frightens me," Kathryn snapped. "Leave me alone."

"I am the master here," Hugh shot back, his voice colder than a winter's day. "You are still my wife and will act the part."

"Please, you don't understand," she pleaded.

Hugh's voice softened. "Then, tell me why you are so troubled."

"I—I—Turlough *touched* me."

Hugh tensed. Why did she taunt him with that? "I know what Turlough did," he said, "and see no good reason to dwell on it."

"But—"

"Madam, I am aware of what he did and choose to put it aside. What's done is past."

"*You* choose to put it aside?" Kathryn echoed, incredulous. She stood up and faced him, saying, "How easy it is to set aside, but it was done to me, not you!"

Determined to see his will out, Hugh loomed over his diminutive wife. "I fail to see the relationship between what was done by him and supping with me."

Kathryn's shoulders drooped. Apparently, victory would not come easily on this night. "Those men in the hall know and—"

"I will remain by your side," Hugh promised. "Leaving this chamber will be easier after tonight. Trust me?" Hugh held out his hand and waited.

Kathryn looked from his hopeful gaze to his offered hand but lost her nerve. "I—I cannot."

"Take my hand and walk into the great hall with dignity," Hugh threatened, "or I will drag you there by those copper tresses."

Kathryn gulped nervously. "You wouldn't."

"Try me," he challenged.

Kathryn stood her ground for one brief moment and then brushed past him to the door. She opened it but shrank back as if slapped by the noise drifting up the stairs.

Turning back like a frightened child, Kathryn asked, "Hold my hand?"

Hugh felt an insistent tug at his heart but refused to soften his expression. If his resolve weakened, she would refuse to go down.

With hands entwined, Hugh and Kathryn walked down the stairs. The cacophony of supper's sounds grew louder with each step forward and Kathryn's face grew paler.

"Together, we will make it through this," Hugh said,

stopping in the foyer to plant an encouraging kiss on her forehead. "I promise."

Still clutching his hand, Kathryn squared her shoulders and nodded once. With that, Hugh led her toward the great hall, her desperate grip on him causing more than a little pain.

With their heads held majestically high, the earl and countess of Tyrone strode into the great hall like arriving royalty and walked toward the high table.

The O'Neill warriors greeted Hugh and smiled at Kathryn as they walked past. Relieved, Kathryn returned their smiles, but the smile died on her face when Liam stood in front of them.

"Good evenin', Countess," he said before stepping aside. " 'Tis glad I am to see you up and about again."

"Thank you," Kathryn murmured.

Wearing his familiar grin, Patrick stood up as Kathryn took her place between Hugh and him at the high table. " 'Tis heartwarmin' to see you're feelin' better," he said, reclaiming his chair.

Kathryn smiled at him, saying, "My thanks, Patrick."

Carrying bowls of meat-laden stew, Maude bustled into the hall from the pantry. As she placed the steaming stew on the table in front of them, the housekeeper said, " 'Tis grand seein' you back in your rightful place, my lady."

"You never brought my tray," Kathryn teased, a smile flirting with the corners of her lips. "You forced me to come down or starve."

" 'Tis a servant's lot to follow the master's orders," Maude said. Casting a sidelong glance at Hugh, she added, "Which is what I was doin'."

Maude made a hasty retreat and Kathryn rounded on her husband. Hugh raised his hands in feigned innocence.

"I vow that blasted woman never took orders from anyone," Patrick grumbled, making them laugh. "And she raised her daughter the same, but I'm supposin' it's too late to remedy the fact."

Fighting a smile, Patrick leveled his gaze on Kathryn and loosed his wit upon her. "Women are all the same—nag, nag, nag. By the way, Katie, you appear to have added some weight since last these tired eyes of mine rested upon your slight frame."

Hugh hooted with laughter, and Kathryn rewarded him with a withering look.

"My husband forgets this bulky frame has fattened his purse," she said. "Soon Hugh will be a proud papa, and Ireland will have the third earl of Tyrone."

Hugh choked on his wine. "It could be a girl," he reminded her.

"No, it's definitely a boy," Kathryn said, breaking a large piece of bread and smothering it with butter.

Patrick's spoon halted en route to his mouth. Swallowing his laughter, he glanced at Hugh who cast him an "indulge-her" look.

As she reached for her wine, Kathryn looked up and paled. Liam stood in front of her. In his arms was a squirming, stormy-gray ball of fur.

"Countess, I bring you greetin's from Daisy," Liam said.

Bewildered for a moment, Kathryn cocked her head to one side.

"The pups are weaned," Liam explained, holding up the squirming ball of fur. "This is the one no good for huntin'. Have you changed your mind?"

"No good for hunting?" Hugh asked.

"The poor boy is lame," Liam answered, pointing to one hind leg. "See here. It's deformed."

Hugh and Patrick leaned across the table and examined

the dog's shriveled leg. The frightened pup whined piteously.

"Give him to me," Kathryn ordered. Clutching him to her breast, she stroked the top of his head and clucked, "You poor baby."

The pup responded to this gentle attention by licking Kathryn's chin, making her giggle. Finally, he snuggled close and rested his head in the crook of her neck, as a baby would, then gazed with dark, doleful eyes at his new mother.

Pleased, Kathryn pinched a piece of stew meat and offered it to him. The pup gobbled it up and then resumed his new position in life upon her breast.

"Though he be lame, that dog is no fool," Patrick observed, making the others laugh.

"His name is Vulcan," Kathryn announced.

"Vulcan?" Patrick and Liam echoed.

"A most appropriate name," Hugh agreed. "I'll help you train him."

"Enlighten me," Patrick said. "What kind of name is Vulcan? 'Tis foreign soundin', but not English."

"It's Roman," Hugh told him.

"Roman?" Liam arched a brow.

"Vulcan was the mighty god of fire and the son of Jupiter, the undisputed king of the Roman gods," Kathryn explained. "Something akin to your Irish 'ard ri'. Jupiter kicked Vulcan out of heaven, and when he fell to the earth below, Vulcan broke one of his legs. After that, he became the lame god."

"But, why did this Jupiter banish his own son?" Patrick asked.

Unable to recall, Kathryn turned questioning eyes on her husband. Hugh looked at Patrick and grinned, saying, "I've forgotten."

"You weave an interestin' tale," Patrick muttered, "and then leave us hangin'."

Kathryn shrugged her shoulders in apology. "Thank you for Vulcan," she said as Liam turned to leave.

"The pleasure was mine," he returned.

Lifting one of the pup's forelegs, Kathryn waved it at Liam in farewell.

The conversation drifted to other topics, but Hugh and Patrick never mentioned Turlough. Drowsy, Kathryn was unable to stifle a yawn. Cuddled against her breast, Vulcan yawned too.

"I believe it's time I escorted you upstairs," Hugh said to her. "Give Vulcan to Patrick to put down for the night."

"No," Kathryn refused, coming to life. "Vulcan is sleeping with me."

Certain that Patrick would laugh in his face, Hugh refused to look at him. But a dog sleeping beside his wife when he was not? Hugh knew he'd never live this one down.

"Very well," Hugh muttered, unwilling to spoil the cheerful mood of the evening.

Inside her chamber, Kathryn set the pup on the floor. Vulcan scurried about as fast as his crippled leg would allow and explored his new surroundings.

Kathryn looked at Hugh and smiled sheepishly. "I'm sorry I behaved so dreadfully earlier. Your thinking was correct."

"It always is," Hugh teased. "You should heed my words of wisdom more often."

Kathryn grinned.

"Pleasant dreams, sweet," he whispered, drawing her uninjured hand to his lips, then left the chamber. Retracing his steps downstairs, Hugh went to his study where

Patrick and several hours of deciphering the estate's badly kept accounts awaited him.

Much later, Hugh said good night to Patrick and went upstairs to his own chamber. He sat on the edge of the bed and pulled off his boots, but on impulse, decided to check on his wife and her canine waif.

Hugh opened the connecting door quietly and padded across the chamber to the bed. What he saw made him smile. Kathryn slept peacefully with the pup snuggled against the warmth of her body.

Leaning over, Hugh brushed an errant lock of copper hair from her forehead and planted a light kiss there. He glanced at the dog whose dark eyes watched him warily. "You won't be sleeping in my place for long, mutt," Hugh whispered.

As if he understood, Vulcan curled his lips back in a silent snarl of displeasure.

"Mind your manners or be banished from this chamber," Hugh whispered in a stern voice, pointing a scolding finger at the pup. "*I* am master here, not you."

Vulcan closed his eyes.

Satisfied with the pup's apparent submission, Hugh sought his own bed.

17

During the following week Kathryn became increasingly restless. She remained within her chamber by day and only ventured out in the evening to sup with Hugh in the great hall below, but her growing restlessness was unable to defeat her fear of facing the O'Neill men-at-arms.

Even worse, the guilt she felt about Tim's untimely death festered deep within her soul. Kathryn had caused the boy's death but never tended his grave. What sorry excuse for a woman was she?

April's weather warmed into May. Each passing day found Kathryn standing at her chamber window. She yearned for the freedom to feel the warmth of the sun on her face, but tried to content herself with stitching baby clothes.

Though she loved him dearly, Vulcan added another frustrating dimension to her world. Try as she did, Kathryn experienced difficulty in training Vulcan to the simplest command, and the pup was the cause of a growing rift between Maude and herself.

Kathryn insisted the housekeeper escort Vulcan to answer his frequent calls of nature. With each passing day, Maude became more vocal concerning this extra task.

Kathryn knew she was being unfair, but without Hugh beside her, she could not face any of his men.

Turning away from the window, Kathryn walked across the chamber to the bell pull. It was again time for Vulcan's outing. Several moments later, an obviously disgruntled Maude appeared.

"Vulcan needs to go out," Kathryn said.

"Take him out yourself," Maude snapped. "I won't be playin' nursemaid to that worthless cur."

"I am the countess of Tyrone," Kathryn said, drawing her frame to its full height. "Obey my order or seek employment elsewhere."

"I won't valet that beastie, nor will I seek other employment," Maude returned, drawing her larger frame to its full height. "The earl is master here, not you."

Glaring at each other, the two women stood ready for battle. It was Kathryn who backed down.

"I am unable to take Vulcan outside," she confessed, sudden tears welling up in her eyes. "I would if I could."

Maude's expression and voice gentled. "Why not?"

"I—I am afraid."

"There's nothin' to fear," Maude assured her. "I've seen you at that window and know you long to be outside. You cannot dally in this chamber for the rest of your life. Take Vulcan for a walk through the gardens."

Kathryn chewed her lower lip in nervous indecision. "I could take flowers to the graves," she said finally. "Where is my husband?"

Maude hesitated. The graveyard might not be the best place for what ailed Kathryn. "The earl is in his study."

Followed by a wildly excited Vulcan, Kathryn emerged from the safety of her chamber and descended the stairs alone for the first time since that fateful day that now held sway in her dreams. Reaching the deserted foyer, Kathryn started down the corridor to the study.

Hugh had just finished instructing Patrick to leave for Dublin in the morning. Patrick and a contingent of O'Neill men-at-arms would escort Polly, Maeve, Shana, and the girls' nursemaid Nellie to Dungannon posthaste.

"Enter," Hugh called, hearing the knock. When the door opened, Vulcan scurried into the unexplored territory of the study.

Kathryn smiled at the two men. "I hope I'm not interrupting anything important," she said. "I can come back later."

"Come in," Hugh said. Perhaps, his wife was finally emerging from the emotional strain she'd been under, and all would be well.

"May I gather some flowers for the graves?" Kathryn asked.

"This is your home," Hugh told her. "You need not ask my permission to go anywhere."

"Of course, I only wanted to be certain." An embarrassed blush stained her cheeks. "I'm sorry to have bothered you."

"Go with her," Hugh said to Patrick when Kathryn had gone. "The graveyard is not the best place for her to be alone, especially on her first venture outside these walls. Katie considers you a friend."

Patrick nodded and left.

Vulcan scampered through the gate into the graveyard, but Kathryn hesitated. Could the recent dead rise up against her? She scanned the deserted graveyard. A chill of fear tickled her spine, and she shivered in spite of the sun's warmth.

Mustering her courage, Kathryn stepped inside, and when nothing happened, exhaled the breath she hadn't realized she'd been holding. Kathryn walked toward Shane's grave. Her senses were sharp, alert to every sound.

Kneeling in front of the grave, Kathryn removed the long-dead flowers she'd left there and arranged the fresh ones she'd brought. She made the sign of the cross and prayed for her late husband's departed soul.

Patrick appeared several moments later, and afraid that he'd frighten her, called out a greeting as he approached. He knelt beside her, made the sign of the cross and mumbled a quick, half-forgotten prayer.

"Shane and I grew from boyhood together," Patrick said. "Loss is the only sure thin' in life for an Irishman."

"Amen to that," Kathryn replied. "My sisters teased me that Ireland was a heathen place, but actually it tends more to bittersweet. For every ounce of joy we're granted, we must return a pound of sorrow."

Patrick stood up and helped Kathryn rise. When he turned in the direction of the graveyard's entrance, Kathryn shook her head and led him across the graveyard.

"Did Hugh send you?" she asked as they walked along.

"Yes, he worried that somethin' would mar your visit."

"Oh."

Patrick glanced sidelong at her. "The earl is guilt ridden."

"Why?" Kathryn asked, surprised.

"He feels responsible for leavin' you unprotected."

"Hugh could not have forseen—"

"I'm glad you're of that mind," Patrick interrupted. "You might consider tellin' him that."

"Here we are," Kathryn said, stopping at another grave. She knelt and arranged fresh flowers, then prayed.

"Tim?" Patrick exclaimed, realizing who lay beneath the sod. "He was only a boy. What happened?"

Ignoring his question, Kathryn stared at the grave. How

could she confess responsibility for Tim's death? What would Patrick think of her? Hugh would find out, and what would *he* think of her then? Hot tears streamed down her cheeks.

Patrick knelt and placed a comforting arm around her shoulders, saying, "Tell me what's wrong?"

"It was my fault," Kathryn sobbed. "I caused Tim's death."

Certain that she was incapable of harming anyone, Patrick held her close until her tears were spent. "Tell me what happened."

"Tim befriended me and tried to help me escape, but I hesitated. Turlough—" she broke off, unable to continue.

Vulcan, wearied by his wanderings, limped over to them. Kathryn lifted the pup into her arms, and he licked the salty tears from her cheeks.

"Turlough laid the boy low," Patrick said. "It wasn't your fault, and don't be carryin' his sin around with you." Then he added, "And have you ever known me to lie?"

"Yes, I have." Kathryn's chuckle was watery.

"Correct, but not about this." Patrick tapped the tip of her upturned nose, making her smile. "Give me Vulcan and I'll carry him back to the courtyard."

"Enjoy him while you can," Kathryn said, handing him the pup. "Wolfhounds don't stay babies for long."

Patrick held Vulcan close to his face and kissed the pup's wet nose. "In a few months' time, Vulcan will be carryin' me upon his back."

As they left the graveyard, Patrick stole a worried glance at Kathryn. Yes, he could order her to not feel guilt, but a world of difference lay between the ordering and the doing.

Standing in the courtyard with Conal and Liam, Hugh spied Patrick and Kathryn walking down the path from the graveyard. He noted her puffy, red-rimmed eyes and knew she'd been weeping. That troubled Hugh. Did she weep for what had been done to her or for Shane? More than anything else, Hugh wished his wife would confide in him.

"I've been waiting for you," Hugh said as he lifted the pup from Patrick's arms. "It's time Vulcan began his training."

"Behold, your comeuppance is at hand," Kathryn teased. Her husband, she knew, was about to find himself in a battle from which he would not emerge the victor. After all, hadn't she been closeted with the pup for a week and made no progress?

Patrick, Conal, and Liam chuckled at their lord's expense. Several other warriors who stood nearby hid their smiles.

"Would any here, including my most supportive wife, care to place a wager upon the outcome?" Hugh challenged.

"We wouldn't think of stealin' your hard-earned coin," Patrick quipped. Everyone in the courtyard, including the earl's most supportive wife, laughed.

Maude, grumbling about the terrible sin of wasting good food on a dog, appeared at that moment and handed Hugh a platter of tempting morsels of meat. Ignoring her, Hugh wafted the platter of meat beneath Vulcan's nose. It twitched with anticipation.

"*Sit* and *stay* will be Vulcan's first lesson," Hugh announced, passing the platter to Kathryn.

Hugh set Vulcan on the ground, shoved his backside down and ordered, "Sit." He reinforced his command by rewarding the pup with a piece of meat. Vulcan learned this lesson quickly.

To *stay* was a little more difficult. Hugh ordered Vulcan to sit and stay, then made a small trail of meat leading away from the pup. As fast as Hugh placed the meat on the ground, Vulcan attacked and gobbled it up.

Those watching were beside themselves with laughter at this debacle. Hugh scowled, annoyed with the pup but not really angry. He would gladly perform cartwheels around the courtyard if it elicited his wife's laughter, yet annoyance was the only emotion visible in his expression.

"If my lady believes she would meet with greater success, she's welcome to try," Hugh challenged, cocking a brow at her.

After handing the platter of meat to Patrick, Kathryn stepped forward and knelt beside the pup. She looked at Hugh, saying, "Walk some distance away and set a piece of meat down."

Just as Vulcan was about to go after the meat, Kathryn held him back. "Stay," she said softly.

Vulcan squirmed for freedom and whined.

"Stay," Kathryn ordered in a stern voice, and the pup quieted.

Kathryn removed her restraining hands. Vulcan cocked his head at her and wagged his tail but stayed where he was, obedient to her command. Pleased, Kathryn praised the pup and rewarded him with a piece of meat.

Kathryn told Hugh to bring the forbidden morsel closer and repeated the whole procedure again and again. When the forbidden tidbit lay untouched in front of Vulcan, Kathryn gave it to him.

"He needed a mother's gentle touch," she said.

Hugh frowned at this unexpected turn of events. He had hoped to gain his wife's appreciation by training her beloved pet.

"Vulcan must learn to *come*," Hugh announced, then ordered the pup to stay and walked a short distance away.

Holding up his hand, Hugh waved a piece of meat in the air and commanded, "Come."

Vulcan cocked his head to one side and lay upon the ground, resting his head on his forelegs. The courtyard filled with laughter.

"I think Vulcan is tired," Kathryn called, then fell prey to a fit of giggling.

"Or full," Patrick added. Everyone but Hugh laughed.

"We'll save something for tomorrow," Hugh said, offering his arm to his wife. "Shall we go inside?"

Kathryn accepted his arm, but Vulcan refused to be roused. "The poor baby is exhausted," she said, casting her beguiling green eyes on her husband. "Would you carry him?"

Hugh stooped to lift the recalcitrant pup into his arms. In midair, Vulcan answered an urgent call of nature.

"You miserable beast!" Hugh bellowed, then rounded on Kathryn. "He's wet on my boots!"

The men in the courtyard laughed so hard their stomachs ached and tears dampened their faces. Imagine, a less than worthless cur pissing on an earl!

As he glared at his wife, Hugh's expression suddenly changed. He smiled and stepped closer.

"Hearing you laugh again is grand," Hugh said. Flustered, Kathryn flushed a deep scarlet. Unexpectedly, Hugh dropped Vulcan into her arms and turned to walk inside.

As the men in the courtyard drifted away, Kathryn's outraged voice rang out, "Vulcan's wet on my skirt!" This was followed by Hugh's howl of laughter and then Kathryn's.

Early the next morning, Kathryn raced into the courtyard. She'd insisted on rising at dawn to bid farewell to Patrick as he began the journey to Dublin to retrieve her daughters. Breathless from the exertion, Kathryn stood beside her husband and looked up at Patrick, already astride his horse.

"You'll be careful?" she asked. "How long will it take?"

"There's nothing to worry about," Hugh said, placing an arm around her shoulders.

"I'll protect the little ones with my life," Patrick assured her. "We'll be back in Dungannon within the month."

Kathryn reached out and touched his hand, saying, "Godspeed, my friend."

Hugh shook his man's hand and wished him fair weather. He glanced at his wife as the men rode away. Kathryn stood motionless, staring after them. Her brow was creased with worry and her expression pure anguish.

Hugh hoped Maeve and Shana's arrival would encourage Kathryn's full recovery and push the awful events of the past from her mind. For his part, Hugh intended to spend a great deal of time with Kathryn for the next few weeks.

"What troubles you, Katie?"

"Do you think they've forgotten?"

"Of whom do you speak?"

"My daughters." Kathryn raised questioning eyes to Hugh, searching his for the truth. "Do you think Maeve and Shana have forgotten me?"

"Forgotten their mother?" Hugh smiled. "Highly unlikely."

"But, it's been so long since I've seen them."

"It only seems like a long time," Hugh said, his embrace tightening around her. "Besides, who could ever forget you?"

In the early morning light, Kathryn's copper hair caught the sun's rays and bathed her in a fiery glow. Her enormous green eyes sparkled like perfect emerald jewels, and her enticingly rosy lips begged to be kissed.

Hugh lowered his head, intending to taste the promised sweetness of her mouth. Kathryn froze, rigid with fear and mentally recoiling.

"I'd never hurt you," Hugh said, drawing back just as his mouth would have claimed hers.

"I'm sorry," Kathryn apologized, regretting her icy response, but the wariness in her eyes remained.

Hugh forced himself to smile and changed the subject. "Though it's still quite early," he offered, "Vulcan could have his lesson now."

Humor replaced the wariness in Kathryn's eyes. "It was much too early for the king of canines to awaken," she said. "Vulcan still lies abed in my chamber."

Hugh smiled, and his hand dropped to her swollen belly. "Perhaps you should join him. To carry such a burden for so long a time is tiring."

"I admit I'm enlarging," Kathryn said, "but we still have three months to wait."

"Soon you'll be waddling like a duck, my weighty wife," Hugh teased her, escorting her inside.

"A duck?" she gasped. "How dare you suggest such a thing? I've never waddled like a duck."

"When you carried Shana, you most definitely possessed the gait of a duck," Hugh differed as they climbed the stairs to her chamber.

"I never did!"

"Have you seen yourself from behind?" Hugh asked. "From the look of you, the duck's gait will arrive even sooner this time."

Kathryn's eyes sparkled with anger, but then she remembered Fiona's complaint and smiled. Apparently, the time of her own comeuppance was at hand. Her husband was trying hard to make her laugh and forget her problems.

Guilt at having recoiled from his touch washed over her, and Kathryn tried to amend her earlier reticence. "Would you care to break the fast with me in my chamber later?"

"Yes." Hugh kissed her cheek and turned to leave.

Kathryn stared after him, then raised her hand to the lucky cheek his lips had brushed. *Could he love me?* she wondered in utter elation. Almost instantly, her fears reigned supreme, and her shoulders sagged as if pressed down by the heaviness of her thoughts. She was unworthy of his love. Turlough's vile touch had soiled her.

As he walked downstairs, Hugh mentally rubbed his hands together. His wife had made an overture of friendship, and he would seize the opportunity before it slipped away. Progress was being made, albeit slowly.

The following afternoon as Kathryn knelt in front of Tim's grave, the most dreadful feeling of being watched assailed her. Fear refused to let her look around, but her motionless body belied the frenzied tingling of her nerves.

A man's shadow fell across the gravestone. Screaming, Kathryn whirled around and threw up her arms as if to ward off an attacker.

"It's me," Hugh said, grabbing her hands.

Trembling, Kathryn lowered her face to his hands and panted with relief. It took her several long moments to regain her composure.

Almighty God! Hugh thought. *What horror had she witnessed that would make her cringe at shadows?*

"You shouldn't sneak up on people," Kathryn said, willing her heart to return to a normal beat. "You gave me a fright."

"I wasn't sneaking, but I'm sorry I startled you." Hugh glanced at the grave's marker, then said, "I thought you visited Shane's grave."

"Sometimes I do," Kathryn answered, releasing his

hands. She turned back to the grave and gathered the flowers she'd left there the previous day.

"Who was Tim?" Hugh asked. "Why do you tend his grave?"

Kathryn pretended deafness. What could she say? If she spoke the truth, she would lose him forever. No sane man desired a murderess for his wife.

Undaunted by her silence, Hugh knelt beside her. "Answer me."

"Didn't Patrick tell you?" she asked, refusing to look at him.

"Patrick would never betray your confidence. And I ask you again, who was Tim?"

Kathryn searched her mind for an acceptable, believable answer. How could she reveal the truth? What chance she had to regain her husband's love would be lost. Finally, she said simply, "Tim was a stable boy."

"A stable boy is of no importance." Hugh knew there was more to this than she was willing to share. "Why do you tend his grave?"

Silence was his answer.

"Please, Katie, do not shut me out," Hugh persisted. "I would share whatever burden you carry."

It was then Kathryn realized she would not escape the moment without revealing the truth. She accepted her sad and lonely fate. "The burden of murder cannot be shared."

"Murder?"

"I killed Tim."

Hugh shook his head in disbelief. He was certain she was incapable of murder except, perhaps, in her own defense. Besides, Hugh would have loved Kathryn even if she'd cold-bloodedly slain a thousand crippled, unarmed men. What bothered him was her torment.

"Tell me all," he said. "Leave nothing out."

Staring at the boy's grave, Kathryn related the details of her abduction and his death. When her tale ended, she bowed her head in shame.

"You blame yourself unjustly," Hugh said, tilting her face up, forcing her to meet his gaze.

"You don't hate me?" Kathryn asked.

"I *love* you," Hugh said, his heart wrenching at the unguarded hope in her eyes. Hugh drew her into his embrace, and Kathryn rested her head against his comfortingly solid shoulder.

The fault was his, Hugh decided. His inability to protect Kathryn was the root of this mess. He vowed that would change now.

During the next few weeks, Hugh courted Kathryn who, in spite of two marriages and three children, had never been courted. Talking is what they did most. They shared childhood experiences, their hopes for the children, and Hugh's plans for Ireland.

Hugh professed his love constantly and teased Kathryn without mercy about her widening girth. By slow degrees, he saw her emotional torment fade.

As part of their daily routine, Hugh visited Kathryn in her chamber each evening until she retired. Some nights they spoke without pause. Other nights nary a word passed their lips. They were content to share each other's company.

As Hugh saw it, there was only one problem with this arrangement. He had no wish for a platonic marriage.

Patience is a virtue, Hugh told himself constantly, *and there is a place for me in God's heaven.*

Seeking escape from the drudgery of sewing, Kathryn decided to enjoy a walk in the gardens one warm afternoon. Calling to Vulcan, she left her chamber and walked down the corridor.

As she descended the stairs to the foyer, Kathryn hoped no one would witness her escape. Her husband had somehow been transformed into a hovering mother hen and would scold her for leaving her chamber during her usual resting time.

With Vulcan by her side, Kathryn scurried across the deserted foyer and swung the door open. Her heart sank at what she saw.

"Why aren't you resting?" Hugh asked, apparently just entering. "Are you ill?"

"I'm going to sit in the garden," Kathryn explained, blushing at having been caught. "The air is beneficial to our baby, you know."

"Ah, Katie, you're my own true mate," Hugh said with a smile, offering her his arm. "I was about to walk in the garden too." He didn't bother to explain why he was on his way *inside* when she'd opened the door.

They strolled leisurely through the garden for a while. Then Hugh spied a bench where they could sit. "Would you like to rest here, sweet?" he asked.

"No, but if *you're* tired, I could be persuaded to sit under that tree," Kathryn replied.

"But, there's no bench."

"What keen eyesight you have," she teased him. "We could sit on the grass."

Hugh escorted her to the tree, and as if she would shatter, helped her down.

"I'd offer my lap for your pleasure," Kathryn said, "but I fear I'm without one at this time."

Seeing the way clear for her afternoon rest, Hugh smiled and said, "I have a lap and insist you use it."

Kathryn lay back and rested her head in his lap. Content, she smiled up at him when he lightly caressed her face.

Vulcan approached and lay down beside his mistress, then rested his head against the mound of her stomach. When Kathryn began stroking Vulcan's head, Hugh had the absurd wish that he could be the dog.

"It's kind of you to spend so much time with me," Kathryn said. "Shane never did."

"Shane was too busy making war."

"And you have no plans in that direction?" That was something Kathryn found difficult to believe. The Irish thrived on war. How would they occupy themselves if there was no war? *Probably start one,* replied an inner voice.

"I fought the Maguire out of necessity," Hugh said, choosing his words with care. "I won't fight my own kind again, certainly not for the queen."

"Will you make war against the English?"

"I didn't say that," Hugh evaded her question. "You'd never make a good diplomat. I am content to live as we are. The peaceful road is always preferable to journey upon. Besides, we can extend our power base through marriage when Maeve and Shana—"

"They're only babies," Kathryn said. Suddenly, Vulcan leapt to his feet, barked at her belly, and limped away.

"What's wrong with him?" Hugh asked.

"The baby kicked him. Give me your hand." Kathryn guided Hugh's hand to her stomach and watched his awe-struck expression as the babe moved beneath it.

"Being this large is becoming a bit uncomfortable," she complained. "Imagine what I'll look like by the time the babe is delivered."

"You've never been more beautiful," Hugh told her.

"It's a boy then," Kathryn announced. "Boys enhance their mother's beauty, or so I've been told."

Hugh laughed and shook his head, then insisted she

close her eyes. Kathryn relaxed, and when her breathing evened, Hugh knew she slept.

Idly, Hugh studied the face that was forever etched in his memory. Kathryn's crown of fiery tresses accentuated her flawless, silken complexion. Divine eyes, created in the image of the most brilliant emeralds, hid behind delicate eyelids. Beneath her small, upturned nose, rosy lips beckoned him to taste their sweetness.

Resisting the invitation, Hugh forced himself to look away, but all too soon his gaze was irresistibly drawn back. Kathryn was a beauty, a fairy princess, a temptress. *Damn it! She was his wife!* Love glowed in Hugh's eyes, and something more.

Without thinking, Hugh leaned down and kissed the lips that taunted him. Dazed by sleep, Kathryn sighed and her lips parted in further invitation. The kiss deepened and awakened her.

"*Do not,*" Kathryn ordered.

"It's natural for a man to feel affection for his wife," Hugh said, his lips merely inches from hers.

"That's lust, not affection. Besides, I—I cannot respond as a wife should."

Hugh grinned down at her, saying, "But you just did."

Kathryn flushed. "I don't want to respond. Truly, if you looked elsewhere, I would understand."

"You are the worst prevaricator I have ever met," Hugh said, playfully tapping the tip of her upturned nose. "And do not forget to confess such a lie to the priest."

In spite of herself, Kathryn smiled.

18

"Hugh!"

Kathryn raced down the stairs as quickly as her seven-month pregnancy would allow, her belly leading the way. Alarmed by her shout, Hugh dashed out of his study and was standing in the foyer by the time she reached the bottom of the stairs.

"My girls are here," Kathryn cried as she flew past him.

Chuckling at her obvious joy, Hugh hurried outside and caught her by the upper arm. "Remain calm," he ordered as they watched the approaching coach and men-at-arms. "Excitement is no good for the baby."

Hugh stepped forward when the coach came to a halt and opened its door. Childish squeals of delight sprang forth as Maeve and Shana threw themselves into his welcoming arms. Hugh gave each little girl a resounding kiss on her cheek and turned to face his watery-eyed wife whose eyes feasted upon the sight of her daughters.

Six-year-old Maeve was a miniature of her mother. Her copper hair had been neatly plaited, only a few fiery wisps set free from her bone-crushing hug with her stepfather. Her green eyes were almost too large for her tiny, oval face, and her nose tilted up at the end, giving her a mischievous appearance.

Two-year-old Shana was the feminine version of Shane O'Neill, stunning those in the courtyard who'd never seen her. Her father's blue eyes shone from her face, and her sensuously full lips hinted more at the wanton than infant. Crowning her head was a lustrous mane of black hair, the braids now in wild disarray.

Hugh set the squirming children down. Squealing with happiness, they ran toward their mother. Kathryn knelt and embraced both, hugging them close and weeping openly.

"Mama, are you sad?" Maeve asked.

"They're tears of joy, princess." Kathryn sniffled, loosening her grip on the two little girls. "Having you in my arms fills me with joy."

Unable to equate weeping and joy, Maeve frowned. *How puzzling!* She cried only when she was sad or hurt. Before she could question her mother, her sister's voice rang out.

"Look!" Shana pointed at her mother's belly.

"Your new brother or sister is growing inside," Kathryn explained. "Just as Maeve and you grew." A doubtful expression appeared on Shana's face as she digested this astounding information.

"All mothers grow big bellies, you goose," Maeve informed her sister. "When the baby comes, the belly disappears like magic."

The courtyard resounded with laughter at her simplistic view of motherhood. Maeve cast a displeased look at those laughing and caused even more merriment, so much did she resemble her mother when angered.

"Maude, come and meet my daughters," Kathryn called. Maude approached and smiled at the two little girls. At last, the housekeeper thought, Dungannon would echo with the divine sound of children's laughter. Lord, but it had been so long!

"You were no bigger than a mite the last I saw of you," Maude said to Maeve. "Now you're almost grown up."

Maeve beamed with pride. Unaware of social position, she dropped the housekeeper a becoming, if a bit unsteady, curtsey. Smothered chuckles filled the courtyard, and Maeve glanced around, trying to discern who would dare laugh twice at her.

"And this is Shana," Kathryn introduced her youngest.

When she bent to get a closer look at the child, tears welled up in the housekeeper's eyes. "It's like lookin' into the face of Shane," Maude choked, overcome by emotion and memory.

Taking a cloth from her apron pocket, Maude blew her nose loudly, then added, "I'll be prayin' she grows with your temperament. 'Twouldn't do for her to grow as wild as her da."

Beneath Hugh's restraining hand, Vulcan had been sitting, whining and aching to investigate these new arrivals. Breaking free, he lunged forward and licked Maeve and then Shana. With his recently added weight and larger size, Vulcan nearly toppled Shana over in his exuberance.

"Sit," Kathryn commanded. Vulcan obeyed, but his wagging tail betrayed his excitement.

"Maeve and Shana, this is Vulcan," Kathryn introduced the dog with mock seriousness. "Vulcan, these are my daughters."

If a dog could experience human ecstasy, then Vulcan did at that moment. Giggling with delight at such a marvelous toy, Maeve and Shana threw themselves upon the pup, stroking and kissing and being licked in return.

Kathryn smiled and asked Maude to supervise the three,

then stood to greet her tiring woman. She hugged and kissed Polly, then went to Patrick who stood beside Hugh.

"All that you asked for has been brought," Patrick was saying.

"What is it you've had brought?" Kathryn asked.

"Nothing of importance," Hugh evaded.

Accepting her husband's words, Kathryn smiled at Patrick and clasped his hands in gratitude. Standing on tiptoes, she planted a kiss on his cheek. "Thank you for bringing my girls home safely. You've always been a good friend."

Patrick grinned. "Then, you won't mind me sayin', you look like you swallowed somethin' whole."

Kathryn smiled and turned to Hugh, saying, "Will you carry Shana? I don't have the strength."

"We'll speak later," Hugh said to Patrick. He lifted Shana into his arms and followed his wife inside, but his placid expression masked furious thoughts.

First, my beloved wife refuses to be touched, Hugh fumed. *Then, she'll be touched but won't grant me my husbandly rights. I give the order to bring the children home, but she gives Patrick a kiss in gratitude. The minx knows how the sight of her torments me. And now it's too late! She's too far gone with child to endure my lovemaking. I'll wait until she's recovered from childbirth, but no longer. I am her husband, and she'd better decide to yield.*

At supper time, Kathryn walked downstairs with Maeve and Shana in hand while Vulcan followed behind. In the few short hours since her daughters' arrival, Kathryn's almost constant look of anxiety had vanished as though it had never been. She positively glowed with happiness.

"Shall we eat here?" Kathryn asked, entering the small family dining chamber.

Hugh nodded, saying, "Our first night together again as

a family should be a private affair. We won't be missed in the great hall."

Stepping forward, Hugh patted Maeve's head and lifted Shana into his arms. Not to be outshone, Vulcan whined for his share of attention. Hugh frowned at the dog but patted him anyway.

"Dog," Shana chirped, pointing at Vulcan.

"That's right, nestling." Hugh smiled with approval at Shana, then cast her mother a meaningful look. "Vulcan is a dog, not a family member."

Ignoring her husband, Kathryn smiled at Shana and said, "Vulcan is a dog *and* a family member."

"Patrick tells me Lord and Lady Burke send their warmest regards," Hugh said, ignoring *her* words. "Fiona has been delivered of a daughter, Grania."

"How wonderful," Kathryn said. "We must send a gift."

"Arrangements have already been made. Shall we eat?"

Supper was a cozy affair with just the four O'Neills and Vulcan. To her mother's annoyance, Maeve soon discovered the advantage in having Vulcan attend her during the meal, and Vulcan quickly learned the advantage in staying close to the girls while they ate. Though Maeve tried to hide her covert activity, much of the beef on her plate ended in Vulcan's waiting mouth. After dessert, Shana climbed up on Hugh's lap and promptly fell asleep.

"Let's deliver these imps into Nellie's capable hands," Hugh suggested when Maeve yawned.

"Maeve, would you care to sleep with me tonight?" Kathryn asked.

Hugh frowned at the offering. He wished his wife would extend the same invitation to him.

"No, Shana will miss me," Maeve said drowsily. "May Vulcan sleep with us?"

Hugh chuckled. Kathryn sent him a repressive frown.

"If Vulcan is willing," Kathryn answered her daughter, "he's welcome to pass the night in your chamber."

After tucking her daughters into bed, Kathryn kissed Maeve and a still-sleeping Shana. Hugh did the same. They said good night to Nellie and started to leave, but Kathryn stopped and retraced her steps across the chamber.

"Watch over my girls," Kathryn whispered, scratching the dog's neck. "I'll miss you."

Vulcan answered by licking her hand.

Outside his wife's chamber, Hugh raised her hand to his lips. When her free hand caressed his cheek, Hugh looked up and gazed into disarming green eyes filled with love.

Kathryn entwined her arms around his neck and leaned against him. "Thank you for bringing my girls home," she said, the sweetness of her breath tickling his neck.

"They're my girls too."

"So they are," Kathryn agreed.

Hugh tilted her chin up to gaze deeply into her eyes. Without warning, his lips swooped down, capturing hers, and long-denied passion overruled caution. Kathryn pressed herself provocatively against the muscular planes of his body and surrendered to his ardor, returning his kiss with equal passion.

Hugh's lips blazed a fiery trail down the silken column of her neck, and a low moan of pleasure welled up from Kathryn's throat. The husky sound of it brought an abrupt awareness of what was happening.

"The b-baby," Kathryn stammered, stiffening within his embrace.

Hugh released her and stepped back a pace. "What excuse will you use when the babe is delivered?" he asked, then turned and walked away.

With an aching heart, Kathryn stared after him.

Inside her chamber, Kathryn found Polly and a steaming tub of hot water in front of the hearth. She embraced her tiring woman, saying, "How can I ever repay you for taking care of Maeve and Shana in my absence?"

"Bah! 'Twas my pleasure and I had plenty of help," Polly said, noting the sadness shadowed within her mistress's eyes. "Come on now. After such an excitin' day as this, a hot tub will be relaxin'."

Kathryn disrobed, unbound her hair and soon sat in the scented water. The moist heat subdued some of her tenseness, and Kathryn closed her eyes with the pleasure of it.

Maude was correct, Kathryn decided. There was nothing as soothing to the soul as a long soak in a steaming tub.

"Are you truly well?" Polly asked, interrupting her reverie.

"Yes, and I won't be needing you further tonight," Kathryn answered. "Seek your own bed."

"If you don't mind, I'll stay to see you safely in bed," Polly said.

"Oh, but I do mind," Kathryn insisted. "Off with you now."

Polly smiled. "Is the earl still in trainin' for my job?"

"You may as well know, my husband sleeps in his own chamber."

"How kind," Polly remarked on her way out. "Most considerate of your condition, *I think.*" The door clicked shut behind her.

Kathryn sank lower in the steaming water, half hoping she would shrivel up, nevermore to be seen. Yes, she thought, her husband *had* been considerate of her needs and sensitive to her feelings. But, how considerate had she been of his?

Not at all, answered an inner voice.

Unable to concentrate on the estate's accounts, Hugh

pushed aside his unfinished paperwork and left the study. Determined to confront his wife and lay down the law, Hugh headed for the stairs. After the babe arrived, they would again share a bed. That was unnegotiable. He was the master of Dungannon, wasn't he? How dare Kathryn impose her will upon him! To serve his needs without complaint was his wife's duty, and no longer would she neglect it.

And yet—

Hugh hesitated outside the chamber, but hearing the faint sounds of her voice, opened the door and stepped inside. Unaware of his presence, Kathryn relaxed in the tub and mumbled almost inaudibly to herself.

Hugh folded his arms across his chest, leaned against the door, and admired the silken splendor of her back, bathed in the glow from the hearth. Faced with his wife's unclad beauty and the fact that she'd withheld it from him, Hugh grew even angrier.

Mumbling to herself, Kathryn caressed her distended belly. It was then Hugh realized she was cooing to their unborn child. His seething anger evaporated like mist beneath a scorching, noonday sun. A lazy smile spread across his face. There was no other woman on God's earth to whom Hugh would entrust the nurturing of his son.

"Mustn't kick Mother so hard, my prince," Kathryn scolded her belly as she stood up in the tub.

At her incredible display of beauty, Hugh's breath caught raggedly in his throat.

One shapely leg went over the edge of the tub, but as the other leg followed, Kathryn lost her balance. Strong, steadying hands grasped her thickened waist and prevented the fall. Surprised, Kathryn looked up into angry brown eyes.

"You have a nasty habit of sneaking up on the unsus-pecting," she teased,

"With such awkward movements, you shouldn't be bath-ing unattended," Hugh snapped. "Do you realize what could have happened if I hadn't been here to catch you?"

"You're right," Kathryn agreed, "but I had no heart to keep Polly from Patrick."

"And how do you think Polly would feel if something had happened?" Hugh asked, his tone gentling.

"I did not think. It won't happen again." Suddenly aware of her nakedness, Kathryn blushed a brilliant scar-let. Slowly, the blush spread downward and stopped just short of her heavy breasts.

Hugh's mesmerized gaze followed the blush's progress, and then dropped lower. Kathryn's breasts were heavy with her advanced pregnancy, their nipples darkened and enlarged. Filled with his seed, her belly was nearing tre-mendous size. Hugh's long-neglected manhood tingled and stretched as if awakening from a long, long slumber.

"Standing naked in front of your husband is no cause for shame," Hugh chided, forcing a light note into his voice. He reached for a towel, hoping to divert his growing pas-sion.

It did not help.

Hugh quickly wrapped Kathryn within the folds of the towel, led her to a chair, and sat down. Drawing her be-tween his thighs, he gently patted her dry.

Why was he tormenting himself? Hugh wondered, eye level with Kathryn's breasts. Teased beyond endurance, he leaned forward and captured one impudent nipple with his lips.

Kathryn recoiled.

"Damn you!" Hugh stood up and jerked a night shift over her head, then led her like an errant child to the bed

and tucked her in. Without a word, he strode purposefully to the door connecting his chamber with hers.

Consumed by guilt, Kathryn watched him retreat. She loved him, she knew, but needed more time. Why couldn't he understand that? And now, because of Maeve and Shana's need, she risked hurting him even more.

"Hugh, may I speak with you a moment?"

"Now?"

"Yes."

Hugh walked back and sat on the edge of the bed. Kathryn sat up, and clasping his hands in hers, brought them to her lips. She pressed her cheek against them, her simple gesture tugging at his heart.

"I am sorry," she said.

Hugh nodded, acknowledging—if not technically accepting—her apology.

"I need a favor," Kathryn began, choosing her words carefully. "I am uncertain if Maeve remembers Shane, and you're the only father Shana has ever known. I want to show them his grave. It's the least I can do to honor his memory and fitting they should learn of their sire."

"Are you asking for my permission?" Hugh asked coldly, removing his hands from hers.

"No, your cooperation." Kathryn reached out and touched his hand. "I want you with us to tell them about Shane—only the good—unless you prefer not. I don't want Shane to become a forbidden subject in their childish minds. The longer I knew Shane, the more I despised him. Though he was a bad man in his personal life, Shane tried to be a good father to Maeve. When they are older and realize who sired them, Maeve and Shana will wonder why we've never spoken of him. If we can speak openly of him, perhaps . . ." Kathryn broke off, uncertain if she was expressing herself clearly.

"I will cooperate," Hugh said, gathering her into his arms. Laughter lurked in his voice when he added, "I'll speak so highly of Shane, the girls will consider him a saint. Of course, I'll need to see the priest afterward and confess my outrageous lies."

"Da!" Shana insisted, pointing a tiny finger at Hugh, who in mounting frustration cast a sidelong glance at his wife.

"Shana may be too young to understand." Kathryn tried to pacify him. She looked at her oldest daughter who stood solemnly in front of her father's grave. "Maeve understands. Don't you, princess?"

"Yes," Maeve chirped, then recited, "Lord Shane O'Neill was my father and a very great man, indeed, but now I have a new father." Here Maeve smiled, recognizing Hugh—the chosen one—who hid a smile and nodded gravely at the distinct honor bestowed upon him.

"That's correct," Kathryn said, beaming with pride at her oldest. Her gaze shifted to Hugh who was wondering if Maeve really understood the words she had so prettily regurgitated.

"Da!" Shana pointed a demonstrative finger at Hugh's face when he lifted her into his arms. Hugh pretended to gobble Shana's finger and nuzzled her cheek with his nose. The little girl laughed uproariously.

"We'll try again when Shana's older," Hugh said to his wife. "Let's deposit these imps with Polly. I've something of interest to show you at the stables."

Followed by Vulcan, the four O'Neills left the graveyard and walked back to the courtyard where Polly was speaking with Patrick. After leaving the girls in their care, Hugh led his wife in the direction of the stables. Kathryn shook her head at his secrecy but went along.

Hugh beckoned Kathryn into one of the stables and led her to the last stall where an exquisite black mare was quartered. He opened the stall and led the sleek-looking mare outside.

"What do you think of her?" Hugh asked, once in the stable yard.

Kathryn slowly circled the horse, carefully examining the beast. Inside the dimly lit stable, she would have sworn the horse was black, but in the bright sunlight, glorious highlights of red appeared in the mare's glossy coat.

"Magnificent," Kathryn said, standing beside her husband.

"Like you," he said, leaning over to peck her cheek. "And she's yours."

"Mine?" Kathryn's mouth dropped open in amazement.

"Yes, yours." Hugh had the absurd wish to trade places with the horse when she reached out and lovingly stroked the mare's flank.

"Seamus, fetch me a saddle," Kathryn called to the head groom.

"Forget the saddle," Hugh instantly countermanded her order, then rounded on her. "You're seven months pregnant and won't be using a saddle until the child is born."

"But Hugh—" Kathryn began to protest, a mulish expression appearing on her face.

"Do things my way," Hugh interrupted, "or the mare will be returned to Dublin."

"As you wish." Kathryn yielded sullenly.

"After I've gifted you with this outstanding piece of horseflesh," Hugh said, "you could, at the very least, gift me with one of your smiles."

Grinning in pure delight, Kathryn entwined her arms around his neck and drew his head down to her level. She kissed him lingeringly and murmured her thanks.

Unsatisfied with the meager reward, Hugh knew he had to wait several months for what he really wanted. Events, however, seemed to be progressing as he'd envisioned while plotting strategy to woo his wife into his bed. Knowing her as he did, Hugh had correctly surmised that one marvelous piece of horseflesh was worth more than a thousand priceless jewels.

"What will you name her?" Hugh asked.

"A special horse needs a special name," Kathryn said. "I'll call her Sable. May I visit her?"

"Of course, but no riding."

Several evenings later, Hugh and Kathryn sat together in front of the hearth in his study. Maeve and Shana, accompanied by Vulcan, had reluctantly left with Nellie for bed.

"Enter," Hugh called, hearing a knock at the door.

"Excuse me," Polly said, then looked at Kathryn. "Your bath is ready. Should I have more water heated?"

"I'll come now," Kathryn answered.

"Polly, take the rest of the evening for your own pleasure," Hugh said, drawing a surprised look from his wife. "I will play the tiring woman tonight."

"But—" Kathryn began to protest.

"Go on with you, Polly," Hugh said, ignoring his wife.

"Thank you, my lord." Polly hurried out before he could change his mind.

Rising from his chair, Hugh looked at Kathryn and smiled, then asked, "Would you heartlessly keep Polly from Patrick on the first anniversary of their marriage?"

"Oh, I'd forgotten."

The steaming, scented tub of water stood in front of the hearth in Kathryn's chamber. After removing his jerkin, Hugh rolled up the sleeves of his shirt and helped his wife undress. As he handed her into the tub, Hugh smiled inwardly.

"Washing me is quite unnecessary," Kathryn said when he reached for the washing cloth and scented soap.

Hugh bowed with exaggerated gallantry, saying, "But I insist."

Hugh massaged her face and neck, then rinsed, being careful no soap neared her fabulous eyes of green. When he stepped to the side and lathered her back, Hugh awakened sensations in Kathryn that she'd thought long dead.

Hugh moved to the front once more. His anticipatory grin reminded Kathryn of a starving man at a sumptuous feast.

Setting aside the washing cloth, Hugh lathered his hands with the soap and began massaging her breasts with seductive motions, then lifted each so the underside would not be neglected. Cupping the water in his hands, Hugh rinsed each breast and the deep valley between them.

Kathryn gasped at the sensation. Hugh chuckled, but when his groin tightened, he had cause to fear for his sanity. Why did he torture himself this way? Even if she was willing, Kathryn was much too large to endure the rigors of his lovemaking.

Hugh lathered his hands once more and began massaging Kathryn's belly. Unexpectedly, he felt the babe move beneath his hands and looked up at her in awed surprise. Kathryn nodded and smiled placidly. An unguarded look of love passed between them, leaving them shaken, humbled by the emotion and feeling unworthy of the other's devotion.

"I think my bath is complete," Kathryn whispered, placing her hand on his.

Hugh helped Kathryn stand and reached for the towel.

After wrapping her in it, he helped her out of the tub and patted her dry, then pulled a night shift over her head.

It did not ease his torment. The sheer silken garment clung tantalizingly to Kathryn's rounded flesh.

"Sit here," Hugh said in a choked voice. He disappeared into his chamber and returned a moment later, chiding, "Don't frown, Katie. It will mark the babe."

"What are you about?" Kathryn asked, casting him an unamused look.

"This . . ." Hugh produced a small chest from behind his back and opened it beneath her upturned nose.

"My jewels!"

"Direct from Dublin," Hugh said with a smile.

Kathryn accepted the box, then stood and placed it on the chair. She wrapped her arms around his neck and drew his head toward hers, saying, "Your thoughtfulness is more dear to me than the jewels themselves."

Their lips met in a lingering, devastating kiss.

Suffering extreme frustration, Hugh ran a hand through his hair. "If not for the babe, I'd bed you this instant, willing or no. However, I've no wish to disturb my own son."

"Or daughter," Kathryn said with a satisfied smile. "You know, I could be wrong about a boy."

With a vile oath, Hugh hurried his wife into bed and yanked the coverlet up to her chin.

"Safely tucked away am I," she teased him.

Hugh brushed his lips against hers, warning, "Safe for the moment, dear heart, but not forever."

19

Rubbing the dull ache in her back, Kathryn stood in front of Sable's stall as she'd done each day for the preceding two months. She produced an apple from the pocket of her skirt and offered it to the mare. Sable nuzzled her hand and accepted the treat.

Kathryn stroked the mare's nose. Sable nuzzled her hand, searching for another apple.

"Tsk! Tsk! You'll end by growing as tremendous as I am," Kathryn chided. She turned to leave, calling over her shoulder, "Seamus, take good care of my Sable."

"Yes, my lady," Seamus answered from another stall where he was grooming one of the horses. "You'll be ridin' her before long."

"Or else I'll surely burst," Kathryn called, making the old man laugh.

Unusually large, Kathryn appeared on the brink of toppling over any moment, belly first. To see her waddling to and fro made even the most courageous of the O'Neill warriors anxious. Even Hugh seemed nervous, forbidding her to wander around alone.

Would her husband consider Vulcan a proper escort? Kathryn wondered, leaving the stable.

Vulcan, who'd been awaiting her reappearance, wagged his tail and followed behind. Kathryn plodded along the path leading to the courtyard and wondered where her husband was at that moment. If only she could sneak back to her chamber without him discovering she'd disobeyed his orders!

Kathryn opened the front door and peered inside. The foyer was deserted. Relieved, Kathryn crossed on silent feet to the stairs, and Vulcan limped behind her.

"Countess," Patrick called, just as she was about to start up. "Your husband requests the honor of your presence in his study."

Damn! Kathryn felt like the hapless fox caught in the henhouse.

"Thank you," she said with forced dignity.

Patrick leaned against the wall and folded his arms across his chest. As Kathryn and her canine partner in crime passed by, Patrick tried to suppress his mirth. If he wasn't mistaken, the countess was muttering unladylike curses, and the usual flurry of activity in this area seemed to have vanished. With infinite wisdom, men-at-arms and servants had removed themselves from the dangerous path of the oncoming storm.

Standing in front of the study, Kathryn screwed up her courage and rapped lightly on the door. Carrying the babe tired her, and she'd few reserves of energy with which to do battle with Hugh who never yielded. Kathryn knocked on the door again, louder this time.

"Enter," sounded a growl from within.

Unlike Shane's, Hugh's ire was slow to rise, but once aroused, avoidance was the best path to follow. Kathryn hesitated and wished she could disappear upstairs.

"Damn you, I said enter!" Hugh jerked the door open.

Kathryn gulped with apprehension. No warm smile greeted her.

"Come in," Hugh said, and stepped aside so she could pass. *"Get out!"*

Kathryn whirled around to face him. "But . . . ?"

"Not you. *Him!*" Hugh pointed a finger at Vulcan. When the door closed behind the dog, Hugh turned to Kathryn, saying, "Madam, be seated."

"I do not wish to sit."

"I said, sit down!" Hugh shouted. Those within hearing distance of the study made the sign of the cross and thanked a merciful Lord that they were not wearing the countess's slippers.

"Very well, but I require assistance," Kathryn said, seemingly unruffled by his outburst. She had become adept at currying sympathy from her overanxious husband, the proud father to be.

Instantly, Hugh was at her side and assisted in the lowering of her bulk onto the chair. Unable to find a comfortable position, Kathryn squirmed this way and that while Hugh towered above and watched her wriggling about.

"Last week I asked you to cease wandering around alone," Hugh began.

Feigning meekness, Kathryn bowed her head and studied her belly.

My wife actually believes if she lowers her gaze, I'll think she's biddable and ever so repentant for defying me, Hugh thought. *Sly little witch! Who would know better than I how rebellious she is?*

"Traipsing about is unwise," Hugh went on. "You could begin your labor any moment. Have you no sense?"

Pompous, insufferable ass! Kathryn thought mutinously, her meekly lowered eyes glowing with suppressed rage.

Does he actually believe that pregnancy has addled her wits? Who would know better than I how I feel?

"You're ridiculous," Kathryn snapped, looking up and dismissing his concerns with a wave of her hand.

Kathryn tried to rise from the chair, but Hugh placed a firm hand on her shoulder and forced her to remain where she was. Husband and wife glared at each other for a long moment. Only Vulcan's low whining on the other side of the door disturbed the heavy silence.

"You will obey me," Hugh said in a voice deceptively low.

"I'm not your prisoner," Kathryn insisted.

"I will be obeyed!" Hugh shouted, silencing her. "You are not to leave the house without escort."

Kathryn opened her mouth to protest but closed it when Hugh threatened, "And if you argue further, you won't go out at all."

"As you wish." Kathryn yielded, casting him a sour look. She lifted her upturned nose into the air in an insulting gesture of dismissal.

Kathryn tried to stand but was unable to gather enough momentum to propel her ponderous body out of the chair. Hugh squelched the urge to laugh and helped her to her feet.

"Thank you," Kathryn said, mustering what little dignity she could. Ducklike, she waddled toward the door, but as her hand touched the knob, her husband's voice stopped her.

"Katie?"

"Yes?"

"Children and dogs are unsuitable escorts."

Without looking back, Kathryn nodded once and left. The door slammed shut behind her. Hugh started after her but then thought better of it.

Running a hand through his hair in frustration, Hugh walked across the chamber and poured himself a whiskey. He downed it quickly and then poured another. In his mind's eye, Hugh pictured Kathryn trying unsuccessfully to propel herself out of the chair. He threw back his head and shouted with laughter.

The following afternoon found Kathryn sitting in front of the darkened hearth in her chamber, an unusually hot August precluding the need for a fire. Kathryn's almost constant backache had made her restless and irritable, and she'd had little patience for Maeve and Shana. Kathryn had sent them off with Nellie lest they be subject to her cross mood.

Hearing the distant rumble of thunder, Kathryn pushed her massive body out of the chair, tugged on the bell pull and moved to the window. The air, capped by an ominously dark sky, was oppressively heavy.

"Hello," Kathryn said when Polly walked in a few minutes later. As Kathryn turned to greet her tiring woman, a brilliant flash of lightning illuminated the dark sky behind her.

"Was there somethin' you wanted?" Polly asked, relieved her mistress's mood had lightened.

"As a matter of fact, there is. You know, Sable is highly strung, and I wondered if the approaching storm has frightened her."

"Should I have word sent to Seamus? Patrick will—"

"I wouldn't want to interfere with anyone's regular duties," Kathryn interrupted, absently rubbing the small of her back.

"Are you ill?" Polly asked, noting the movement.

"I'll be fine." Kathryn grinned mischievously. "Yes, I'll be excellent once we've checked on Sable's welfare."

"We can't go out now," Polly cried.

"Why not? Do you fear the rain?"

"No, I fear the earl."

"There's no need to worry," Kathryn assured her. "My husband said I could go out when accompanied by an escort. He said nothing concerning fair weather. We'll need our cloaks in case the rain beats us back here."

Polly shook her head. If the earl discovered them, he would dispatch her without a qualm. Her mother and husband would probably help him. No, she positively refused to be a party to this.

Several moments later, Kathryn and Polly were wrapped in their cloaks and headed down the corridor toward the stairs. Polly led the way.

"I'd prefer to remain unseen," Kathryn whispered as they reached the top of the stairs.

Polly nodded with understanding. "Wait here," she ordered. "I'll signal if the foyer is clear."

Polly walked downstairs and looked around, then waved her hand in the air. Kathryn raced down the stairs as quickly as her bulk would allow, and Polly followed her outside into the deserted courtyard. A spectacular bolt of lightning flashed above them, and a sudden blast of wind slapped their faces harshly.

"We'd better return inside. We won't make it back before the storm," Polly whined. "If we had any sense, we'd . . ."

Kathryn silenced her with a withering glance. Turning to the right, Kathryn walked toward the chapel and side gardens.

"Where are you goin'?" Polly demanded, tugging at her arm. "The stables are the other way."

"We'll travel the long way around to lessen the chance of being seen," Kathryn said. "Follow me."

Slowly, due to Kathryn's inability to perform the most simple maneuver, they cut to the right and passed the gardens, the kitchen, and the garrison quarters. They reached the stable yard just as the first droplets of rain hit their heads. *Success!*

Kathryn, still rubbing her back, stood in front of Sable's stall with Polly and Seamus. Polly surmised she wasn't feeling as well as she pretended.

"As you can see, Sable is in capable hands," Polly said. "If the storm makes Sable nervous, Seamus will calm her. And we can return to your chamber."

"Don't be frettin' over the mare," the groom added. "This pretty lady is a particular favorite of mine."

"You win," Kathryn said. "Let's go."

Wrapping their cloaks around themselves, Kathryn and Polly pulled up their hoods and left the safety of the stable. The heavy, windswept rain slashed mercilessly against them. Kathryn decided to take the most direct route back. After all, there was nothing Hugh could do now except rant and rave like a madman.

Suddenly, Kathryn cried out in pained surprise as a severe cramp gripped her lower abdomen. She fell to her knees, and mud splattered all over her.

"Oh!" Polly cried. "I'll fetch help."

"Calm down, you ninny, and help me up," Kathryn shouted above the wind. "I refuse to spend the rest of my days listening to Hugh's ravings."

Polly helped Kathryn up. Arm in arm, they walked the remaining distance to the courtyard.

Hoping to enter undetected, Polly opened the front door a crack and peered inside. The foyer was deserted.

Kathryn and Polly, confident they'd managed to escape the earl's ire, crossed the foyer on sodden shoes that squished with each step forward. As Kathryn placed her foot upon the bottom stair, a voice boomed out like thunder and paralyzed her.

"What is the meaning of this?" Hugh shouted, glaring at the mud-covered apparition that was his wife.

Kathryn smiled winsomely and looked past Hugh at Patrick whose face contorted with the herculean effort to hold back his laughter. "I was about to retire," she said.

"You've been out," Hugh accused her.

Kathryn glanced at her cloak and knew it would be useless to lie. Her gaze shifted to her husband's angry countenance. "How perceptive! It's a quality I've . . ."

Hugh raised his hand to strike her but stopped when Kathryn flinched. Slowly, he lowered his hand and studied her for a long moment. Silence reigned in the foyer, and feeling guilty, Kathryn shifted uncomfortably beneath his stare.

"Do you care so little for our baby?" Hugh asked quietly.

"I—I—I did not think."

"Bypassing logical thinking is a nasty habit of yours," he countered. "Don't you realize you could begin your labor any moment?"

"It's begun." Kathryn grimaced with the sudden cramp gripping her lower regions. As she panted for breath, Kathryn reached for her husband.

Hugh swore and lifted her into his arms. "Get Maude!" he shouted, starting up the stairs.

Both Polly and Patrick ran to find Maude. In their excitement, they collided.

"Leave off, you bumblin' oaf," Polly snapped.

Patrick stepped aside to let her pass, but his eyes narrowed at the insult. He leaned against the wall and watched her hips and derrière in swift retreat.

The earl's willful countess was exerting a powerfully bad

influence on his wife, Patrick decided. What his usually sweet-tempered wife needed was a swollen belly that rivaled her mistress's.

Patrick chuckled at the thought, and a smile spread across his face. As soon as the present crisis was over, he would toil night and day to fill his wife's belly with his seed. And that would shut the wench's mouth! Whistling a spritely tune, Patrick sauntered into the great hall to drink while he awaited the arrival of Dungannon's heir.

"Put me down. The pain has passed," Kathryn said as her husband carried her into the bedchamber.

For a moment Hugh looked doubtful but then gingerly set Kathryn on her feet. He removed her muddied cloak and tossed it aside.

"Where are you going?" Hugh demanded when she started toward her dressing closet.

Kathryn stopped short, taken aback by the panic in his voice, and looked at him in surprise. "I want my blue night shift, and then I'm going to wash the mud off my face."

"I'll get the night shift," Hugh said. "Go to bed."

"No!" Kathryn paled beneath the mud spots. "I won't go to that hellish place of agony before my time."

"Come," Hugh said, his shaking hand grasping hers. "Sit here."

Hugh led Kathryn to the chair in front of the hearth and then raced for her dressing closet. In mere seconds, he reappeared with the blue night shift in hand. Hugh helped her stand and discard her dirtied skirt and blouse, as well as her undergarments, then pulled the night shift over her head. Carefully, he eased her back onto the chair.

"Bring water," Kathryn ordered. "I cannot meet my new son while my face is dirty."

Hugh smiled and hurried across the chamber to do her

bidding. Moments later, Hugh found Kathryn doubled over in the chair, grimacing against the pain.

As if he could share his strength, Hugh knelt in front of Kathryn and clasped her upper arms, yet he could do nothing but watch helplessly as she panted against the contraction.

At his comforting touch, Kathryn looked up. Beads of sweat glistened upon her forehead and above her upper lip.

Almighty God! Hugh cursed inwardly. *Why must the young be brought forth thusly?* The birth of his child was an occurrence for which Hugh had no strategy, and he suffered horribly for it.

With the passing of the contraction, Kathryn breathed with relief. "Once the babe is in her arms, a mother forgets the agony," Kathryn said as Hugh began washing the mud from her face. "Until the next time."

The chamber door swung open, admitting Maude and Polly on the run. "Polly, start a fire in the hearth and heat the water," the housekeeper ordered, heading toward the bed to make the necessary preparations.

"She refuses to go to bed," Hugh complained.

"She'll go soon enough without forcin' the issue," Maude said, then laughed at the strange sight of the earl in a high panic. "You'd better go downstairs. You don't look well and may not possess the stamina to endure this."

"I'm staying."

"I want to walk for a while," Kathryn said.

"Walk?"

"Yes."

Muttering to himself about the stupidity of women, Hugh helped Kathryn rise, and they began pacing the chamber. Lending support, his arm encircled her back. For a long, long time Hugh and Kathryn paced the chamber, stopping only when the contractions came, and in her agony, she leaned heavily against him. When the pain receded, they resumed their pacing.

"You appear unwell," Kathryn said, gazing at his pale face. "Go downstairs and wait with Patrick."

"I am going to see my son born," Hugh insisted.

"Then, it's time I—"

Much stronger than any previous, another fierce contraction gripped Kathryn, cutting off her words. Hugh held her as she buried her face against his chest. When the pain passed, Hugh lifted her into his arms and carried her to bed.

"Hold me," Kathryn cried, catching at his hands as another contraction seized her. Her panic rose with the increased intensity of pain.

Hugh eased onto the edge of the bed and leaned against the headboard. He gathered Kathryn into his arms, and she rested her sweat-dampened head against his chest.

Maude shoved the blue night shift above Kathryn's distended belly, baring her from breasts to feet. "The babe's a big one," the housekeeper said. "Must be a boy."

Kathryn smiled weakly at Hugh who kissed her sweaty brow. Almost instantly, another contraction seized her, and through the pain Kathryn felt a warm wetness gushing between her thighs.

"Here's the water," Maude called from the foot of the bed. "Katie, push when I tell you but not before."

Kathryn's pain was constant now, so close together were the contractions coming. The pain swirled around and around Kathryn like a heavy mist, enveloping her until she was oblivious to all but the voice of authority.

"Push!"

As if from a great distance, Kathryn heard the word and obeyed.

"Here's the head," Maude called. *"Push!"*

Kathryn writhed and pushed. Hugh's gaze was riveted upon the high drama being enacted between his wife's shuddering thighs.

"I have the shoulders," Maude cried. *"Push!"*

With one agonized wail, Kathryn bore down and the baby slipped from her straining body. Maude cleared the mucus from the baby's mouth, forcing air into the small lungs, then whacked the infant's backside. Wearing a broad grin, Maude held the squalling infant high so Hugh could see the tiny masculine appendage.

"A son!" Hugh cried.

Maude gently placed the babe upon his mother's belly to rest for a moment. Protesting his rude expulsion into the world, the babe continued wailing his displeasure.

"He has your voice," Kathryn said, glancing at Hugh who smiled at his perfect wife.

Maude cut and tied the cord, then handed the baby to Polly, whose task it was to wash and make him presentable for viewing. Maude would see to Kathryn.

Hugh kissed his wife and murmured his thanks. As if drawn by a more powerful force, he followed Polly across the chamber to better study his son.

Soon, Kathryn nestled her sleeping son within the safety of her arms.

"Thank you for my son," Hugh said, planting a kiss on her cheek.

"Our son," Kathryn corrected. "Is he not perfection? Why, I believe he resembles you. His hair and coloring are yours, not to mention his temperament."

"I'm positive I've never seen a more perfect baby," Hugh agreed, drawing a chair close to the bed. The proud parents proceeded to watch the most exciting event they'd ever seen, their child sleeping.

"What shall we name him?" Kathryn asked, breaking the silence.

"Shall we be politic or not?"

"I'd like to name him for your father," Kathryn answered. "Matthew is a fine name."

"Matthew *Timothy* Conn O'Neill," Hugh murmured, his eyes filling with emotion.

"Thank you, my love," Kathryn said. "The future earl of Tyrone should have close connections on both sides of the Irish Sea. Why not appoint two sets of godparents?"

Hugh smiled, pleased with the idea, and suggested, "Lord and Lady Burke would make excellent godparents."

Kathryn nodded in agreement, saying, "My brother is a favorite at court and would be an excellent choice for Matthew's English godfather."

"And his godmother?" Hugh asked. "Would you like to name your sister Brigette?"

"Brigette is by marriage a Scot," Kathryn replied. "Why not think great? The queen could hardly repudiate her own godson, the nephew of one of her favorites. Besides, it's an honorary position at best. The queen will be Matthew's English godmother."

"My dear, you think more like me with each passing day."

"You weren't saying that earlier," Kathryn reminded him. "You said I bypassed—"

"We'll forget all about that," Hugh interrupted her.

"Until the next time."

Hugh laughed, knowing the truth of her words. "Is it permissible for Matthew to accompany me to the great hall?"

"Yes, but only for a few minutes and he must be warmly swaddled." Kathryn winked at him. "Polly will go with you.

Perhaps Patrick will heed a subtle hint." Across the chamber, Polly blushed scarlet and Maude laughed.

Accompanied by his wife's tiring woman, Hugh carried his son downstairs. The O'Neill warriors and servants filled the great hall to overflowing. Cuddling his son close to his chest, Hugh walked toward the high table's dais, and an expectant hush descended upon those watching.

"Gentlemen!" Hugh called out, then grinned. "I give you Matthew Timothy Conn O'Neill, Dungannon's heir."

Wild cheering erupted from the men and servants. Hugh looked with pride at his son, whose eyes were startled open for a brief moment by the rousing din. Hugh gaped at the baby. Clear blue eyes, certain to change to emerald green, watched him from his son's wizened face.

The hair and the coloring are mine, Hugh thought, *but those eyes are his mother's. This one is a true blending of the stallion who sired him and the mare who bore him.*

Hugh raised his son into the air so all could view the tiny miracle he had wrought. Another rousing cheer arose, and Matthew Timothy Conn O'Neill wailed at being disturbed.

"It's fitting at Matthew's time of life to be with his mother," Hugh said, passing his screeching son to Polly. He winked at her, adding, "I intend to toast my *first* son's birth with each and every one of my men."

Polly smiled at his use of the word *first* and walked the length of the hall. Near the entrance, Patrick lounged against the wall and watched the proceedings. He especially admired the way his wife looked with a baby cradled in her arms.

Polly blushed furiously as she walked past him. There was no mistaking *that* smile or the gleam in her husband's eyes.

Turning to watch her retreat, Patrick admired her swaying hips and backside. It wouldn't be long, he decided, before his own son would be suckling at his wife's teats. With that satisfying thought, Patrick walked toward the high table to congratulate Hugh and toast Dungannon's heir.

It was very late when Hugh, on wobbly legs, climbed the stairs and went to his wife's chamber. He entered silently and crossed to the bed, then gazed through love-filled eyes at his wife and son.

Hugh sat down in the chair beside the bed and for a long time watched his family sleep. Stifling a yawn, he stood finally and bent to kiss his wife's forehead.

"Don't worry, son," he whispered. "Many brothers and sisters will follow you."

Hugh smiled at his sleeping wife. In no time at all, Kathryn would be sharing his bed.

20

"Damn her ice-sheathed heart," Hugh grumbled, alone and brooding in his study.

Kathryn had recovered from giving birth, but her fears concerning the marriage bed still held her in thrall. God in heaven knew how hard Hugh had tried to conquer her fears, but she always ended by crying and pleading for more time. Who would have imagined that Turlough could reach out from the grave and destroy his marriage? Dungannon would soon be filled with guests for Matthew's christening, and he would have no opportunity to woo his wife into his bed.

The door opened unexpectedly. Kathryn stood there, her unparalleled beauty taunting him.

Kathryn wore a forest-green skirt created from rich velvet and a peasant-style white linen blouse with billowy sleeves gathered at the wrists. The blouse's neckline and sleeves, as well as the skirt's hemline, were embroidered with golden threads. Her shining, copper hair was parted in the middle and woven into two braids that looped around her ears and were held there with clasps of gleaming gold. She wore no jewelry except her wedding band.

A becoming flush, caused by the flurry of activity surrounding the preparations for the christening, adorned Kathryn's cheeks. Following the birth of her son, Kathryn's figure had returned to its former petiteness, but nursing the baby had added a hint of voluptuousness. Her youthful face and body belied the fact that she had borne three children.

"Lord Burke's entourage has been sighted," Kathryn said.

"I'm coming." As if weighted down by the heaviness of his emotions, Hugh rose slowly from his chair. Together, they walked outside.

A large entourage of men-at-arms, baggage carts, and the Burke coach halted in the courtyard. Apparently, Lady Fiona did not travel lightly. The O'Neill retainers descended upon the carts and lent a helping hand to the Burke servants.

From astride his stallion, Lord Burke dismounted. With an exaggerated flourish and a roguish grin, he bowed in Kathryn's direction before turning away to help his wife out of the coach.

Dressed in a dark blue velvet traveling gown with a matching fur-lined cloak, Fiona looked as beautiful as ever. Always lush, her figure tended toward pudgy since the birth of her daughter.

Seeing Kathryn, Fiona squealed with feminine excitement and ran toward her. She threw herself into her friend's embrace, simultaneously laughing and crying and kissing and hugging.

With her attention on Fiona, Kathryn missed what happened next. Lord Burke turned back to the coach to assist someone else. Hugh rushed forward to greet his friend and this unexpected but incredibly lovely guest.

The vision alighting from the Burke coach was of average height and blessed with a complexion created from peaches and cream silk. Her hair was spun gold and her eyes sapphire blue.

"Greetings, and congratulations on the birth of your son." Lord Burke grinned and shook Hugh's hand.

"My thanks," Hugh said, then smiled at his unknown guest. "Welcome to Dungannon. I'm certain these ancient walls of stone have never seen a fairer face or form."

Flattered by the outrageous compliment, the young woman smiled. A blush stained her cheeks, enhancing her beauty.

"May I present Lady Aisling O'Brien, Fiona's cousin," Lord Burke introduced them. "I believe Aisling and her husband attended your wedding."

Aisling extended her hand artfully, saying, "Meeting Ireland's greatest earl is an enormous pleasure."

So sweetly did she smile that Hugh was reminded of an angel.

"May I be so bold as to say," Hugh returned the gallantry, "you are, indeed, worthy of your name—a dream."

"A pleasant dream, I hope," Aisling murmured, the blush on her cheeks deepening as she raised her eyes to meet his interested gaze.

"An exceedingly pleasant dream," Hugh said.

"Fiona wanted a traveling companion," Burke interjected, "and Aisling is recently widowed."

"Madam, my condolences on your loss," Hugh offered.

"Thank you, my lord, but I loathed my late husband," Aisling, replied, then laughed at the shocked surprise on Hugh's face.

The dulcet tones of Aisling's laughter caught Kathryn's attention. Fiona drew Kathryn toward her husband and cousin.

"This merry young lady is my cousin Aisling," Fiona

introduced them. "Aisling, may I present the countess of Tyrone, Lady Kathryn."

"We're pleased you could be with us for our son's christening," Kathryn welcomed her.

"Thank you," Aisling said, assessing Kathryn with a calculating stare. The countess of Tyrone was lovely but lacking when compared with herself. "The birth of a first son is such a joyous occasion."

Aisling turned back to Hugh, saying, "I wonder if the boy resembles his attractive father."

Hugh preened at the compliment. Kathryn's gaze narrowed speculatively on the beauty. Was her imagination playing games with her? Or was Aisling coldly aloof toward her and overly warm toward Hugh? By the expressions of those around her, no one appeared to think anything amiss.

"Madam, may I escort you inside," Hugh said, offering her his arm.

"You do me great honor, my lord," Aisling returned, accepting his arm. "Call me Aisling. There should be no formality between close friends. May I call you Hugh?"

Hugh grinned and nodded.

"I understand Dungannon is absolutely steeped in history," Aisling went on. "I insist on a complete tour before I depart, Hugh."

"You shall have it," Hugh replied. "And anything else you desire."

Ignored, Kathryn stared after them. Remembering her duties as hostess, she smiled at the Burkes and escorted them inside.

Hugh ushered them into the great hall and led them to the chairs in front of the hearth. Chasing October's chill from the journeyers, a blaze crackled in the hearth. At

Kathryn's nod, a serving girl brought the O'Neill's finest whiskey for the men and mulled wine for the ladies.

Maeve and Shana scampered into the hall. A ribbon-bedecked Vulcan followed behind them.

Having practiced diligently for more than a week, Maeve dropped the guests a curtsey as befitting royalty. Shana followed suit but only managed to fall with a heavy thud on her rump. Vulcan sympathized by licking her face, and the little girl giggled, making everyone else laugh. Shaking his head, Hugh lifted Shana onto his lap and planted a kiss upon her cheek.

"What lovely children!" Aisling exclaimed.

"Thank you." Kathryn wondered if her first impression of the woman could have been mistaken.

"The girls are the countess's but not yours?" Aisling asked in a sugary voice, casting her gaze in Hugh's direction. "Am I correct?"

Hugh stole a glance at his wife, then cleared his throat and said, "Shane O'Neill was their sire, but I'm the only father they can remember and I consider them my own. Needless to say, I could not love them more. Right, my beauty?" He planted another kiss on Shana's cheek. The two year old cast sultry blue eyes on her stepfather and wrapped her arms around his neck.

"I love you," Shana declared, nose to nose with Hugh. She gave him a noisy smack on his lips and laid her head possessively upon his shoulder. With a feminine maturity beyond her years, Shana silently challenged all those ladies present, including her mother, to attempt usurping her place.

Hugh chuckled, and Kathryn smiled with indulgence at her daughter. She couldn't help but wonder if Shana's rare beauty and flirtatious manner would one day bring the girl to a bad end at the hands of an unscrupulous man.

"Generosity and kindness are noble traits rarely found in the very great such as yourself," Aisling said to Hugh.

Kathryn, in the act of sipping her wine, choked suddenly and gasped for breath. Realizing she was laughing at his expense, Hugh flicked her an irritated glance. Fortunately, Nellie carried Matthew into the hall at that moment.

"Here's my prince," Kathryn announced, lifting Matthew from the nursemaid's arms. As women are wont to do, Fiona and Aisling cooed over the boy whose startling emerald-green eyes watched their unfamiliar faces warily.

"What a beautiful baby," Fiona gushed.

"Yes," Aisling agreed.

Kathryn smiled with pride, pleased with the compliments to her son.

"I suppose I must make good on our wager," Lord Burke remarked.

Hugh chuckled with glee. Kathryn looked up at him. Hugh seemed to be staring at Aisling's exposed cleavage as she leaned forward to see the baby. It was then that insidious jealousy began weaving itself around Kathryn's heart and mind.

"Why, I believe this handsome boy resembles his sire," Aisling said. Aware the earl was enjoying her apparent charms, Aisling leaned forward in a bold invitation.

Hugh smiled but glanced at his wife. Riveted on Aisling, Kathryn's green-eyed gaze marked the other woman for certain destruction. Lord Burke, sensing the nasty undercurrent, cast an accusing look at his wife. Fiona lowered her gaze. Bringing Aisling along had been a grave error.

"You must have been relieved that Lady Kathryn managed a boy after producing only girls," Aisling said to Hugh in a voice that dripped innocence. "One can never tell, you know."

Beauty is as beauty does, Hugh decided, revising his opinion of Aisling. *And this beauty's jibes make her ugly.*

Kathryn opened her mouth to reply, but Matthew chose that moment to wail loudly. Hugh tried to clear the tense atmosphere with humor, saying, "Though my son has inherited my handsome face, he unfortunately possesses his mother's disposition."

It was the wrong thing to say. Everyone but Kathryn laughed. She smiled stiffly and rose from her chair.

"Matthew is hungry," Kathryn said as his tiny mouth frantically sought her nipple through her blouse. "If you will excuse me?"

"I'm surprised Lady Kathryn hasn't acquired a wet nurse by now," Aisling said.

Leaving the hall, Kathryn glanced back at that remark and caught sight of the blonde smiling at Hugh.

"Katie is an excellent mother and enjoys nurturing the children," Hugh defended his wife.

"How quaint," Aisling remarked. "But, would you not agree that a hungry infant interrupts so many interesting activities, especially at night?"

With her lips curled in a silent snarl, Kathryn glanced back a final time. In the next instant, the snarl disappeared and a smile tugged at the corners of her lips.

Apparently unhappy with her father's attention on another woman, Shana opted for a more direct approach to satisfy her needs. She reached up and forcibly turned his face in her own direction.

"I love you, Da," Shana vowed as her mother stepped into the foyer and dissolved into giggles.

At supper time, Hugh strolled through the connecting door into Kathryn's chamber and found her standing beside the bed where she'd placed her jewelry box. He noted the special care she'd taken with her toilet, her appearance being especially lovely that night.

Deep in contemplation of her jewels, Kathryn was a vision in peach. Her gown, designed to catch and hold the eyes of all, had a tight-fitting bodice and daring neckline that displayed her slim waist and lush breasts to best advantage.

Hugh sat in the chair in front of the heart. He only hoped her mood had improved.

"I'm almost ready, dear," Kathryn called over her shoulder.

At the sweetness in her tone, Hugh looked in her direction and wondered what devilment she was planning, but Kathryn seemed intent on selecting her jewels for the evening. Hugh relaxed, stretched his legs out, and watched his oblivious wife.

Dipping into the jewel box, Kathryn removed a necklace of perfectly matched pearls and held it up to her gown. She decided against them and put them back.

Watching her, Hugh smiled. He could well imagine the wrinkling of her upturned nose.

Next, Kathryn chose an exquisite opal necklace with jeweled clasp. After thoughtful consideration, she discarded that too.

"I don't like Lady Aisling," Kathryn remarked. "What do you think?"

"I think, judging a person on the basis of one meeting is unfair," Hugh said.

Kathryn frowned at his reply. Then she saw it, the perfect necklace to complement her gown, and smiled mischievously. From her jewel box, Kathryn removed the ancient Celtic torc of gold that symbolized the O'Neill's chosen woman. Not only would the torc complement her gown, but a significant message would be sent to that scheming woman and her own illustrious husband. The chest of jewels closed with a snap, and Kathryn turned around and smiled at Hugh.

"Will you help me with this?"

Hugh stood up and walked across the chamber. Taking the necklace from her, he turned her around.

"Do you think she's pretty?" Kathryn asked as he placed the torc around her neck.

"Who?"

"Lady Aisling." Kathryn fought to control her temper, but an exasperated note entered her voice. "Well?"

"Quite lovely." At first puzzled by his wife's obvious anxiety, Hugh fumbled with the clasp when a sudden realization startled him.

Kathryn was jealous.

Hugh smiled inwardly. It was true that human nature desired what others wanted. The attention that Lady Aisling had fixed on him apparently made his wife jealous.

"Are you jealous?" he asked.

"Lady Aisling has nothing I would desire," she replied.

Experimentally, Hugh let his fingers linger longer than necessary on Kathryn's neck. With skillful hands, he kneaded her shoulder blades and whispered close to her ear, "So tense, my love?"

"Probably the excitement of the christening festivities," Kathryn murmured, leaning against him when his lips brushed the side of her neck. Like an old friend, that familiar tingle raced throughout her body, starved as it was for her husband's touch though her mind resisted it.

Hugh turned Kathryn to face him and pressed his lips to hers. He smiled and offered his arm, saying, "Let's join our guests."

The great hall was a buzzing hive of activity. Arm in arm, Hugh and Kathryn strode toward the high table.

Along the way, Hugh called a greeting to one or another of his men, and Kathryn, respected and loved by all, smiled and nodded her head.

Reaching the high table, Hugh smiled at Kathryn and lifted her hand to his lips. As she returned his smile, Kathryn glanced at Aisling and noted with satisfaction that the blond beauty was watching this display of husbandly devotion. It was then Hugh gifted his wife with the first of several disappointments she would receive during the following days.

"Ignoring our guests won't do, sweetheart," he said, releasing her hand. "We should mingle and play the gracious host and hostess."

Without another word, Hugh ushered Kathryn to a seat beside Fiona at one end of the table. Turning, he walked away and claimed the seat between Aisling and Burke.

From her vantage point, Kathryn gazed down the length of the table and couldn't help but notice the immodesty of Aisling's gown and the shocking amount of flesh it displayed. Kathryn frowned when Hugh leaned close to whisper into Aisling's ear.

"Is anything wrong?" Fiona asked.

"No, I was thinking of the striking resemblance between you and your cousin."

"Really?" Fiona was surprised. "Except for the color of our eyes, I am unaware of any similarities."

Kathryn smiled wryly, saying, "Tell me about Grania."

Throughout what seemed like an endless meal, Kathryn kept a stiff smile pasted on her face. Politely, she listened to her friend's incessant chatter about her daughter from the moment of conception until the day the Burkes left for Dungannon. Hawklike, Kathryn watched the attention Hugh gave Aisling, and by gradual degrees, glumness marred Kathryn's expression.

When supper finally ended, Hugh glanced down the high table for the first time that evening and signaled Kathryn to leave the men-at-arms to their own entertainment. Along with their noble guests, they planned to retire to the study. Standing, Hugh offered his arm to Aisling and left his wife to follow behind with the Burkes who exchanged worried glances.

In the study, Hugh handed Lord Burke a whiskey and noted his wife's growing vexation. Aisling had adeptly refused to relinquish her place beside Hugh, and miserably, Kathryn felt like an outsider in her own home.

"You have superb taste in jewels," Aisling said to Hugh. "I do admire your wife's necklace."

Hugh opened his mouth to reply, but Kathryn's tongue was faster.

"My thanks," Kathryn said, teasing the other woman's envy by leisurely fingering the priceless torc. "It's *absolutely steeped* in history and has been passed down through generations as the symbol of the O'Neill's chosen woman. Only she may possess it—as she possesses the O'Neill."

There was no mistaking Kathryn's warning, and Aisling looked at her through sapphire slits of displeasure. Hugh choked on his whiskey.

"What's the news from Dublin?" Hugh asked his friend, trying to move the subject to safer ground.

"P-pardon?" Lord Burke was trying valiantly to control his merriment at the sight of two noble felines baring their claws at each other.

It was Fiona who *almost* saved the day, saying, "Katie, I've the most delicious gossip to—"

"By far the most delicious gossip of all was Lady Kathryn's abduction," Aisling interrupted.

Stunned to silence, the O'Neills and the Burkes gaped

at Aisling. Hugh glanced at Kathryn and was dismayed to see her leveling a decidedly murderous look on the other woman.

"How terrible it must have been for you, Hugh," Aisling went on. "Having one's wife achieve such notoriety can hardly have been pleasant. Indeed, it's disgraceful."

"Aisling, how dare you say such a thing!" Fiona cried. "Katie did not *ask* to be abducted."

Kathryn paled. Her expression became the saddest mixture of rage and pain.

How dare this sorry excuse for the gentler sex, this bloodthirsty she cat wound my lady! Hugh fumed, itching to throttle her. Unfortunately, Aisling was their guest and must be treated courteously.

Despising himself, Hugh forced a smile and said, "What do you say, Aisling? Tomorrow would be a good day for the grand tour of Dungannon."

"I'd love it," Aisling gushed, casting Kathryn a triumphant look.

"It's almost time for Matthew's feeding," Kathryn announced, rising from her chair. She leveled a disparaging look on her husband and said, "I must see to the needs of Dungannon's heir." Kathryn retreated with her head held high and an unyielding set to her shoulders.

Much later, having dismissed her tiring woman and retired for the night, Kathryn was unable to sleep. She rose from her lonely bed to pace back and forth across the chamber. Finding herself in front of the connecting door, Kathryn knew it was the only real barrier to her husband's love, yet the courage to pass through it evaded her.

How beautiful Aisling is, Kathryn admitted to herself. And how she would love to send the blond bitch back to Dublin or anywhere else away from Dungannon.

It wasn't actually Aisling's fault that she was attracted to

Hugh. He did possess many fine traits—handsome, charming, titled, rich and, Kathryn hoped, honorable and faithful.

And it wasn't Hugh's fault that he was attracted to another woman, Kathryn thought. Aisling was exceptionally lovely and offering the very thing that she had been withholding from him. All would be well if she could deliver herself into her husband's hands.

Kathryn reached for the doorknob with a trembling hand but quickly snatched it back. Frustrated and unable to go on, Kathryn pressed her forehead against the connecting door as a sob escaped her throat, breaking the dam of tears she'd held back all evening.

In his own chamber, Hugh heard the muffled sobs and padded across the chamber to stand in front of the connecting door. Yearning to comfort Kathryn, Hugh reached for the doorknob, but when his hand would have made contact, he yanked it back as if scalded by fire.

Let her cry, Hugh decided, steeling himself against the pitiable sobs. Kathryn would never yield if he offered her sympathy.

Hugh retraced his steps across the chamber and got into bed, but still those distressing sobs seeped through the door to torture him. Rolling onto his stomach, Hugh pulled the downy pillow over his head to block out the sounds of his tormentor.

Late the next morning, Hugh and Aisling strolled into the stable yard on the last part of her tour of Dungannon. Finding vast amusement in the fact that a refined young noblewoman wanted a tour of his stables, Hugh hid a smile as he ushered his lovely guest inside.

For her part, Aisling hoped no one would be in the area so she could further her cause to make Hugh her lover. If successful, she would become the pampered, privileged mistress of a powerful man when he traveled to Dublin. Naturally, his wife and children would be left to languish in Dungannon while she enjoyed his priceless gifts.

Sable, Kathryn's most prized possession, drew Aisling's attention. "I've never seen a more beautiful horse," Aisling said.

"Sable was a gift to Kathryn," Hugh told her, following her gaze to the magnificent mare.

"How generous you are," Aisling murmured. Her sapphire-eyed gaze glowed with adoration, and a blush rose upon her perfect complexion.

"Would you care for an early morning ride tomorrow?" Hugh asked.

"I'd love to ride Sable," Aisling replied, thinking the earl was more than a little interested in what she had to offer. But how could it be otherwise?

"Well . . ." Hugh hedged, reluctant to hurt his wife's feelings. After all, Sable belonged to her.

"I'm certain Lady Kathryn won't mind a short ride," Aisling insisted. "I will, of course, ask her permission."

"Very well," Hugh agreed against his better judgment.

Hugh offered Aisling his arm. Chatting about inconsequential matters, they walked back to the courtyard where he sent her off to join the ladies.

Meandering through the garden, Aisling spied Fiona and Kathryn. They were seated upon a bench with their backs turned to her approach. Something in their manner suggested a confidential conversation. Hoping to glean information that would benefit her cause, Aisling hid behind the shrubbery and listened.

"I know something is troubling you," Fiona was saying. "Is it Aisling?"

"Partially," Kathryn admitted. "I know she's cast her eyes upon my husband."

"I'm sorry," Fiona apologized. "I never imagined this would happen. After the christening, I will insist we leave immediately for Dublin."

Hiding behind the shrubbery, Aisling curled her lips in displeasure.

"Much of the blame rests with me," Kathryn said.

"What do you mean?"

Kathryn opened her mouth to speak but hesitated and looked away in embarrassment. Taking a deep breath, she confessed, "Hugh and I are not intimate."

"Oh, my poor dear! I'm so sorry."

Kathryn's head snapped back to her friend. "It's my choice, not his."

Fiona's mouth dropped open in surprise. "It's obvious you love Hugh. Why deny him his place in your bed?"

"I—I am afraid," Kathryn answered. "Turlough—" Unable to embellish her answer further, she broke off.

Intimacy was the one thing Fiona had never feared. "What happened?" she asked in a hushed tone, stunned that her friend could be thus afflicted.

"I—" Kathryn flushed hotly. "He touched me."

"You were his prisoner."

"But I loathed Turlough and feel so—so unclean," Kathryn explained. "What if Hugh—you know—and I can't . . . ?"

The most incredulous expression of relief appeared on Fiona's face and was followed by a smile. Then she chuckled. That tiny chuckle grew into a hearty laugh until uncontrollable tears streamed down her cheeks. Finally, Fiona hiccuped and managed to catch her breath while one hand soothed the ache in her belly.

Horrified, Kathryn stared at her. How could a friend find humor in such a terrible predicament?

"Katie O'Neill, how is it possible you've married two

virile men and borne three children yet remain utterly naive?"

Bewildered, Kathryn asked, "What do you mean?"

Superior in her expertise, Fiona arched a brow at her, saying, "I was no maid on my wedding day. Would you also consider me unclean because someone other than Michael had touched me?"

"Well," Kathryn hedged, unwilling to answer lest she hurt her friend's feelings.

"Thank you very much," Fiona said dryly, then grinned. "Though my husband should know better, he believes I am as pure as a virgin. Well, almost. And Hugh feels the same way about you. Men in love can be such fools."

In spite of herself, Kathryn smiled.

"My advice is to bed your husband immediately," Fiona said.

At the sound of another's approach, the two women looked around in surprise. The most placid of smiles masked the fury Aisling harbored toward her cousin at that moment. With any luck, Lady Kathryn would not heed Fiona's advice.

Many of the castle folk were just rising from their beds as Kathryn marched toward the stables early the next morning. She'd passed another long and sleepless night in her chamber, and dark smudges of fatigue beneath her eyes gave proof to her anxiety. As if by magic, the countess had been transformed into a scruffy boy, dressed in a shabby riding outfit of tight breeches, shirt, cap, and comfortably worn leather boots.

A long ride on Sable would sweep the cobwebs from her mind, Kathryn thought. Then she could handle that simpering harlot who dared to invade her home.

Walking into the stable yard, Kathryn stopped short at

the sight that greeted her. Hugh was mounted on his stallion, and that simpering harlot perched regally at his side.

Aisling noticed Kathryn first and gave her a triumphant, condescending smile. To the casual observer, Aisling was the countess and Kathryn her bedraggled groom.

Kathryn's gaze dropped to the horse on which Aisling perched, and her eyes widened in angry surprise. "What is the meaning of this?" she demanded.

At the sound of his wife's voice, Hugh turned and smiled at Kathryn, but then noticed her attire. Up and down, Hugh inspected Kathryn's boyish appearance with disapproval, then glanced at Aisling as if comparing the two. A discouraged shake of his head conveyed the message that his wife did not measure up to the impeccable vision at his side. Hugh's gaze locked on Kathryn's.

"Aisling and I are going to ride," Hugh answered. "Would you care to join us?"

"Sable is mine," Kathryn insisted. "Get her off my horse."

Hugh snapped his head around to look at Aisling, who refused to meet his gaze. Apparently, the lady had lied about receiving his wife's permission to ride Sable. Well, there was nothing to be done for it now. Hugh realized he was neatly caught between the proverbial rock and a hard place. He would appeal to his wife's genteel upbringing and then try to placate her later. What else could he do?

"Katie, the stables are filled with horses," Hugh said, gesturing to the barn. "Pick another."

"I want Sable." Kathryn stamped her foot for emphasis.

"Sable is yours because I chose to gift you with her," Hugh returned, becoming angry. "You forget that Aisling is our honored guest. Apologize at once."

Long moments passed as Kathryn and Hugh stared at

each other. Finally, Hugh cut the tense silence, saying, "We are waiting."

"Go to hell!" Kathryn exploded, shaking her fist at him. "And take your honored guest with you!" With that, she whirled away and stalked off the way she had come.

"Get back here!" Hugh shouted. At the sound of his command, Kathryn quickened her pace and then broke into a trot. Watching her, Hugh fought against an admiring smile. Those tight-fitting breeches displayed his wife's delectable derriere to best advantage.

"I'm sorry to be the cause of such trouble," Aisling apologized, gaining his attention.

"Nonsense," Hugh said, suppressing the urge to throttle her. "Please accept my apology on behalf of my wife."

Aisling smiled. "And how could I possibly rebuff such gallantry from so handsome a man?"

Drawing curious stares from loitering servants, Kathryn stormed into the foyer, raced up the stairs, and slammed her chamber door. She crossed to the window and looked out.

"Here she is." Maude's irritated voice sounded from the doorway as she hurried into the chamber. "I thought you couldn't find her?"

Kathryn turned toward the voice. Noting her expression of misery, Maude lifted a squalling Matthew from Nellie's arms and shooed the nursemaid out.

Kathryn sat in the chair in front of the hearth and bared her breasts. Without a word, she took her angry son from the housekeeper and offered him a nipple. Matthew quieted instantly, having reached his hunger-inspired goal.

"I'm losing my husband," Kathryn moaned, raising her anguished expression to Maude. Her bottom lip quivered in the battle to hold back her tears.

"That's not surprisin'," came the housekeeper's matter-of-fact reply. "After all, it's no secret you're not sharin' the earl's bed."

"Mind your own business," Kathryn snapped.

"Like it or not, you'll listen to what I have to say," Maude shot back. "I welcomed you here as Shane's bride, and when he died, helped you bury him. I delivered two of your babies and nursed you through the loss of another. And I was the one who cared for you while Turlough was doin' his worst. Why, I've been more mother to you than your own, and I will be heard."

Kathryn hung her head sheepishly, saying, "I'm sorry."

"That's better," Maude snorted. "Tell me, do you love the earl?"

"Yes."

"Then fight for him."

"But how?"

Maude smirked. "You already know the answer to that."

"I cannot."

"Expectin' him to live like a monk is unfair, not to mention unnatural," Maude said. "He loves you, but even love has its limits. Go to him and he'll use you gently. Believe me, Hugh O'Neill is no Turlough."

"I'll think about it."

Maude nodded and started to leave, then paused at the door, warning, "Lady Aisling's a real beauty. Don't be thinkin' too long or all will be for naught." The door clicked shut behind her.

Kathryn frowned. She looked down at Matthew whose eyes were half closed with the pleasure of suckling upon his mother's nipple.

"Still hungry?" she cooed. "Feast upon its mate now." Nearly satiated, Matthew protested feebly when she shifted him to the other side.

"What say you, my prince?" Kathryn asked, watching him. "What should Mama do?"

Drawing upon the teat, Matthew opened his eyes at the sound of her voice but said nothing.

21

Dungannon's chapel was filled to overflowing with honored guests, O'Neill kinsmen, men-at-arms, and retainers to witness the baptism of Matthew Timothy Conn O'Neill. One day the infant would be the lord of all that surrounded them, assuming the English did not steal it first.

The O'Neills and the Burkes stood in front of the village priest at the flower-adorned altar. Holding a fidgeting Matthew in his arms, Lord Burke and his wife stood between the proud parents. Kathryn stood on Fiona's left and Hugh to the right of Lord Burke.

As the priest began his litany, Kathryn looked at Hugh and unconsciously perused his body from black leather boots upward. Lingering on the spot of her husband's masculinity, her green-eyed gaze glowed with the remembrance of past passions.

If she did not soon return to his bed, would she lose him? Kathryn wondered, her gaze drifting upward to his chest, hidden beneath silk shirt and velvet doublet. Loving him so, how could she endure his loss?

Kathryn's gaze reached his face, and she reddened with embarrassment. The corners of Hugh's lips turned up in an enigmatic smile. His intense, smoldering gaze held her in thrall.

Almost lazily, Hugh perused the length of *her* body. His dark eyes lingered on her supple curves and proud peaks.

Kathryn felt positively naked. A familiar and urgent sensation throbbed between her thighs. A hot blush colored her cheeks when Hugh, aware of the effect of his lusty scrutiny, grinned knowingly at her.

My God! Kathryn thought, unable to tear her gaze from his. How could he do this to her while they stood before a man of the cloth and a whole chapelful of people? It was indecent!

Annointed with the holy water, Matthew kicked and screeched in anger, breaking the sensual spell Hugh had cast upon Kathryn. Lord Burke gladly handed the squalling infant to his godmother. To Kathryn's relief, the ceremony soon ended and everyone walked to the great hall.

A festive atmosphere reigned as the enormous chamber filled with guests. Lifting Matthew from Fiona's arms, Kathryn stood beside Hugh to welcome their son's many well-wishers. Proudly, they exhibited Dungannon's heir-apparent to all.

"Great God above," Hugh whispered. "It seems there are more O'Neills in Ulster than paupers in London."

"The Irish are prolific, to be sure," Kathryn said with a smile. "But, I'm certain they came as much to peek at the greatest of earls as they did to honor our son."

"Perhaps they wanted to see you," Hugh countered. " 'Tis an uncommon wench who's capable of capturing the hand of two O'Neills in marriage."

"If you will remember, dear, I was the captive and you were the captor."

Hugh opened his mouth to parry, but Matthew wailed, proclaiming his hunger.

"Your son's disposition resembles yours," Kathryn said. "Try to set a better example for him in the future. If you will excuse me, I must feed our hungry son."

There was no mistaking what the heated glow in his wife's eyes meant, Hugh thought as he watched her climb the stairs. His reluctant wife was ready to return to his bed. If he could just manage to get her alone, Kathryn would be sleeping beside him that very night. *Or sooner.*

Hugh scanned the crowded hall, and locating Patrick, went to speak with his man and enlist his aid in getting Kathryn alone. Unaware that he was another's quarry, Hugh left the great hall and headed for the gardens. His predator, Lady Aisling, followed him out.

Upstairs, Kathryn fed Matthew and left him with Nellie in the nursery, then retraced her steps downstairs to her guests. Somewhere between ascent and descent, Kathryn made up her mind to place herself in her husband's hands and return to his bed. Reaching the great hall, Kathryn searched the crowd for Hugh.

Greeting first one guest and then another, Kathryn made her way slowly through the crowd toward Patrick. "Do you know where my elusive husband is?" she asked, sidling up to him.

"I believe he stepped out for a breath of air."

"Stepped out where?"

Having seen Aisling following Hugh, Patrick hesitated for a brief moment, then answered, "I—I think the gardens."

"Thanks, I'll find him."

As she stepped away, Patrick had second thoughts and grasped her arm, halting her progress. "Shouldn't one of you stay here to host your guests?"

"It's important I speak with him," Kathryn said, shrugging off his restraining hand. She glanced around at the crowd, saying, "My guests seem to be enjoying themselves without my help." With that, Kathryn headed for the foyer.

Whatever happened was not his fault, Patrick decided as he watched her exit the hall. After all, he had tried to stop her.

Patrick sauntered toward the foyer. He would position himself there to discourage the curious and, if need be, assist the wounded.

Outside, Kathryn walked down the garden's main path. Though the days of sunshine were warm, the autumn chill of October's early twilight made her shiver.

Reviewing in her mind what she would say to Hugh, Kathryn stumbled upon the couple before she was aware of their presence. At the sight, Kathryn's lightheartedness turned to lead and sank to her stomach.

On the path in front of her stood Hugh and Aisling, locked in a passionate embrace, their bodies and lips pressing together as one. Unfortunately, fury blinded Kathryn to the fact that her husband was struggling to free himself without injuring his ardent assailant.

Kathryn curled her lips in a snarl and a growl escaped her throat. Without thinking, she grabbed a handful of blond hair and yanked savagely, wrenching the couple apart. Her boiling anger unappeased with that, Kathryn flung the stunned woman to the ground.

"You may have ridden my horse, but you won't be riding my husband," she hissed. With that, Kathryn rounded on her fascinated husband, mute with shock.

"Adulterer!"

Like a sudden and fast-moving tempest, Kathryn whirled away and ran back down the garden path.

"Katie!" Hugh shouted. With an oath, he chased her

through the side gardens, the courtyard, and into the foyer.

At the base of the stairs, Hugh reached out and grabbed her arm, spinning her around so roughly their heaving chests collided. Kathryn leapt back from the contact as if he were a vile and unclean thing, but Hugh refused to release her.

"You were kissing Aisling," she accused.

"No, Aisling was kissing me," he insisted.

"What the bloody hell is the difference?" Kathryn hurled at him, struggling to break free.

Hugh gave her a hard shake and shouted, "I love you, Katie!"

Kathryn stopped struggling and Hugh's hands dropped away, releasing her. Kathryn's anguished gaze held his prisoner and judged him guilty. She raised her hand, and with all her strength, slapped him. With her fury spent and her shoulders sagging beneath weighty pain, Kathryn turned and climbed the stairs to her chamber.

Dejected, Hugh watched her retreat. When she'd vanished from sight, he lowered himself onto the bottom stair and rubbed his smarting cheek. His wife's right hand carried a pretty good wallop.

Black boots appeared in front of him, and Hugh looked up at his man's commiserating expression. "Beware," Hugh warned. "I'll see your ugly head adorning a pike at Dublin Castle."

Patrick sat down beside him. "All is not lost," he said. "Once Katie's calmed down, she'll reconsider her actions. After all, you did tell her—and everyone in the hall—you loved her. What woman doesn't want her husband to shout his love for her to the world?"

Hugh stared at his man but said nothing.

"All of Ulster is titillated," Patrick went on. "Imagine,

the great earl professing his love for his wife in such loud terms."

Hugh scowled, his tolerance for the other man's humor at an all-time low.

"Retire for an hour or two," Patrick advised, heedless of consequence. "The guests will think you and your wife are consummatin' the great love you share."

"Go to hell," Hugh growled, then stood and went to his study where he could find whiskey and peace.

The bewitching hour found Kathryn, hurt and confused, pacing the floor in her chamber. Barefoot and clad in an ivory gossamer night shift, she never felt the chilly warning of winter's approach that invaded her chamber through the open window. Misery numbed her to such earthly discomfort.

I've lost Hugh forever, Kathryn thought. Striking him after he'd professed his love was unforgivable. After all, her husband wasn't a god but a man with a man's need. Suffering the lonely consequence of hesitating too long would be her punishment.

"Damn my stubborn pride!"

At the sound of her own voice, Kathryn looked up and found herself in front of the connecting door. *Dare I approach him now? What would he say? Does he want me or Lady Aisling? There is only one way to find out.*

With a trembling hand, Kathryn opened the connecting door, stepped inside and, blocking a coward's retreat, closed it behind her. Kathryn reached for the straps of her night shift, and like a flower shedding its petals, the gossamer gown fluttered off her body to the floor. Magnificently naked, she stood with her eyes riveted on the form of her sleeping husband.

Taking several deep breaths, Kathryn summoned her courage and approached the bed. Long moments passed as she stood in naked splendor and gazed at her husband, but ultimately the powerful fear of rejection overwhelmed her. Kathryn turned away, intending to return to the refuge of her own chamber. Without warning, a hand shot out and yanked her down on the bed.

"Are you coming to bed?" Hugh asked, nose to nose with his surprised wife. "Or was there something urgent you wish to discuss?" A smile lurked in his voice.

"Bed," she murmured, relieved, and pressed her lips to his. Kathryn poured all her love and long-denied need into that single, stirring kiss.

Hugh answered her in kind, then whispered, "You're cold, my love. Let me warm you beneath the covers."

Accepting his invitation, Kathryn slipped beneath the coverlet. They lay side by side and reveled in the exquisite sensation of flesh against flesh. Hugh drew Kathryn on top of him, and his erection teased the softness of her belly.

"Does your face hurt?" she asked.

"Not anymore," he answered, caressing her cheek. "Are you afraid, my love?"

"Not anymore."

Hugh rolled over on top of her. His demanding kiss halted all speech, his tongue seeking and finding entrance to the sweetness beyond her rosebud lips.

Leaving her mouth behind, Hugh rained feathery-light kisses upon her temples, eyelids, nose, and throat. Kathryn arched in primal submission and offered her neck to him. Hugh moaned at her gesture and buried his face against it, inhaling her fresh scent. Casting her fears away forever, Kathryn held him close, wanting and needing to mingle and mesh with him into one divine being.

"Easy, love," Hugh whispered. Worshiping her, his lips dipped lower to her breasts and licked her weeping nipples. "My son's breakfast—"

Cupping her swollen breasts, Hugh lowered his mouth to suckle her mother's milk from one large nipple, then gave his attention to the other. With each delicious drawing upon her nipples, Kathryn felt a throbbing between her thighs.

Weaning himself, Hugh slashed his tongue downward and licked the softness of her belly, leaving in his wake a riot of fluttering like the beating of a thousand airy butterfly wings. Bypassing her silken womanhood, Hugh sprinkled kisses down one leg and up the other. Reaching her moist silkiness once more, Hugh flicked his tongue back and forth across her throbbing pearl until kittenish mewling sounds welled up from her throat.

"Take me," Kathryn panted.

With his manhood poised to pierce, Hugh reared up between her thighs and plunged deep, making her cry out with the pleasure of it. Kathryn entwined her legs around his waist and, driven beyond reason, met each powerful thrust of her husband's. Thrashing wildly together, they became one maddened creature caught in the throes of unspeakable passion.

"*Hugh!*" Kathryn exploded, her throbbing depths enveloping, drawing his seed.

Hugh groaned and shuddered, then fell upon her and buried his face against her neck. At this weakest of life's moments, Kathryn held her love tightly and shrouded him from all that lay beyond the kingdom of their bed. As their panting eased and their heartbeats slowed, Hugh and Kathryn fell into the drugged sleep of the contented . . .

"Mmmm," Kathryn murmured in her sleep. Wrapped in the comforting warmth of her husband's arms, she buried her face in the mat of dark hair covering his chest. In the next instant, pandemonium descended on the chamber like the frenzied Furies of fable.

The chamber door swung open with a loud bang, and Maude barged in on the run. Close on her heels came Patrick, followed by Maeve and Shana and Vulcan. Hugh bolted up in the bed, and in the process, dumped Kathryn back out of sight of the intruders.

"Lady Kathryn is missin'," Maude cried. "And Matthew is squallin' to be fed."

"I've checked the gardens and stables," Patrick added. "Sable is where she should be."

A head of copper hair peeped over the coverlet on the other side of Hugh. "Fetch Matthew here to me," Kathryn instructed Maude and sat up, carefully holding the coverlet up to her chin.

With his lips quirked in a smile, Patrick looked at Hugh who raised his brows at his man and broke into a devilish grin. Spying his mistress, Vulcan barked and leapt onto the bed so suddenly the coverlet dropped, exposing her bare breasts. With a reddening face, Kathryn snatched it back up. Hugh chuckled and relaxed against the headboard as Maeve and Shana raced toward the bed to greet their mother.

"If you please, Maude," Kathryn repeated, "bring my son to me." The older woman hurried away.

"You're not wearing clothes, Mama," Maeve observed. "What are you doing?"

Hugh chuckled, earning himself a quelling glance from his wife.

"I'm playing with Da," Kathryn told her oldest.

"Me play too?" Shana asked.

Hugh threw back his head and roared with laughter. Patrick joined in.

" 'Tis grown-up games we're playing, my beauty." Kathryn smiled at her youngest daughter.

"Who would like a pony ride?" Patrick asked, and the

two little girls squealed with delight. "Then, come along with me to find Soot."

Without needing a second invitation, Maeve and Shana dashed out of the chamber and Vulcan gave chase, almost knocking over Maude who was on her way in with a howling Matthew.

"Patrick, tell Polly I won't need her services until later," Kathryn said as he turned to leave.

"My wife will be happy to hear that bit of news since at this very moment she's draped across the chamber pot."

"Polly's ill?" Maude asked, instantly alert.

Patrick grinned at his mother-in-law. "No, sweet Mother, she's breedin'." Then he was gone but the sound of his laughter drifted back to the three in the bedchamber who stared dumbly at the empty doorway.

"Humph!" Maude snorted, passing Matthew to his mother. "That good-for-nothin' finally did somethin' right."

Kathryn pushed aside the coverlet and offered a nipple to her hungry son. Matthew suckled on it as though it were his last meal.

Hugh smiled at his wife and son, then called out to Maude as she turned to leave, "Tell our guests not to look for us before supper. If any problems arise, see Patrick."

"Yes, my lord." The door clicked shut behind the housekeeper.

Contented, Hugh watched his son suckling upon Kathryn's breast. "Greedy, is he not?" Hugh remarked.

"His resemblance to you is uncanny."

Hugh smiled at that and his arm went around Kathryn's shoulders. Cuddling close, he nibbled upon her sensitive neck, making her giggle at the sensations he was creating.

"I should see about hiring a wet nurse," Kathryn said, her voice a fair imitation of Aisling's. "A hungry babe interrupts so many interesting activities. What say you, my great earl?"

Hugh gently turned her face toward him and tilted her chin up. As he smiled and stared into her mesmerizing green eyes, his mouth descended to hers and claimed it in an earth-shattering kiss.

"My sweet countess," Hugh breathed against her lips. "I love you."

Reckless abandon. Intrigue. And spirited love. A magnificent array of tempestuous, passionate historical romances to capture your heart.

Virginia Henley

☐ 17161-X	The Raven and the Rose	$4.99
☐ 20144-6	The Hawk and the Dove	$4.99
☐ 20429-1	The Falcon and the Flower	$4.99

Joanne Redd

☐ 20825-4	Steal The Flame	$4.50
☐ 18982-9	To Love an Eagle	$4.50
☐ 20114-4	Chasing a Dream	$4.50
☐ 20224-8	Desert Bride	$3.95

Lori Copeland

☐ 10374-6	Avenging Angel	$4.99
☐ 20134-9	Passion's Captive	$4.99
☐ 20325-2	Sweet Talkin' Stranger	$4.99
☐ 20842-4	Sweet Hannah Rose	$4.99

Elaine Coffman

☐ 20529-8	Escape Not My Love	$4.99
☐ 20262-0	If My Love Could Hold You	$4.99
☐ 20198-5	My Enemy, My Love	$4.99